THE END

Elba Rae Van Oaks never intended to die at the church that night. But being the only decedent in the history of the Litton County Medical Examiner's Office to be officially deemed dead from drowning while apple-bobbing in the fellowship hall of the First Avenue United Methodist wasn't even her greatest pinnacle of notoriety. It was, in fact, what people remembered the least and discussed most seldom except, understandably and excusably, as it came up in the natural progression of conversation about Elba Rae Van Oaks in general—which was most likely and always the result of someone remembering and discussing something else about her all together.

The fine citizens of Buford and the greater Buford area would usually say it was simply Elba Rae Van Oaks's own fault if she was the subject of conversation and of discussion and of more than the occasional embellishment because she did, after all, bring it on herself. Maybe she hadn't set out to do it that way, but her antics were documented as fact, just as much as the records at the courthouse were or the particulars of the establishment of Litton County were known and taught. And, some felt, far more entertaining than either.

It's not that people wanted to gossip, as it were; they were just repeating what they'd heard. So sometimes for the lack of any new discussion-worthy event in Buford, the stale ones got replay that a good affair-laden divorce or bankruptcy filing would easily have bumped. Elba Rae Van Oaks's name had a habit of coming up that way.

She was only sixty-five years old when the doctor pronounced her gone on a colder than usual evening back in 1988. Another few degrees and Elba Rae probably would have skipped the Fall Festival of Fellowship at the Methodist church all together and left her Ford ensconced in its single carport at the efficiently maintained ranch house out on Highway 29, but since the whole idea of a festival had practically been born of her utter disdain for what had theretofore always been known as the Halloween Youth Party, she was, certainly, obliged to partici-pate. And as long as she was going to the trouble of installing herself into the set of Ultra-Sheer Ladies Thermals she had ordered from the JCPenney and driven all the way to the catalog outlet store some forty-four miles round trip to pick up so as to avoid the extra charge for shipping and handling, then she wanted to make the event as memorable as possible.

That would, to her great and everlasting misfortune, entail stepping forward with enthusiasm when the Dawson girl called her out to lead off round one of the apple-bobbing competition. Elba Rae Van Oaks thought she was no more than about to dip into an aluminum washtub filled three-fourths of the way with Methodist tap water and topped off with the most festive red and green apples the Buford Piggly Wiggly had to offer. She did, instead, enter immortality.

THREE GRAPES AND
A COLD BISCUIT

THREE GRAPES AND A COLD BISCUIT

A Novel

ROBERT F. HASTINGS

iUniverse, Inc.

New York Bloomington Shanghai

Three Grapes and a Cold Biscuit

iUniverse books may be ordered through booksellers or by contacting:

iUniverse
1663 Liberty Drive
Bloomington, IN 47403
www.iuniverse.com
1-800-Authors (1-800-288-4677)

Because of the dynamic nature of the Internet, any Web addresses or links contained in this book may have changed since publication and may no longer be valid.

This is a work of fiction. All of the characters, names, incidents, organizations, and dialogue in this novel are either the products of the author's imagination or are used fictitiously.

ISBN: 978-0-595-48620-5 (pbk)
ISBN: 978-0-595-60714-3 (ebk)

Printed in the United States of America

For my grandmother, Margaret.
Your gift of laughter endures always.

Dishing it Out

Howard Bailey's office was small and smelled much like the library, which Elba Rae Van Oaks assumed was due to an impressive collection of old books bulging from each shelf of the big credenza behind his desk. It somehow lent the room and its occupant an air of authority that may or may not have truly been from an accumulation of dust, since she didn't imagine anybody had been to the top shelf to clean since Mr. Bailey had unpacked when he moved in and assumed his duties as principal of the Homer T. Litton Grammar School. Back then, they'd only had the one grammar school in Buford; it had been enough.

Since then, the population of Buford and surrounding Litton County had finally convinced the Superintendent and the school board they needed to provide a second. It was a strange passage for Elba Rae Van Oaks to conceive, at first, having grown up in Buford and lived there all of her life because she imagined somehow things would always stay the same, even down to the number of grammar schools. She knew changes like that must happen all the time in the big Alabama cities like Montgomery and Huntsville and certainly Mobile, but Buford had always seemed so far removed from the places like that.

There was the Square which hadn't materially changed in the decades since the courthouse was completed, even if some of the stores surrounding it had come and gone over the years. But the Mosses still had the hardware store there, and it was still just around the corner from where the Fikes sold their clothing and accessories.

There hadn't been a new church building of any consequence erected in forever, as long as you didn't count some of the nondenominational congregations who met in mostly temporary quarters and who Elba Rae Van Oaks generally found to be suspect. The same folks who'd always gone to Buford Baptist would always go to Buford Baptist, just like the Presbyterians would not likely lose any significant number of their flocks to the First Avenue United Methodist where Elba Rae Van Oaks was a member just like her parents before her.

And even though the county had justified the addition of a second facility, the young mothers of Buford found comfort in knowing they'd for the most part send their second and third borns off to the Homer T. Litton Grammar School for an education delivered by the same faculty as had welcomed their firsts. Elba Rae Van Oaks would be waiting for them once they reached fifth grade. It was but one of the qualities, simply, making life in Buford what it was. The idea of ever living anywhere else never even came to most.

"Now, Ms. Van Oaks, this is a serious matter," Howard Bailey said. Elba Rae suddenly noticed the eight-by-ten framed photograph of Mr. Nixon positioned on one of the credenza shelves next to an American History book. She wanted to ask him when he planned to update it with a glossy of President Ford, but didn't. "Do you understand that this is serious?" he repeated.

No matter her demeanor that morning, Elba Rae Van Oaks knew it must be serious, else she wouldn't have found herself sitting across from Mr. Bailey in his office with the door closed behind her. But she'd not yet grasped the full gravity of the situation. There just hadn't been time. At one moment, Elba Rae had been concluding the last lesson before the lunch bell, which was always reading and comprehension, and looking forward, as was the custom, to the association with her coworkers and faculty members at what had long been a tradition at the Homer T. Litton Grammar School, the first Thursday of the month potluck. She had gone to the teacher's lounge to retrieve the Pyrex dish containing her Chicken Florentine casserole from the faculty refrigerator so as to transport it to the industrial oven in the cafeteria kitchen for heating, and had been no more than usually irritated to see, among others, first-grade teacher Mrs. Patsy Simpson in the lounge. Patsy Simpson was speaking in her typical hushed whisper of a tone of voice to anyone who would listen—which that day happened to be Irma Young, a matronly woman with the patience of Job (which was of course necessary to teach, as Irma Young had, the Special Education class at the Homer T. Litton Grammar School for the past twenty-two years). It was Elba Rae's goal in life to avoid Patsy Simpson whenever humanly possible.

And now, somehow, still completely unreconciled to her, she sat transported in Mr. Bailey's book-filled office with its picture of a recently banished president while he read his report that seemed to say so much more than was possible to have transpired in the short time since the lunch bell rang. It sounded like he was talking about someone and some place else because he was using words like "aggressive" and "irreparable grease damage" to describe the carpet in the teacher's lounge. Elba Rae Van Oaks considered she might be dreaming and was, though only momentarily, relieved by the possibility she'd likely wake up and realize she hadn't even left for school yet and that her Chicken Florentine casserole was still in her own refrigerator, not even road-ready in its portable Pyrex.

Mr. Bailey's voice was so vivid, though, Elba Rae thought—much too clear and concise for one of her regular dreams which tended toward bizarre some nights. And it just didn't seem like he was ever going to stop.

"Ms. Van Oaks?" He wasn't even sure she was hearing him. "Do you have *anything* to say to me?"

"She lied about me." There, she thought. Now she'd said it.

The stiffness in his back almost relaxed when Mr. Bailey realized Elba Rae Van Oaks really was not in a state of catatonia. "Well now, good, I'm glad you've decided to speak up for yourself and say something because I really do want to hear your side of the story. I have to say, I'm shocked that something like this has even happened at our school because I think as a rule we do have a very dedicated group of teachers and administrators here who only—"

"She lied about my chicken! What are you planning to do to *her* about that? Do you have a report for lying?" It was, they both knew, a question for which neither expected a simple answer.

What some folks just never did understand or take the time to find out or ever even feel responsible for researching in the least was the unignorable fact Elba Rae Van Oaks had been provoked beyond restraint that Thursday morning in the teacher's lounge of the Homer T. Litton Grammar School. Else, she would have never been party to the "assault;" she would have never acted out in a most unladylike fashion; nor would she ever—under any act of self defense or threat of war—reduce one of her Chicken Florentine casseroles in its portable Pyrex to a mere weapon. But that's what happened, really, even though Elba Rae would not for the rest of her life accept most witnesses's account of the "assault" or agree to the word "weapon" in the Principal's Incident Report. Not her Chicken Florentine casserole, the one made from the recipe passed on to her from her own mother who had written it down for Elba Rae just before she married Fettis Van Oaks. That anyone would believe she had committed such a sacrilege was absurd.

"Ms. Van Oaks, I—"

"She stood right there in the middle of the lounge in front of everybody and told a bold-face lie! I have never used canned chicken in my casserole! My mother never uses canned in hers but then I guess they never had any back then to use when she learned to cook if she'd wanted to, but she wouldn't have used them if they had and I never have either! Mine has always been fresh chicken! That's as much a part of the recipe as the spinach!"

Howard Bailey was unaccustomed to such sessions. He was used to dealing with undisciplined children who talked out too much in class or whose seemingly innocent scuffles on the playground transgressed into third-grade versions of fist-fights. He was not, however, routinely prepared to impose sanctions on one of his teachers. Certainly, if ever, on one as much an institution as Elba Rae Van Oaks. It was a strange morning indeed.

"So," he said, not sure what would come out next, "why were you and Ms. Simpson discussing your cooking?"

"We weren't discussing my cooking, Mr. Bailey! We weren't discussing anything at all!" As though she'd broken through a thick and blinding fog, Elba Rae Van Oaks was suddenly lucid on the other side of it. "She took it upon herself to announce I make my Chicken Florentine casserole with canned meat and it's not true! Never has been!"

"I see," Howard Bailey commented, although he surely did not. "There was some controversy regarding the ingredients of your food?"

"No. There's no controversy. And there wouldn't have been any doubt, if she'd bothered asking. But she didn't. She just took it upon herself to say I use canned meat in my casserole and I don't. Do you understand me? I do not!"

"Ms. Van Oaks, how in the world did this even come up? I mean, how could it have come to this?"

"How should I know? She's the one who started it. With her lie. I'm sorry, Mr. Bailey, and I hope the Lord will forgive me, but that's the only way to call it. She's a liar!"

In the interest of her defense, Elba Rae supposed it was morally acceptable not to quantify the entire history of her casserole baking by admitting, in fact, there had been that one lone time when Jack Moss's brother Earl died and she had been forced to present her condolences with a Chicken Florentine casserole made from canned stewed chicken in tow. It had only happened once and it just didn't seem like it would serve any purpose to tell Mr. Bailey about the duress Earl Moss's unexpected passing had caused her. It bore no relevance, after all, to the situation at hand from strictly a matter of motive.

Mrs. Ethel Maywood had taught her daughter Elba Rae not only the mechanics of cooking but had also incorporated into the lessons certain practical matters like always having the ingredients on hand to make a casserole to take when a neighbor or a church member or even some far-off distant relative of either who you'd never met died, because you knew no matter who they were or what their beliefs they'd need a dish. And with a specialty that called for fresh chicken to be boiled on the stove before it could be cooled and then deboned and merged with the rest of the ingredients that would make it a funeral favorite throughout the county, Mrs. Maywood had emphasized it was okay in some cases to keep a ready-made casserole supply in the deep freeze for when the time between the notification of death and the correct time to make the delivery did not permit a proper fresh boiling. That happened more times than most people uneducated in such condolence cooking matters would think, especially when the deceased went to glory so late in the evening or so very early in the morning that sufficient word just wasn't spread until up into the next day. By then, the family was gathering and Elba Rae Van Oaks, like her mother, was never one to take a dish on the actual day of the funeral. That showed a lack of concern and respect of which the Maywoods had never been guilty. It was okay to be frozen, her mother had ensured, as long as it was taken in a timely manner. After all, it was fresh when it was frozen.

That particular distressing spring week some while back when the Earl Moss family had become the recipient of a Chicken Florentine casserole made with stewed chicken from a can had been neither strictly an example of inadequate warning nor a relaxing of the proper death-to-dish rules. It was more because that week had seen a cumulative death count in Buford unmatched since typhoid had been a problem before Elba Rae was born.

There had first been Martha Betty Maharry's mother, Miss Nita, who was quite elderly and whose death had been expected ever since she'd somehow man- aged to get the railing down on her bed at the Restful Haven Care Home in an attempt to walk out the front door at two o'clock in the morning. She had, instead, plunged directly to the tile floor below and broken what remained of her left hip. The doctors didn't begin to suggest setting it, at her age and in her already compromised condition, so the only prognosis was to try to keep her comfortable. That show of medical mercy had both spared Miss Nita the trauma of surgery as well as allowed Elba Rae the luxury of an unscheduled visit to the Piggly Wiggly for fresh chicken so that by the time Miss Nita drew her last breath two days after the fall, Elba Rae already had a pot of water on the stove just wait- ing to turn on the coil. Martha Betty Maharry was a member of the First Avenue United Methodist Church as well as a neighbor on Highway 29, the combination of which certainly warranted and almost dictated a fresh casserole even though Elba Rae had two perfectly good ready-made ones in the deep freeze. Whenever she had occasion to use one of those, she was diligent about making another to replace it. But since Miss Nita had been thoughtful enough to linger a full two days after her aborted escape from Restful Haven, there had been no need to rely on frozen.

Elba Rae had still been in the carport having just disembarked from her Ford Galaxie after paying respects at the Maharry house two miles south down the highway when she heard the phone ringing inside. She managed to get up the three concrete steps in the carport to enter through the kitchen door and grab the black wall-mounted phone in time to answer. It was her cousin Hazel calling to tell her Dewey Richardson had died that afternoon at Litton County Memorial Hospital. Yes it was sad, bless his heart, and he's better off that's for sure and no she didn't realize the cancer had spread as badly as it had because yes she had heard he had cancer of the lung but she'd thought he'd just gone in the hospital for some tests and yes that's right what they say you go into that hospital you're just likely to not ever come out so she guessed they'd better take a dish.

Dewey Richardson had never been a member of the First Avenue United Methodist Church nor any other Methodist church that Elba Rae knew of, or of any evangelical denomination whatsoever for that matter, but he had lived in Buford all of his life and his people had been from Buford and she didn't care what had happened to him in the war, she was sure whoever was gathering that evening at the Richardson house would need nourishment. And with two frozen Chicken Florentine casseroles in stock, her genuine show of concern and support had required little original effort.

Elba Rae did not attend services for Mr. Dewey Richardson, which were held in the chapel of the Buford Memorial Funeral Home two days after his passing. She had taken food, double-checking to make sure the masking tape that bore her name was secure on the bottom of the dish in case no one in the Richardson family had been assigned to keep up with such things, so there was no cause to make an additional appearance at the funeral. But before she had even recovered her Pyrex dish from the Maharry house two miles down the road, news came that W.F. Millford, Doctor Millford's father, had dropped dead of a heart attack while trying to remove a wasp nest from the eave of his tool shed. Thank goodness she had one last casserole on hand, she'd mused.

Replaying the whole sequence of that week's events as she sat in Mr. Bailey's office at the Homer T. Litton Grammar school while he went over the P.I.R. (as those in the profession knew it), Elba Rae would have, in hindsight, opted to just mail the Richardsons a sympathy card in lieu of delivering a casserole. That she would have, no doubt, had she any possible hint or warning that Jack Moss's brother Earl was going to choose that week to fall out of his john boat and drown outright while trolling for catfish on Warner Lake. If only she hadn't wasted a perfectly good frozen Chicken Florentine casserole on that nut Dewey Richardson, who never was right after the war, she'd have had one to take to poor Mabel Moss in her hour of need. It certainly hadn't helped matters that Earl's body hadn't floated to the surface until just before dark which meant sufficient word didn't quite spread about the recovery of the remains until well into the evening and in some cases not until the next morning, but in all cases it had most assuredly not been during the retail operating hours of the Buford Piggly Wiggly. Clearly it would have been distasteful to present food at the Moss house while Earl was still underwater and there existed, if in no one else's mind except Mabel's, the hope he might be found alive so those who adhered to the proper death-to-dish schedule were left to scramble.

Elba Rae hadn't wanted to open the can that had rested so patiently on the shelf of her pantry for just such a crisis, but she'd had no choice. Earl Moss had been fished from Warner Lake some fourteen hours earlier; if she hadn't gotten to the Moss home within the next three to four, well, there wouldn't have been any point in showing up at all. Not unless she intended to take a dish the day of the funeral, and she just wasn't going to succumb to such compromises. It had been bad enough she was caught with no fresh chicken in the house; she was forced to compensate for the sake of timeliness.

As Mr. Bailey babbled on about the cohesiveness of the faculty and staff at the Homer T. Litton Grammar School, Elba Rae didn't suppose there was any way possible he had been privy to her one counterfeit Chicken Florentine casserole that had been delivered to the Earl Moss family. After all, he wasn't related to any of the Mosses, and, as far as she knew, he had no business stopping by the Moss house in any capacity and certainly not in one which would have warranted lingering long enough to fix a plate. So Elba Rae felt justified in her fresh-chicken-only declaration and frankly just didn't have the heart to blame anything on poor dead Earl Moss at that point, especially when—from a technical standpoint—the blame fell squarely on Dewey Richardson anyway. Nut.

"Ms. Van Oaks, am I to understand the dispute between you and Ms. Simpson began over a casserole you brought for the potluck today?" Mr. Bailey, a patient man who'd made a career teaching children—some of them unruly—before he matriculated to the administration side of the business, was losing some of the diplomacy he'd long been credited with during his tenure as principal of the Homer T. Litton Grammar School.

"I just told you, Mr. Bailey," Elba Rae retorted. "It began when she stood in the lounge and started her whispering and her pointing and leaned over to Irma Young and said I make my Chicken Florentine casserole with canned meat! And it's not true! It's just not! And it wasn't fair of her or right to be able to say that!"

"I understand why you might have been ..." He carefully searched for the right word. "Offended. But I can hardly condone your reaction, Ms. Van Oaks. And I certainly cannot condone your actions that followed. You ... you ... you threw your dish at Mrs. Simpson, striking her from what I'm told. That is simply unacceptable. Not to mention the brawl that followed."

"She has never liked me since the first day you hired her," Elba Rae responded with no hesitation or prompting needed. "She's never wanted to teach the first graders, and she's told everybody here that'll listen she took the opening just to get her foot in the door. And ever since, she's been waiting for me or Louise Kinney to quit or get fired or drop dead in the cafeteria so she can have one of our classrooms. She's undermined me, she's whispered in the halls about my students and their marks and how I can't make them behave, and if she's told it once she's told it a thousand times—she taught fifth grade in Kentucky before she had to move down here so her husband could take over his daddy's farm. For heaven's sake, you'd think she invented the fifth grade! You can ask Irma Young if you don't believe me. Irma's just better at ignoring her, that's all. So she tends to leave Irma alone. She doesn't talk about Irma's cooking."

For all the drama that had transpired on the campus of the Homer T. Litton Grammar School that morning, Mr. Bailey knew there was truth in the unfolding confession of Elba Rae Van Oaks, and the fact that she was leaving out a good half or more of the relevant exposition didn't make the circumstances any less sad. Mr. Bailey was well aware of the animosity between his first grade teacher Mrs. Patsy Simpson and his veteran fifth grade educator Mrs. Elba Rae Van Oaks. He was the principal of the school, after all, and as such had heard the pair never mixed well from the first season Patsy Simpson was on board six years earlier. It was true, as Elba Rae had so passionately mentioned, that Ms. Simpson had adamantly desired a position teaching a grade other than first. However, her untimely relocation from Paducah to the greater Buford area had unfortunately not coincided with the Litton County Department of Public Instruction's need for a fifth grade teacher—neither at the Homer T. Litton Grammar school nor at the newer Walnut Hills Grammar school in the south part of the county—so Mrs. Patsy Simpson had settled for what was available because she was too scared of her husband's farming skills not to.

Thus had begun, although probably not to the degree Elba Rae Van Oaks professed it to be, a campaign for Patsy Simpson to rectify the side effect of the move which had resulted in her spending long days calming the new first graders of Litton County and acclimating them to the finer arts of hand raising and organized restroom breaks, when, that is, they actually waited until they were in the restroom to let go. Meanwhile, her greater calling to influence the developing youth of America was surely being unanswered, she felt strongly, by the insipid Louise Kinney and the frustrated prude Elba Rae Van Oaks, who hadn't modified her teaching methods since the Scopes monkey trial. Patsy Simpson had once even come to Mr. Bailey's office, having scheduled an afterschool appointment, to discuss the possibility that perhaps Mrs. Van Oaks's skills and teaching methods would be better served in a lower grade of, say, maybe first, and that if Mr. Bailey were to ever agree with such an assessment that Mrs. Patsy Simpson would be willing to fill in the gap in the fifth grade faculty. Mr. Bailey, who most definitely had his office door closed the day Elba Rae Van Oaks threw a Chicken Florentine casserole in its portable Pyrex at Mrs. Patsy Simpson and then sat in his office discussing the Principal's Incident Report of which she was the subject, did more often that not actually keep his office door open, making it unavoidably possible yet terribly convenient for his secretary Hazel Burns to ingest most everything that went on within. Patsy Simpson had not only been brazen enough to make an appointment with Mr. Bailey for the exact purpose of suggesting he reallocate Elba Rae Van Oaks to a first grade teaching position, but she had altogether ignored the fact Hazel Burns and Elba Rae Van Oaks were first cousins on Elba Rae's mother's side as well as both members of the First Avenue United Methodist Church, and she had certainly not considered that Hazel Burns would nearly sideswipe two mailboxes on Walnut Road trying to get home with a quickness to phone Elba Rae with the unsettling news of the meeting. Mr. Bailey had long suspected Hazel Burns worked after regular school hours unnecessarily.

"Ms. Van Oaks," Mr. Bailey continued, "there are witnesses to this morning's unfortunate sequence of events who have already informed me you attacked Ms. Simpson. Now whether you felt justified at the time, I just cannot overlook the fact that you … struck the first blow."

"I—"

"And when I say blow, I mean when you turned your chicken casserole up and emptied it onto Ms. Simpson."

"I—"

"Ms. Van Oaks, please. I need to finish. I have seen a lot of things in my own years in the classroom as well as since I've been principal. But I have never known of an occurrence when two teachers had to be physically separated and restrained from a fist fight in the lounge. And over a casserole, no less. What kind of example is that for the children?"

Elba Rae took a deep breath, and exhaled it slowly. Mr. Bailey had made a viable point, and the realization of it began to settle in her stomach like a heavy piece of Irma Young's dry meatloaf which, were there truth in advertising, would have been called breadcrumb loaf.

In fact, Elba Rae had finally had all of the snippy Patsy Simpson she could stand that morning in the lounge. She had, as the witnesses would recount, been suddenly overcome by the purposely audible can whisper and turned quickly to confront its source. There was no pause or hesitation (and the movement was even quite graceful, in a way) as Elba Rae twirled on her heels, methodically removed the lid from the casserole dish while simultaneously marching in Patsy Simpson's direction, and overturned its contents approximately three inches from the peak of her teased and frosted hairdo. Even Irma Young, in a state of shock that lasted through the weekend, was able to contribute to the Principal's Incident Report that Elba Rae had clearly screamed, "*It's fresh chick-e-e-en!*" as the first bits of chopped spinach slid down Patsy Simpson's face.

Whether Elba Rae expected Patsy Simpson to just stand there with cold Chicken Florentine casserole collecting in a puddle at her feet without attempting retaliation was never really known and, at any rate, wasn't something Elba Rae was afforded time to ponder. With her frosted hair decidedly depressed in the center of her scalp due to the concentration of chicken chunks, Patsy Simpson lurched forward and grabbed Elba Rae by the shoulders and gave her a shake, whereupon Elba Rae grabbed onto Patsy Simpson's shoulders and gave her the same. The shaking had soon given way to shoving and general hair tugging (at which Patsy Simpson had the clear advantage, since Elba Rae's own auburn hair was food-free and more readily held onto and Patsy Simpson's hair was just too slippery at that point to get a good grip) with some ear pulling thrown in by both but on a random basis.

In spite of the outcome, most present had commended Claude Pickle for the inaugural effort he launched to separate the two combatants and break up the fight. Mr. Pickle had entered the teacher's lounge at just about the instant the unheated Chicken Florentine casserole had made initial contact with Mrs. Patsy Simpson; he didn't even know the nature of the dispute, but felt innately compelled without the luxury of discovery nonetheless to prevent the possibility of mortal injury which seemed imminent before him. In the melee, the Principal's Incident Report was inconclusive as to whose blow it was exactly that had knocked Claude Pickle out of the arena all together, thrusting him backward into the cold drink machine with such force that a chilled Fresca dispensed.

Mercifully, Miss Gunther, the girls's P.E. teacher, had heard the *chick-e-e-en!* declaration in the gymnasium all the way around the corner from the entrance to the teacher's lounge and had come forth to assist. Miss Gunther hovered approximately seventeen inches over Claude Pickle, who taught Arithmetic and had always been somewhat leery of Miss Gunther, who was then known as 'athletic' but would, in her later years, be downgraded to 'husky.' Miss Gunther had never married. She cut her own lawn and painted her own house. She was as physically fit a specimen as was on the campus of the Homer T. Litton Grammar School and just the person one would hope for in such a time of need to disengage the ensuing brawl in the lounge. What had proven no fair match for Claude Pickle was easily disarmed by Rosemary Gunther. She calmly stepped in between the two teachers and raised both arms straight out from her side, displacing both women and thus centering herself in the impromptu ring. Whatever resistance either one of them thought about offering was soon squelched with Miss Gunther's baritone, "Ladies! Please!"

"Do you see what she did to me? Look at my hair! She—" said Patsy Simpson.

"She has lied about me for the last time! I've taken it from her for years, but this—" said Elba Rae Van Oaks.

"I don't care who did what to who," Miss Gunther said to both. "That will be a matter for Mr. Bailey to decide." She paused to survey the room for spectators. "Did anyone hit the intercom?"

"I did," Irma Young replied sheepishly.

"Good." Miss Gunther felt it safe to drop her arms back to her side, though she maintained her firm stance in position on the lounge's indoor-outdoor carpeted floor just in case things were to again escalate out of control before Mr. Bailey could arrive on the scene. There was suddenly silence in the room, interrupted only by the kerplunk of some chicken as it became free from the belt buckle of Patsy Simpson's navy dress and hit the floor, although by the time Mr. Bailey entered the lounge, Claude Pickle had regained enough air in his lungs to produce a light cough.

Elba Rae had not thought of crying in front of Mr. Bailey as he began the conclusion of his report. She wouldn't give him the satisfaction, nor would she want Hazel Burns—cousin or not—to feel tempted into repeating the vision of her red eyes and streaked face departing the office.

"In light of today's events, and based on the accounts of the people in the lounge during the incident, I have no option but to immediately suspend you,

Ms. Van Oaks. Suspend you until such time as I can review the case with the Superintendent to determine further action, if any, that he may feel is warranted."

Elba Rae slumped in the chair opposite Mr. Bailey in his office, digesting the unspeakable menu of repercussions the fight with Patsy Simpson would have. The smell of the old books seemed heavier than it had when she'd first entered. She was deflated and weak from the surge of adrenaline that had left her body in the teacher's lounge and, more telling, by years of anger and frustration and resentment raging inside of which no witness could have even known.

"Furthermore, I would like you to go immediately to your car and leave the school property." Not knowing Elba Rae's decided constitution, he automatically paused in the event there were to be tears. Seeing no signs, he continued.

"If there are any personal items here you need from your classroom, or your empty casserole dish, perhaps, let me know and I'll have Miss Burns … I'll get your cousin to gather them and drop them at your home."

"Well," Elba Rae said as she stood up in front of Mr. Bailey's desk. "I will need my dish. You never know when someone might die unexpectedly."

With that, Elba Rae Van Oaks collected what fragment of her pride remained intact and walked out the door, past Hazel Burns who knew best not to look up.

*   *   *   *

Although classes were by that time back in session after the lunch break and the grounds of the school were quiet and peaceful, Elba Rae couldn't help but feel the stares of many sets of eyes on her through the windows as she walked toward the faculty lot and her awaiting white Galaxie 500 with its red interior. Her head swirled and she wanted to run but knew better. There would be enough made of her confrontation with Patsy Simpson without throwing in a final climax of her fleeing like a fugitive. She just wanted to get in her car, start up the motor, and drive away like it was the end of any regular school day, with the only difference being the compelling desire to drive eighty miles an hour and directly toward the bridge that crossed over the railroad tracks that went to Birmingham. She could swerve off the side of the road right before the bridge, and by the time the Galaxie hit the tracks below, her troubles would be over. Except, of course, suicide was sinful and disgraceful and no one in the Maywood family had ever committed suicide nor had anyone in the Van Oaks family, although surely some of them had been more wont to contemplate it, but Elba Rae wasn't willing to shame either side, not her biological or her married one.

She took deep breaths as she drove out of the faculty parking lot and they seemed to help, and by the time she turned onto Highway 29 she was almost feeling vindicated over her cruel insult and practically smiled at considering that Patsy Simpson's way too short navy dress with the too big buckle in the front would probably never come clean. Had only she not spied the pale green Rambler waiting in the driveway at her house, the presence of which meant with certainty that Ethel Maywood had already heard the news, Elba Rae might have been deluded into thinking that Thursday couldn't have turned any worse.

Mrs. Ethel Maywood had let herself into the tidy house with the spare key Elba Rae wished she'd provided to someone (anyone) else for safekeeping. When Elba Rae entered, her mother was sitting stoically on the center cushion of the brocaded sofa in Elba Rae's living room beneath a large faux painting of a tranquil mountain stream, her hands crossed on her lap. Elba Rae wanted to leap into the painting and disappear on the other side of the stream beyond some big moss-covered rocks. She imagined it was quiet there.

Two Victorian reproduction wing chairs sat opposite the sofa in the living room and Elba Rae lowered herself into one of them without saying a word of greeting to her mother. She slowly raised her eyes upward until they met Ethel Maywood's.

"I just don't know what to say, Elba Rae," Mrs. Maywood said. Elba Rae knew oxymoron when she heard it since she imagined her mother had practiced plenty of things to say on her way over in the Rambler and that she herself would get full benefit of all of them plus a few new ones that would come to her mother on the spot once she got going good.

"I've been in shock ever since I got the call from Aunt Ruby." Aunt Ruby was Ruby Burns, mother of Hazel Burns, secretary to Mr. Bailey, and who, for all the discretion that Hazel Burns had ever practiced, may as well have been in the office with Elba Rae during the entire recital of the Principal's Incident Report. Hazel was nothing if not quick. Like a lightning bolt, she was.

"Aunt Ruby was just sick and didn't even want to tell me." Whatever trumped oxymoron, Elba Rae knew she'd just had a serving of that, too. "But I'm glad she did because at least I heard it from someone in the family and didn't have to hear it on the street."

'Road' was the more common and accepted term to refer to public transportation right of ways in Buford, Elba Rae knew, but didn't suppose her mother would soften much by being corrected. "What exactly did you hear, Momma?" Elba Rae suspected there would be no way to downplay the version Aunt Ruby had conveyed, especially since it had been generated from the school secretary herself, but it was worth a brief exploration.

"Don't try to fool me, Elba Rae. I know what happened at school this morning and I know Howard Bailey's had to fire you."

"He didn't fire me, Momma. It's just a suspension."

"Same thing."

"No, actually, it's not the same thing. And if that's what Hazel told Aunt Ruby, then she must not've been listening as good as I thought she was."

"Don't sass me, Elba Rae. And don't try to take this out on your cousin and make like it's her fault I know about it. For heaven's sake, it's not like I wouldn't have found out anyway."

Elba Rae knew that was surely true. It was, perhaps, the first time she'd ever wished she'd fulfilled her teaching career in the public school system of New York City. Or maybe Canada. Anywhere but Buford.

"I'm not sassing you, Momma, but I didn't get fired from the school. It's just a suspension. It's temporary."

"Until when?"

"Mr. Bailey just has to talk to the Superintendent and they'll probably go over the report and then I'll be back at school. And probably Patsy Simpson will have to answer for a thing or two in the meanwhile."

"What possessed you, Elba Rae? Can you answer me that? Do you know? Were you just gone insane?"

"Oh, Momma, please ..." Elba Rae stood from the chair, almost involuntarily, and began to walk out of the room.

"Where are you going? I'm not near through talking about this!"

The walk was over and Elba Rae sat back down. She was in the other Victorian reproduction wingback chair this time. "I'm not insane, Momma, and I don't appreciate your saying I am."

"Well I'm just trying to understand what could come over a grown woman, a teacher in the schools, a churchgoing, upstanding woman who wasn't brought up that way, that's for sure, to fall prey to the behavior they're talking about."

"They?" Elba Rae inquired. "Don't you mean Hazel?"

"Well I'm sure it's not just Hazel by now, Elba Rae. The whole school was there, weren't they? In the teacher's lounge?"

"It wasn't the whole school, Momma, it was just a few of the teachers. And it was that—that *witch* Patsy Simpson who started it!"

"Elba Rae Maywood! I don't want to hear talk like that!"

"Well it's true. You know she's hated me since she started teaching at the school, and today she went too far and I'd just had it. I wish it hadn't happened like it did, but in a way I'm not sorry about it either. She's had it coming and for a long time, too."

"You always were a willful child, Elba Rae. I couldn't stop you if you wanted to do something, even if it was wrong. And Lord knows your daddy never did give you the time of day. But you just never did learn there could be consequences sometimes. And now look at the mess you're in. What if you lose your job? What then? Are you going to be sorry then? Huh?" Elba Rae leaned her head back and stared at the ceiling.

"It'll be too late to be sorry then, Elba Rae. When you've been fired from the only job you've ever known and you're disgraced in the community. What are you going to do then, huh? Did you think about that when you were wrestling Patsy Simpson?"

"She said I put canned chicken in my casserole."

At last there was a reason for Ethel Maywood to take pause. She leaned back on the sofa cushion and processed the new information. "That's ridiculous."

"I know."

"We've never made Chicken Florentine casserole with canned meat. I never taught you to make it that way."

"I know, Momma, but Patsy Simpson decided today she'd stand in the teacher's lounge and announce to Irma Young and anybody else that was listening that my dish was made with canned meat."

"You must have misunderstood her."

"No, I didn't misunderstand. I walked in the lounge and as soon as I did she leaned over to Irma Young and said, 'Well, you know she just mixes that up with some Sweet Sue and then runs it in the oven.'"

"What would make her say such a thing?"

"Because she hates me, Momma, I told you. She's always hated me."

Ethel Maywood suddenly lowered her tone of voice to a more pleasing and less threatening pitch that could've almost passed for compassion. "Elba Rae ..."

"What?"

"This doesn't still have anything to do with that business of her and Fettis, does it?"

"Oh, Momma, please. I don't want to dredge all that up again. Not today."

"But does it?"

"No, it doesn't."

"Then what else would cause Patsy Simpson to just up and decide she's going to insult your cooking, out of nowhere like that? Have you two been at it again?"

"Momma, I am not talking about all of that anymore. It was years ago and Fettis is dead and there was never anything to it and what has that got to do with my Chicken Florentine casserole anyhow? She's just mean, that's what it is. She was mean when she got to Buford and truth be told, I bet she was just as mean when she was still in Paducah. She's just mean-spirited and that's all there is to it. She's a mean woman. She doesn't want to live in Buford and she doesn't want to teach first grade and she probably doesn't want to have to bring a covered dish to the potluck but she does it anyway because she's too snooty to not be in it but since she hates it all so much she decides she may as well make everybody else as miserable as she is. That's what I think."

"Oh, Lord, Elba Rae. Lord ... Lord ... Lord ... What are you going to do?"

"I'm gonna go in the kitchen and see what I'm gonna fix for supper tonight and then I'm gonna look at my lesson plan for next week like I do every Thursday afternoon when I get home and then I'm gonna fix my supper and I'm gonna get my TV tray out and eat my supper and watch *The Waltons* like I do every Thursday and then I'll go to bed. And probably by tomorrow Mr. Bailey will have talked to the Superintendent and straightened this whole thing out and he'll call me on the phone and tell me to be back at school Monday morning."

With that, Elba Rae Van Oaks felt empowered enough to really walk out of the room and leave her mother sitting alone on the sofa with nothing but the distant sound of the refrigerator door opening and shutting for company. Elba Rae studied her lesson plan for the week to follow and that evening enjoyed a Salisbury steak smothered in onion gravy while Pa Walton struggled with a most complicated dilemma regarding use of the family barn to house some traveling carnival workers which apparently did not sit well with any of the Walton womenfolk, and so confident was Elba Rae that the tempest would be short lived she slept better that night than most. And the next day, right on the queue practically willed by Elba Rae Van Oaks herself, the call came from the principal of the Homer T. Litton Grammar School, Mr. Howard Bailey, who had, indeed, spoken with the Superintendent and reviewed thoroughly with him the Principal's Incident Report and who with the recommendation of Mr. Bailey did agree termination was not the appropriate action to take against such a heretofore devoted employee of the Litton County school system with good reviews and even some written letters of praise from parents past.

Yes, Elba Rae thought, while she patiently allowed Mr. Bailey to play out the formality of asking her back to school, she'd shown Patsy Simpson what was what and the next time she caught Hazel Burns alone she was going to give her a piece of her mind as well. She nearly blurted out that she'd see him at school first thing Monday morning but was suddenly caught off guard by a change of plans most unanticipated.

"Therefore, it is at the Superintendent's explicit direction that you are to report to the Board Tuesday afternoon at two for your first meeting with Dr. Yardley and thereafter as often as Dr. Yardley shall deem necessary. Until then, your suspension will remain in effect."

"Doctor … *who?*"

"Ms. Van Oaks, are you listening to me?"

"I am, Mr. Bailey, but I must have misunderstood something you said about going to the Board—on Tuesday afternoon?"

"That's right. And may I just say, Ms. Van Oaks, and this is really off the record for as much as it pertains to my official follow up to the P.I.R., it's very fortunate timing for your sake that the Board brought Dr. Yardley into the system just so recently. Without this as an option, I'm not so sure we wouldn't be having an altogether different conversation right now if you know what I mean."

"I … I don't think I do know what you mean, Mr. Bailey."

There was only enough of a delay for Howard Bailey to conclude it was no time to spare bluntness or feelings. Not after everything that had transpired, and not when the eyes of the entire Litton County education community were on him to see just how well he'd handle the most unprecedented situation.

"I mean if counseling sessions with Dr. Yardley hadn't been an option to consider at this time, the Superintendent would have recommended termination. It's just that simple, Ms. Van Oaks. Neither the Superintendent nor I can give the appearance we will tolerate violence in our schools. Especially not amongst the teachers."

"You want me to go to … counseling?!"

"It's your choice, Ms. Van Oaks. Either report to Dr. Yardley's office on Tuesday afternoon, or deliver your letter of resignation to me by end of school on Monday. That's it."

"But this man … Mr. Yearley, is it?"

"It's Yardley, and it's not Mister, it's Doctor. Dr. Marvin Yardley. Maybe you should be writing some of this down."

"No … no … I got it, Mr. Bailey, but a doctor? You need me to go see a doctor?"

"Really, Ms. Van Oaks, I'm beginning to think you haven't heard a word I've said. Marvin Yardley is a psychologist. He has a doctorate degree from the University of Georgia—a double doctorate, I should say—one in education and the most recent in psychology. That's why the Board decided to hire him. As an expert in both fields, he's going to be invaluable for the new curriculum the Board's planning in the high schools for next year. It's a stroke of fortune for you he's already here."

"Okay, Mr. Bailey. If that's what you want. I'll go to the appointment. Tuesday afternoon? All right. And then do I—"

"And then you will do as Dr. Yardley instructs you to do. If his schedule will permit and he wishes to see you each and every day, you will go every day. The Superintendent is taking a personal interest in this, Ms. Van Oaks, because the very idea of introducing this new curriculum was his, after all, and he's proud to have Dr. Yardley on staff and to be able to offer this to you as an alternative. He will be conferring regularly with Dr. Yardley, I suspect, about your progress and will report back to me the ultimate outcome of your suspension when they both feel the time is right. Now, are there any questions?"

"I don't know if … I mean, what …"

"Yes?"

"No, Mr. Bailey. I don't have any questions."

"Very well," he concluded. "I'm glad you understand the gravity of the situation, Ms. Van Oaks, and … well … good luck to you. Please take advantage of this opportunity."

And then the conversation was over. The first thing Elba Rae realized was that she wished she had a sleeping pill, knowing the night to follow would not be so restful.

AFTERMATH

Elba Rae woke up early that next morning. She was used to it, for school if not usually on Saturdays, but by six she was in the kitchen and making coffee. The boy that threw the paper on her route probably hadn't been there yet, she thought, but while she waited for the percolator to heat up she decided to check out front anyway and was glad to see it at the end of the driveway so she wouldn't have to make another trip later.

She was on the way back toward the carport when she thought she noticed something over on the steps at the front door. The sun wasn't really up yet, and it was hard to make out the shape at first, but it appeared Elba Rae had a package. Odd, she thought, not so much that someone would leave something at the door without knocking or ringing the bell, because that was just like Martha Betty Maharry to deliver a sack of tomatoes or a bushel of beans or some eggplant from her garden down the road, but because anyone who'd regularly drop something by at the door would have left it at the carport door, the one Elba Rae more frequently used and where she most always received visitors. The front door was used by strangers who stopped to ask directions or by Reverend Bishop sometimes, though not by his wife Edith who always felt at ease coming to the back through the carport.

Elba Rae went down her front walk toward the door and as she got closer, she could make out perfectly well a paper sack. Maybe she'd parked the Galaxie too close to the kitchen door, Elba Rae surmised, and Martha Betty'd not had room to bestow her neighborly gift there. Or maybe, Elba Rae sort of started to shake her head yes in realization, it was just time for the new phone book again and the carrier had put it in a sack. She walked up her steps and picked up the sack. There was a note inside, on top of what did appear to be some kind of packaged food. Confused, she carried it around and back in the house through the carport door and into the kitchen where there would be sufficient light to make out the note.

"What in the world?" she said as she set the sack on the kitchen table and took the note out. She unfolded it and even after reading it three times didn't readily understand the message.

> *We thought you could use these next*
> *time. They're more fun to throw than chicken.*

And then she slowly looked into the sack again and pulled them out. Two pies. One chocolate meringue, the other clearly a coconut cream. The Piggly Wiggly BAKERY stickers still affixed, as a proud declaration of their origin.

Elba Rae stood perfectly still, as though someone were watching her and would see if she made a move. Did everybody in Litton County know what had happened in the teacher's lounge on Thursday afternoon? How would she face her friends again, and how, she started to worry, would she be able to go to church the next morning? Maybe she wouldn't go. She'd get word to Hazel that she'd woken up with the upset stomach and had stayed home to try and settle it. Yes, that sounded good. But would anyone believe it? Now? Since she'd been victim to even random pranksters leaving pies and a vile note on her very front door in the dark of night? Some big old high school boys, no doubt, out riding around on a Friday night in their daddies' cars looking for something to get into. She hoped the law would catch them at it the next time they thought about prowling around decent people's houses in the night, she did. She looked over on the counter where the coffee was pounding madly in the top of the percolator. For the next hour, she sat at her kitchen table and sipped slowly first one and then the next cup, the newspaper still perfectly folded, creased, and untouched.

On Sunday morning, Hazel Burns, who had neither seen nor spoken to her cousin Elba Rae since school on Thursday, got a phone call just as she was about to put on her petticoat for Sunday School. Elba Rae was relieved when Hazel picked up herself after two rings, because she wasn't ready yet for an awkward conversation with her aunt Ruby with whom Hazel still lived.

"It's my stomach, Hazel. I don't know what it was but something didn't agree with me, that's for sure."

"Well what did you eat last night, Elba Rae?"

"Nothing much, really. I had a pot pie for supper but you know I'm not sure how long it's been in the deep freeze. I need to give that thing a good cleaning but when do you have the time?"

"You think the meat was bad in your pot pie?"

"I guess it could have been old."

"Was it beef?"

"No, it was the chicken one."

"I expect it could have been, Elba Rae. Frozen or not. If they left it out too long at the factory before they froze it, it wouldn't matter if it'd been frozen or not. You know chicken's bad to turn on you. I mean ... oh—" She cut herself off. "Oh, I'm sorry, Elba Rae."

"Sorry for what? I was just saying ..." And then Elba Rae realized the delicate poultry territory she and Hazel were broaching, inadvertent and unplanned, especially since Elba Rae had not actually even entertained a pot pie for supper the night before, not the beef variety and certainly not the chicken one, but had enjoyed in reality a bacon, lettuce, and tomato sandwich with lots of black pepper and a full complement of mayonnaise.

"Well, whatever, Hazel, I'd better let you finish getting ready before I make you late. I just wanted to tell you why I wouldn't be there today in case anybody asked you. You know, so they'd know nothing was bad wrong, but just tell anybody that asks I'll be all right in a day or two."

"I will."

They stayed on the phone for a few more awkward seconds without saying anything to each other, and then Hazel had to ask.

"Elba Rae?"

"What?"

"You won't be back at school tomorrow, will you?"

"No, Hazel. I won't."

*   *   *   *

Customarily, when a long-standing and regular member such as Elba Rae Van Oaks was not in her pew on Sunday, concern would naturally arise amongst the congregation of the First Avenue United Methodist Church, spurring talk, and questions, and depending upon the thoroughness of the answers, there could be phone calls to the missing party throughout the afternoon following the absence.

"We missed you at Sunday School and preaching this morning. Are you all right?" was standard dialogue, and would be anticipated from any number of close friends or distant relations.

The Sunday Elba Rae Van Oaks stayed home from church due to the unsettled state of her stomach, the telephone did not ring. By four o'clock, at which time news of her recovery should have been what was being spread throughout the community, Elba Rae realized the error of her judgment in hastily selecting a pot pie as the source of her misery when obviously more lethal fare had been in order, something like spaghetti or some hot tamales with a little diarrhea thrown in for good measure, as distasteful as that was to repeat. Hazel Burns did not even call, and Elba Rae's own mother, it seemed, was avoiding her too.

Elba Rae turned and tossed most of the night into Monday morning and could just imagine what the faculty would have to say in the lounge when they realized she wasn't there nor was she expected back any time soon. Patsy Simpson would be gloating, she was certain, and would milk it for all it was worth. Elba Rae wondered who Mr. Bailey had gotten to substitute for her room and was hoping it wasn't Irma Young's sister, Inez, who'd done little more than sit at Elba Rae's desk and give the children busy work a couple of winters before when Elba Rae had been out with the flu, completely disregarding the lesson plan.

Elba Rae had gone to peeking through the living room sheers first thing in the mornings to survey the front door step before going outside to fetch her newspaper, not really expecting a repeat of the anonymous pie prank but afraid not to look all the same. The pies were still in her refrigerator Tuesday because it seemed a shame to throw out perfectly good food that hadn't even been touched. She had no intention of consuming any of the chocolate one, whose meringue had wept well past the edible stage, but was tempted on and off again by the coconut cream, although in the end, she knew she'd never bring herself to touch either one of them because they were tainted.

When she gathered the newspapers up with the other kitchen garbage in the house mid-morning, she broke down and put both pies in the big bag and took them to the trash barrel out back to burn with the rest of the rubbish. She'd stared at them long enough, she thought, and it was time to turn her attention to the appointment awaiting her that afternoon at the Litton County Department of Public Instruction. The one with Dr. Marvin Yardley.

*   *   *   *

It had been quite a while since Elba Rae had been at the Board, she realized as she drove the Galaxie into the Visitors Only parking lot. The bricks were still the same stark gray they'd always been, but something about the one-story building looked a little different nonetheless. Maybe it was the trim, she thought. They must have painted it since the last time she'd been there for a meeting. She looked nervously at her watch after putting the car in park and decided she'd just sit there quietly instead of going in fifteen minutes early.

At one minute before the stroke of two, Elba Rae Van Oaks took a deep slow breath and exited the sanctity of her Galaxie for the unknown within the gray bricks. There were two desks inside the lobby just through the double glass doors. Mary Alice Hankerson sat at the one on the right, because it was in front of the Superintendent's office and Mary Alice Hankerson was the Superintendent's secretary, having once been a secretary at the high school before advancing. Mary Alice had off and on again gone to the same ceramics group with Elba Rae, which was also attended by Hazel Burns, Willadean Hendrix, both Moss wives (Mabel and Florine), and Dr. Bud Millford's wife, Virginia, who always livened things up although her painting and attention to detail reflected by far the poorest skill level in the class. All Virginia ever wanted to make, it seemed, was ashtrays, and even if she every once in a while opted for a ginger jar or a decorative platter, its design would inevitably be ruined by the big "M" with which she insisted on monogramming everything. Elba Rae wondered if she herself would ever return to the group which met on Tuesday nights, and if not, what fate would befall her current project which had, by the unanimous opinions of the group, been the most ambitious undertaken to date. There had been other attempts at lamps, some successful and quite the showpiece, with some looking painfully amateurish and unsaved by even an expensive shade, and of course over the years there had been any number of clocks completed, including wall models for practical use as well as fanciful French reproductions that always looked good on a guest room dresser or which served well as an elaborate Christmas gift. But no one had wanted to try the clock lamp combination piece again after what everyone secretly agreed had been the debacle created by Mabel Moss.

It wasn't enough for Mabel to have wanted to be the first to try the clock lamp combination piece. No, she had decided, against the advice of Pauline McGreggor who owned the kiln and served as both hostess and instructor for the classes, to paint—freehand style, no less—the face of Jesus on the front of lamp base, just below the inset for the clock. Pauline had warned against it, since the pre-molded lamp definitely did not have the face of Jesus, or the face of anyone else for that matter, etched into the plaster, and attempting freeform painting was just too risky and ill-conceived a notion on a large, signature piece like the clock lamp combination. Mabel Moss disregarded the warning, foolish as it was since Pauline McGreggor had been conducting ceramics classes in the shop behind her house for years and was certainly considered an expert in the field, and carried on with the dubious support of the group.

Elba Rae and her cousin Hazel Burns could hardly wait to get to Pauline McGreggor's the week after the piece had been put to the kiln. For as much as Pauline McGreggor tried to offer encouragement and constructive criticism to everyone who attended her classes, there were no consoling words for Mabel Moss to offset the obviously disappointing outcome. In the car on the way home that night, having ridden together as they often did, Hazel Burns remarked that the color the lips had turned after baking made the face look overall more like Mama Cass Elliot than it did Jesus, whereas Elba Rae Van Oaks was adamant the stringy hair and completely unholy eyes bore an eerie and downright sacrilegious resemblance to Charles Manson and hoped Mabel would have the good sense to destroy it properly with a sledgehammer the first chance she got, even if she had to borrow one from Pauline McGreggor.

As Elba Rae stood in the lobby of the Litton County Department of Public Instruction, staring at the MARY A. HANKERSON nameplate on the desk, she wished whatever the future of her ceramics class attendance that Mabel Moss not be allowed take over her unfinished lamp. She might have even hinted as such to Mary Alice had Mary Alice been at her desk, but she wasn't; instead, Elba Rae had to talk to the woman sitting at the desk on the left side of the lobby whom she did not recognize.

"Can I help you?"

"Yes. I have an appointment. At two."

"And you are?"

"I'm Elba Rae Van Oaks. From the grammar school."

"I see. Well I don't believe the Superintendent is here at the moment, but as soon as Mary Alice gets back to her desk, she'll be able to help you."

"Well, that's all right. You can help me. My appointment isn't with the Superintendent anyway. It's with Mr. Yardley. Or, Dr. Yardley I guess it is."

"Oh. I see. Well—oh … you must be the teacher who …"

Elba Rae had by then overcome just enough of her nerves to raise one eyebrow in the direction of the unknown secretary. "The teacher who has the appointment with Dr. Yardley. Of course, Ms. Van Oaks. Just have a seat. Here, at my desk if you'd like. And I'll go let him know you're here."

"Thank you," Elba Rae said, while slowly retracting her brow.

"Can I get you some coffee?"

"No, thank you."

"Well, all right then. Just have a seat and I'll be right back."

Elba Rae stood firm in the middle of the lobby floor and had no intention of taking up a seat at the unknown secretary's desk. If it were to be so long a wait to see this Dr. Yardley man that she needed to sit, considering an appointment had been made on her behalf by the Superintendent himself, she'd just forget the whole thing and walk out the door. There was just so much she could be expected to endure, after all: Patsy Simpson and her hateful disposition, a humiliating lecture from Mr. Bailey, the ridicule of cruel kids playing jokes, and being spurned by her own church. She wasn't going to sit in the lobby of the board for everybody to notice as they passed through to add insult to her growing collection of injuries.

Fortunately, the wait was brief as the unknown secretary reappeared momentarily followed by a tall, middle-aged man with a short cropped gray beard and matching yet somewhat receding hairlines. He wore a three-piece suit with the coat unbuttoned, and on the top of his head rested a pair of narrow-rimmed reading glasses.

"Mrs. Van Oaks?"

Elba Rae answered, although the question seemed condescending and it irritated her. Of course she was Mrs. Van Oaks. It was Tuesday and it was two o'clock and even if it wasn't, she didn't doubt for a second she'd been properly announced by the secretary at large.

"I'm Marvin Yardley," and he reached out to shake her hand, which Elba Rae reluctantly took. "Can I get you some coffee before we go in?"

"No. Thank you." Elba Rae wondered what they did at the Board all day besides trying to push coffee off on anyone who wandered in. She wasn't there for the refreshments.

"All right then. Will you follow me, please?" He was so proper, Elba Rae thought. He was acting like she'd made the appointment with him of her own accord and free will instead of being forced into it by Howard Bailey and the Superintendent. Like she was there to get her hair done instead of be held captive for what would probably be another spin on Howard Bailey's previous speeches.

He led her down a short hall off the lobby and to a large office near the rear of the building. From the looks of the bookshelves and the walls around them, he'd not quite completed his unpacking, and as if he noticed right off the unsettling atmosphere the disorder created, he apologized to Elba Rae.

"I'm sorry for my office today, Mrs. Van Oaks. I've been so busy since getting to Litton County, working with the Superintendent on a new curriculum we're developing, that I've not had time to get my office completely set up. But I promise it'll be in order before our next meeting."

Elba Rae already did not like the turn the appointment was taking. Even though Mr. Bailey had alluded to the possibility of multiple visits with Dr. Yardley, she was holding out hope of a single trip. The fact that Dr. Yardley was already speaking of their future together seemed to negate those intentions. "I'm sure it will be really nice once you've got it all fixed up," Elba Rae said, without looking around anymore.

"I hope so. And as much for your sake as my own."

"How's that?" Elba Rae asked.

"I want you to feel comfortable here, Mrs. Van Oaks. For our visits. I think a comfortable environment can only enhance our sessions. Won't you sit down?" He said, as he did so himself.

"Our ... sessions?" Elba Rae warily lowered herself into a chair which felt too big for her.

Dr. Yardley leaned back in his. "You seem ill at ease, Mrs. Van Oaks. Are you sure there isn't anything I can get you? A glass of water?"

"No, thank you. I'm fine."

"All right then. Perhaps we should start off today by just getting acquainted with one another."

"Okay," she said. And so they began, with Dr. Yardley reciting his litany of credentials and touching briefly on the different places he had lived to earn them, followed by a summary in reverse chronological order of his various employments, and then concluded with a return to the present by which he explained how he'd come to move to Litton County and just how delighted he'd been with the decision thus far. Elba Rae supposed it was necessary to hear so he could feel validated. "Now tell me a little bit about yourself, Mrs. Van Oaks."

Elba Rae was nervous and didn't care for the getting acquainted segment of their meeting in the least, especially since her own background paled so when put up against the impressive Dr. Yardley's. She didn't think a graduation from Buford High School and a teaching certificate would do much to enhance a resume that consisted of one job with the fifth graders, but she reluctantly told him anyway.

"So you've lived in Buford all your life, is that right?" It was hard sometimes for Elba Rae Van Oaks not to spew the sarcasm she'd perfected from an early age, particularly when presented with an unspoiled opportunity, but she didn't want to peeve the great Dr. Yardley, as she could already tell she'd need him on her side if the Superintendent and Mr. Bailey were ever to be convinced she was ready to return to school. Nonetheless, she was tempted to point out to Dr. Yardley that nowhere in the story she'd just told had she made reference to a move, another town, a different job, nor had she included any innuendo whatsoever to suggest she'd lived anywhere but Buford. Instead, she just said, "That's right."

"It's a pretty town, from what I've seen. And the people are so friendly. I think they must know I'm new to the area."

"Probably do," Elba Rae concurred, "since most everybody knows everybody else around here. Of course, half of us are related to the other half some way or another, if you go back far enough."

"So you have a lot of family here?"

"Some. My momma is here, and I've got an aunt. They're both widows. My first cousin, Hazel. We're more like sisters than cousins. I have a sister, but she lives in Birmingham now."

"I believe the Superintendent may have mentioned you're a widow also."

"Yes."

"I'm sorry to hear that. My wife, Isabell, passed away about two years ago." Elba Rae did not respond.

"Anyway," he continued, "what I'd like to do today is talk to you about the Principal's Incident Report from last week." Elba Rae stiffened in her chair. "Now I know Mr. Bailey went over it with you before you left the campus Thursday, and I've read it, but it doesn't really tell me much, Mrs. Van Oaks." Elba Rae thought that comment odd, since from what she could recount from the unpleasant talk in Mr. Bailey's office prior to the suspension, the report had been quite vivid as Principal Incident Reports generally went. "Please don't be distressed, Mrs. Van Oaks. I'm not here to pass judgment on you, or scold you, or berate you. I'm sure you must feel like enough of that has been done already. I truly want to help you. And I think the best way I can start to do that is to hear about this … incident, as it's referred to, from you. Because I have a strong feeling there's a lot more to it than what I've read on this piece of paper."

Elba Rae shifted in the chair. "I … uh … I'm not sure what you want me to say. I thought Mr. Bailey put it all down."

"Mr. Bailey wrote up a report, because he's the principal and that's what he was supposed to do. But all it tells me is that he got a call on the intercom last

Thursday morning to come to the teacher's lounge because there was a—" He pulled the glasses from the top of his head and put them to work on his nose, as he held up the actual report. "A 'disturbance.'" He looked over the glasses at Elba Rae. "Now that's an awfully formal word for a food fight, don't you think?" Dr. Yardley wasn't positively sure that moment, though he would recall it later to be true, but he thought he almost saw Elba Rae Van Oaks smile. He returned his attention to the report. "Says here upon arrival in the lounge he observed a member of the faculty, a Miss Gunther, standing between you and another faculty member, a Mrs. Simpson, and that both of you had what appeared to be a ..." He paused to find the exact line in the report, and touched it with his finger. "'A chicken casserole' on your clothing, but that most of it was observed to be on Mrs. Simpson." He put the paper back down on his desk. "And the rest of it is basically the testimony, if you will, of some other teachers in the lounge either during or after the alleged incident. Besides Miss Gunther there was a Miss Young, and I think I recall some input from a Mr. Pickle."

"Well, " Elba Rae said softly, "that's about it."

"I don't believe you."

"I beg your pardon?"

"I said I don't believe you."

"Well, it's right there in the report."

"No, it's not."

"I don't understand what you mean, Dr. Yardley."

"You know what's in this report, Mrs. Van Oaks? It's the statements from Miss Gunther, who talks about hearing some noise coming from the lounge, and from Miss Young, I believe it is, who talks about being in the lounge getting ready for your monthly potluck lunch, and from Mr. Pickle, and of course there's the complaint from Mrs. Simpson, saying she was ... I think 'attacked' is the word she used."

"Yes."

"No," Dr. Yardley replied, and Elba Rae was perplexed. "Do you know what's not in this report? Isn't it obvious?" Elba Rae shrugged one shoulder and said nothing more.

"Your statement, Mrs. Van Oaks." He paused, for effect, and to allow her to absorb his revelation. "Sure, your signature is at the bottom of the report. You've acknowledged receipt of your copy. But this report is all about what other people had to say. This report doesn't tell me one thing about what *you* had to say."

"Well ..." Elba Rae was reluctant to speak up. Retelling what happened in the teacher's lounge wasn't going to help make it go away or be forgotten so she could get back to school. "Mr. Bailey and I sort of talked about it. But he'd already written up his report, so ..."

"Exactly," Dr. Yardley proclaimed, with somewhat of a legal authority in his voice Elba Rae thought. "And that doesn't give me one hint about what could possibly have precipitated the events of last week. About what would cause a devoted, well-respected teacher such as you to become involved in what sounds like a childish scuffle. Mrs. Van Oaks, do you know you could have been fired, on the spot, for what happened at your school?"

"I—"

"There's no need to answer. Because of course the answer is yes. Heck, in most school districts, you probably would have been. There might have been one of these incident reports written up, but I guarantee you we wouldn't have been sitting around discussing it in a setting like this the next week. It would have been handled much differently." Elba Rae didn't bother attempting a reply, since apparently Dr. Marvin Yardley was good at answering his own questions anyway. He took off his glasses and leaned forward across the desk. "I'm going to help you, Mrs. Van oaks. Do you believe that?"

"I—"

"We're going to work through this. We're going to work through whatever it was that really happened at your school last week, and we're going to get you back in the classroom where you belong. Where Mr. Bailey wants you to be, and where the Superintendent would rather you are, and, I'm quite sure, where you'd prefer to be."

"I would, Dr. Yardley. I feel like I need to be there now maybe instead of doing ... this."

"In due time, Mrs. Van Oaks."

"But—"

"We'll talk more next time, Mrs. Van Oaks. Friday morning, at ten?"

*   *   *   *

Instinctively, Elba Rae Van Oaks wanted to exit through the rear door of the building and walk around front to the Visitors Only lot and the Galaxie, because after her inaugural appointment with Dr. Marvin Yardley, she was no longer in the mood to encounter Mary Alice Hankerson and didn't even much care anymore if Mabel Moss took over her clock lamp combination piece at ceramics and painted all twelve disciples on it, but Dr. Yardley's escort down the hall and toward the main lobby had made a discreet departure too awkward to attempt.

"See you Friday," he said in a parting gesture, before turning around back toward his office, leaving Elba Rae but a few feet away from Mary Alice Hankerson's desk with Mary Alice Hankerson at it.

"Well hey, Elba Rae," Mary Alice said in what Elba Rae felt was a friendly tone.

"Hey, Mary Alice. How are you?"

"I'm fine. You?"

"Just fine."

"That's good. How's your momma doing?"

"Oh, going strong. As usual."

"Good."

"Well, I guess I better get in home. My wash isn't gonna do itself."

"I know what you mean. We'll see you tonight, then."

"Tonight?"

"For ceramics."

"Oh, I'm glad you reminded me, Mary Alice. Will you do me a favor?"

"Sure."

"Tell Pauline I won't be there tonight. I hate to miss, but I've got so much work piled up at the house, I just can't seem to catch up."

"All right. But I hate you're going to miss."

"Oh, me too. But you'll let her know when you get there, will you?"

"I sure will."

"Thank you."

"Then we'll see you next week."

"Well, I hope so. I'll see you, Mary Alice."

"Bye."

Elba Rae Van Oaks made her way to the Galaxie and drove home, hoping the worst was over.

*   *   *   *

It was not expected by many people, certainly no one in the immediate family and under no circumstances by Elba Rae Van Oaks in particular, that Ethel Maywood could keep a low profile for long, scandal or not, and so Elba Rae was not surprised in the least when her mother phoned in the early evening following Elba Rae's first appointment with Dr. Marvin Yardley; Elba Rae had known it would only be a matter of time before Ethel's curiosity would get the better of her deliberate attempts to distance herself from the talk going around Buford. Elba Rae was right, and Ethel Maywood wasted no time getting brought up to date.

"Did you get it all straightened out this afternoon? Is Howard Bailey going to let you go back to school?"

"Not yet, Momma."

"What do you mean, not yet?"

"I have to go back to the Board on Friday."

"What for?"

"To talk to Dr. Yardley."

"I thought that's who you were going to see today."

"It was."

"Well didn't you go?"

"Yes, Momma, I went."

"Did you see him?"

"Yes."

"Then I don't understand, Elba Rae. I thought you said this was just some kind of suspension or something and all you had to do was go to the Board today and then it'd be over and you'd go back to school."

"It is just a suspension, Momma, like I've been telling you. And I will be going back to school. Just not yet. I have to go see Dr. Yardley some more."

"That doesn't make a bit of sense. How long should it take to clear all this up and get it over with?"

"It's up to Dr. Yardley, I guess."

"Dr. Yardley? What does he have to do with this, and why does he get to have the say?"

"Because he just does, Momma."

"What aren't you telling me, Elba Rae?"

"Nothing."

"I don't think so. Exactly what kind of doctor is this Yardley man?"

"He's a psychologist."

"A what?"

"A psychologist."

"You mean some kind of mental doctor? Good Lord, Elba Rae, what have you gotten yourself into?!"

"He's not a mental doctor, Momma, he works for the Board. He's developing a new curriculum for the high schools and he just happens to have a doctorate degree in psychology."

"Well, then, what's he doing talking to you? Shouldn't be any of his business who the Superintendent lets work in the schools and who he doesn't. Unless they think you're just so crazy they've got to have you under a doctor. He didn't try to give you any shots, did he? Or pills?"

"Pills? Oh, Momma, for heaven's sake, you don't even know what you're saying."

"Elba Rae, I've lived a long time and I've seen a lot. Some good and some not so pretty. That's just life. But I've never seen any good come of people going to those kinds of doctors. You know they tried all kinds of treatments with that oldest sister of Dewey Richardson when she was young and didn't any of it ever settle her. They dragged her to every doctor within a hundred miles of here and wouldn't any cure ever take. They doped her up and gave her the shock paddles and she still ended up in the nut ward down there in Montgomery. Still there, far as I know."

"Momma, Veenie Richardson had a lobotomy because her daddy was afraid she was a sex maniac. You know all she ever wanted to do was chase after married men. That's what was wrong with her. That, and the fact she was a Richardson in the first place and you know none of them has ever been right in the head."

"Well I don't care. I want you to promise me right here and right now, Elba Rae, that you won't let them talk you into those treatments, no matter what they threaten you with. Even if it means losing your job. It's not worth it. Better to try and find another way to make a living than to be electrocuted into some sort of babbling fool that can't sit up in the chair less she's tied to it with a rope. You'll end up just like Veenie Richardson down there in Montgomery in the nut ward."

Through the years, Elba Rae Van Oaks never completely abandoned her fantasy that the world was populated with parents—mothers, especially—who comforted their children, as a matter of ingrained habit, yes, but who with their love and tenderness and sheer physical presence lent even more support during occasions of particular strife. Some days the fantasy was harder to cling to than others.

"You've got it all exaggerated as usual, Momma. Dr. Yardley is a psychologist. That's not a real medical doctor. He couldn't give out pills even if he wanted to. It's not his job. All he wants to do is talk. Period."

"About what?"

"About what happened last week at school!"

"Well everybody knows what happened at the school, Elba Rae. Don't think they don't. Just because you're staying shut up in the house and not going to church doesn't mean people aren't talking."

"I'm sure they are, Momma."

"Does he just want to make sure you're sorry? Did you promise nothing like this will ever happen again?"

"You know, Momma, Dr. Yardley actually seemed like he was a little more interested in it than just making sure I was sorry. Seemed like he might just want to know how I felt about what happened. That maybe something I had to say about it might be important, too. As important as whatever lies Patsy Simpson told."

"Well for goodness sake, Elba Rae, don't go making it any worse than it already is."

"How can it be any worse, Momma?"

"I'm sure you'll find out if you go up there and continue to do nothing but argue and fuss and carry on! They'll think you're as crazy as Veenie Richardson, and they're liable to never let you back in the school! Now just tell them you're sorry! Tell them you won't cause any more trouble, and you need your job back! Don't be so stubborn for once in your life!"

"I don't think it's gonna be that simple with Dr. Yardley. He may want to see me for some time yet."

"And what are you going to do in the meantime? Lay out of school? Hole up in your house?"

"I don't know, Momma. It's out of my hands."

"You know it's not easy for me, Elba Rae. I won't stay home from church. It's not right to do the Lord that way. And I can't stay shut up in my house. I still have to get out and go and face people on the street. What am I supposed to tell them?"

"I'm sure something will come to you, Momma. It always does."

*   *   *   *

Friday came around much sooner than Elba Rae wanted—sooner, it seemed, than in other weeks, as though it had skipped a day even to get there. Mary Alice Hankerson said hey when Elba Rae Van Oaks walked in the door at the Litton County Department of Public Instruction but before they could begin a conversation in earnest, about the latest developments at ceramics class or anything else, the unknown secretary whose name Elba Rae Van Oaks still had not learned just went ahead and told Elba Rae to go on back, that Dr. Yardley was expecting her. Elba Rae did as she was told; she didn't feel at liberty to keep the doctor waiting, although she was back to worrying about her clock piece and whether it had fallen into the hands of Mabel Moss by default.

Dr. Yardley was pleasant, as he was throughout their time together. But he didn't wallow too long in the small talk before plucking a nerve or two with Elba Rae.

"So have you been out much since you were here with me on Tuesday?"

As would so many occasions be the case, Elba Rae was hesitant to answer. She thought about her replies too long to suit him, of course, and he could always tell she was filtering the options. "Out?" Even she thought it lame.

"Yes. Shopping? To lunch with a friend, or your mother perhaps? To get your hair done?" She immediately ran her hand along the back of her hair, checking for damage to her coiffure, since—as she suspected he knew—Elba Rae had cancelled her regular beauty shop appointment. And not because her hair could afford to miss.

"Well, I've been real busy around my house, Dr. Yardley. You wouldn't think one person could make for so much work around a house, but they can."

"I would understand if you were reluctant to throw yourself into certain social situations at the moment, Mrs. Van Oaks. In fact, that's why I asked."

"I'm not reluctant, I just haven't had the need to really be anywhere except around my place, that's all."

"I see."

"Well, it's the truth." His instincts irritated her to no end. "I mean, there was the Book Club Wednesday night, but there wasn't any need for me to go to that."

"Is it something you normally attend?"

"Most of the times. But like I told Hazel, I wasn't getting myself ready and dragging all the way over there for a program I've seen ten times already."

Elba Rae Van Oaks was stretching the count a bit but it wasn't like she hadn't actually seen them before, which made for a convenient decline when she'd phoned Hazel Burns to convey her regrets.

"Who did you tell me was giving the program?" The conversation had gone.

"Mabel Moss," Hazel had replied.

"Ye gods, Hazel, you know she can't ever get up anything for a program except to pull out those slides."

"Surely she'll have something different," coaxed Hazel.

"Why, I bet she won't. I saw those at the regional Circle meeting at the Baptist church when they hadn't been back home a month, and then she wagged them to the Book Club Christmas party like we hadn't already seen them at the Circle, and then I had to sit through them again when she took Willadean's turn on the program at the Home Demonstration when Willadean was in the hospital with the shingles last spring."

"Well, they are right impressive, Elba Rae. If you haven't seen them before, I guess."

Hazel Burns had not anticipated from the very onset of the call Elba Rae would relish yet another opportunity to view slides of the Mosses' trip to the Holy Land, since Hazel Burns was fairly well sick of them herself and admittedly she'd not sat through them as many times. But her intention, of course, had not been so much to force Elba Rae to see the Moss travel pictures while Mabel offered what had become rote commentary seemingly catalogued perfectly to each and every slide but to just get her out of her own house. Hazel was worried.

"Would you think about going?"

"No, ma'am, I won't. I can sit here in my own den and close my eyes and see every one of those slides. And I can just hear Mabel now, when she gets to the one of Earl riding on that old nasty camel: 'Earl said if the gas prices had kept going up they way they were, he was going to see about us trading the car in for one of these!' That wasn't funny the first time I heard it and I'm not sitting through it again."

"Well, okay. I just thought I'd ask since—"

"And if I was Mabel, the least I'd do if I was gonna pull all over the county peddling those slides would be to get a decent projector. That one she's got must have come over on the Ark. It takes her an extra thirty minutes to get set up because she's always fumbling with a piece of paper trying to fold it up just so under one corner so it'll sit level. Last time I saw them, I didn't know if I was looking at a pyramid or The Leaning Tower of Pisa."

"Maybe I'll see if Momma wants to go," conceded Hazel, thinking all the while Elba Rae's protest was a bit excessive.

"That's a good idea," Elba Rae had concluded.

"Did you think about what we talked about the other day, Mrs. Van Oaks?" Dr. Yardley asked, after Elba Rae had quit trying to justify her newfound reclusiveness.

"Think about it?"

"Yes."

"Well, yes, I guess I did." Elba Rae was unsure of the best answer, but feared little Dr. Yardley would correct her were she not following his intended lead.

"Good," he said, seemingly pleased. "Because from now on, we're going to talk about you." Elba Rae shifted in her chair, unsure she would ever get comfortable with the imposing man sitting behind the desk.

"I want to know a little more about you, Mrs. Van Oaks. Not so much about your teaching background or about your credentials—I know you're a good teacher. I believe that in my heart."

"Thank you."

"Let's talk about your personal life."

She stared at him, waiting for him to continue and at least hoping he'd say something. But he didn't. "I'm not going to pry, Mrs. Van Oaks. And there's no purpose in you talking about things you're uncomfortable with, but if we're to make progress, I need to know more about you. Do you understand?"

"I guess so."

"Good. So why don't we start with …" He was pausing, as if he were trying to come up with a subject, but Elba Rae did not doubt in the least he already knew what he wanted to say. "… Your husband. Mr. Van Oaks. Why don't you tell me about when you were married?"

Elba Rae Van Oaks was suddenly cognizant of the conversation she'd had with her mother a few days prior, when Ethel Maywood had dared pose the possibility Elba Rae might need to abandon the teaching profession all together and seek her livelihood elsewhere. And at that moment, it seemed like a good idea to Elba Rae, rather than indulge whatever foolishness this man was forcing on her.

But she was trapped in the circumstance and locked inside Dr. Yardley's office, if not literally by a chain on the door then certainly by the doing of her own hand; namely, it seemed, the hand that had carried the Pyrex dish over to confront Patsy Simpson.

"Does it make you ill at ease to talk about your marriage, Mrs. Van Oaks?"

It was not so much the subject of the late Fettis Van Oaks which caused Elba Rae discomfort as it was the question being posed by a stranger who, in any other setting whether social or business, would surely have been recognized as just rude for asking. "No, it's not unpleasant for me, Dr. Yardley. It's …"

"Then what?"

"Well, it's just that it was so long ago, and I don't know when I've ever talked about my wedding."

"Then why not? I'd like to hear. Tell me about when you got married."

"Well … okay. If you think it will help anything." She had to think about it for a minute before launching full force into the story and was deliberate about which details she mentioned aloud to Dr. Yardley and which ones she muted as they came up in the story.

It had not been hot by Buford standards on that first Saturday in June in 1953 when Elba Rae Maywood pledged her troth to Mr. Fettis Van Oaks at the altar of the First Avenue United Methodist Church, yet the coolness of the breeze had not prevented the small beads of perspiration from forming just at the peak of Elba Rae's forehead, nor under, she was certain, her arm. She knew she was nervous because she was to be the center of attention for at least the next two hours, because she was about to enter forth into a phase of life she felt deficiently prepared to ford, and because as long as she was making the soon-to-be-public declaration of said fording she wasn't entirely convinced that Mr. Fettis Van Oaks was the most absolute and final candidate for which no man should be put asunder. Not that there were alternatives at hand, and not that she'd have felt any less sweaty if another groom were waiting in the sanctuary. The fact was Fettis Van Oaks had genuinely and properly proposed marriage to her and she'd guessed that was just going to be that. At twenty-eight, she was already eight years older than her younger sister Lila Mae had been when she'd stood before friends and family with her six attendants and one bridesmaid to join her hand in marriage with Bucky Fessmire of the Birmingham Fessmires. And yet, Elba Rae was still somewhat younger than the groom-elect.

Raymond Maywood had been heard to joke more than once to no one in particular that he was just glad someone was finally taking his eldest daughter off his hands. Ethel Maywood's overall impression of the forthcoming marriage announcement had been, instead, tempered by her innate opinion that Fettis Van Oaks had come courting the unmarried Maywood daughter because of the one endearing quality separating her from the other similarly seasoned maidens in the community, of which there was quite the bountiful crop that year: Elba Rae was employed. She was then, as she was still that Thursday in the teacher's lounge on the day she would become the subject of a Principal's Incident Report, one of the two fifth-grade teachers at the Homer T. Litton Grammar School. Fettis Van Oaks was so well ahead of his time, some would speculate years later, when he had readily declared his absolute wish not to take Elba Rae from the career she had so diligently pursued after graduating from Buford High School.

Ethel Maywood declared at least to Raymond and to Elba Rae that she thought Fettis Van Oaks never intended to have to work a day in his life. And while Elba Rae had chosen to ignore those clouds that hovered over her approaching nuptials, she couldn't help but think—as she stood in the minister's study of the First Avenue United Methodist Church, awaiting the knock to let her know it was time to go to the back of the sanctuary where she would join her father for the short stride to the altar that bore Mr. Fettis Van Oaks and his father the best man—that her mother's voice was taking the shape of many tiny beads of sweat under her arm and at the peak of her forehead. And it frustrated her so.

When the moment came, she met her father at the back of the church, entwined her arm in his, and tried to remember what Reverend Bishop had said about taking slow steps to get to the front of the sanctuary. In the entire scheme of things, it had taken such a scant few moments of her life to be joined as one with Mr. Fettis Van Oaks that later on the memories of the actual experience would be gleaned more from the several black-and-white photographs taken immediately afterward than could be recollected from having been there in person as the bride.

She did always remember, without even the assistance of the glossy visual aids, how pretty her matron of honor, the former Lila Mae Maywood who was now a Fessmire of the Birmingham Fessmires, had been, how happy she appeared and how even then eight years into her own marriage Lila Mae was the most free of anyone in the church.

Elba Rae did also always remember, hard as she might try to forget, how her groom's father the best man had, without warning or provocation, been stricken with a most unfortunate occurrence of flatulence during her vows which put a special strain on her for which no amount of rehearsing the night before would have helped overcome. Standing before Reverend Bishop and her own parents and the gathered congregation at the First Avenue United Methodist Church, Elba Rae had said, "I do," while simultaneously surmising that her almost father-in-law's discomfort must surely have been the consequence of the inferior size of his suit pants in direct relation to the circumference of his girth. She felt sorry for him then.

The pity lasted but just through the fall of that first year, however, which was about as long as it took to be party to a few holiday gatherings with her new in-laws. To her further disappointment and disgust, Elba Rae would conclude pant size was irrelevant to the Van Oakses as a general indicator of impending flatulence, and that for some Van Oaks family members in particular, whom she never publicly named, the act itself took on a near prideful trait. She had prayed through most all of the year 1954 that amidst the glory and the splendor of the Christmas Eve candlelight service at the First Avenue United Methodist Church no one in surrounding pews had taken note that her mother-in-law Helma Van Oaks's own flame had turned a most cobalt shade of blue.

The new Mr. and Mrs. Fettis Van Oaks had driven to the Georgian Terrace Hotel on Peachtree Street in Atlanta for their honeymoon, and the next afternoon they drove home to Buford, where they pretty much stayed for the rest of their lives. Elba Rae taught school and gradually learned some breathing techniques from Miss Gunther the girls's P.E. teacher that would serve her well during Thanksgivings and birthdays.

Fettis Van Oaks had worked, of course, first on a crew with the Litton County Road Department before the wedding and later at the meatpacking plant on the outskirts of town, during which time the couple qualified for the loan to build their new house on Highway 29. Fettis was on the job at Buford Slaughter and Packaging when the accident occurred which permanently and forever extracted him from the greater Buford workforce, leaving Elba Rae solely to fulfill their mortgage obligation.

Ethel Maywood had been slow to embrace the full and complete nature of her son-in-law's disability, nor could she ever, to her satisfaction, conjure a picture in her mind of exactly how it was he had not been able to flee in time the path of the heifer's suspended carcass as it rolled down the cable. Fettis Van Oaks was alive and mobile; the cow was dead and impaled on a hook. She just didn't think it made sense that he should be knocked sideways with such debilitating force that his back and his neck but mostly his back would never again be able to endure the sufferings of full time work.

"What was he doing just standing there, anyway?" Ethel Maywood would repeat to her husband Raymond for years to come without ever wanting him to answer.

"I guess he wasn't thinking."

"What's to think? There's a dead cow flying your way, you'd best move. I bet he just stood there and waited for the nasty thing to hit him."

"Oh, Ethel, now—" he would attempt to interrupt the first few times he heard the rendition.

"Oh now nothing. He just stood there. He stood there and he waited and when he got the chance he took it. And Elba Rae will be hobbling to the chalkboard when she's eighty to keep a roof over their heads and food in their mouths! I hope she gives him hamburger meat every meal!"

As bovine-induced disabilities went, Fettis Van Oaks as it turned out perhaps did not have the most severe of cases. He had managed thereafter to attend enough meetings of the Lodge to retain his membership and on most mornings did enjoy the camaraderie of the other, albeit older, Buford retirees who gathered at Jack Moss's hardware store on the square to drink coffee and discuss the political scene, both local and beyond, and talk about health issues that may have been of concern to those present and those who weren't but that as a rule centered around digestive issues and the prostate. One unsubstantiated account even had him on a bowling league in Tallapoosa County but no one ever dared question Elba Rae about his recurring absences from the house on Tuesday nights.

Yes, Fettis Van Oaks had held his head high knowing he was an example to other disabled Bufordians who didn't the make the same efforts he had when it came to returning to normal life, as best he could, after the untimely accident that had struck him down in his prime. He had persevered in spite of it all and accepted that he was an inspiration to his community. He did his inspiring mainly from Monday through Saturday because he could not—according to Fettis at the suggestion of his own physician—attend with regularity any services at the First Avenue United Methodist Church due to the intolerable strain the uncushioned pews put on his back and his neck, and in this instance the misery was pretty much divided equally between the two.

Elba Rae didn't realize at first how much time had lapsed since she'd started the involuntary reminiscing about her wedding at the First Avenue United Methodist Church and about her one night at the Georgian Terrace Hotel in Atlanta and about all the farts that followed. Dr. Marvin Yardley, however, was among his other virtues an indefatigable timekeeper.

"I appreciate your candor, Mrs. Van Oaks. On some level it must appear I'm just being nosey."

"Well ..."

"But there is a purpose. I assure you. Eventually, it will perhaps be more evident than it is today."

"Eventually?" She'd said it quite slowly, making clear her apprehension.

"Yes," he said. "At some point, before our time together is over."

"And when do you think that might be, Dr. Yardley? I mean, how long is this going to take?"

He removed his glasses and set them on the desk before reclining slightly in the large accommodating chair. "Until we get to the bottom of this, Mrs. Van Oaks."

"I don't understand."

"It's quite simple, just as I explained in our first meeting. I believe there's a reason you snapped in the teacher's lounge. And it's now become my duty to find out what that reason was, to hopefully be able to isolate it, and to assure the Superintendent and Mr. Bailey you belong back at work."

Elba Rae Van Oaks let out a little sigh that was the combination of a slight moan and a fret as she leaned back in her own chair. It had begun. The day and, perhaps, the days Elba Rae Van Oaks realized she might spend away from her classroom became a week which soon begat two and eventually grew to six during which, to her later surprise, she did actually reveal some things to Dr. Marvin Yardley she'd not previously disclosed to others on a wholesale basis.

He'd started the next week wanting to know about life in Buford and some of the people Elba Rae Van Oaks knew, some of them relatives, some church members, and some she just happened to know because she lived in Buford, but he'd eventually learn a thing or two about Elba Rae Van Oaks, too. She had tales to tell, as it turned out. For Dr. Marvin Yardley, they produced an amusement previously devoid from his career but which served well in the carefully veiled memoir he composed upon his retirement that, incomplete and somewhat indiscriminate, ultimately went unpublished before or after his death. Perhaps mercifully so.

DEWEY RICHARDSON

Though she never became unguarded with Dr. Marvin Yardley by any interpretation of the word, Elba Rae Van Oaks did eventually displace a small quantity of her initial apprehension with just enough trust to allow forth the clarification of some details leading up to the unfortunate confrontation with Mrs. Patsy Simpson. Both Dr. Yardley and Elba Rae considered it a milestone of sorts when she disclosed what had immediately precipitated the messy disagreement, namely the slur relevant to her casserole ingredients. But it was actually well into week three of their sessions together before Elba Rae Van Oaks would willfully confess she had, in fact, once made her signature dish with a canned product just as Patsy Simpson decreed, although not before repeated assurances from Dr. Yardley that the content of their conversations was strictly confidential.

"It must have been sad for you," he offered.

"Sad?" She didn't seem to follow.

"Yes. That week you speak of. When you lost so many of your friends and neighbors, so close together."

"Well, yes, it was sad I guess. But you know Miss Nita Perrymore was past ninety, bless her heart, and Dewey Richardson ... well, he just never was right."

"Oh?"

"No," she confirmed.

"Was he ill?"

"In the head he was." By the stern reaction Dr. Yardley suddenly wore on his face, she supposed the remark had sounded flippant and callous. "What I mean is, he never was right after he came back from the war."

"In what way?"

It was Elba Rae Van Oaks looking at the clock that particular afternoon, hoping Dr. Yardley would soon call time. She found it absolutely pointless to spend the day in his office rattling on about poor dead Dewey Richardson because, after all, he was dead, and he wasn't the one who'd tussled with Patsy Simpson and he wasn't the one who needed to get back to teaching. Yet, she had to indulge him.

"He just did things, you know? That weren't right."

"Such as?" He almost seemed insulted, as if he'd known Dewey Richardson and was taking personal offense at the unflattering assessment of his character. So be it, she thought. And she told him what she knew to be the truth about Mr. Dewey Richardson, secondhand though most of it was.

*   *   *   *

"Good Lord, have you heard?" Hazel Burns was breathless, and sounded panicked. "Dewey Richardson had another spell this afternoon and it's so bad, they've had to call in Shirley from Baton Rouge!"

Elba Rae had been, up to the point of Hazel's phone call, having a relatively peaceful evening as she was on the TV thoroughly enjoying watching the very talented and the lovely Miss Kitty Carlisle banter with the just as lovely Miss Arlene Francis as they both attempted to guess the profession of Mr. Ed Zork, a door-to-door lingerie salesman from Schenectady, who was on the verge of stumping the night's panel. Elba Rae had not particularly wanted to be disturbed with panic, or death, or news in general, or any other situation that would necessitate extra energy or concern. It had just been an evening when all she wanted to think about was Miss Kitty Carlisle and Miss Arlene Francis and exactly what nature of lingerie Mr. Ed Zork of Schenectady might be selling and how she bet she'd never have cause or opportunity to open the door to him in Buford.

But all hopes of such were over as soon as she heard the subject of her cousin's urgent ring, since there had not typically been a call placed or received about Mr. Dewey Richardson for years that would leave the caller or the receiver unaffected enough to continue with television-watching once it ended, not even when enticed with the combined loveliness of Miss Kitty Carlisle and Miss Arlene Francis nor with the intrigue of a native northerner who went from house to house pulling lurid attire out of a satchel in front of perfect strangers. Dewey Richardson was a figure to pity in the community, one most people wished they could ignore. The trouble was, Dewey Richardson didn't try in the least to be ignored because being ignored and doing the things he did were a contradiction no Bufordian could reconcile.

"It's worse than the night Earl and Mabel Moss went to his house and he … well, you know," Hazel Burns forewarned.

It was a fact Dewey Richardson had never been the same since returning to Buford from the First World War. Oh, in the beginning the signs went unnoticed, at least outside the immediate Richardson family, and any perceived idiosyncrasies were attributed to his readjustment to civilian life and sometimes also to the fact that the Richardsons had, through the generations, always had just a touch of insanity in the genes. Between the war and his natural lineage, no one could quite blame Dewey Richardson himself if his conversations didn't always make exact sense or if sometimes, walking around town on a Saturday afternoon, he might be prone to tug suspiciously at parts of his clothing that a normal person wouldn't touch in public (or at least not in full daylight right there on the Square). It was only later that Dewey Richardson's actions would thrust him into the lives of those who may have once sought to look the other way with one of the most notable intrusions of all delivered directly unto Earl and Mabel Moss.

"You know, I don't think poor Mabel's ever gotten over it," Hazel recounted on the phone while Mr. Ed Zork from Schenectady coyly answered a question from Miss Francis, who Elba Rae couldn't exactly hear anymore. "And I know it was a long spell before Earl even wanted to go calling again. Momma said the only way Mabel ever agreed to even go with him after that was if he promised to never mention Dewey Richardson's name again!"

"Well I don't blame her, Hazel," Elba Rae sympathized. "If I was them, I'd have just got in home and sat down and never knocked on another door."

"Isn't that the truth?" Hazel Burns agreed.

The Mosses had always been good to call on new arrivals to Buford, and on old arrivals who weren't, to their knowledge, regular church members, and on those they knew to be former regular church members who it might be known were experiencing an estrangement from their particular congregations for whatever the reason. The Mosses went calling so that they could, as part of their duty as members of the Mission Committee, persuade the potential sinners to seek salvation and fellowship at the Buford Baptist Church. Earl Moss worked at the Litton County Farm Bureau, when he wasn't busy being a deacon in the church, and Mabel kept house.

The Tuesday night Earl and Mabel would call on Dewey Richardson, Mabel Moss had expressed a desire to instead report back to the committee the following night at Prayer Meeting that she and Earl were saddened by their inability to make any calls that week but had felt it best to avoid all contact with the public what with Earl's nasty and most likely contagious virus. Earl Moss overruled his wife's agenda and felt it best to extend the right hand of fellowship to all of God's people, even if one of them was Dewey Richardson, and just what kind of example would they be setting when it would be obvious to all that Earl Moss had been robust and healthy at church just two days before with clearly the absence of disease or infection.

"Well, what if he decides to come to church?" Mabel Moss inquired of her husband as they backed out the gravel driveway of the two-story frame house Earl Moss's father had built before the turn of the century. Earl Moss put his right hand on his wife's knee in a reassuring gesture as he sometimes did and steered the Chevrolet Bel-Air toward the road.

"It'll be all right, Mabes. Dewey's harmless. He might seem a little strange to you sometimes but he's a good soul. Jack says so all the time."

"Jack would say so about the Devil himself as long as he spent six days a week drinking coffee in that store and gossiping about heaven only knows what."

"Mabel," Earl said, slowing the Bel-Air to almost a crawl and looking her directly in the eye. "It's the Lord's work."

She thought about the Lord's work long enough for Earl to turn out onto the road and get headed in the general direction of Dewey Richardson's house in one of the original sections of Buford.

"If the Lord wants to save Dewey Richardson, I wish He'd coordinate it through the Methodists and leave us out of it. That man hasn't been right since the War and that's all there is to it." Her assessment was met only by the chorus of *Blessed Assurance*, which Earl Moss had begun to whistle, prompting Mabel to close her eyes and then roll them into the back of her head.

As a general practice, the Mission Committee of the Buford Baptist Church did not specifically believe it necessary to contact those in the community selected for salvation that week to schedule a visit in advance. The committee preferred, for better or worse, to approach the recipients of their witness unannounced so as to disarm any preparations for pretense—which also served, proportionately, to increase the likelihood they might be home and answer the door. No one ever really knew with certainty whether phoning ahead would have made a difference in the Richardson case, and there were always those who believed outright it may have even aggravated the situation had Dewey Richardson known to be expecting guests and, in particular, guests who were on a mission from the Baptist church. Either way, the outcome of the Mosses's call had been the talk for days and even made Earl Moss regret dismissing the illness alibi his wife had proposed.

That night, Mabel Moss had felt her buttocks tense on the cool vinyl of the Bel-Air's front seat when she realized they were turning onto Dewey Richardson's street and would probably soon be in his actual living room, a prospect that did hold some curious anticipation as she had, unexpressed but surely not alone, always wondered just what the inside of that house must look like. "I bet it's nasty as buzzards," she recalled Elba Rae Van Oaks having once surmised. The outside of it was unthreatening enough and best described even as just ordinary, and some of Dewey Richardson's own neighbors had even been known to comment amongst themselves that didn't he always keep his yard up nice and couldn't he grow the prettiest roses anybody'd ever seen. But horticulture aside, the exercise of trying to make small talk with someone known to walk around the Square on Saturday afternoons doing vulgar things with his pants made Mabel desperate.

"It's not too late. Not if you don't slow down enough for him to notice the headlights." Mabel Moss thought it worth one last appeal to her husband who, on that night, she knew was out-sainting her and wouldn't have turned back if Satan had been standing on the lawn between the curb and front door holding a flaming pitchfork and spewing brimstone.

"Mabel, we are not turning around now," he replied in a tone that was beyond stern and crackling with irritation at her. "We are going to the front door and ask for a few minutes of this man's time to talk to him about the Lord just like we've done on every other mission call before. This one is not going to be any different."

He parked the Bel-Air in the driveway and turned off the motor. "Are you ready to go with me?" He asked.

Mabel opened the car door and stepped out without answering, and then she waited for her husband to round the car and join her, slightly ahead, up the walk to the front door. She'd decided right then and there she wasn't going to say another word, that he'd been the one who insisted they go through with it, and he could just lead the way to the door, knock on it, explain to Dewey Richardson why they'd come to be standing on his porch step without so much as an invitation or the pretense of any genuine friendly acquaintance, and that way she would face no liability whatsoever when the subject would come up in her Circle meetings, as surely it would, when someone would later question whose idea it had been anyway to invite Dewey Richardson into their congregation. She hated to turn on her husband like that, since she did love him and all, but that was her strategy and she was sticking to it.

The Mosses stood at the front door in darkness and although Mabel recognized hesitation in her husband's pause before knocking, she didn't dare observe it out loud. That would have been contrary to her plan, no doubt about it. Earl Moss did knock on the door, and even though Mabel thought the knock definitely too light for anyone inside the house to possibly hear unless he was already standing in the living room with one ear pressed up against the door, she didn't observe that out loud either. Moreover, she knew if Dewey Richardson never heard them at the door, they could report back his absence from the house the following night at Prayer Meeting and everyone involved could save face and be safe and Earl could continue to silently pride himself on being the better Christian which Mabel Moss even most of the time believed to be true herself. She had subconsciously turned her left foot slightly back in the direction of the Bel-Air when they were both noticeably startled by a flash of light in their faces that was the porch light switching on from inside. By then it was too late, she knew.

Mabel Moss glanced in the direction of her husband just enough to notice he was taking in a deep breath and preparing his demeanor for a greeting to the person who'd be on the other side of the door. She was still looking at Earl when, oblivious to the swish that had been the door opening, she thought Earl must have been having another spell of the angina, because his plastered smile was suddenly distorting itself into a mildly painful-looking grimace and his eyes were opening larger and larger. At first, it hadn't occurred to Mabel that she needed to be looking straight in front of her if she wanted an explanation for her husband's sudden transformation but hours later, as she relived the moment while sitting at the Formica table in the sanctity of her own kitchen while nursing a lukewarm cup of Sanka, she realized she'd just been afraid to look for herself.

When she finally had taken her gaze off the motionless Earl and turned to force eye contact with their mission for herself, there he was. Dewey Richardson. Expressionless. His left arm by his side, his right hand raised forth grasping a can of Old Milwaukee poised for the next sip. Bathed in the golden sunlight hue that his yellow porch light bulb rendered on the door stoop and to just inside the living room. Calm, un-startled. And buck naked.

Mabel Moss's head jerked and her eyes blinked quickly as though she had just swallowed a potent medicine. She thought she could hear something that was no more than muttering coming from her husband, but couldn't be sure. She was frozen in a block of ice and was dipped in a vat of cement and was chained in padlocks to Dewey Richardson's front door in such a way that any attempt to turn away was pointless.

The first distinguishable word she'd been able to recall Earl saying was, "Hello." In retrospect, "hello" seemed somewhat inappropriate for the occasion. "Hello" was, in fact, just downright stupid, she thought. "What the hell?" is really what Mabel Moss had been thinking at that moment—but of course this was not something Mabel Moss would ever have said out loud, live at the scene or in any recounting thereafter.

If there could have been any more inadequate follow up to "hello" than "How are you, Dewey?" Mabel Moss was never able to imagine it later. She briefly wondered if the sight of Dewey Richardson posing nude in his front door drinking a beer and looking jaundiced by the unflattering color choice of porch light bulbs was all in her imagination and hers alone. But, alas, the remarkable circumstance was real.

Mabel Moss didn't want to stand there making small talk on the door step with Dewey Richardson! She wanted her husband to melt the ice with a blow torch and chisel the concrete away with a jackhammer and chop the chains with an axe and yell, "Run, Mabel, run!" as they simultaneously leapt to the safety of the awaiting Bel-Air, the getaway car that would extract them from a crime in progress and which they'd be able to reach in one big thrusting jump. But no. Earl Moss, instead, was looking Dewey Richardson right in the eye and inquiring as to his health. Mabel Moss looked at his eyes, too, and even if it was the one and only voluntary function she could control, she was determined not to look anywhere else. Even so, with her constitution strong, Mabel absolutely couldn't help but notice how surprisingly fit Dewey still was physically even at his age and with his obviously diminished mental capacity, though she knew right then there would never be any benign way of introducing her observation into polite conversation.

Dewey Richardson said nothing yet Earl Moss blathered on. "We uh … we didn't mean to come at a bad time, Dewey … uh … me and Mabel. You know my wife, Mabel, don't you?" Mabel nodded to Dewey as though she owed him at least the courtesy, but she remained careful not to look down nonetheless.

"We didn't want to take up much of your time, Dewey, but we had just wanted to talk with you for a minute or two and—"

"—But we can't stay!" Mabel said. Earl Moss looked at his wife. "We did want to visit with you, Dewey, but we can see that this just isn't a good time. I mean … not see … but we can tell. I mean, we should have called first and the next time we surely will. Call first. Before we come. Earl?"

"Uh … excuse us, Dewey. We'll be getting on now and let you get back to … your business."

"Y'all take care, now," Dewey Richardson finally offered, and then he closed the front door right back where it had been. Earl and Mabel Moss stood in the yellow light, speechless, before Mabel took her leave and started walking back to the still-warm Bel-Air. They were halfway home before the shock of it all had worn off enough to discuss.

"Well, what's happened now, Hazel?" Elba Rae was defeated. The panel was saying goodnight to each other and she hadn't even seen how much cash Ed Zork from Schenectady had pursed.

"Are you sitting down?"

"Yes, Hazel, I'm sitting down."

"Well, it was about dinner time this afternoon. You know that Wrigley girl that married one of the Templetons from up around Eagle Gap?" Elba Rae did not readily know the Wrigley girl and admitted as much to Hazel.

"You know those Wrigleys, Elba Rae. There were three of them. Let's see, there was Melanie, she was the oldest, and then I believe next was Ruth. She's the one that married that Cole boy that ran off with that girl … oh, what was her name … the one that was in all those Litton County Chorale competitions they used to have. They said she was wanting to get to New York and try to be some kind of singer and that fool just wagged right off behind her and left poor Ruth high and dry. But now, Ruth was sort of the homely one in that family."

"If she's the one I'm remembering," Elba Rae offered, "she would've had to slip up on the bucket to get a drink."

"Well, I know it, but poor thing. I don't know what gets in to people, Elba Rae, do you? Except that they're men. I guess that's it. Melanie always was the most sensible one of them but—"

"Hazel, is there—"

"And then there was Lou Anne. She married one of those Templeton boys that lived up around Eagle Gap."

"Well I do sort of remember some Templetons," Elba Rae recollected. And even if she hadn't, she would have said so anyway to unstick her cousin Hazel from the rut she'd slipped into that was clearly impeding the story at hand.

"Lou Anne Wrigley married a Templeton and they moved into an old house up there on Delight Lane, right across from Dewey Richardson." Finally they were getting somewhere, Elba Rae thought.

"About dinner time, Lou Anne went to the mailbox to get the mail and she heard the lawnmower going across the street and it was Dewey. Well, she said she didn't think much about it at the time because Dewey's always been good to keep up the yard and cut the grass and she said it seems like he's always out there with the mower and it sounded like he was around the side of the house. Well, just about the time she got to the box and was getting their mail out of it, she said she heard the mower coming from the side of the house toward the front and then there he was cutting clean across the front yard—right there on the street—and do you know what?"

"What?"

"He didn't have a stitch on from the waist down!"

It had certainly been a night for picturing strange images, Elba Rae somehow first thought, what with the introduction of Mr. Ed Zork from Schenectady and now this. So unusual a report was it that Elba Rae didn't even know what to say, although she'd heard a lot and heard often from her cousin Hazel Burns, who was always so good to call when there was news in the community.

"What did she do?" Elba Rae wanted to know next.

"She said she didn't know what to do so she just grabbed the mail and went back in the house, and she said she was hurrying so to get in the door she dropped her new *Good Housekeeping* on the porch and it fell under her peony bush and she didn't even bend down to get it."

"My heavens, Hazel."

"I know," Hazel continued. "She said she didn't want to get mixed up in any confrontations with anybody, not that I think she's scared of Dewey, but you know how he is and he's just not right and everybody knows it and I don't blame her for wanting to get in the house and shut the door."

"So what'd she do?"

"She called Jimmy at work and told him to get home. He works up there at the Tool and Dye, you know. Got a good job, I think. Somebody told me he was some kind of supervisor on the line or something so he must make good money. I don't think any of the rest of them have ever hit a lick but at least he's tried. You know, Momma ran into Willadean Hendrix getting a prescription filled not long ago and they got to talking about this and that and who's what and Willadean told Momma that oldest Templeton was in jail somewhere, in Montgomery County maybe, 'cause he'd gotten mixed up in some kind of stolen tractor parts mess."

"I didn't know that. Which one was he?"

"What was his name … Timmy? No, it wasn't Timmy."

"Tommy?"

"No, I don't think it was Tommy."

There was silence on both ends of the phone line as Elba Rae Van Oaks and her cousin Hazel attempted to conjure the birth name of the oldest Templeton boy who'd been unfortunately introduced to the justice system and was now incarcerated due to his ill-fated farm implements caper.

"Well, it doesn't matter," Hazel Burns resolved, certain it was time to shelve the genealogical background of the bit players because she was, anyway, much too anxious to pick up the story at hand which had been left off with a traumatized Lou Anne Wrigley Templeton inside the house calling her husband, having surrendered to her peony bush possibly forever the latest edition of the *Good Housekeeping.* "They never were any count except for Jimmy."

"Did he come home?"

"I don't think he really believed her at first but she was upset and carrying on so over the phone that he came rushing and when he got there, do you know what?"

"What?"

"Dewey was still in the front yard just mowing the grass like he didn't have a care in the world."

"What did Jimmy do?"

"Lou Anne said she was watching out the window just waiting for him to get home and when he did, he parked the truck in their driveway and went straight over across the street."

"What did Dewey do?"

"She said he stopped the mower and from the window it looked like Jimmy and Dewey were talking like any two people would. She said Dewey was just as calm and didn't ever raise his voice or anything."

"She could hear what they were saying?"

"Well, I think she cracked the window a little in her front room so she could check on Jimmy, I guess."

"Yeah."

"Well, Jimmy talked to him for a good bit and then came on across the street into the house, but he didn't even get in the door good until they heard the mower crank up and Dewey went right back to cutting the grass."

"He's a nut, Hazel! That's all there is to it! There's none of them that's ever been right."

"I know it. But anyway, Jimmy didn't know what else to do so he called the Sheriff. I think he hated to call the law on his own neighbor, but you know there are children all up and down that street and poor Miss Nita Perrymore still lives up there in her house and she's so decrepit anyway and what if she'd come out in the yard and seen that old fool over there just exposing himself in the street like some kind of ..."

"Nut! That's what he is!"

"I know it."

"Well what happened? Did the Sheriff come?"

"They sent that Fowinkle boy."

"Who?"

"You know, that boy of Myron and Helen Fowinkle. The one that had such a hard time in school. They had to keep him back a year and practically threaten to put him in Irma Young's class to get him to study his arithmetic."

"I'm not surprised at any child having to struggle with arithmetic when all they've got is Claude Pickle trying to teach."

"I thought he'd gotten better."

"Oh, he'll never be any better, Hazel. He's silly as a goat and none of the children pay him any mind, and how can they when half of them are bigger than he is?"

"Elba Rae, you're a mess," she chuckled. Even though Hazel Burns was an employee of the Homer T. Litton Grammar School, which shared a campus with the Homer T. Litton High School, she often relied on her cousin Elba Rae to find out what really went on behind the scenes. Mr. Bailey was too often prone to close his door and lower his voice when he was on the phone and did not fully inform his secretary of important matters.

"That Fowinkle boy was always such a timid child in school, I can't imagine him wanting to be on the Sheriff's Department," Elba Rae picked up.

"Well, I heard the service wouldn't take him."

"Is that right?"

"You know Helen Fowinkle used to be in the book club with Momma and she told Momma he had some kind of spastic colon problem that nobody ever knew anything about until he tried to sign up for the Marines and they did a good physical on him and they found it out."

"That's a shame."

"Well, I don't think it really affects him much. He goes with some girl from Tuscaloosa and Helen said he just has to stay away from nuts. Of course, the first time he went over there to meet her people, what do you suppose they wanted to serve?"

"What?"

"Peanut brittle. Said it was something the girl's grandmother was famous for and they put on so about it and said the grandmother couldn't much see anymore, but how she'd fussed over the stove anyway just to make it for the girl cause her beau was coming to meet the family and she nearly put a can of pinto beans in it instead of peanuts cause she couldn't see so the boy felt like he had to take it when they offered and act like he liked it."

"Goodness. Did it hurt him?"

"Helen said she didn't think it did, but he had to stop at every gas station between there and Buford on the way home so he could use the restroom."

"Such a young boy to be having problems like that."

"Well, I think he finally got up his nerve to tell the girl he just couldn't go those nuts, and after that he didn't have any more trouble. Helen said they had to put the grandmother in the nursing home anyway because she was blind as a bat and still trying to cook and they were afraid she was going to burn the house down 'cause she couldn't read the settings on the stove and would just turn everything up on high and then forget she'd done it."

"I dread the day I've got to face that with mine, Hazel."

"Oh, I know, Elba Rae. But Aunt Ethel's so tough I bet you don't have to worry about that for a long time."

"I hope you're right."

"You know what I mean. She and Momma are two peas in a pod like that. They're both too stubborn to ever take leave of their senses."

"That's true," Elba Rae said and then she and her cousin Hazel laughed together, followed by a simultaneous sigh because neither one of them believed they'd be spared the anguish of caring for their respective elderly mothers some day. Elba Rae speculated to her own self that of the two of them, Hazel would be at the disadvantage because she was the meeker, while Elba Rae was surely better equipped to suffer the consequences of a strong-willed but failing parent.

"Well anyway," Hazel continued, "the Fowinkle boy was on duty and got the order to go over there when Jimmy Templeton called."

"I hope they arrested Dewey Richardson and put him some place where he belongs!" Elba Rae was quick to refocus on the drama at hand.

"When the Fowinkle boy got there, what do you think Dewey was doing?"

"What?"

"He was still cutting that yard."

"He's a nut!"

"I know it. Lou Anne said Jimmy waited in the house till Jimmy saw the Sheriff's car pull up, and then he went over there and made the complaint. The Fowinkle boy wanted to talk to Lou Anne in person since she was the one that had first witnessed it, but Jimmy said there wasn't any way he was going to let her come back out in the front yard because Dewey was still standing there with nothing on but a dirty T-shirt. They finally convinced him to go in the house, but not until he'd put the mower up and he wanted to sweep the sidewalk, but the Fowinkle boy put his foot down."

"Good for him."

"They got to talking inside the house, and Lou Anne said Jimmy said that the Fowinkle boy asked if maybe they could avoid making an arrest for indecent exposure—because that's what it would have been—indecent exposure—if they could call somebody in the family to come over and see about Dewey and if in the meantime, Dewey would promise not to go back out in the yard, even with his clothes on."

"Did they call Dewey Junior?"

"No, that's the thing. They couldn't find Dewey Junior, because somebody said he'd gone off to the lake and nobody could get hold of him so the Fowinkle boy didn't know what else to do but call Shirley in Baton Rouge."

"I'm surprised Dewey had enough mind to give anybody the phone number."

"Well, that's just it, Elba Rae. What doesn't make a bit of sense about the whole thing."

"What?"

"Well, I know Dewey Richardson hasn't been right since Lord only knows when, and Earl and Mabel Moss can tell you this isn't the first time he's been up there without any clothes on, but sometimes he can be so sensible, it's hard to understand why he's out in the yard without a stitch on."

"What do you mean?"

"Jimmy told Lou Anne that after they went in the house and the Fowinkle boy got to asking Dewey how come he'd be out in the front yard without his pants on, that Dewey walked over to the divan and started shuffling through some papers and then came back and handed them to the Fowinkle boy."

"Papers?" Elba Rae wanted to know. "What in the world, Hazel? Is he just mad as a hatter?"

"Well Lou Anne said that Jimmy said that at first the Fowinkle boy wasn't much paying Dewey any attention with the papers, but Dewey was insisting almost so he started to sort of study them for a minute. To keep the peace with Dewey, you know."

"He should have slapped the handcuffs on him and packed him in the back of the patrol car. That's what he should have done. And given him a little extra whack with the billy club for good measure. Forget the papers!"

"Well, Elba Rae, can you imagine what Dewey Richardson had up there in that house? Spread out on the divan in the broad open daylight, like it was the *TV Guide* or something?"

"What?"

"Papers and pictures and some kind of halfway filled-out application to join something called the Natural Society. Have you ever heard of it?"

"Oh, for heaven's sake, Hazel!"

"Is it some kind of cult, Elba Rae? Because that wouldn't surprise me a bit to know Dewey Richardson was mixed up in some kind of cult. That might just explain a lot, you know."

"Well, I don't think it's really what you'd call a cult, exactly, but …"

"But what?"

"It's for people who don't want to wear clothes, Hazel. And who don't think anybody else should be wearing them either. And they all want to go live together in a big commune and be naked together."

"Well, isn't that a bird."

"It'd be a bird if they were so hard up for members they'd take in Dewey Richardson!"

And with that, the cousins could no longer sustain their collective indignation, their shock, or their disgust, and they burst into the kind of boisterous laughter only two long-suffering friends and sometimes a few select family members can openly share. Hazel Burns eventually made the wheezing sound she was apt to induce when she became too amused to sufficiently inhale; usually, it was up to Elba Rae to reintroduce composure to the conversation once it crossed that measure.

"I guess we ought to be ashamed, Hazel, and try to remember insanity's always been in that family. He was bound to get it one way or another. How did they ever track down Shirley?"

"Lou Anne said the Fowinkle boy tried to get hold of Dewey Junior to come up there and see about his daddy, and when he couldn't, she said Dewey told him to call Shirley just as pretty as you please like she'd be glad to hear from them. And when the Fowinkle boy was on the phone with her, she was asking all sorts of questions, of course, as you can image she would getting a long distance call out of the blue like it was, and from the law at that, and she couldn't understand exactly what had even happened or why her daddy was out there without his pants on but he was wearing some old grimy T-shirt."

"Well, you know, I was gonna ask you before why did they think he was out there with a shirt on and nothing else. But he's such a nut I didn't think it would make any difference."

"That's what I mean about him being so sensible sometimes, Elba Rae. You can ask him a question about something, and he can answer you just like he's got good sense."

"Did he tell the Fowinkle boy why he was wearing the T-shirt?"

"He did."

Elba Rae waited, in the natural volley of their conversation, for it was her cousin Hazel's turn to return the ball into Elba Rae's court. But something was wrong, it seemed, on Hazel's side as there was no response.

"Well what did he say? What did he tell the Fowinkle boy?"

"Oh, Elba Rae … now I really should be ashamed. I shouldn't be repeating a word of this. Because it's downright sad, that's what it is. Poor thing can't help it if he wasn't right to start with and then he went off in the war and got so scrambled up he can't make rhyme or reason sometimes. But do you know what he told the Fowinkle boy? It's really right pitiful."

"What?"

"Jimmy told Lou Anne that Dewey said ever since he'd been in the army, people had teased him about his big bosoms. And that's how come he wanted to keep them covered out in the yard. Now isn't that sad?"

"I've never noticed his bosoms."

"That's because he's always been so careful to keep them covered. You know some men just get them as they age. If you think about it, old man Richardson was big-breasted, too."

"Yeah, I guess he was. But he was more heavyset."

"And Dewey just doesn't have the weight anywhere else to hide 'em. Just something else they've handed down through the generations."

"That family hasn't had a prayer in a hundred years!"

"Now Elba Rae, don't get me started again or I'll have the hiccups and I'll have them all night."

"Well, I don't want you to be up all night," Elba Rae said as a diversion so as not to send Hazel into another wheezing fit of hysteria. "Did they leave him alone until Shirley came?"

"The Fowinkle boy told Dewey that if he'd promise not to go back out in the yard until Shirley got there from Baton Rouge, he wouldn't be arrested for indecent exposure–because that's what it would have been. Lou Anne said Jimmy told the Fowinkle boy they'd keep an eye out for him, too, just to be on the safe side, and Lou Anne said after Jimmy got back across the street he didn't leave their front room for the rest of the afternoon. Shirley finally pulled in there around supper time and Lou Anne said it was a good thing she did because Jimmy nearly had the Thumps from keeping watch."

"What in the world is she gonna do with him, Hazel? Do you think she'll take him back to Baton Rouge?"

"Who knows? I guess she and Dewey Junior will have to put their heads together and figure something out. I'm just glad it's not my decision to make."

"Me too."

And with the crisis resolved, at least to the degree it was within the jurisdiction and the concern of Elba Rae Van Oaks and her cousin Hazel, the ladies bid one another a good night and rested again the hand pieces of their phones back onto their respective cradles for the evening, after which Elba Rae Van Oaks took her leave to do the same with herself, since by then she surmised certainly even Miss Kitty Carlisle was applying a cold cream and wrapping her beautifully styled coiffure in a sturdy and protective yet surely elegantly adorned sleep cap.

Shirley from Baton Rouge returned home two days later without so much as a passenger, leaving the responsibility of their father primarily to her younger brother who promised to step up his diligence and monitor with greater frequency the activities of Dewey Senior, who never until his dying day gave up the enthusiasm for the cause he so wanted to promote. But for all of his solicitations and enticements and downright advertisements, Dewey Richardson was forever the sole member, charter or otherwise, of the Buford chapter of the Naturalist Society of America, although Irma Young was once rumored to have requested a brochure.

Virginia Millford and the Fall of Miss Nita Perrymore

Litton County had for years been blessed with access to superb medical facilities, what with the Litton County Memorial Hospital for those in acute need of attention, surgeries, and other long-term care, but also with the Buford Clinic for those in Buford proper who did not find themselves in life-threatening peril or in need of general anesthesia since neither was well served by its limited staff. The Clinic, as it was more simply referred to since everyone in Buford knew the clinic was *in* Buford and thus didn't feel the necessity of geographically distinguishing which clinic they meant when mentioning it, was home to Dr. Bud Millford, who was called Dr. Millford by practically no one except strangers who didn't otherwise know everyone just called him Dr. Bud.

Dr. Bud would answer his phone at home late on a Tuesday night and before Sabbath School early on a Sunday morning when a patient needed his assistance outside the normal operating hours of the clinic. He would make a house call if it was understood the patient was just too sick to sit up in the car but not so very critical that he or she required transport to the Litton County Memorial Hospital, which was referred to as the Hospital since everyone in Buford and even those not knew there was only the one. Dr. Bud had delivered babies before the hospital was built. He could stitch a cut with such precision that it hardly left a scar.

And he would pronounce Elba Rae Van Oaks dead one October night when she succumbed in the fellowship hall of the First Avenue United Methodist Church.

There were through the decades other doctors on duty at the clinic who were politely received by most Bufordians when it was not possible to see Dr. Bud, although it was pretty much understood Dr. Bud was their physician of choice. He was gray before his time and perhaps that helped endear him even sooner to a generation of citizens who revered him as much as they did Reverend Bishop of the Methodist Church and Brother Lumpkin at the Buford Baptist and even other area religious leaders of lesser-known denominations.

And then there was Dr. Bud's wife, Virginia. She and Dr. Bud met as freshmen at the University in Tuscaloosa when Dr. Bud was still just Bud and when, to that point, Tuscaloosa was the southernmost point Virginia had traveled to from her home north of Chattanooga. By the time sophomore year rolled around neither would ever date another, and it had been expected by both sides of their family they would marry after graduation, so it lessened the shock somewhat to all when during the Easter holidays of junior year they arrived in Tennessee and announced to Virginia's parents their elopement. Virginia left the university not long thereafter and everyone rejoiced in the birth of the first Millford child, Bud Junior.

Homesick for either end of Tennessee, Virginia celebrated with her new husband and her new son when the former was accepted to medical school in Memphis. An internship followed in Nashville, then a residency in Raleigh, and by the time Wendall Fairchild Millford, Senior, returned to Buford, he was officially and forever Dr. Bud. Virginia Millford dutifully followed her husband, having not planned especially to settle in Litton County per se, but by then Bud Junior was sibling to younger brother Ben and little sister Ginny and Dr. Bud was pursuing his life's passion to return home and start a practice.

It was noted by some native Bufordians that their young doctor's bride appeared standoffish and less social than regular people, with the more charitable ones allowing that she just wasn't from around there and it would surely take a while before she fit in. At first, the family rented a roomy, rambling old house within walking distance of the Square where Dr. Bud set up his office. But as the practice flourished, so did Virginia's opinion that the Millford domicile should properly mirror the stature and respect afforded by her husband's position and by the time the new and improved Buford Clinic was completed on Highway 29, the land had been cleared and construction was underway on the striking colonial that would house Millfords young and old for ages to come. It was the biggest house in town—everybody knew that, even the folks who'd never actually been inside—but it was also the most prestigious because it was the doctor's house. And Virginia was the doctor's wife.

Virginia Millford sported about town in sometimes a new Cadillac but never less than a Buick, and gradually, as most of her domestic and child-rearing duties were undertaken with great skill by the faithful Gussie Mae, she was free to engage in more church activities at the First Avenue United Methodist and in cultural organizations such as the Litton County Historical Association and the Buford Home and Garden Society. It was a meeting of the latter that first bore the talk of Virginia's peculiar behavior.

The January meeting of the Buford Home and Garden Society wasn't just any meeting like the rest of the monthly ones, where a presentation was made featuring indigenous specimens of the season coupled with a discussion of such, and which concluded with refreshments typically consisting of coffee, mixed nuts, a festive punch, and an assortment of cakes and cookies expected to be homemade but sometimes courtesy of the bakery department of the Buford Piggly Wiggly, depending on that month's hostess. The January meeting historically drew the club's highest yearly attendance due to the special business of installing new officers who had been elected at the December meeting, which drew the year's second-largest attendance numbers due to the casting of votes and due naturally to the general surge in socializing that Christmastime brought. It was not unusual at all to see members at the January meeting that hadn't been seen at one since the January prior. The year Virginia Millford's demeanor was more the topic of discussion than the fact Florine Moss was elected Treasurer (notable since everyone knew full well the reason Florine had never worked with her husband Jack at the hardware store was because she couldn't for the life of her make correct change) happened to also coincide with the last public appearance of Miss Nita Perrymore.

Martha Betty Maharry was always good to look after her mother Anita Fay Perrymore, affectionately known to all as "Miss Nita," especially as she aged into her eighties. Martha Betty phoned her daily and dropped by almost as frequently at Miss Nita's house on Delight Lane. She would take Miss Nita to church, when she felt up to it, or to a wedding if it was a family member of at least blood cousin status, and she did—without need of any persuasion to speak of—convince Miss Nita to accompany her to the garden club meeting that day since, of course, as a founding member and former three-time president, it was important for Miss Nita to witness the installation of officers even if no one anticipated her presence at any other meetings throughout the year. Everyone knew Miss Nita just didn't get out much anymore ever since the palsy had gotten the better of her.

At the January meeting of the Buford Home and Garden Society, it was understood the normal menu of snacks would defer to more of a luncheon variety since the crowd would be larger, and thus the meeting time was changed from the second Wednesday of the month at ten A.M. to the second Wednesday at eleven to accommodate the heavier servings, although most members never really knew which variable had precipitated which. There was even a committee assigned to collectively furnish the meal so as to relieve the hostess of the extra burden of cooking while also hostessing. With holiday celebrations over, the January meeting offered a highly anticipated event in what was elsewhere a non-eventful month and everyone was always extra pleased when they knew Edith Bishop was on the food committee because it meant they'd be treated to her delicious pea salad.

Many of the members had already arrived for the meeting by the time Martha Betty Maharry and her mother Miss Nita entered Willadean Hendrix's two-story Federal-style house out on the Hendrix road, which was really old Litton County Route 6 but had never much been known as such since Hendrixes of one fashion or another had lived out there for so long. Miss Nita's entrance, as expected, caused a light stir as was usually the case on account of her near shut-in status. A few ladies flocked over to receive her, being diligent to extend their sincerest of welcomes whilst showing due care not to compromise Miss Nita's balance at the same time because of her obvious frailty. Unable to mask her trembling, Miss Nita thanked all for their warmest of greetings and was soon escorted to her seat in the parlor off the front hall where the gavel was banged and the meeting was called to order.

The club president was halfway through her opening remarks by the time the front door swung open one more time and Virginia Millford paraded into the room wearing the glorious mink coat Dr. Bud had gifted her with just weeks before. Seated beside one another, Ruby Burns and her sister Ethel Maywood looked at each other and communicated perfectly clearly between them, without so much as moving a lip, the message that the temperature that afternoon in Buford was expected to be near sixty. Ruby Burns, in fact, glanced at her sister Ethel with a look of concern several times during the meeting that day, and not only when Florine Moss was taking her oath as Treasurer, but also every time it seemed there was conversation and chuckling coming from the rear of the room where the last available folding chair had been taken by Virginia Millford. Virginia certainly was enjoying herself, Ruby said to Ethel, without actually saying anything to her at all.

After the longer meeting necessitated by officer installations was over and adjourned, the level of chatter in the room rose to a point such that neither Ruby Burns nor her sister Ethel Maywood could justifiably pinpoint any irregular noise attributed solely to Virginia Millford, who still did, however, appear to be having a more joyous day of it than was reasonably justified by a meeting of the Buford Home and Garden Society, even if it was the January one with a full luncheon.

Willadean Hendrix's dining room was beautifully decorated, as always, for the buffet that had been provided by Edith Bishop and the food committee, and soon the house was full of members holding punch cups and members holding just coffee and members holding plates heaped with tea sandwiches and stuffed celery and some who mastered all three with grace and ease as they made their ways back to the folding chairs which had by then been disbursed from their row formations and curved into two distinct semicircles. No one particularly noticed that Virginia Millford was already sipping on her second cup of punch by the time Martha Betty Maharry got Miss Nita resettled into her chair before going to the buffet table to serve both of their plates. The benefit of retrospection, however, would enhance Ethel Maywood's recounting of the day's events considerably when that evening she phoned her daughter Elba Rae Van Oaks to discuss the meeting and the strange goings on with Virginia Millford and the pitiful spectacle that had been Miss Nita Perrymore and the fact that they may as well have dissolved the club if they were expecting Florine Moss to keep up with the money.

"I didn't think Miss Nita left her house anymore," Elba Rae observed with the phone receiver wedged between her ear and her shoulder while simultaneously stirring a skillet of frying okra just plucked from the deep freeze.

"She doesn't," Ethel Maywood confirmed. "But you know she's been a member of that club since they started it and she's served in every officer capacity at least twice so I guess Martha Betty felt like she had to try and drag her if she wanted to come, bless her heart."

"Martha Betty is a saint, that's for sure."

"I know it," Ethel agreed, "but I just knew something like this was going to happen, I could tell when they walked in the house."

"What do you mean?"

"Miss Nita is so teetery, Elba Rae."

"Well, Momma, for heaven's sake—she's been teetery for years. She hasn't been able to drive since I don't know when, and the last time Martha Betty brought her to church, she was shaking so bad she couldn't hold the song book. It made *me* dizzy just watching it."

"Which is exactly why Martha Betty should have put her foot down and left her at home this time."

"Well you can't blame Martha Betty for trying to get Miss Nita out, poor thing."

"Maybe not, but I'm here to tell you right here and right now and I'll tell your sister the same thing next chance I get. When I get so feeble I can't stand up on my own two feet without holding the wall, I want you to leave me at home!"

"We'll see about that," Elba Rae Van Oaks said, smugly.

"There'll be no seeing about to it! If it wasn't long distance, I'd hang up this phone right now and call Lila Mae and tell her the same thing!"

"Okay, Momma. All right. Now what happened with Miss Nita that was so bad? She didn't fall, did she?"

"No, but that's a miracle the way everybody rushed up to hug her and grab her and shake her hand and put on so, and don't you know Evelyn Marshall was leading the pack, putting it out on one leg and wiping it off on the other."

"Oh, I bet it made Miss Nita feel good to know so many people remember her and were glad to see her."

"I guess. But you know how put on Evelyn Marshall is. She wouldn't have helped pick poor Miss Nita up off the floor if she had fallen unless somebody else thought of it first."

"She means well, Momma."

"Anyway, Miss Nita didn't fall because Martha Betty's at least good about keeping an eye on her whenever she tries to get up for anything, and makes sure she's got a good clutch on her arm when they're walking. But the worst of it was after the meeting, when were having the lunch."

"What happened?" Elba Rae was, by that point, stretching her phone cord to its maximum flexibility in order to rip a sheet of paper towel from the wall-mounted rack opposite her stove so she could lay it on the counter and take up her okra.

"Well, the food was all delicious. We had some chicken salad sandwiches that Willadean had made with pecans in them, even though the committee is supposed to furnish all the food for the hostess in January, but you know what a good cook Willadean Hendrix is. She puts up pecans every year from all those trees they have, and there's just nothing she can't do with one. And Mabel Moss made a coconut cake that was out of this world. I heard somebody say she uses goat's milk in the icing, but I never got to speak to her long enough to find out for myself, so many people were asking her for the recipe and all. Evelyn Marshall brought some kind of lemon squares and they had so much powdered sugar on them I thought I was going to choke. And they were so dry your aunt Ruby got tickled at me because I took a bite of one of them and told her it was clinging to the roof of my mouth so, I didn't think Willadean had enough punch made for me to be able to swallow it."

"Oh, Momma."

"She never could cook. I don't know why they'd put her on the committee for January of all times."

"Did Miss Edith bring her pea salad?"

"Yes, Lord, and that's what I've been trying to tell you."

"What?" Elba Rae had successfully sprinkled just the right combination of salt and pepper onto her steaming hot okra.

"Well after they shuffled the chairs around and got Miss Nita back seated, Martha Betty went to the buffet and fixed Miss Nita a plate before she went off to get her own. I couldn't see everything Martha Betty put on it, but I noticed right off she'd piled up a serving of that pea salad Edith Bishop always makes."

"I always look forward to it at the church suppers."

"I do too, but then I'm still in a little better shape than Miss Nita."

"What do you mean?"

"Oh, Elba Rae, it was just pitiful. Everybody was enjoying themselves and talking and laughing—especially Virginia Millford, I can tell you—and there was poor Miss Nita balancing the plate on her lap with one hand and struggling to hold a fork with the other. And of all the things for her to have, she was trying to eat that pea salad."

"Could she not manage it?"

"I don't think she ever got the first pea. I could see her from where I was in the dining room. She'd try and try, and she'd finally hem up a few peas on the fork. And then she'd try to get the fork up to take a bite, and by the time it was half way to her mouth, every pea had shaken off. And then she'd try again. She'd hem them up, and she'd shake them off. Hem them up, shake them off."

"That's awful, Momma."

"I know it. I counted a couple of dozen at least that hit the floor and rolled under Willadean's piano bench. I'll bet she's wondering about now why her living room smells like vinegar."

"Where was Martha Betty?"

"I don't know. In the kitchen visiting or talking to Mabel or somebody, I guess. I know she can't watch her momma every minute, but I just felt so sorry for Miss Nita I couldn't stand there and do nothing."

"Did you go find Martha Betty?"

"No. I decided anybody near ninety years old that's lived as long as Miss Nita and still trying to get up and go deserves to keep what little dignity she's got left. So I walked right out there where Miss Nita was sitting and I took that plate off her lap and I said, 'I'll be right back, Miss Nita' and I carried it in the kitchen and set it down on the counter, around toward the back porch where I didn't think anybody would see me."

"You took Miss Nita's food away from her?" Elba Rae couldn't resist one bite of okra even though it was still too hot to properly chew.

"No! When nobody was looking, I went over to the sink where Willadean's got one of those paper cup dispensers stuck on the side of the cabinet and I pulled one out of it. And then I got a spoon out of the drawer, and I shoveled every bit of that pea salad into the cup and I put the cup on the plate. And then I took the plate back out there to Miss Nita pretty as you please and I said, 'Here you go, Miss Nita. I think this will be a little easier for you.' And I walked off, sort of nonchalant like, so it wouldn't draw any attention."

"You put her pea salad in a paper cup?" Elba Rae had her hand on another piece of okra but was now too distracted to think about putting it to her own mouth.

"Well, the only way she was ever going to get a bite was to drink it. She'd have been there all day trying to round it up with a fork! Not to mention the mess it'd made on Willadean's floor! She's liable to have the ants as it is!"

"Did anybody say anything?"

"Not a word. They just thought Miss Nita was having extra punch," Ethel Maywood proudly recalled the victory to Elba Rae, oblivious to the unprecedented spike the completely unanticipated and swooping extraction of the buffet plate from her diminutive lap had caused to Miss Nita's trembling.

The conversation between Elba Rae Van Oaks and her mother didn't last much longer that night, as Elba Rae had within moments remarked to her mother that her supper was getting cold and her mother had remarked to Elba Rae that she needed to go anyway because she'd decided she was going to call her other daughter Lila Mae Fessmire, of the Birmingham Fessmires, whether it was long distance or not. About the time the call had terminated, Ruby Burns was just getting started good with her own report of the club's meeting to her daughter Hazel who, like her cousin Elba Rae, was excluded from participation in so many things due to a full-time career at the Homer T. Litton Grammar School. While Ruby Burns had not yet been fully briefed about the sad deterioration of Miss Nita Perrymore's table manners, thanks, no doubt, to Ethel Maywood's advanced skills in nonchalance, she was anxious to share her observations about

Virginia Millford's overly friendly behavior that seemed all too connected to her suspicious number of trips to the punch bowl.

"Was it that frozen punch we had at the church when the Dawson girl married? The one with the lime sherbet?" Hazel inquired.

"No, it was red. And a little too sweet to be able to drink much more than a cup. That's why I was surprised to see Virginia Millford going back so often. You'd'a thought she'd been out on the desert the way she was gulping it down. And the more she had, the louder she got."

"Well, maybe she was just happy to be there. And anyway, it's not like Willadean Hendrix was serving spiked punch."

"Well, of course not, Hazel. But there's something about that woman. I don't know what it is, but there's something about her that hasn't been told."

"What do you mean?"

"First of all, she was late getting there. The meeting was already going on when she sashayed in wearing a fur coat. Said it was her Christmas present from Dr. Bud, so I guess she felt like she had to show it off even if it wasn't cold enough to be wearing any fur coat today. Probably had to ride out there with the car window down just to keep from burning up in it."

"O-o-o-o-h-h ... I bet it's pretty."

"I'm sure it's the best money can buy. You know Virginia Millford's not gonna have anything second rate."

"Does it go all the way to the floor?"

"No, no, I don't think it's a full length. But I'm sure it cost a pretty penny nonetheless."

"Well, they've got the money. They may as well spend it."

"That's fine with me. It's his money to spend as he sees fit. I'm not criticizing."

"So what did she do that was so bad? Besides be late that is."

"She shouldn't have been late, to start with. That's just rude to whoever's trying to conduct the meeting. And especially in January, when there's so much business. But that's not even it. Aunt Ethel and I could hear her the whole time—during the meeting, and the installing of the officers—talking out loud and giggling about first one thing and then another. She was sitting in the back right next to Mabel Moss, and I glanced back there one time and poor Mabel looked like she was so embarrassed she could've just sunk right into the floor. But it didn't seem to faze Virginia in the least. She had a comment about practically everything that was going on."

"That's kind of odd, really."

"I should say it is. After the meeting was over and before the lunch was served, she went over to Miss Nita Perrymore and gave her such a hug, I was afraid she was going to knock her right off her chair. I'm surprised she didn't crack a rib."

"Miss Nita was there?" Hazel was genuinely surprised.

"Martha Betty brought her, bless her heart. She's so frail. But everybody fussed over her and put on so, I hope it made her feel good."

"How old is she?"

"Oh, goodness, she's got to be near ninety by now. Eighty-eight, eighty-nine, somewhere in there."

"And still living by herself."

"Yeah, well, I think Martha Betty looks in on her nearly every day. Just to check on her."

Still, Hazel Burns was momentarily impressed by the longevity of their fellow citizen, uninformed of the debacle that had been Miss Nita's attempt to ingest Edith Bishop's famous pea salad. After the January meeting of the Buford Home and Garden Society, Anita Fay Perrymore would not again leave her house on Delight Lane until the day she was forced to do so some five months later, and only then to seek immediate medical care at the Litton County Memorial Hospital. She never again attended a meeting of the Buford Home and Garden Society or of the Litton County Historical Association, nor did she ever again participate in services at the First Avenue United Methodist Church, which did serve at least to spare Elba Rae Van Oaks the threat of nausea induced by a wiggling hymnal. It was only by the grace of her neighbor Lou Anne Templeton that Miss Nita did not meet death right there in the yard of her house on Delight Lane but was preserved for a bit longer courtesy of the Restful Haven Care Home where she unavoidably was sent to recover and convalesce after the debilitating fall that fractured her left hip.

Lou Anne, out in her own back yard to hang a load of sheets on the line to dry, knew distinctly she was hearing the wails of a human that afternoon as she clipped a clothespin onto the sewn end of an extra-long white pillowcase. She instinctively dropped her clothes basket and traveled in the direction of the distress, only to find Miss Nita Perrymore collapsed in a heap at the bottom of her back door stoop, an unopened bottle of Excedrin still clutched in her fist.

It seems Miss Nita was suffering from a touch of the bursitis and had sought relief from her discomfort with some of the drugstore remedy. Trouble was, Miss Nita could not—racked with pain or otherwise—see to get the top off the bottle in the inferior light produced by her kitchen fixture's two forty-watt bulbs and had reasoned, therefore, it would be a good idea to step outside the back door into the natural sunlight in order to crack open the Excedrin. So concentrated was she on the task at hand that she had not at all paid attention to the mop handle resting against the back of the house and had, in the confusion, entangled her right foot between the wall and the mop handle while twisting without success the Excedrin cap which, cumulatively, had brought the whole sequence of events to a conclusion most unpleasant to Miss Nita Perrymore who then had more than the bursitis to think about.

Lou Anne Templeton tried to comfort Miss Nita and at least had the peace of mind not to pull her up on her feet while they waited for the ambulance to arrive so as not to do any more damage than was already done by the fall off the door step—and since it was a warm day as June went in Litton County, it wasn't like Miss Nita should have been cold lying there in the soft yard on any account. Lou Anne Templeton tried as she might to distract Miss Nita by recounting stories, some recent and some not, that she thought Miss Nita might enjoy reminiscing over, such as remembering the day they had to call the law on Dewey Richardson when he was mowing the front yard without his trousers on. Miss Nita did not smile at that story, Lou Anne would tell her husband Jimmy later in the evening, but then again Lou Anne couldn't recall Miss Nita ever finding humor in the unsavory carryings-on of their neighbor Dewey Richardson.

Martha Betty had made the only decision she could, everyone knew, and relegated Miss Nita to the ranks of the crippled and the infirm and the senile that populated the halls of the Restful Haven Care Home. There was no way Martha Betty could look after Miss Nita at home, they all said, and Restful Haven was a nice place, they all knew, clean and certainly much better than anything in a big city. That Dr. Bud Millford was on the board of the facility lent validity to a decision that mostly never troubled Martha Betty, except during the particularly disturbing period when Miss Nita insisted with convincing regularity that Mrs. Lady Bird Johnson had come to speak in the day room of the nursing home as part of her nationwide beautification campaign. While Martha Betty was well beyond skeptical at such a claim, having read no such story about it in any newspaper circulated in Litton County nor having heard any discussion whatsoever amongst any group of her peers, Miss Nita was nothing if not lucid and downright credible as she described in vivid detail the fabric of the First Lady's pale yellow suit with the half-length sleeves.

Martha Betty was eventually tempted to inquire of a random staff member of the Restful Haven Care Home as to whether the First Lady of the United States had visited Buford on what very well could have been her tour across the country, but was overruled at every urging by her own common sense and her noble desire to maintain at least the illusion that her mother wasn't crazy as a loon. Martha Betty had, however, gone so far as to compose a letter to the White House in an attempt to clear the matter up once and for all, thoughtfully enclosing a self-addressed stamped envelope in hopes it would encourage Mrs. Johnson to reply. She threw it promptly away the afternoon she visited Restful Haven and Miss Nita had introduced her new roommate in the other bed as Lady Bird Johnson, who Martha Betty knew without hesitation or need of introduction to be Mrs. Geneva Pickle, Claude's mother, who had been a resident at Restful Haven since long before Miss Nita got entwined with a mop and flew off the back door step.

Thereafter, Miss Nita rested mostly at peace in the nursing home, until one night a couple of years later when, confused by the combination of an all-too-vivid hallucination and a sleep-numbing narcotic, she momentarily forgot she wasn't safe at home in her bed at the house on Delight Lane she'd shared for so many years with her late husband who, she thought, if only in a dream, had asked her to bring him a glass of milk. The attempt to take it to him would be her last motion on earth.

*   *   *   *

Virginia Millford, on the other hand, was just hitting her stride the day she slipped her gin-filled monogrammed flask into the interior pocket of her new mink coat before venturing out on Hendrix Road for the January meeting of the Buford Home and Garden Society. Gussie Mae had been late to work that morning, and Virginia had nearly missed the meeting by the time she got ready herself and drove the big Buick out to the Hendrix place. It was a pretty day, for winter, but that hadn't stopped her from sporting the beautiful gift she'd picked out for herself on a shopping trip to Atlanta before Christmas. Her husband was much too busy at the clinic to Christmas shop, she knew, and after all if he'd said it once he'd said it a hundred times: Illness doesn't know a holiday. He seemed happy just to know she'd gotten something she liked, whether he was in on the selection or not.

He always seemed happy, for that matter, whether in Virginia's opinion or his patients's or anybody else's around Buford. And why shouldn't he be? His life was everything he'd ever wanted and everything he'd planned—right down to the attractive and doting wife who held court over hearth and home and three heirs and a steadfast maid named Gussie Mae. The countless hours spent at the clinic with vomiting children and their coughing parents weren't work to Dr. Bud, not in the sense it was work for Hazel Burns to type all day and answer the phone and take dictation from the principal of the Homer T. Litton Grammar School, or in the sense it was work for Patsy Simpson to recite the same *Primary Reader* to the new first graders year in and year out, or in the sense it would have been for Fettis Van Oaks to process cattle parts at the packing plant had Fettis Van Oaks actually worked. Virginia Millford, though, was living her husband's life and not her own, and she knew it. It didn't matter at all by the time she was implanted in Buford and rearing three children and busy being the doctor's wife that she, unlike so many of her classmates, really had meant to graduate from the university rather than leave early to do the right thing and get married before the reason why she had to was more blatant than not.

During her earliest years of settlement in Buford, Virginia did not so much enjoy attending the many social functions to which she and Dr. Bud were invited. It seemed everyone in Litton County knew her husband and was anxious to lend prestige to whatever event they might be planning by having him accept. But Virginia graciously accompanied Dr. Bud wherever they needed to go, and looked forward to their special time together just before departure when the two would enjoy a toast of martinis or a glass of port before driving off into the night and the gathering at hand. Dr. Bud did not drink alcohol at the parties at which he and his wife were guests, most usually because libations were not offered but always because he did not feel it proper to be seen in public or in the private that was someone else's home imbibing spirits of any type. He was a doctor, after all, and just because the clinic was closed didn't mean he might not be needed before morning, and it was not a good idea to have his friends and his neighbors and his fellow church members, all of whom were patients, ever wondering about his faculties. Virginia too would not be seen in Buford or anywhere in Litton County at any event with a beverage in her hand containing a liquid stronger than iced tea. To the naked eye, her fortitude came from within.

But the years passed and the people who had once been strangers to Virginia Millford became her friends and her neighbors and her fellow church members as well, and many were also associated with the numerous organizations to which Virginia lent her time. And by then, the silver-plated flask that fit so compactly in the lining of her Christmas mink coat wasn't so much put there for courage as it was to maintain the calm that otherwise would have given way to her fragile nerves. At no time was that ever put to more of a test than the day half the population of Buford witnessed a most unfortunate mishap involving the statue of Homer T. Litton, which stood mounted on limestone in front of the courthouse in the middle of the Square, and Virginia Millford's shiny black Buick Electra 225.

It was the spring of 1972, and spring was the busy social season in Buford. And if there was one thing Virginia Millford could bet on, it was that if her husband had at all been involved in the birth of a Buford baby—be it from the initial diagnosis of the pregnancy or the delivery of the newborn itself—Dr. Bud would be invited to the child's wedding. It seemed an unspoken tradition that few dared to buck. The necessity of a new frock this day which had brought Virginia to F & F Fashions in downtown Buford could be blamed on a bride neither Virginia nor her husband even knew, other than to speak to if passing on the street, but that didn't matter. Her closet needed replenishing if she and Dr. Bud were to be seen at the wedding planned at the Buford Baptist Church which ensured, Virginia knew, the reception would follow not at the country club but would instead, without fail, be held in the basement of the church and would feature dry cake, greasy nuts, stale mints, and sour punch as their reward for coming.

On the afternoon Virginia set out to procure her new outfit, F & F Fashions was as adequate a source as was warranted by the relevant occasion. Kathleen Fike, one half of the F that was F & F, the other so named for her husband, Lloyd, who knew little about fashion in and of itself the year his wife talked him into the venture that was now their clothing business, knew all her customers by name and greeted everyone who entered her establishment with such familiarity that even the ones whose names she couldn't readily recall never realized it. Virginia Millford was a regular, of course, but also was one of a rare breed who Kathleen knew did not rely exclusively on her stock of merchandise for total wardrobe needs and who did, it was known, travel to larger venues even out of state for no other purpose sometimes than to buy things. The bell tied to the handle of the store's front door alerted Kathleen Fike that a customer was in her midst.

"Why Virginia, how in the world are you? I've missed seeing you lately here in the shop."

Virginia Millford strolled into the store with a firm grip on the large pocketbook which hung at her side. "I'm fine, Kathleen, just fine. How are y'all doing?"

"Goodness, we're busy as beavers. But it's just that time of year."

"Lloyd doing okay?"

"He is, thank you. He ran out to get something to eat a while ago but I expect he'll be back after while. Dr. Bud all right?"

"He's fine."

"That's always good to hear. I don't know what we'd do around here if he wasn't." She followed her pleasantry with a polite chuckle which Virginia reciprocated out of habit.

"Anything special you're looking for today?"

"I need something for a wedding, Kathleen. That McGibbon girl's getting married Saturday after next and Bud and I got an invitation."

"Oh, yeah, I've been fitting the two bridesmaids for it. They picked the most darling periwinkle dresses and then wanted to go and raise the hemlines so high I wouldn't be surprised if Brother Lumpkin refused to perform the ceremony. But, like Lloyd always tells me, I just sell the clothes. I don't have to wear them."

"I'm sure they'll be beautiful, Kathleen. You always have such pretty things in your shop."

"Well thank you, Virginia. We try to carry the nicer lines but the dresses have just gotten shorter and shorter till it's hard sometimes to keep the place stocked with something decent."

"That won't be a problem for me, Kathleen. I don't plan to wear a miniskirt to a wedding at the Baptist Church, or anywhere else for that matter." This time the laughter that followed was more genuine than not.

"I know you'll want to see my upper-end dresses, Virginia, so let me show you a couple of things I just got in. I know you're going to love them."

With that, the ladies sauntered to a rack of dresses located closest to the shop's storefront window overlooking the Square, the wooden floorboards creaking beneath them with informality along the way. Kathleen Fike was surprised, though pleased, that Virginia happily accepted the first selection as a candidate to try on.

"Do you want to pick out another two or three to try?"

"Oh, I will, I'm sure. But let me go ahead and slip this one on for size."

"All right. You know where to go."

"I surely do. I've spent more than my share of time in your fitting rooms, Kathleen."

"And I thank you!" The chuckle meter was back to polite mode.

"Why don't you leave your purse with me and I'll put it under the counter? That way you won't have to worry with it in the dressing room."

"Oh, that's okay," Virginia said. "I'll hang onto it."

"Of course." Kathleen Fike did not understand why anyone would need the contents of her pocketbook while trying on clothing, but her many years of retail service had taught her not to question. "Take your time," she followed. By then,

Virginia Millford was closing the curtain on the changing room in the rear of the store.

The afternoon progressed with Kathleen Fike pulling first one dress and then another, while Virginia Millford gleefully tried them all on. "Oh, I like this one, Kathleen, but I'm not sure of the color," she'd say before retreating to the dressing room to model the next selection.

"It's an unusual fabric, Kathleen, but it may be too loud for a wedding—especially with the Baptists!" She roared with laughter while Kathleen Fike remained more solemn. Although Kathleen did not attend Buford Baptist church herself, she was not necessarily at ease mocking those who did. Why, just the day before, she had sold Mabel Moss two pair of stockings, a white blouse, a scarf, and some undergarments. The Baptists were her customers, too, she thought to herself.

"Well Kathleen, this one's probably going to be it," Virginia announced as she burst through the only partially opened curtain of the changing room. It was a green satin two-piece ensemble that Kathleen Fike thought entirely too fussy for the low-key event she expected the McGibbon wedding to be. "I knew you'd love that one," she said instead. "Will it need any alterations? If it does, I can have it for you in plenty of time for the wedding."

"I think it'll be fine just the way it is, Kathleen, thank you. You can put it on my charge and I'm gonna take it with me. It's so pretty I've a mind to wear it home but I guess I won't!"

Kathleen Fike's laughter now was more nervous than polite. "It might be a little formal for cooking supper."

"Oh, Gussie Mae'll have all that done by the time I get home. Bless her heart. She's a treasure."

"All righty then, will you be needing any accessories? Are you okay on shoes, Virginia?"

"I'm better when I'm not on them! But I don't guess it'd do to show up at the church barefoot! But no, I've got a pair to put with it I'm sure."

"Okay. Then if you'll just slip that off I'll get it wrapped up for you."

"Slip I will! I'll be out in a jiffy," and then Virginia disappeared one more time to the rear of the store.

Kathleen Fike was perplexed at the jovial attitude of her customer and felt a sense of relief when she heard her husband Lloyd entering through the stockroom door off the alley.

"Am I glad to see you!"

"Been busy?" Lloyd inquired. He did not, as rule, spend his time at the store actually on the floor where ladies came to shop. He referred to his second floor space as the "business office" and made a point to mostly be there. "I don't see any customers."

"Shhhhh ... Virginia Millford's in the dressing room taking off a suit she's buying."

He lowered his voice. "What's so bad about that?"

"I don't know, exactly. But I was starting to feel a little uneasy with her."

"Virginia Millford?"

"Shhhhh!"

"Virginia Millford?" He said, in a deliberately husky whisper.

"It's not funny," Kathleen Fike said. "She's been in here an hour trying on first one outfit and then another. I thought she was going to try on every piece of inventory we've got."

"Well, since when, may I ask, can *any* of y'all make up your mind in a hurry and get something bought? I thought browsing was supposed to be part of the fun."

"Fun's one thing. But the longer she stays, the more she's acting like she's a little ... off, if you know what I mean."

"I don't."

"I mean, she's been—Virginia! Here we are! Let me get that wrapped up for you!"

Virginia Millford had indeed returned to her civilian clothes, the kind one would not have worn to a wedding but would have found perfectly acceptable to wear in search of some that one would. "Well, hello there, Lloyd, I didn't hear you come in."

"How are you, Virginia?"

"Fine. And you?"

"I'm fine, thank you."

"Dr. Bud okay?"

"He's fine. Just busy like always. People don't ever stop being sick, you know."

"Guess that's good—for him." Virginia Millford and Lloyd Fike laughed. Kathleen Fike did not and her terse snap at the perforation of the plastic garment wrap wasn't coincidental either.

"Here you are, Virginia, and we thank you!"

"I thank you, Kathleen. Take care, Lloyd."

"Come back to see us," he said, which is what he always said to a departing shopper, whether a purchaser or not.

"Enjoy the wedding," Kathleen offered as the jingling bell signaled Virginia's exit. Then she added, "Something about her's just not right, Lloyd."

"Oh, I don't know. She seemed perfectly all right to me."

The couple watched out the front window as Virginia Millford swung open the back door of the Electra and momentarily searched for the hook before hitting it with the crook of the hanger which held her new green satin outfit that would be worn first and possibly only to the McGibbon girl's wedding. Virginia shut the back door and proceeded to take the driver's seat, slinging the big pocketbook across to the passenger's side of the car. When she started the engine, the people strolling by on the sidewalk heard the motor screech just a little, the way it would if the ignition were held too long after being started, but otherwise noted nothing unusually strange.

"She's gonna wear that motor out cranking it like that," Lloyd Fike observed.

"And when she does," Kathleen said, "she can get a new one. Will you listen for the door a minute? Virginia coming in here reminds me I need to go call one of those bridesmaids and tell her we need to fit her one more time before the wedding."

"How long are you going to be?"

"Just long enough to make one phone call. I'll be right back." Kathleen Fike left her husband with his gaze still focused on the street in front of their shop, knowing his disdain for being caught alone on the sales floor when a customer might happen in—but she couldn't be there every moment their doors were open, after all, and it wasn't like everybody in Buford didn't know he owned the shop with her. He was always so silly about that, she thought, as she disappeared into the back room where a phone hung on the wall. She was fumbling through a sequence of names and phone numbers in a stenographer pad where the McGibbon wedding details were collectively contained when she heard the outrageous squeal coming from the front of the store. "What in the world?" She said to no one.

By the time Kathleen Fike rushed back to front of her establishment, her husband Lloyd stood still in the position she'd left him, his eyes wide open and his mouth agape. "What is all that smoke? What happened?" Kathleen asked.

"Did you see that?!"

"No, I didn't see it. I was in the back! I just heard the screeching! What was it?"

"She ..." Lloyd Fike was all but speechless. "She just tore out of here! Backwards!"

"Who?"

"Virginia Millford!"

"What?"

"Backwards! All the way across the street, and onto the Square!"

"Oh my goodness, Lloyd, is she hurt?"

"We'd better go see."

The magnitude of the situation not yet assessed, Lloyd Fike moved slowly around the counter which held their cash register, with the kind of caution and dread that surely forewarned of a tragedy. Without a word to one another, he and Kathleen jingled the bell on the front door and walked out front, where the smoke still hovered and the air smelled of rubber. Across the street on the court-house lawn and just several yards from the south entrance of the imposing old building, Virginia Millford's long black Buick had come to rest against the base of the Homer T. Litton memorial statue. Upon impact, the car's trunk lid had flung open and raised completely, as though eager to accept a frivolous cargo of luggage and beach umbrellas for a carefree trip to the shore. Homer T. Litton himself, most fortunately, had remained stationary on his perch overlooking the lawn that was quickly filling with those who had seen the vehicle race from its parking spot in front of F & F Fashions backward across the street, those who had been practically on the other side of the Square and not witnessed the crash itself but had heard the screeching and the squealing, and those who had been between the curb and the south entrance of the courthouse just prior to the ama-teurish cranking of the car's motor and who were now in various degrees of a daze, some praying aloud in thanks to one another that the Lord had spared them death or dismemberment from the errant Electra.

The chaos inside the courthouse, at least on the southwest corner, was no less felt than on the lawn itself since the first floor windows offered an unobstructed panorama of that side of the Square. It was in the County Register's office that the Fowinkle boy had been visiting with a clerk he felt more than mildly giddy about while waiting to be called into traffic court on the second floor to state the facts of a speeding ticket issued to a violator on Highway 29 one month prior when, with a trained lawman's instinct, he reacted immediately to the commo-tion outdoors and ran to the scene. Virginia Millford sat stoically in the driver's seat of the Buick with both hands still gripping the wheel.

"Is anybody hurt?" The Fowinkle boy attempted to ascertain amidst the con-fusion. "Does anybody need an ambulance?" A quick survey of the immediate surroundings did not readily indicate pedestrian injuries. Being a man about the community, as his job dictated he be, the Fowinkle boy did not even need access to the license plate number from the rear of car, which was good since it was molded around the base of the Homer T. Litton memorial statue, because even before approaching it he knew it to be the vehicle of Mrs. Virginia Millford. He rushed to the wreckage and opened the driver's side door.

"Ms. Millford! Are you hurt?" She opened her mouth, paused, then closed it again saying nothing.

"Ms. Millford! Talk to me! Are you hurt?"

"I ... don't think so."

"Are you able to get out of your vehicle?"

She turned her head for the first time left to face him. "Why?" She wanted to know.

"I need to see if you've been hurt."

"No ... no, I think I'm okay."

"Do you want us to call Dr. Millford at the clinic?"

She turned to face him again. "Why?"

"Ms. Millford, please. I need you to try and get out of the car."

"I'd rather just go home now, but thank you."

In the fresh air of the courthouse lawn on a spring afternoon, the Fowinkle boy had not at first detected the odor of an intoxicant coming from inside the vehicle. But as he leaned closer in toward the subject behind the wheel, the smell was suspicious. "What happened, Ms. Millford?"

"Well ... it was all so fast." The Fowinkle boy, trained to be patient during the interrogation process, knew to let his subject do the talking. "I just bought a new outfit. Over there, at Kathleen Fike's." She raised her right index finger to point but otherwise did not let loose of the steering wheel. "I came out and I hung it up in the back." She interrupted herself long enough to look behind her to see that the clothing was still hanging up, obstructing the onlookers's view into her back seat. "And then I got in, and I started the car, and I was just going to back out of the parking space and go home."

"Ah-huh," the Fowinkle boy confirmed, just to maintain the flow of information.

"I was backing up ... and I tapped on the brake a little ... and I think my foot must have slipped off the pedal and onto the accelerator. But I guess I didn't realize it was the accelerator, because I kept stepping on it harder, but the harder I stepped, the faster I was going. And then ... and then I guess I must have bumped into this statue before I could get stopped all the way."

"Ah-huh," the Fowinkle boy said, which that time meant he understood clearly the only thing that had kept the Buick from propelling inside the south corridor of the courthouse itself had been the granite memorialization of Mr. Homer T. Litton, whom Virginia Millford was referring to as a bump. He looked around the scene at the gathered crowd, some of them standing in the fresh tire tracks cut into the grass. And then he looked at the passenger side of the Buick's front seat which held the scattered contents of a rather large pocketbook. On the floor, a silver flask lay on its side and glistened in the sunlight when he cocked his head at just the right angle.

"Ms. Millford, please exit your car," he directed in a voice not intended to sound like a request. "We need to step inside the courthouse."

"I'm sorry, Mr ... what is your name?"

"It's Deputy Fowinkle, Ma'am."

"Deputy Fowinkle. But I don't have time to stop and go inside with you now. I've got to get home."

"I'm afraid you can't do that right now, Ma'am."

"I have to. It's nearly three thirty already and Gussie Mae likes to leave before four o'clock. She's got her own supper to cook, you know, not just mine, and I do try to be understanding about it even if we are paying her more than a decent wage to work for us and it wouldn't kill her if she had to stay late every once in a while."

"I can't let you leave, Ms. Millford."

"What?"

"I can't let you go."

"What do you mean you can't *let* me? I told you what happened. My foot slipped off the brake pedal and I hit the gas by mistake. Is that a crime? Do you want to write me a ticket?"

"It's not about a ticket, Ma'am," the Fowinkle boy said just as calmly as he knew how.

"Well, do you think I've caused some damages?"

"Frankly, Ms. Millford, I'm sure you have caused some damages to county property but that's not the reason we need to—"

"For goodness sake, do you know who I am, young man?" She was becoming indignant.

"I know exactly who you are, Ms. Millford, but—"

"Then do you not think I'm capable of paying for any repairs the county decides it needs? Do you think I can't afford it? Do you think I'm going to run off and not make good on it?"

"No, Ma'am, that's not it. I'm sure you'll be able to make full restitution for the damages."

"Good! Now I told you—I'm in a hurry and I need to get home!"

"You can't go home right now, Ms. Millford. We have to go inside and sort this thing out."

"Deputy Forgey, let me tell you something!"

"It's Fowinkle, Ma'am."

"Well I don't care if it's J. Edgar Hoover! Let me tell you something! I am Mrs. Bud Millford, and you're not gonna order me around like a criminal! Now get out of my way and let me get home!"

"Ms. Millford, I'm going to ask you one more time. Get out of the car."

"No! I will not get out of the car!"

"I'd rather you didn't force me to take action out here, Ma'am, but you're not giving me any other choice." He reached into the car with both hands and put them on her shoulders.

"Get your hands off me! Do you hear me? Let go!"

"Will you get out of the car peacefully, Ms. Millford?" He reasoned as he released her and stepped back.

"I will not get out of the car period because I'm going home!"

Aware that he was detaining the wife of one of Litton County's most distinguished citizens but well, he knew, within the confines of his duty, the Fowinkle boy's negotiation session was over. He reached forward with both hands out, planning fully to grab Virginia Millford by the upper arms and wrest her from the vehicle, not anticipating her next act of contempt. Just as he stepped toward her, she grabbed the door handle and slammed it shut, grazing the Fowinkle boy's shin along the way. Immediately, she struck the automatic control on the door panel which locked all four of the sedan's doors; by 1972, conveniently, a standard feature on the Electra model.

And there they were. The spectators, the actual witnesses, the near-victims, the deputy from the Litton County Sheriff's Department. Kathleen and Lloyd Fike who, by then, stood in the midst of it all. And the star of the afternoon herself, Mrs. Virginia Millford, sitting behind the wheel of her disabled yet secured Buick. It was, the Fowinkle boy knew, a stand-off—a situation he was not entirely unfamiliar with given the nature of his work and the usual sector of the population it brought him in contact with. Only those people had never been named Millford before.

With his professional reputation on the line, the Fowinkle boy tried not to ooze obvious relief when he observed the Litton County Sheriff Department vehicle rounding the Square, which meant back up was on the scene. It was a delicate problem, all right, and one perhaps better dealt with by some senior officers. The crowd watched silently as the uniformed officer disembarked from the patrol car and the whispering amongst themselves didn't erupt in earnest until the first onlooker realized the officer was actually Sheriff Porter himself. Thank God, the Fowinkle boy thought.

"Deputy," Sheriff Porter stated routinely as he arrived at the base of the Homer T. Litton statue and the crumpled up Buick. "What's going on here?"

"Well, Sheriff, I was inside the courthouse waiting on my call to appear when I heard the loud screeching of the suspect's tires burning—"

"Hold on there, boy." He looked around the lawn and smiled at a few of his constituents. "Let's just get the facts before we go calling anybody a suspect."

Yes, Sir." He rethought his next sentence. "Well, like I was saying, I was inside the courthouse when I heard the screeching of the ... of some tires, and when I looked out the window I observed the sus ... the vehicle crash into the statue. Backwards."

"Ah-huh," Sheriff Porter nodded.

"I immediately made the scene ... well, since I was already here and all, and surveyed the crowd for injuries before ascertaining the sus ... the victim's ... before attempting to ascertain Ms. Millford's condition."

"Ah-huh," the Sheriff said. "And being as how Ms. Millford is still inside her vehicle, can I assume she does not need immediate medical attention?"

"No, Sir," the Fowinkle boy affirmed.

"And you could determine that with certainty while Ms. Millford is inside her vehicle with the door shut and the windows rolled up?"

"Well no, Sir. I mean ... the door *was* open, for a while, and the susp ... and Ms. Millford was cooperating with me. She doesn't appear to have sustained any injuries, Sir."

"Why is the door shut now, Deputy?"

"She closed it, Sir. Refused my repeated requests to exit and slammed the door shut when I attempted to remove her for questioning. Hit my leg with it, too." The Fowinkle boy offered forth his right shin as evidence, black grease on the pant leg of his county issued trousers.

"Do you need medical attention, Deputy?"

"No, Sir."

"And did Ms. Millford give you any reason for not wanting to step out of her vehicle?"

"Kept saying she needed to get home. Said she was running late and her maid was gonna be leaving and that I should just let her go. Stuff like that. But I don't believe it's the truth, Sheriff."

Sheriff Porter processed the information. He digested the Fowinkle boy's statement as well as the visual evidence before him. When he looked at Virginia Millford through the car window, he observed a woman who seemed unconcerned by the ruckus surrounding her. She remained motionless on the seat and her hands were back on the steering wheel as though she were traveling down a distant highway all by herself.

"Virginia?" Sheriff Porter called to her through the closed window. "Are you all right?"

"I'm fine," she said without looking at him.

"If you'll just step out of the car, we'll get this whole thing straightened out and we'll have you on your way home."

"I could go home now if all these people would get out of my way."

"But I need to talk to you first," the Sheriff replied.

"Some other time, Norman. I'm late. Gussie Mae needs to get home."

Without prolonging the dialogue between them, Sheriff Porter reached swiftly to the door handle and attempted to open it. "It's locked, Sir," the Fowinkle boy proclaimed, news he then immediately realized was unnecessary. The Sheriff gave him an exasperated look.

"Sir, if I could have a word with you. Over here," the Fowinkle boy motioned.

Sheriff Porter was unaccustomed to disregard for the law. He was most assuredly unaccustomed to seeing the wife of the town doctor in a wrecked vehicle on the lawn of the courthouse in the middle of the Square. He hoped the Fowinkle boy was going to shed more light on the case as he stepped over to consult.

"Sir," the Fowinkle boy lowered his voice as much as possible, "I have reason to believe Ms. Millford may be intoxicated." Sheriff Porter glanced back at Virginia and considered for the first time she might be a suspect.

"Go on."

"While I was questioning her, I detected the odor of liquor coming from her vehicle. And Sir," he hesitated, "there's what appears to be a flask on the floorboard of the passenger side."

Sheriff Porter knew then he had a bona fide situation on his hands. A delicate one, which would serve him well not to blunder. What not even the senior law man in the county realized was how quickly word had spread of what only just then he'd accepted as a bona fide situation.

*   *   *   *

Elba Rae Van Oaks had not long been home from school when her cousin Hazel Burns called with the news.

"Have you talked to anybody that's been up on the Square this afternoon?"

"No," Elba Rae affirmed. "I just got in from school. How'd you get home so quick anyway? I thought Mr. Bailey was trying to get all the materials ready for teachers' meeting next week."

"He is, but I'm pretty near through with all the mimeographing. Anyway, Willadean Hendrix just called Momma because she was up at the dime store getting some navy blue thread and a new lint brush and saw all the commotion herself."

"What commotion?"

"On the Square! Have you really not heard? Momma didn't believe it at first, but Willadean was right there and saw it all! Well, not all I don't think—she was inside the dime store when it happened—but she was out front on the sidewalk when the Sheriff got there."

"Got where? What are you talking about? I had three pupils staying after today to make up some lessons and I—"

"To the Square! Right in front of the courthouse! Right under the statue of old man Litton!"

"I haven't heard a word about anything, Hazel. I just this minute got in the house."

"Well, they said Dr. Bud had to come up there to get her out of the car! The law came and—oh, I think it was that Fowinkle boy at first, bless his heart—Norman Porter finally had to come and they eventually had to call Dr. Bud at the clinic."

"Get who? Out of what car?"

"Virginia Millford! She drove right up to the courthouse steps and smack into the statue of old man Litton! And then do you know what?"

"What?"

"Virginia wouldn't get out the car!"

"For heaven's sake! Was she hurt? Did they take her to the hospital?"

"Not according to Willadean. Virginia finally got in the car with Dr. Bud and they drove off."

"Well, what in the world, Hazel?"

"Nobody seems to be saying much. There were a lot of people on the Square, and some of them are lucky to be alive according to Willadean."

"Did Virginia have to swerve to miss somebody else? Another car or something?"

"I don't think so. From what Willadean heard, Virginia had been at Kathleen Fike's for the longest trying on clothes and when she finished there, she got in the car and backed all the way across the street and onto the courthouse lawn!"

"In reverse?"

"Backwards."

"All the way across the street?"

"And into the statue of old man Litton. Willadean said if she hadn't hit the statue, she'd a been inside the courthouse before she got stopped. And then the law came, and they tried to get her out of the car, but she out and out refused! Willadean thought she must have been in some kind of shock or something, but then somebody said no, they were worried she was about to commit suicide!"

"In the car?"

"Yes, Ma'am!"

"With what? Was she going to hang herself with a coat hanger from Kathleen Fike's?"

Hazel Burns did not understand her cousin's lack of appreciation for the pure gravity of the situation, especially since she'd not even yet heard the outcome. "Well, I don't know, Elba Rae, I wasn't there of course myself. I'm just telling you what I heard."

"Well, Hazel, now really. Are you sure you heard right? I can't believe Virginia Millford would go up on the Square and threaten to take her life!"

"She wasn't trying to take her life, as it turned out. But they were afraid she was gonna crank the car back up and just plow right over that Fowinkle boy, and on through the crowd. You know, what's that they call it? Amok, like."

"Oh, Hazel!"

"Well, Willadean was right up there in the dime store and saw the whole thing with her own two eyes! She said Virginia tried to hit the Fowinkle boy with the car once before the Sheriff ever got there, but thank goodness somebody pulled him out of the way in the nick of time!"

"Do you think she's had a stroke?"

"Between you and me, I think she's had something. But I don't think it's a stroke."

"Oh, Hazel, no."

"Well, Willadean was gonna go over to Kathleen Fike's after it was all over, just to get the details on the whole thing and all, but do you know what?"

"What?"

"About the time she was gonna walk over there, Norman Porter and that Fowinkle boy went in the store with Lloyd and Kathleen. Kind of escorting them like. And Willadean said it looked like they meant business."

"What do you suppose that was all about?"

"I don't know for sure. But they said Virginia was acting a little funny at Kathleen's. Before she ever drove up on the Square. And in reverse!"

"You don't think she'd been drinking, do you?"

"Well, certainly I'm not the one to say. But you think about it, Elba Rae. What would get into somebody that's supposedly able-minded and capable of driving a car? What would make her drive all the way across the street and up on the Square until she hit a statue? And in reverse?"

"Maybe the accelerator got stuck or something. I've heard of that happening before."

"Well, maybe it did. And I hope it did, really, if not for Virginia's sake then at least for Dr. Bud's. Lord knows he doesn't deserve this."

"I hope it's something like that, Hazel. I'd hate to think she's so out of it she'd be up on the Square, drunk, in the middle of the afternoon."

"But you know what, Elba Rae?"

"What?"

"I really don't think it'd be the first time. Everybody knows it. Half the time anybody sees her some place she acts like she's not all there. What else could it be?"

"I don't know, but I'd just rather not think that."

"Don't you remember the way Momma and Aunt Ethel used to talk about her? The way she'd come to the club meetings and disrupt things and be loud?"

"Surely not, Hazel."

"I'm just telling you what they say, Elba Rae. I'm not making any of it up."

"Maybe she's had a stroke. One of those mini kind you don't know about until later."

"I would think Dr. Bud would know it since he lives with her every day. He is a doctor, after all."

"Do you think he knows she drinks?"

"How could he not? I just feel sorry for him, you know. I really do. Dr. Bud's a good person and I hate for him to be under this kind of burden."

"Well, he's a smart man, Hazel. And a doctor. He ought to know what to do. If that's the problem with her. And I'm not saying it is. But if it is, he ought to know what to do."

In reality, it was a combination of the calming effect Bud Millford had always had on his wife, as well as the inevitable subsiding of the Beefeater's influence on Virginia, that brought the incident to a peaceful resolution that afternoon on the Square. Sheriff Norman Porter wasn't the least interested in pressing charges against Virginia Millford or having her name be in the newspaper because some nosey reporter from over at the *Litton Times* happened to be perusing the police blotter. Once the facts were sorted out and Dr. Bud understood how much the county would appreciate him doing his rightful part to spruce up the courthouse grounds and the limestone of Mr. Homer T. Litton, he didn't imagine there would be any need to write up much of a report. He'd have to have a talk with the Fowinkle boy, he expected, but the boy was smart and a good deputy and he'd understand.

Without need of advice from Elba Rae Van Oaks or her informative cousin Hazel, Bud Millford did, indeed, think he knew best what to do about his wife Virginia and her problem that could no longer be concealed. He would plant the seeds before dark that afternoon for Virginia's alleged trip to Tennessee to nurse her ailing mother back from the sudden attack of her gall bladder, so unexpected yet clandestine not even Gussie Mae knew their true destination when they set out early the next morning.

In all the excitement that spring afternoon on the Square, no one even noticed Dewey Richardson had been resting in the shade of an ancient oak tree on the far side of the lawn or that his pants were partially unzipped throughout most of the ordeal. Somewhat after the crowd had dispersed and well after the tow truck had pulled Virginia's Electra off of Homer T. Litton, Dewey Richardson strolled casually over to the scene to observe the damage for himself. The memorial had taken quite a lick, he smiled to himself, and then laughed out loud when he recalled the sight of the frustrated deputy getting his leg smacked by the car door. That was when he noticed the object in the trampled grass. He bent down and picked up a numeral 5 from the dirt below the statue's base, a clear indication Virginia Millford now owned the only Buick Electra 22 in Litton County. Dewey dropped it into his pocket and walked on home with the souvenir.

SIMPLE BEGINA

"Tell me about the rest of your family."

Elba Rae Van Oaks watched Dr. Yardley pour himself a glass of water from the medicinal-looking thermal pitcher he kept on the edge of his desk before, as he customarily did, offering her a serving which she, always, politely refused. She didn't know why he continually made the gesture other than to be mannerly which, forced upon her or not, she'd decided he was.

"Who do you want to know about?" She asked, completely disinterested in talking about any Maywood or Van Oaks relatives.

"Well, you've mentioned your mother in passing quite a few times, and how unsettling your suspension has been on her. And of course your cousin, who you seem very close to. And your mother's sister."

"Ruby."

"Yes. Ruby. Are there others?"

"Here in Buford?"

"Or elsewhere. Doesn't matter."

"Well, elsewhere, there's my sister, Lila. Lila Mae. She lives in Birmingham. And I have another aunt on my daddy's side still living. She's in Hattiesburg."

"Not too far away, I don't suppose," he commented, as though it were a good thing.

"But far enough, thank God."

"I beg your pardon?"

"I'm sorry. I guess that sounds ugly."

"You don't have to apologize to me, Elba Rae. Apparently you're not close to this particular aunt."

"It's not that. It's just … well, she was always a little peculiar, and then we could never get a visit from her without her daughter coming along, but I don't guess it matters much now because she doesn't get outside Hattiesburg anymore. Her mind's not good."

"I'm sorry."

"It's okay. Really. Because whatever keeps her in Hattiesburg will keep my cousin there, too."

"You dislike your cousin?"

"No, I don't dislike her. She's sweet. In her way. But I'd dread knowing she was coming for a visit, that's for sure."

"Why is that?"

Elba Rae felt guilty before even opening her mouth, like she was telling family secrets not meant to be aired. But if he wanted to know, she was going to tell it. Because way deep down, she bore no ill will toward her daddy's sister or her cousin as long as the both of them stayed in Hattiesburg. Dr. Yardley would surely understand, she thought.

*   *   *   *

Elba Rae Van Oaks never did think of herself as one prone to scheme outright. Not, at least, until the year she and her mother would conspire together for their common good and rid themselves of a visitor to Buford who just didn't know when to go home. They would feel bad about it, Elba Rae knew that before she ever shared the plot with her mother Ethel, but they had to do something. Nature, apparently, would not have taken its course otherwise.

The day the disruption began, Elba Rae Van Oaks was enjoying with unusual delight the first full week of her summer break from teaching fifth grade at the Homer T. Litton Grammar School. She was planning to put up some corn and some beans and some okra too, assuming her neighbor and friend Martha Betty Maharry shared the bounty from the Maharry garden as she always did, but that wouldn't come until a bit later in the summer. The first week off was always Elba Rae's official vacation, when she did very little and practically didn't leave the house. Her husband, Fettis, might be underfoot from time to time, but the rhythm of their years together—during school sessions and not—was habit to them and they each knew how to live with the other. Most mornings Fettis would be gone before Elba Rae even got up, and sometimes he didn't come home until dinner time.

She had been thinking about what she was going to fix Fettis for dinner but really hoping to herself he'd call and say he was getting a bite at the Litton Café and Bait Shop and not to wait for him. It wasn't because Elba Rae Van Oaks didn't like to cook or that she didn't sometimes enjoy the domestic duties of her seasonal housewife role; it was because of Lisa Hughes, the blond vixen so entrancing on Elba Rae's favorite afternoon serial. It had been months since Elba Rae had the luxury of watching TV in the daytime—it had been since school started the fall before to be exact—and getting reacquainted with Lisa and all her men and all her troubles was part of the relief the school year's end brought. By twelve thirty, having not heard from Fettis, she made herself a grilled cheese sandwich and got settled in the den in front of her set. The cheese was still hot and soft when her telephone rang. It was Elba Rae's mother, Ethel Maywood.

"I was running the vacuum and nearly didn't hear the phone. If I'd known who it was, I would have kept on vacuuming," Ethel declared quickly.

"Who was it, Momma?"

"Have you got company, Elba Rae?"

"No."

"I thought I heard voices."

"Must have been the TV."

"Elba Rae, I hope you're not watching those trashy stories on the TV. My goodness, school hasn't been out a week good and you're already looking at those trashy stories."

"I'm not looking at anything, Momma, the TV's just on. Fettis left it on when he went out this morning and I just haven't cut it off."

"Well I'm glad somebody's got enough money to play their TV all day just to keep up the electric company."

"Momma, who was on the phone? Who called you?"

"Your aunt Laveetra."

"Oh, Lord, what did she want?"

"Well, first off, she acted like she didn't want anything. But that's how she always does, you know. I'll go six months and not hear a word from her and then she'll call up out of the blue and chit chat about nothing and then she'll eventually get around to letting you know what she really wants. She always has done that, especially when your daddy was still alive. She'd wait six months and then she'd call and talk forever about nothing and finally she'd get around to it and she'd say, 'Put brother Ray on the phone for a minute, will you Ethel?' and then we'd be stuck. Again."

"She asked you for money?" Elba Rae was now more excited by the potential drama on the phone than she was the possible controversy Lisa Hughes was stirring up on the TV.

"She wouldn't have the nerve to ask me for money. Not with your daddy gone. But before it's over, we might've wished that's all it was."

"Well, what did she want?" Just as Elba Rae anticipated the menu of answers, there was a swell of organ music from the TV, signifying both the crucial climax of a scene and the pending transition to an important message from the sponsor who would announce breakthrough remedies for a waxy build up on the linoleum floor or at least a new and improved fresher-scented detergent to fight even the toughest stains.

"Elba Rae, I know good and well that's one of those trashy stories on TV you're listening to. Fettis didn't any more leave that on than I did."

"I don't know what it is, Momma, because I haven't even been paying attention." Elba Rae Van Oaks lied sometimes, but that was her business.

Ethel Maywood had once suffered herself from an unhealthy devotion to the *Love of Life* but was now reformed and felt with unfailing conviction that gave her not only the right to counsel others but that it was her duty. "It's the Devil's workshop, Elba Rae. Watching those people on there carrying on with each other's wives and husbands and having babies and not even knowing who the father is and having relations before they marry. Those shows are full of sinful people and the people watching them are no better!"

"I am not watching TV, Momma! Now what did Aunt Laveetra want?"

"And another thing, Elba Rae. I hope you and Hazel aren't gonna be going up on the Square three times a week to see those trashy movies they run at the picture show these days."

"I don't know what you're talking about, Momma."

"They didn't even make movies like that in my day, you know, and if they had, no decent person would have been caught dead paying good money for a ticket!"

"Momma, what does the fact Hazel and I might want to enjoy ourselves every once in a while and go to the show have to do with anything? Is that what Aunt Laveetra called you about? Because she wanted to know if Hazel and I had plans to go to a movie?"

"Well certainly not, Elba Rae, and I don't appreciate this tone a bit! Not one bit! I'm upset enough as it is!"

"About what?!"

"Your aunt Laveetra, that's what! And that simple daughter of hers! But at least I know she won't be talking you into going to any trashy movies while she's here."

"While *who's* here? Begina? She's coming here? Oh, Momma, no. Not again. Wasn't she just here? It's not time for her again!"

"Well, that's what I was thinking—at first. But then Laveetra somehow reminded me it'd been two years since they drove over for the reunion, so I guess we were due."

"Well, I'm not."

"It doesn't matter. She's coming."

"Is Aunt Laveetra coming too?"

"No, thank heavens, at least we've got that to be grateful for. It'll just be Begina. Oh, I think deep down Laveetra probably wanted to come, cause she never wants to miss anything you know, but she made up some excuse about her leg having the cramps so terrible she just can't stand to ride in the car for too long at a time."

"Well, she always has leaned to one side when she walks."

"If she'd wanted to come bad enough, she'd ride all the way to Buford with her leg sticking out the car window. No, she just doesn't want to bother because there's not a Maywood reunion involved or a wedding or anything pleasant. It's that cousin of your Uncle Sammy's. The one that's been up there in the nursing home around Anniston so long. He's finally passed and she's sending Begina to the funeral."

"I thought he was dead."

"And I guess he is, else your Aunt Laveetra wouldn't be sending Begina over for the funeral."

"No, I mean I thought he'd been dead."

"That's wasn't Sammy's cousin. You're thinking about that brother-in-law of his that had the stroke. He did die a few years ago. Don't you remember? They held up burying him till he was nearly mortified because they had to wait for one of the sons to get back from France or England or Europe or somewhere. Over there playing in a golf tournament or some foolishness such as that."

"Well then who was this one?"

"This is Sammy's cousin, Willie Lynn. The one they always called W'lynn. He was your Uncle Sammy's last first cousin, on his daddy's side. He was old as Methuselah and I don't think he's known any of them for years."

"But I thought he was already dead. Are you sure you heard Aunt Laveetra right?"

"Laveetra said W'lynn had died up in the nursing home and she was sending Begina over to represent the family at the visitation and the funeral and she'd be so indebted if we could go with her because she just doesn't like Begina to go off that far from home by herself. I know what I heard."

"But don't you remember going up there for his funeral already? When Daddy was still alive? Don't you remember how we laughed cause he made us leave two hours too early and then we got lost anyway?"

"Yeah, I do remember us getting to laughing about being lost. And the more we did, the madder he got."

"And it was on the way to W'lynn's funeral."

"Oh, I know what you're talking about, Elba Rae. That wasn't for his funeral. That was when they buried his leg."

"His leg? Oh, yeah … now it's coming back to me. Didn't he end up having the other one cut off too?"

"I believe he did, because you know he always was just eat up with the diabetes. But I don't recall them putting on a graveside service for it. Else, we'd have gone to it, I'm sure."

"It was a little child's coffin, wasn't it?"

"What was?"

"The coffin they put W'lynn's leg in when we had to go out to the cemetery and bury it."

"I believe it was. Course, there was no sense wasting a perfectly good full-sized one for just a leg. Unless they were planning to put the rest of him in it eventually, but you know there's something unseemly about that, Elba Rae. Even if it was just a leg. You oughtn't to be digging anything up once it's been proper buried."

"Well do you think they'll put him all together now? I mean, in one coffin?"

"It'd seem like the appropriate thing to do, but surely they'll have all that decided before we get to the funeral home for the visitation. I'm gonna try not to think about it."

"Uncle Sammy's family always was a little on the strange side. It's no wonder Daddy thought Aunt Laveetra married beneath her."

"Your Aunt Laveetra's no prize either, Elba Rae, but at least she's doing us the favor of staying home this time. But mark my words, she probably hadn't thought to send Begina over here with the first sign of any food for us to take up there. And you know we can't just land in on them for a visitation without taking a dish."

"Well that's all right, Momma, because I've got a casserole in the deep freeze I can carry up there if we need to."

"Is it in one of your good dishes?"

"It's one of my Pyrexes."

"Well you'd better put masking tape on the bottom to write our names on—from the Ray Maywood family, I mean—if you've any hopes of ever getting it back."

"It's okay, Momma. I've got several and if I have to lose one, then that's that."

"I don't care. Put our name on it anyway."

"All right, Momma. When will Begina be here?"

"Laveetra said she'd have her off from Hattiesburg first thing in the morning. And just pray she makes it and we don't get a call somewhere from the side of the road."

"Why? Does she think her car's not reliable?"

"Well you know it's that old piece of Laveetra and Sammy's. I'm surprised the Smithsonian Institute hasn't offered to buy it. If I was your aunt Laveetra, I'd be ashamed to send my daughter off down the highway in some old piece of car, especially with her already being simple-minded to start with. I'd be a nervous wreck till I knew she'd gotten where she was going."

"Then make sure you get Begina to call Aunt Laveetra as soon as she gets to the house," Elba Rae thoughtfully suggested.

"Well, be sure and tell her when she gets there, hear?"

"When she gets where?"

"To your house. Well, didn't I tell you? Laveetra was carrying on so about how Begina was grieved about W'lynn and all, because he was just about the last of her daddy's family I guess, but how she couldn't help but look forward to the trip cause she always loves getting over to Buford and seeing all her kin here. So I told her Begina should stay with you."

*   *   *   *

Elba Rae Van Oaks was still seething with fury when her husband Fettis parked his truck in the driveway, which actually wasn't officially the driveway but more of a path he'd worn in the grass off to the side of the real driveway which led him to the shade of an elm tree. He came in the house and put his keys up on the shelf over the kitchen sink where he always kept them. Elba Rae might waste time in the morning, wondering which pocketbook she'd dropped her car keys in the last time she'd had them, but not him, no sir. He heard the shuffling in the den off the kitchen and was on his way to investigate when he spied the saucer on the counter with what appeared to be a grilled cheese sandwich waiting.

"You needn't have made me any lunch, Elba Rae. I thought you'd know by now if I wasn't home I wasn't coming in time to eat." He got no immediate response. "Elba Rae?"

"What?!?" came bellowing from the other room.

"You in there?"

"No, Fettis, I'm not in here! Miss Donna Reed is in here and she's the one getting this house all cleaned up! Of course I'm in here!"

"Well, you don't have to bite my head off! I was just saying, you didn't have to fix me any lunch."

"I didn't fix you any lunch, Fettis! That was supposed to be my lunch! But now I don't have time to eat it 'cause I've got to get this house in shape for company!"

Fettis Van Oaks, unsure he wanted to know the rest of the story, did dare to venture into the den nonetheless. "For what company? It's not time for the church women again, is it?"

"I wish it were just the Circle! At least they'd go home after the lesson! Oh, no. We're having real company. From Hattiesburg."

"Oh, shoot me, Elba Rae. Not your aunt Laveetra and that daughter of hers."

"Well, you're part right. The good news is Aunt Laveetra's not coming. The bad news is, Begina is. And my momma thought it was just fine to tell them Begina should come on here and stay with us instead of going to Momma's. How do you like that? So now I'm trying to get the house cleaned and the sheets washed in the spare room because she'll be here tomorrow. Just in time for us to pile in the car—with Momma—and drive up to Anniston to the funeral home cause W'lynn finally died."

"Uncle Sammy's cousin, W'lynn?"

"Yes!" Elba Rae was slapping a rag onto the surface of an end table more so than she was just dusting it.

"I thought he was dead."

"I did too."

"Didn't you go to his funeral already?"

"No. That was just for his leg. Did you eat any dinner?"

"I got a bite at the café and—"

"Well then, could you get the mower out and do something with that front yard? If you wait another day, we can sell it for hay."

"Elba Rae, why are you trying to put on for that dim-witted cousin?"

Elba Rae stopped her slapping and stood firm with one hand to her hip. "She does the best she can, Fettis. She can't help it if she's a little slow. And even if she is, that doesn't mean I'm gonna let her come in here to a dirty house with stale sheets on the bed and a yard that looks like nobody lives here and then go back to Hattiesburg talking about how filthy we are. She's family and we're going to make her feel welcomed in our home if it kills me. And you too. Now can you get to the yard or what?"

"All right, all right!" He turned around to head out the back door and toward the shed where his mower and countless other belongings were stored. "But dang it, Elba Rae," he declared as he walked off, "you haven't even been home a week and already you're into some mess."

Elba Rae was slapping the table again before the screen door had the chance to bounce once off the frame. By the time she heard the mower crank, the sheets were already stuffed into the washing machine.

*   *   *   *

Not surprisingly, Fettis Van Oaks was the first to arrive at the Moss Hardware & Supply store for coffee and fellowship the next morning, having wanted to clear the house just as soon as was possible. He would get his fill of cousin Begina, he felt sure, without being present for her arrival and certainly without even hinting that he'd consider accompanying the group on their condolence visits to Anniston where they would witness the last burial once and for all of the late legless W'lynn. The Maywoods could be a cantankerous bunch, he knew, and his wife Elba Rae, it seemed sometimes, had benefitted not a bit nor been diluted in the least from all her years of being a Van Oaks, who were, he knew, by breed a more mellow people.

Elba Rae Van Oaks had risen early as well, not so she could slither out of the house and seek refuge at the coffee corner of the Moss Hardware & Supply like her cowardly husband, but because she still had not decided on an outfit for the car trip and visitation in Anniston. It would have to be something that wouldn't wrinkle too badly and something that wouldn't be too hot since even in the bowels of summer heat her mother, Ethel Maywood, could somehow always complain about the frigid temperature of the air conditioning in Elba Rae's car. And

Elba Rae knew she'd be the one driving, for sure, since there was no way she was leaving Buford in the old piece of Aunt Laveetra's that would bring Begina.

"Is she there yet?" Was Ethel Maywood's first question when Elba Rae answered the phone in the kitchen.

"No, Momma. I told you I'd call you when she gets here."

"Well, be sure you get her to call Laveetra when she gets there. If Laveetra's got any sense, she'll be worried. Begina should have come on the bus. It would have been safer."

"Probably so, but—wait—oh, Momma, I think she's coming up the drive now." Elba Rae strained the phone cord to get to the carport door for a better look. "Yep, she's here."

"Well, thank goodness. I guess. You call me now and tell me what time y'all are picking me up."

"All right, Momma, now I've got to go."

Elba Rae hung up the phone and took a deep breath. She returned to the carport door and got ready to receive her guest.

Cousin Begina on Elba Rae's daddy's side wasn't really supposed to have ever been "Begina" at all. Elba Rae had always found the story of her cousin's random moniker both amusing and yet foreboding, and wondered if she'd been named something different, whether she would have been less affected.

Aunt Laveetra required little prompting to share with anyone who'd listen the details of those most grueling hours of her life—which could have been condensed, but weren't—into the story of the birth of her only child, Begina Marie Chittum. In some versions, Begina's origins began with the courtship of the young Laveetra Maywood from Buford and the eventual ne'er-do-well Sammy Chittum from down around Weoka, but in all of them it ended with a labor that got longer with every telling and ranged anywhere from a day-and-a-half to two weeks.

The unimaginable and naturally unrivaled strain of the delivery had caused Aunt Laveetra to require significant quantities of rest medicine following, doses so powerful in fact it had rendered her for all practical purposes unconscious for nearly three days, which became four or five days in some tellings but which, nonetheless, left her in no mind to fill out the form required by the county to record the child's birth.

After two days, Uncle Sammy had filled out the paper without a thought given to the consideration he'd always received poor marks in penmanship and that his capital Rs always had looked like capital Bs, and it was only later after the certificate arrived in the mail that a semi-recovered Laveetra would discover with horror her daughter Regina did not exist for as much as the Litton County Records Department was concerned. By the time she felt up to doing something about it, the idea of "Begina" aroused a strange appeal to Aunt Laveetra and she decided she liked it as well as, if not better than, Regina anyway, so it must have been the Lord's way of letting her know the child wasn't ever supposed to have been Regina in the first place—although she did question why the Lord had to knock her out for six days on rest medicine to get the message across.

The first thing Elba Rae noticed when the car door swung open in Buford that day was not how much it squeaked from lack of proper lubrication over the years but how large her cousin Begina had gotten since their last visit. The knocking and the pinging of the engine which wouldn't seem to cut all the way off wasn't even distracting. Begina had always been a big-boned girl, having inherited some of that from the Chittums and a bit from her mother Laveetra too, but before she even had both feet firmly out of the car and onto the driveway Elba Rae could tell she'd expanded considerably. The frock she was wearing was most unflattering, and the large floral print did nothing to conceal her size.

"Elba Rae, Elba Rae, come here and give me a hug! I am so glad to see you!"

"And goodness, Begina, you're a sight for sore eyes!" The two cousins hugged, and Elba Rae could tell right away if the old Invicta had air conditioning at all, it wasn't cutting it that day because the back of Begina's big unflattering floral frock was moist with sweat.

"You never change a bit, Elba Rae! You still look just like you did when we were kids. Look at you."

"And look at you," Elba Rae started, but soon thought better. "I know you must be tired from the drive. Come on in the house. Just leave your suitcase in the car. Fettis'll get it when he comes home. Come on in the house and cool off. Did you have any trouble getting over?"

"Oh no," she said as the pair walked through the carport toward the kitchen door. "Mother's car does just fine on the road. I even stopped a little bit before I got into town and filled up so we wouldn't have to get any gas when we start out to Anniston."

"Oh, did you? Well, you're probably so tired from driving already this morning, Begina, I'll be glad to take us in my car."

The two entered the cool house and Elba Rae knew without doubt she wouldn't get much argument from Cousin Begina.

*   *   *   *

Fettis Van Oaks did not come home before the departure to Anniston that afternoon, and Elba Rae knew full well he had no intention to, even if he had to drive up and down Highway 29 past the house to make sure the coast was clear first. She'd left him a note on the refrigerator door under a pineapple magnet to tell him to bring Begina's suitcase and any other belongings from the battered Invicta and into the guest bedroom.

Meanwhile, Elba Rae and Cousin Begina and Elba Rae's mother Ethel Maywood were comfortably motoring north up Highway 21 in Elba Rae's white Galaxie 500 with fully functioning air conditioning, Cousin Begina in the front passenger seat and Ethel Maywood in the back, when Begina suddenly announced she was about getting ready to have some supper, what did the rest of them think? Elba Rae looked at her watch.

"It's a quarter to four now," Begina confirmed. "By the time we get through and back on the road, we'll hit it just about right at the funeral home. Mother said the visitation was from six to eight." Then she turned her head slightly toward the back seat, and raised her voice. "And Aunt Ethel, you just tell me if you're getting worn out tonight at the funeral home and we'll start on back. I figure I can visit with everybody some more tomorrow at the funeral and I don't want to wear you out, sweetie." Elba Rae tried as she might to get a glimpse of her mother in the rear view mirror, knowing as she did that Ethel Maywood would rather to have been called "bitch" than addressed as "sweetie." She'd always hated it, and Cousin Begina was the only person who'd ever called her such.

"I'm fine, Begina. And I'm not that hungry," Ethel responded.

"Are you not?" Begina semi-yelled although Ethel Maywood was not hard of hearing in the least. "Well, sakes, I am. I had a good breakfast this morning before I left home, and Mother packed me some sandwiches, but those just aren't staying with me for some reason." Elba Rae was making many mental notes for the conversation she hoped to have soon with her other cousin, Hazel Burns.

"Begina, if you're hungry now, we can stop," Elba Rae said. "Just as well now as on the way home tonight. Momma?" Elba Rae looked again in the mirror. "Is that all right with you?" Ethel Maywood met Elba Rae's eyes in the reflection and frowned.

"Whatever you all want is fine with me," Ethel deferred while both frowning and sounding pleasant.

"Well good, sweetie," Begina picked up, "cause I've been seeing those signs for this Routy's ever few miles and they've got my appetite whetted up for some bar-beque. I think we've stopped there before, on the way to the nursing home to see W'lynn. Papa said the meat was a little tough but as I recall it was some of the best barbeque I've had."

"It's fine with me, Begina," Elba Rae said even though it was not fine with her and she knew full well it was not at all fine with her mother Ethel and she wasn't hungry in the least and if she were she didn't think a plate of greasy barbeque was necessarily the thing to have when you had to pile back in the car and go to a funeral home. But the trip wasn't about her and it wasn't about her mother Ethel; it was about doing something nice for her simple cousin Begina and some-how maybe that was honoring her own dead father's memory since Begina's mother Aunt Laveetra was her daddy's own sister and maybe if she talked to her-self long enough she wouldn't want to drive the car down an embankment with Begina in it.

The ladies soon stopped at Routy's Hot Pit Bar-Be-Que where the diners were sparse and the supper rush had not yet formed. Elba Rae ordered a barbeque sandwich, small, with some slaw on the side. Ethel Maywood had a glass of iced tea and one complimentary pack of Saltines from the pile which sat atop the nap-kin dispenser of every table in a red plastic bread basket, and vowed as to how she just didn't think she could eat a thing right then. Begina Marie Chittum ordered the barbeque plate with french fries, baked beans, a tossed salad, and extra slaw, and before the dishes were even served, she'd pretty much already consumed the entire supply of hot dinner rolls intended to be shared by all parties. After what she thought had been the conclusion of the meal, Elba Rae prematurely reached to the floor for her pocketbook when she stood corrected and heard Begina allow to the waitress as to how she didn't believe she could pass up a piece of the chess pie that looked so good in the refrigerated case up at the register. Elba Rae dropped her purse back to the floor and made a point of not looking in her mother's direction.

*   *   *   *

Judging from the cars in the parking lot of the Mortimer and Sons Funeral Home, the late W'lynn had drawn more of a crowd than Elba Rae had expected—especially since he was such an elderly man and had been in the nurs-ing home so long. "Will you look at the cars?" Begina seemed to concur. "I'm so happy for W'lynn. I just wish Papa could be here. You know they were more like brothers than they were cousins, Elba Rae."

"Ah-huh," Elba Rae agreed as she stopped at the front door. "Why don't y'all go on in and I'll park the car?"

"Are you sure, Elba Rae?"

"Come on, Begina," Ethel Maywood said as she opened the back door and disembarked. "I just hope it's warmer in there than it is in this car. I've been in a rigor ever since we left that old barbeque place."

"Hold on, sweetie, and I'll help you out!"

Elba Rae knew, though the offer was genuine, that by the time Cousin Begina could maneuver her own self out of the Galaxie and gain her footing Ethel Maywood would already be inside the funeral home signing their names to the guest book. She parked the car and joined them shortly in the room called the Serenity Parlor, where the head and torso of the late Willie Lynn Chittum was dressed and made up and arranged just so under the blue- and rose-colored spotlights in what was obviously yet another new casket.

Not surprisingly to Elba Rae, her mother Ethel was the model of grace and good will as she mingled about the room visiting with apparently more people she recognized than not. Cousin Begina embraced her relatives and wept every once in a while when she'd look over at dead W'lynn in the casket and it made Elba Rae ashamed for all the collection of ill thoughts she'd had since the afternoon before when her mother had interrupted her story and her grilled cheese with the announcement of Begina's impending visit. Cousin Begina was simple, yes, and she was big as the side of the house, it was obvious to all, and the brown and white polka-dot dress with the matching short-sleeved jacket she'd chosen to wear for the visitation was no more flattering than the sweaty flowered muumuu she'd worn for the road trip over from Hattiesburg in Aunt Laveetra's piece of car, but her heart was in the right place. Uncle Sammy was dead and Elba Rae did believe for a fact Uncle Sammy and W'lynn were close as brothers and underneath all those polka dots she knew Begina was probably hurting. She made up her mind that moment she could stand a couple of days to accommodate her cousin, even if it meant driving back to Anniston the next day for the actual funeral service and enduring her mother's subtle snipes about the setting of the Galaxie's air conditioning. Right about then, Elba Rae Van Oaks felt a surge of indigestion that was surely some of Routy's Hot Pit Bar-Be-Que bubbling up in the back of her throat.

*　　　*　　　*　　　*

The third and final interment of Mr. Willie Lynn Chittum was concluded on a Friday afternoon in a picturesque cemetery outside Anniston with fewer spectators in attendance than had signed in at the Mortimer and Sons Funeral Home the evening before, but respectable enough and of course with Elba Rae Van Oaks, her mother Ethel Maywood, and her cousin simple Begina front and center. Since neither Begina nor any of her Chittum kin had made mention of the multiple caskets already occupying the plot, Elba Rae did not feel it appropriate to bring up as a topic of discussion although the curiosity was almost unbearable. At one point, she leaned forward over the open grave just ever so slightly to see what might already be down there, but Ethel Maywood had restrained her with great discretion by pinching onto the bottom of Elba Rae's elbow which served to straighten her right back up. Maybe someday when Begina wasn't grieving so, she'd ask about it somehow, she thought.

On Sunday morning, when Elba Rae expected her to be gathering her belongings and saying her thank-yous and her good-byes, and asking Fettis if he wouldn't mind helping with her suitcase, Begina Marie Chittum instead asked Elba Rae if she still had the old waffle iron that made just the best crispy waffles and did it still work. Elba Rae, momentarily caught off her guard by the query, immediately confirmed in fact she did still have the old waffle iron and by the time she was standing over it mixing up some batter to serve Cousin Begina some good crispy waffles she regretted having not told her instead she'd thrown it down the big gully behind their house some while back because it seemed to have an electrical short in the old cord. She wasn't feeling rushed, as yet, but was mindful that Sunday School would be starting in less than two hours and she had some getting ready to do and didn't really have the time for a large scale waffle cooking which she knew, given Begina's appetite since arriving from Hattiesburg, would naturally be the only conceivable scale.

"Elba Rae, these are the best waffles I've ever eaten."

"I'm glad you're enjoying them, Begina. You sure I can't make you another one? The griddle's still hot."

"No, no, I better not. If I don't get up from here and start getting ready, I'll make us late for church."

"Huh?" Elba Rae dropped the wooden spoon she'd been using to stir the batter into the sink.

"It's still ten o'clock, isn't it? For Sunday School?"

"Yeah ... it's ten."

"Then I'd better get a move on. I'm gonna run a bath, Elba Rae. Is that all right? Is there enough hot water? Will Fettis need to be using the shower?"

"No, Fettis won't be using the shower because he won't be going."

"He won't?"

"Well, no, on account of his back, you know. It hurts him to sit in the pews."

"Oh, Mother's the same way. Except it's her leg, you know. It'll go to cramping and some days we can't get any further than the drug store before she's wanting to go back home. Well, I guess it's just us girls then. I'll try not to be long cause I know you'll be needing in there too." She scooted her chair back and pushed toward the middle of the table a breakfast plate with a syrup lake half an inch deep in its center. Elba Rae stood still at her kitchen sink and looked out the window, which offered nothing of a view other the roof of her Galaxie in the carport. She felt one knee buckle just a little.

The congregation of the First Avenue United Methodist Church loved it when someone had a visitor. The church wasn't small by any means, for Buford standards, but everyone knew everybody else and you couldn't just waltz into Sunday School with a guest and plan to go unnoticed. Most of the members of Elba Rae Van Oaks's Sunday School class had met Cousin Begina before, and those who didn't know her outright certainly knew her by association since she was the niece of Ray Maywood, whose widow, Ethel, was still an active member of the church. Since no one there had attended the visitation for the late W'lynn Chittum at the Mortimer and Sons Funeral Home near Anniston, none of them could know how Cousin Begina had managed to recycle her funeral home outfit into a Sunday School and church outfit by switching to a solid white jacket over the same brown polkadots.

Begina drank in the attention she got after church was over like it was waffle batter, Elba Rae thought, as first one and then another would come up and offer introduction and then more likely than not realize they knew exactly who she was, it'd just been so long since they'd seen her, and how was her momma doing anyway and why didn't she come to Buford with her, and by the time Elba Rae got Begina herded into the Galaxie and away from church she was getting more versed than she wanted to be in the condition of Aunt Laveetra's twitching leg. On the way home, she was anxious to ask precisely when did Begina think she'd have to leave them and head back to Hattiesburg but that would've been just plain rude and she wasn't going to hurt her feelings because Begina was family and Elba Rae knew she was sad about her father's cousin W'lynn with no legs that was more like a brother having finally died, and Elba Rae was determined to live through the visit without unnecessary regret later and if that meant an extra day or so then fine.

Four days later, the only regret Elba Rae Van Oaks had was not knowing the check-out date of her prize houseguest Cousin Begina from Hattiesburg. It had been a week. Long enough for most people to visit, more than enough if the person was Begina Marie Chittum who never seemed to fill up although Elba Rae was steadily providing three balanced meals a day plus an assortment of snacks and sweets and seasonal fruit from both Martha Betty Maharry's orchard and the produce department of the Buford Piggly Wiggly. Fettis Van Oaks for all intents and purposes had moved out of the house, Elba Rae felt, and somehow found something to do most any hour of the day to keep him busy elsewhere. He was filling in on some—any that needed him—bowling teams and it didn't even matter to Fettis if they were the same leagues or not; he was willing to travel. He'd even taken to helping out with odd jobs and chores around the Simpson place, a thoughtful gesture Elba Rae decided on some level since Doug Simpson was busy in the fields and his wife was near helpless around the old farmhouse they were living in since Doug had come back to Litton County, but odd somewhat since Fettis was never too quick to take on any chore around their own house until she'd worried him about it for a month or two first. But Mabel Moss had told Elba Rae how Florine had declared that poor Patsy Simpson just didn't have anybody to help around that old house and wasn't it a blessing Fettis was so handy and able to help her fix a few things.

"I'm telling you, Hazel, I don't know how much longer I can stand this," Elba Rae sort of whispered into the phone one afternoon while keeping a watchful eye toward the hallway leading to the bedrooms.

"She can't hear you, can she Elba Rae?"

"Lord no. Every evening about this time, she takes to her bed and naps till near about supper time. One day she got to snoring so loud, I couldn't hear a bit of what anybody on the TV was saying. I tiptoed down there and pulled her a door to a little, but it didn't do much good. So I just turned up the TV."

"When do you think she'll go back to Hattiesburg?"

"Hasn't mentioned it."

"At all?"

"Not a word. And I'll tell you who's been laying low ever since we got back from Anniston and hardly ringing my phone or darkening my door and that's my momma."

Hazel Burns laughed. "I bet she hasn't, after it was her doing and all that got Begina to stay with you and Fettis instead of going on over there."

"And I wouldn't mind, Hazel, you know I wouldn't. She's my daddy's own niece and I know she can't have much life over there living up under Aunt Laveetra day in and day out, and that can't be easy—for someone in their right mind, much less somebody like Begina. But Lord have mercy, Hazel, I am just worn out with it! This is supposed to be my time off and I've barely had a minute to myself since school was out!"

"Well does she offer to help you with anything, Elba Rae? The dishes? Does she do any wash?"

"She hasn't so much as carried a dish from the table to the sink since she's been here. But I don't know, Hazel, maybe she just doesn't know any better. You know how Aunt Laveetra's always been and Uncle Sammy was no count all his life, so who was there to ever teach Begina anything about going to somebody's house and how to act? And when to go home?"

"You're right, Elba Rae. I don't think she knows any better. And now she's over here staying with you and you waiting on her hand and foot and cooking and cleaning for her and she probably thinks she's died and gone to heaven and landed at the Waldorf Astoria or someplace like that."

"I'm telling you, Hazel, I can't keep it up much longer. Something's got to give. Every morning I'm in here at the stove first thing frying up bacon and scrambling eggs and baking biscuits, and then it's dinner time and she's expecting some fried chicken and creamed potatoes and green beans, and the skillet doesn't even get cooled off before she's asking me what we're having for supper. And then, round about eight or eight thirty every night, she's rustling in my pantry looking for cookies."

"Well, I did notice at church the other day she'd put on some weight."

"Weight *nothing*, Hazel. She is just digging her own grave with a knife and a fork. And I guess I'm helping her do it by feeding her three hots a day, every one with some pie or cake or a scoop of ice cream after."

"Well, what can you do, Elba Rae? You can't not feed her."

"I guess not. But if she doesn't go home soon, Fettis is going to have to take out a note at the bank just so we can buy groceries." Hazel Burns laughed again, and this time it served to lighten Elba Rae's mood just a little. "I'm telling you, Hazel," she giggled, "I don't know what I'm going to do."

First thing the next morning, Elba Rae Van Oaks knew what she was going to do. She was going to call her mother Ethel Maywood and tell her—not ask—that it was time Cousin Begina moved quarters and gave Elba Rae and Fettis a much needed break (although Fettis himself had pretty much already been having all kinds of one, it seemed). Elba Rae dreaded the call at first, but her plan was executed without much resistance from Ethel Maywood whose own guilt left her wide open for the relocation of Cousin Begina. As was usual with any show of attention, feigned or otherwise, Begina was delighted her Aunt Ethel had missed not getting to spend enough time with her since she'd been over to Buford and of course she'd love to come stay a few nights with her at her house. Ethel Maywood offered to come pick Begina up, since the battery on Aunt Laveetra's Invicta had more or less discharged from sitting idle for so long. Elba Rae reciprocated as how that wasn't even necessary, she'd bring her right over in the Galaxie.

Ethel Maywood was accustomed to living alone since the death of Elba Rae's father Raymond, and had long settled into a daily routine not at all conducive to a houseguest expecting the quantity of nourishment required by Begina Marie Chittum, and within three days, Ethel was carrying the suitcase herself out to the Rambler and driving Simple Begina back over to Elba Rae's whose brief respite was over, leaving only Laveetra Chittum to revel, apparently, in a freedom she'd not known for years.

"I'm sorry, Elba Rae, but I couldn't do it. I'm just not able. Someday, you're gonna be my age and you'll see what I'm talking about. Right now you and Fettis are still young enough, and you can take care of somebody staying in your house. I just can't do it." A dump truck whooshed down the highway past the two women who were talking in the driveway outside Elba Rae's house, while Begina was back in her room unpacking and arranging her creams and assorted ointments on the dresser.

"Young doesn't have anything to do with it, Momma, what do you think I'm going to do with her here? What is wrong with her?"

"Now Elba Rae, you know she's simple. She can't help it. I think she got that from those Chittums and it's just a burden she's had to carry. And it can't have been easy for your Aunt Laveetra all these years."

"I bet it's easy for her now! Now that Begina's moved to Buford to live with me!"

"Surely she'll be heading back to Hattiesburg before long, Elba Rae. I would think her momma would need her back over there by now."

"Her momma's probably too busy dancing a jig to notice, cramped-up leg and all!"

"Hush that, Elba Rae. It's disrespectful."

"Well you're the one who said Aunt Laveetra would hang her leg out the car window if she wanted—"

"I don't care what I said. You just need to be nice to her a little while longer, and I'm sure she'll be gone before you know it."

Begina had no immediate plans to vacate and Elba Rae Van Oaks knew that. "In the meantime," Ethel Maywood offered, "I might just give Laveetra a call when I get home and sort of feel her out a little, you know, to see if she knows when she's expecting Begina back. Nonchalant-like."

"Well, let me know. I'm gonna go crazy if I don't know there's an end to this in sight. Not to mention I might as well get a divorce from Fettis for all I've seen him around here lately."

"Stop that kind of talk. Nobody in this family's getting any divorce. I'll let you know what she says. But goodness, Elba Rae, I do hate to have a long distance call on the bill just to talk to Laveetra."

Ethel Maywood returned to her dependable Rambler and left Elba Rae as hostess once more. She went back into the house through the carport door since it was closest to the kitchen, where she knew she may as well wait.

*   *   *   *

Although Ethel Maywood gleaned a plethora of information from her sister-in-law Laveetra Chittum during the course of their long distance call, including the clarification once and for all there had only ever been one child's coffin interred in W'lynn's grave before the main casket with the rest of him in it but which did, however, definitely contain both amputated legs but wrapped separately, she did not learn the point most important to all concerned and that was when Laveetra reasonably expected her daughter to return home to Hattiesburg. When broached, Laveetra gushed with appreciation at the hospitality being shown Begina, who, it was revealed, had mailed her mother a letter extolling as much and how she hated to leave. That news would disturb Elba Rae, Ethel knew, but there was no way around it.

Meanwhile, as the days passed, Elba Rae got reacquainted with assorted Chittum relatives, some from Anniston and some from as nearby as down around Weoka, and some Maywoods Elba Rae had practically forgotten about but all of whom arrived at Elba Rae's house at the invitation of Cousin Begina who was consistently thoughtful enough to have them drop in for visits well after dinner time in the afternoons and closer to supper, ensuring them a hearty meal prepared by Elba Rae, served by her, and naturally cleaned up by her. Fettis Van Oaks was nowhere to be found and Elba Rae wasn't even sure he was still in Litton County.

After one such evening when Elba Rae had fried catfish for nine which included Uncle Sammy's sister's two youngest children, one of their six-year-old daughters, and the daughter's little friend, April Dawn, who did not like fish of any variety unless it contained the word stick after it and who wanted macaroni and cheese instead, Elba Rae lay awake in her bed unable to sleep. Fettis had slipped in through the back door just in case Cousin Begina or any of her guests might still be lingering in the front room and fallen promptly asleep with hardly a word. But Elba Rae could not. She was determined not to greet another morning of servitude without a plan.

The next day, Cousin Begina had barely retreated to her morning bath, a hygiene ritual for which Elba Rae was undeniably grateful, when the last of the breakfast dishes and skillets and pans were stacked in the drainer by the side of the sink. Elba Rae had been in a hurry to get Begina off to her bath that day and didn't even offer her the usual last cup of coffee on purpose. After all, she'd already had three, plus a large glass of orange juice and half a cup of sweet milk in her oatmeal and surely that was enough liquids to last her till lunch. And Elba Rae was anxious to speak on the phone with her mother Ethel Maywood, who would be both privy and party to the agenda Elba Rae was ready to put in motion.

"You want me to do what, Elba Rae?!"

"You heard me. Now I'll do all the talking. You just have to go along."

"I won't have any part of this nonsense, Elba Rae! What's come over you?"

"You know full well what's come over me, Momma! It came in an old piece of car and it's been over me ever since!"

"Well this isn't the way, Elba Rae. It's wrong. And if Begina ever found out what you were up to, it would hurt her feelings something awful. And don't even get me started on your Aunt Laveetra! You know we'd never hear the end of it from her!"

"Do you have any better ideas?"

Ethel Maywood did not have any better ideas and with surprisingly little more convincing, she conceded to Elba Rae and resigned to participate.

✳   ✳   ✳   ✳

That afternoon, Begina awoke from her nap and noticed right off the house was more quiet than usual. Cousin Elba Rae sometimes kept the TV up so loud in the afternoons it was the first thing she'd hear after her rest, Begina thought, and it was strange not to hear it. She walked down the hall toward the den calling out for signs of occupancy. There was no one in the den and the TV wasn't even on with the volume turned down low. It was quiet in the rest of the house, too.

After a quick survey of the kitchen, Begina noticed a paper stuck on the refrigerator door under a magnet in the shape of a banana.

Begina,

Momma had a fall this afternoon and I have gone over to see about her. It's probably nothing but better safe than sorry. Will be back soon.

Elba Rae

At her own house, Ethel Maywood was nervous as Elba Rae glanced at the big clock on the wall in her mother's living room. "She ought to be getting up from her nap about now."

"Well, how do you know she'll see your note, Elba Rae? Did you think about that?"

"She'll see the note, Momma. Believe me. I left it where she'll walk right into it."

"I don't like this a bit."

"I don't care. It's too late now. I'm gonna go call her."

"No—wait!" Elba Rae stopped, but her mother followed up with nothing. "What?"

"Are you sure, Elba Rae?"

"I can either pick up this phone right now and call my house, or I can bring her back over here. And if I do, I'm going to send for Aunt Laveetra just for good measure."

"Oh, all right! But if this ever gets out, Elba Rae, I'll never get over it."

"Hush up, now, I'm dialing the number."

Being as she was practically a member of the Van Oaks household by then, Begina Marie Chittum felt no hesitation in answering the telephone when it rang even if clearly she was the only member home to receive calls.

"Begina! Is that you?"

"Elba Rae? Is that you?"

"Yes! I'm glad you answered! I was afraid you might be resting!"

"Well, no, I was laying down a while ago, but I got up and I saw your note on the ice box."

"Oh, good!"

"What's wrong, Elba Rae? You sound all flustered. Is Aunt Ethel okay? It wasn't something serious, was it?"

"I don't know, Begina. I just don't know! When Momma called me this afternoon, I think you must have gone to lie down, and anyway Momma said she didn't think anything was broken but she wanted me to come on over and check, just to be sure, you know, and, well, you know how Momma is, the least little thing sometimes gets her all excited, but I thought I'd better come over here anyway to ease her mind—and mine, too—but I think she might have really hurt something this time."

"Oh my word, Elba Rae, what happened?"

"It was the bathtub, Begina. I've told Momma and told her again, 'You have got to be careful when you're getting in and out of that tub.' Well anyway, she said she was stepping in the tub to take her a bath this afternoon and her foot just hit the bottom of that slick tub and went right out from under her! And she fell!"

"In the tub?"

"Huh?"

"In or out?"

"In or out of what?"

"Did she fall in the tub, or out of it onto the floor?"

"Well … she of … I guess what she must have said was she sort of fell in it, first, and, uh … then tried to get her balance—but couldn't—and fell out of it, and onto the floor … I think."

"Is she hurt bad, Elba Rae? Do I need to call Mother in Hattiesburg to come?"

"Oh, no, Begina, don't do that! I mean, it's probably nothing serious but I'm taking her on over to the clinic and let Dr. Bud look her over just to be sure."

"Well, bless her heart, Elba Rae."

"Yeah. I know, Begina. But listen, I just wanted to let you know where I was in case you got to worrying, but I should be home real soon. Dr. Bud's good about not making you wait too long if you're really sick or hurt or something like that."

"Do you think you'll be home to eat?" Elba Rae put her left hand to her head and closed her eyes as she rubbed her temples with her thumb and forefingers.

"Well I'll try, Begina. It just depends on Momma."

"All right then. I'm glad you called, Elba Rae. I'd'a been worried."

"Okay, then, Begina, I'll probably see you soon." Elba Rae hung up the phone.

"What did she say?" Ethel Maywood, fully clothed and unwounded, wanted to know.

"She wanted to know what's for supper."

*   *   *   *

The afternoon heat was still hovering when Elba Rae pulled back into her carport even though it was already past six o'clock. Cousin Begina was near-panic stricken when Elba Rae entered the house and it gave her, for a minute, a twinge of guilt. But she had to let that go, she knew.

Elba Rae methodically explained to Begina how the x-rays taken at the Buford Clinic by Dr. Bud did not indicate any broken bones or even the fracture of any bones but that Ethel Maywood could expect, nonetheless, to be severely sore and incapacitated and would need assistance full time for the next several days, if not longer depending upon the natural healing process which sometimes wasn't as forgiving toward the older patients. Elba Rae was sorry, she emphasized, to leave Begina but surely Begina would understand and every once in a while Begina did nod her head in that direction.

The explaining continued on into Elba Rae's bedroom whereupon she took down from the top shelf of her closet a suitcase which never usually had much cause to leave it. It was flopped onto the bed and opened up receiving clothing while Elba Rae assured Cousin Begina she was more than welcome to stay on and that Fettis would be glad to have her and no, he wasn't much cook (and she laughed for effect) but they'd make out just fine, she was sure, because Fettis had done it before and even he was kind of used to it what with Elba Rae staying late at school so many afternoons and let Fettis know and he'd be more than happy to stop by the Litton Café and Bait Shop and bring home a slab of bologna and a wheel of cheese and she didn't care what anybody said about there being flies in the front case where they kept the bologna, what did people think, anyway? It was a bait shop too, after all, and really it was a bait shop long before there was ever a café anyhow and flies were just naturally going to be attracted to dead fish, there was no stopping them.

And then she was off, suitcase in hand, to begin her faux nursemaid's mission. Cousin Begina waved once while Elba Rae was backing out of the drive and onto the highway.

*   *   *   *

Elba Rae Van Oaks suspected she might have to spend one night at the home of her mother and maybe even two if she were to fully execute her script, and she had prepared for such during the packing portion of her performance in front of

Cousin Begina. Begina telephoned the first morning to check on her aunt Ethel's condition, which Elba Rae gleefully reported back to the patient being precise not to leave out a single "sweetie" from the translation, and even offered to come over to sit for awhile after first asking the defrosting instructions for a casserole in Elba Rae's deep freeze but Elba Rae had discouraged company for the time being since poor Ethel just wasn't up for it yet. It took more talking to keep Ethel's own sister Ruby at bay once word of Ethel's tumble reached the Burns household, but Elba Rae knew the charade had to be maintained on all levels for protection. She would discuss it in private with Hazel when the time was right but probably would never tell the truth to Martha Betty Maharry who brought over a big roast with potatoes and carrots to help out and who understood poor Ethel was lying down and didn't feel up to seeing anyone, which was near on truthfully the case after practically being shoved all the way to the bed by Elba Rae who, thank goodness, had heard Martha Betty's car pulling up just in the nick of time right in the middle of washing her mother's hair in the kitchen sink and hopefully Martha Betty hadn't seen the trail of water leading out of the kitchen that Elba Rae hadn't been able to fully contain from Ethel Maywood's dripping head on such short notice.

But at long last, however, Elba Rae received the respite she was after. On the morning of day two, Cousin Begina phoned to lament it seemed like it'd be better if she headed on back to Hattiesburg for now and yes, she sure did hate to leave under these circumstances especially given the delightful visit they'd been having since W'lynn's funeral and all but she didn't want to be a bother to Fettis, who'd already said he'd be happy to hook up the jumper cables, and really she just didn't know how he could eat that old bologna because it sort of smelled like fish on any count.

Elba Rae convincingly conveyed her sincerest of regrets their visit was being cut short such as it was, though in whose mind the visit could have been considered short she had no earthly notion, and please do write when she got back to Hattiesburg to let them know she arrived safely and give all of their bests to Aunt Laveetra and take care and bye-bye. Elba Rae Van Oaks was finally liberated and Ethel Maywood was able to resume her life as a non-invalid although she insisted Elba Rae be the one to return Martha Betty Maharry's dish because Ethel just couldn't face her.

About a week after Begina Marie Chittum had returned to Hattiesburg to live forever with her mother Laveetra, Ethel Maywood received a small package in the mail which did appear at first to have been wrapped with the remnants of a brown paper grocery sack, and after she began to tear it a little she was convinced the *ixie* on the bottom had once belonged to the **Winn D** piece taped on the left side. A note fell out of the box when she opened it.

Dear Aunt Ethel sweetie,

I hope this finds you feeling better and on the mend. I have been worried about you. You are too sweet to be suffering.
Mother and I wanted you to have some of these. We use them and Mother has never taken a spill. Knock on wood. (ha, ha).
  Get well soon,

  Begina

  P.S. The other set is for Elba Rae.
  Like she says, better safe than sorry.
  x x x o o o

Inside the parcel postmarked Hattiesburg were two sets of bright yellow and orange rubber decals shaped like big daisies and sunflowers, some small and some quite large. The backs of the decals had a waxy paper on them intended to be peeled off so the big yellow and orange flowers could be stuck to the bottom of the bath tub. They were guaranteed to be skid-proof and help prevent falls, their package said. Ethel Maywood felt ashamed. But not as ashamed as she meant for Elba Rae Van Oaks to be when she got through with her.

For reasons neither woman ever discussed with the other, they both adhered the decals per the enclosed instructions. Over time, the bright yellow and orange faded from the effects of hot water and bath salts and cleaning products containing bleach, yet they were never removed. Instead, Ethel Maywood and her daughter Elba Rae Van Oaks just continued to step on the non-skid flowers on the bottom of their bathtubs every day for years to come, as a legacy of their deceit.

FETTIS VAN OAKS

She might not have thought so in the beginning, not perhaps on the afternoon she was first escorted into Dr. Marvin Yardley's office at the Litton County Department of Public Instruction, but into the fifth week of visits Elba Rae Van Oaks inevitably knew the time had come.

They had gone around the world to get there, with stops off in the port of Getting Acquainted as well as the village of Tell Me About Your Family. And she had, even if begrudgingly at times, indeed told Dr. Yardley things about them all she'd not necessarily told to others. But then the day came when he was no longer satisfied to just hear the recollections of her wedding to Fettis and he wanted to know what happened afterward. It was as if he had known from the time of their introduction—if not already suspecting just from the content of Mr. Bailey's report—that Elba Rae Van Oaks distrusted Patsy Simpson's motives well beyond the context of an unkind quip about casserole baking.

"I just find it a bit odd, Elba Rae. That you hardly mention him."

"Well, he's been gone for a few years now."

"I can understand that. Although I can't perceive of a time when I won't feel like talking about Isabell … my late wife," he added in case she wouldn't recall. Elba Rae did not reply.

"He apparently was handy around the house."

She pondered the assessment for a few seconds. "He could be, yes."

"As well as other people's houses. No?"

Again, she offered nothing easily.

"But it's true, isn't it?" Dr. Yardley persisted. "He was friendly with the Simpsons? Helped them out at their farmhouse?"

Elba Rae tensed. She had never thought of that period in their lives as one when friendships were being formed. But then, she tried to never think about Patsy Simpson at all.

*   *   *   *

Of all the men who convened with devotion at the coffee corner inside Moss Hardware & Supply on weekday mornings and also most Saturdays, amidst the nuts and bolts and washing machine belts and the shiny virginal garden tools, Lloyd Fike was surely the most likely to linger well beyond the early opening hour of the store and usually after all the other regulars dispersed for the day to carry on with whatever purpose it was their lives served. The kinship Lloyd felt with fellow business owner and proprietor Jack Moss was not the only draw, Jack knew, because anybody who'd ever gotten to know Lloyd Fike in the least knew the last thing he ever wanted to tell a soul was that he owned a dress shop on the Square; he surely deferred that glory to his wife, Kathleen, and would rather have never been seen on the premises.

It was expected on any given morning that Dewey Richardson would be present, and there were many times when he could be spotted somewhere around the Square before Jack Moss himself arrived to open the store. Jack Moss felt an obligation to Dewey like he did his actual customers who bought things from him because he knew his customers needed him, and he was well aware Dewey Richardson did also. Dewey's wife was long gone to parts unknown, though few blamed her; his daughter had moved to Baton Rouge years ago; and his son, Dewey Junior, was more wont to be off fishing or hunting or chasing a skirt to pay any attention to a father who did, everyone knew, bear watching. Jack Moss understood and accepted with pride that he and his store and the fellowship within provided some structure to Dewey's existence, which had not been an easy one for so long.

A couple of summers while school was out, Claude Pickle had taken to coming by sporadically on no specific day of the week in a gesture to mingle with the other Buford men. Claude did not farm for a living and did not own a business, nor did he much ever even shop at Moss Hardware & Supply since he was not inclined to attempt the replacement or repair of anything that could be classified as mechanical. Claude rented his tidy little house out on the Hendrix road from the Hendrixes, who through the years had bought up places to the east and to the west of their own, and when something was broken, Claude called a Hendrix to fix it. He paid whatever student was tall enough that year to cut his grass and didn't even keep a mower for himself. No other regular at the coffee corner was or ever had been engaged personally in the education profession, on any level, which put Claude Pickle's potential contribution to the group at odds with the usual conversations about crops and how the Crimson Tide was looking that fall for football, so it was understandable when Claude's appearances became less frequent and the fact he eventually stopped coming in the summers all together was never discussed in the store as a topic in and of itself, and that is to say if anyone had even noticed.

Lloyd Fike notwithstanding, the most regular and faithful coffee-drinking philosopher of them all was Fettis Van Oaks, who'd been meeting at Moss Hardware & Supply ever since he'd retired from his job at Buford Slaughter and Packaging, which wasn't so much a retirement in the traditional sense as it was an inability to continue working due to an on-the-job mishap resulting in a terrible neck injury. Jack Moss knew he was just about Fettis Van Oaks's best friend and, to a degree, showing up at the store early in the mornings *was* Fettis's job since he'd never held another paying one after the unfortunate whamming he'd taken from a cow at Buford Slaughter.

Fettis Van Oaks was a dutiful patron of the business as well, willing to undertake home repairs obvious to him or those his wife Elba Rae announced were needed. He frequently concluded his morning with a purchase and through the years, his acquired knowledge, skill, and expertise on so many things hardware rivaled that of store owner Jack Moss himself. It was not uncommon at all—if Jack was otherwise engaged or on the phone with a supplier—for Fettis to assist real customers who patronized the store not sure exactly what it was they needed to fix something or another. There was a time when Jack had officially offered Fettis Van Oaks a job in the store, envisioning that he'd be able to go fishing himself every once in a while or go on the vacation his wife, Florine, so often pestered him about without having to close the store, but Fettis steadfastly declined the invitation and Jack knew without asking it had something to do with some permanent disability payments and how they'd likely not be permanent if Fettis were to take up steady employment at Moss Hardware & Supply.

It was on one such morning when Fettis Van Oaks was in attendance and Lloyd Fike was still lingering, after Claude Pickle had abandoned totally the notion of bonding with any males outside of the school setting, that the coffee had gone cold and no one else remained. Jack Moss had been called to the loading dock behind the store to receive a shipment of upright freezers, which was only four, but which in the compact confines of the Moss Hardware & Supply constituted a shipment. Lloyd Fike had been declaring how he just wasn't able to walk distances like he used to because of his dang knee but how that hadn't stopped Kathleen one bit, no siree, from thinking he ought to be stomping around in that dress shop with her all day every day except Sundays and didn't she ever think he had better things to do. Fettis Van Oaks did understand the predicament on the table and did sympathize with Lloyd Fike since he was, at least during the school year, blessed with a wife who got up in the morning and left the house and him alone in it. He was just about to concur with Lloyd's assessment of the species altogether when the front door opened and a customer entered. Both men readily recognized her to be Doug Simpson's wife, Patsy.

Lloyd Fike knew Patsy Simpson, naturally, because she shopped for clothes sometimes at F & F Fashions, the livelihood regrettably bearing half his name, and Fettis Van Oaks knew Patsy Simpson because she taught first grade at the Homer T. Litton Grammar school where his wife Elba Rae was a fixture. Patsy gazed around the store and its contents that morning as if she might not have realized she was even in a hardware establishment and if she did, that maybe she'd wandered into it by mistake. She wore a khaki skirt and a white sleeveless blouse that was untucked, and on her feet were a pair of bright green sandals Lloyd Fike recognized as having come from his stockroom at F & F. Her toenails were painted pink and somehow the gush of hot air she'd let in by opening the front door felt more like a tropical breeze than the merciless reality of an Alabama summer. The way her hair was swept up on her head announced a neck the sun had not often seen.

"Morning, Miss Patsy."

"Oh." She seemed unaware of anyone's presence. "Good morning, Mr. Fike."

"Hot enough for you?"

"I should say it is. If I didn't have air conditioning in the car, I don't know what I'd do. Stay home, I guess."

"We're all a little spoiled these days."

Fettis Van Oaks thought Lloyd's retort to be uncalled for. It was June, in Alabama, where the thermometer in the window already registered eighty-five degrees and would likely near ninety by afternoon, and here was a petite female who'd obviously taken measures to enhance her general appearance before venturing into a hardware store populated by men who rarely bothered.

"It's too hot for most anything this time of year. Spoiled or not," Fettis Van Oaks offered indirectly in her defense.

"It is for me, I can tell you. That's my problem."

"Ma'am?" Fettis asked.

"This heat. And my air conditioner at the house. It's about to go out on us."

"Isn't that just always when they do? When you need 'em the most?"

"I don't know. I guess. It's an old one that was secondhand to start with and it's about had it. There's no point trying to fix it. We just need to replace it. That's what I've been trying to tell my husband since last summer. And now we've waited till it's on its last leg and if we wait till it quits all together, I'm gonna die in that house."

"Then you've come to the right place," Fettis assured.

"Good. Do you work here?"

"Well, no, I don't. Jack's out back taking in some freezers but he won't be long."

"Oh, okay. I'll just look around."

"They're over there." Fettis pointed to the far left wall and Patsy Simpson took immediate note of the units that were turned on with the colorful streamers tied to their vents flapping briskly.

"Thank you," she said as she meandered in the right direction past some pipe and down the aisle with the septic flush and the plungers.

"That's Doug Simpson's wife," Lloyd Fike clarified. "You know he came back to Litton County last year to farm his daddy's place after old man Simpson took sick."

"I know," Fettis Van Oaks agreed. "She teaches at the school. With Elba Rae."

"That's right." Lloyd Fike joined Fettis Van Oaks in watching Mrs. Patsy Simpson locate the air conditioner units on display. "Pretty little thing, isn't she?"

"Huh?" Fettis said.

"I said, she's a pretty little thing. Doesn't look like she's used to being much of a farm wife."

"Then I guess she's about at the right place, cause from what I hear, Doug Simpson's not used to being much of a farmer." The two men laughed, but tried to keep it down enough so as not to distract Patsy Simpson or to be overheard by her.

About then, the back door leading to the stock room flopped open and a big burly man pulling a two-wheeler with a freezer strapped to it rolled into the store followed by Jack Moss.

"Over there with your other one?" The big burly man inquired.

"If you please."

"You got it, Boss." Jack Moss suddenly noticed a customer was in the midst of the morning's activity and strolled over to be of assistance.

"Hi-dy. Sorry I didn't hear you come in."

Patsy Simpson stood still in the path of one of the air conditioners letting its cold stream blow her face. "Oh ... that's all right. They were sort of helping me." She nodded in the direction of Lloyd Fike and Fettis Van Oaks, who hadn't taken their eyes off her.

"Yeah, well they're good for something, I guess," Jack Moss sort of chuckled. "What can I help you with? You needing an air conditioner?"

"I'm afraid so."

"Well that's a good one you're looking at there. Fifteen hundred BTUs. Pretty near keep your whole house cool. Whereabouts you needing it?"

"My whole house. The downstairs, anyway. We've got an old one in the living room and it's about gone. I'd love to have one in my kitchen, too, but I don't know. My husband thinks we should be able to get by with just one. Course, he's not the one standing over the stove in the heat of the day."

"Well, bless your heart. You know, the thing to do might be to get you a good big one, for your living room you know, and it'll cool pretty near your whole house. But then you get you one of these smaller units over here just for your kitchen. It'll have you so cool in there, you won't even know you're cooking."

"Do you think?"

"Just ask my wife, Florine. I have her so cold in the kitchen sometimes, she'll go to cooking just to warm up!" Patsy Simpson laughed.

"He's such a liar," Lloyd Fike said from across the room.

"Maybe," Fettis agreed. "But he just sold two air conditioners."

Patsy Simpson didn't spend much more time that morning perusing the model air conditioners in the Moss Hardware & Supply store, having accepted Jack Moss's recommendation and gone to the counter to write up the ticket for two units.

"And can you deliver them, Mr. Moss?"

"Yes, ma'am. I've got me a boy that comes around in the afternoons to help, and I can get him out to your place with them. Might be tomorrow, though."

"Not before then? He couldn't come today?" She was in the middle of writing out her check when she paused. "I mean, I don't mind paying him a little extra for it. But by the time my husband gets in from the field these days, he's not much good for anything. And if I wait for him to get around to it, I may as well leave them here in the store."

Before Jack Moss could reply to his customer, the telephone at the register rang and he had to stop and relay the message to Lloyd Fike that Lloyd's wife, Kathleen, was needing him over at their own store because she was trying to redecorate the front window display and how did he think she was going to hoist all those mannequins by herself. Lloyd Fike said, "Shit," under his breath and walked out of the store on his bad knee.

"Well, now Miss Patsy," Jack said after the door closed behind Lloyd Fike, "I know I can get him out there late tomorrow, but I can't promise he could get them both in. He's a good boy, don't get me wrong. And he's dependable as the day is long. But he's not the fastest horse in the race, if you know what I mean."

Patsy Simpson stood at the counter staring at Jack Moss and appeared to be entirely uninterested in horses or races or who was the fastest, uninterested really in anything other than a commitment of the exact hour she could expect once again to be cool.

"I don't guess I do know what you mean, Mr. Moss. Can this boy put my air conditioners in or not? Like I said, I don't mind paying extra for it."

"Oh sure, he can do it. But like I said, it might be a day or two before he gets it all finished. He doesn't exactly work for me full time, you see. In fact, he just comes around in the afternoons late to see if I've got some odd jobs for him. And that's when I use him for deliveries, if I've got any. Now, if there's not any problem with your windows, it won't take him that long. But you just never know what you're going to run into putting one of these units in a window where there's never been one before, you know what I mean?"

"No." Patsy Simpson was hot and she didn't want to hear another analogy involving animals.

"Excuse me there, Jack," Fettis Van Oaks joined in. "Seems to me like maybe I could help Miss Patsy out."

"You could?" Patsy was encouraged.

"Well I think I could, ma'am."

"I'm sorry, but when I asked if you worked here when I came in, didn't you tell me no?"

"Fettis doesn't actually work here, Miss Patsy. He's just one of my regulars," Jack said.

"Fettis Van Oaks, ma'am."

"How do you do? I'm Patsy Simpson. My husband is Doug Simpson. Maybe you know his family?"

"Well I do know some of your people. And I believe you must know my wife. She teaches over at the grammar school."

Patsy Simpson took pause. "Van Oaks … Van Oaks! Yes, of course. You must be Mrs. Elba Rae Van Oaks's husband."

"That'd be me."

"Well it's nice to meet you, Mr. Van Oaks. I'm afraid I haven't gotten to know all the teachers at the school as well as I'd like yet, since I just finished my first year there. But your wife is one of the fifth grade teachers, right? With Ms. Kinney?"

"That's right. Been teaching at that school practically since they've had it! Sometimes it's hard to remember which one of them was there first."

"Oh, I doubt that, Mr. Van Oaks," Patsy smiled.

"She's been there a long time, all right."

"She must enjoy it. You know, actually, I used to teach fifth grade myself. Back in Paducah, where we're from. Or where I'm from, anyway."

"Is that a fact?"

"And honestly, I hope one day I'll have the opportunity to teach it again. Not that there's anything wrong with the first graders, mind you. It's just a whole other ball game. Different, you know."

"I expect it is."

"Tell your wife if she's planning to retire anytime soon, let me know first. I want to get my dibs in," Patsy Simpson laughed.

"I sure will, but I don't see her retiring any time soon."

"No?"

"Don't think so."

"Oh, well. It'll all work out someday, I guess. I mean, I took the job at the grammar school because that's all they had. But I plan to look for another opening as soon as one comes available." Patsy Simpson was suddenly aware of Jack Moss's stare.

"Mr. Van Oaks, do you know how to put the air conditioners in right? I'd be more than happy to pay you for your trouble. The main thing is I just want to be cool!"

"Why don't we get them in my truck, and I'll head on out to your place and take a look?"

"Are you sure, Mr. Van Oaks? I hate to impose on you like this."

"No bother, ma'am. I don't have anything pressing at the moment. Be glad to get them in for you if I can. Or see what we'll need if I can't."

"I'd be so grateful if you could."

"Sure thing, ma'am."

"Uh, Fettis," Jack Moss offered, "what say you pull around back and I give you a hand loading them in your truck?"

"I'll do it."

With that, Fettis Van Oaks was out the door and Patsy Simpson was busy folding her receipts up and stuffing them into her purse. Jack Moss was momentarily perplexed, but came to when he heard the chugging exhaust of a struggling old pickup truck nearing his rear loading dock.

*   *   *   *

Fettis Van Oaks followed behind Patsy Simpson's wood-covered station wagon until they turned off the blacktop and onto a gravel road leading to the old Simpson home. It'd been a while since Fettis had cause to be by there, and he could tell right off the place had run down a little since old man Simpson had done the same. There were weeds growing along the road in the front of the house that used to be kept trimmed with the sickle, and where one shutter on the upstairs bedroom window was missing a couple of slats, its mate was off the house all together and lying down below against the side of the porch. The roof still appeared to be in adequate shape, so at least Doug Simpson wasn't living in squalor; it was just more like the homestead had suffered from a few years of neglect the younger Simpsons hadn't caught up with yet. Patsy Simpson stopped her station wagon in front of the house and Fettis pulled up behind her in his truck, followed by the wave of dust that had followed the both of them since they'd turned off the blacktop.

Fettis heard the dog barking before he ever got out. It was an old hound dog that had apparently been resting peacefully underneath the front porch's shade before being called to duty by the arrival of a strange vehicle. It stopped barking when Patsy stepped from the wagon, but resumed when Fettis joined her.

"Hush, Ranger! Hush!" Patsy Simpson commanded.

"Does he bite?"

"No. Well, I've never seen him bite at anybody. He'll settle down in a minute."

"Good watchdog, I reckon."

"Yeah, yeah he is. It's a good thing, too, I guess, being way out here."

Fettis looked about the surroundings while Ranger growled softly and bore just a couple of his teeth.

"I know the house looks like it's in bad shape, but you should have seen it when we got here last year."

"Kind of run down, was it?"

"It was. Still is, but we've made some progress. It's just, right now my husband is in the fields most all day every day."

"Yes, ma'am, I guess he is."

"And his father just hadn't been able to keep things up the last few years. He's bad sick you know."

"I heard he wasn't getting along too good."

"Well, he's a tough old bird. Doug's sister is looking after him right now. Don't know how long that'll last, but for now, it's just me and Doug out here."

"Yes, ma'am."

"Well, I don't guess you want to stand outside in the hot hearing my complaints about this farm. Can I help you get the air conditioners out of your truck?"

"I believe I can manage them. Why don't you just show me where you're gonna be wanting them?"

"Okay," she said and then led him up the porch steps and into the house. "Would you like a glass of tea, Mr. Van Oaks?"

Fettis took a few seconds to ponder. "Why, yes, ma'am. I believe I would. And why don't you call me Fettis?"

*   *   *   *

It had not taken Fettis Van Oaks long to assess the prognosis of the living room window sill housing the nearly burned out air conditioner he was there to remove. It would have been neglectful, he explained to Patsy Simpson, to install the new unit in a window with rotted wood, and while she appeared at first distressed by the delay, Fettis assured her he was proficient enough in carpentry skills to replace the boards and get her cool once more. He had no worries, meantime, getting her new kitchen unit in place and promised he'd return in the morning to tackle the bigger job in the living room.

Doug Simpson was too tired to ask the cost of the new air conditioners by the time he got in the house that evening and accepted without question his wife's explanation that the man from the hardware store would be back to repair their rotten window.

Early the next morning, Jack Moss barely got the time to visit with Fettis Van Oaks, who was too focused on getting the measurements exactly right for the cut of lumber he needed and didn't even want his usual third cup of coffee, and Lloyd Fike had scarcely bid him a howdy-do before he departed.

"Where's he going to put out a fire so early in the day?" Lloyd inquired.

"The Simpson place."

"The Simpson place?"

"That's right," Jack Moss replied. "Seems ole Fettis is helping Miss Patsy get those air conditions she bought yesterday in and running."

"Is that so?" Lloyd Fike did not sound entirely convinced.

"Yeah. He took them on out there for her, but then she had a bad window. He's fixing it for her."

"Neighborly of him."

"I thought so," Jack Moss said.

*   *   *   *

Fettis sawed and he nailed and then he sealed and he painted, and then he told Patsy Simpson he'd be back the next day to install finally her new living room air conditioner, for which she was most grateful and appreciative and offered Fettis some real United States currency as a measure of her sincerity. Fettis Van Oaks steadfastly refused any token of reward and explained to Patsy Simpson as to how it was just the right thing to do, to help a neighbor in a time of need, and then he told her as long as he was planning to stop by Jack Moss's hardware store on his way out the next morning to pick up the new fuses for her fuse box, why didn't he just go ahead and see if Jack didn't have a new faucet to replace the one dripping in Patsy Simpson's kitchen sink that was, in Fettis's professional opinion, compromised beyond what a new washer could rehabilitate.

It was only after taking loose the old faucet that Fettis realized the pipes underneath the kitchen sink were rusted and all but leaking. Patsy Simpson protested to Fettis that she should hire a plumber to see to her problem, that certainly it was not Fettis Van Oaks's responsibility to repair everything awry in the old Simpson place, and she was sure he had more important duties awaiting him at his own home. And it was at that moment in the unfolding relationship between Fettis Van Oaks and Patsy Simpson he did confide to her that while he was, most assuredly, happy to be of assistance to her—and her husband, Doug—she was in fact doing him the favor by giving him some solace during the day from his wife Elba Rae's cousin who had come from Hattiesburg for a visit, interminably so, it seemed.

And so it was the TV antenna on top of the house became Fettis's next order of business because, as he explained to Patsy Simpson one day, it just out and out troubled him each time he pulled up the road in his truck and observed it leaning the way it did and even though Patsy Simpson took issue with Fettis's ascent to the crest of her roof, citing safety concerns, she did confess upon his return to solid ground after a successful straightening that it had been bothering her as well ever since their arrival and declared as to how just the week before she'd not been sure whether she was watching Soupy Sales or Miss Peggy Lee singing on her favorite variety hour, due to the terribly distorting waves in the picture. Fettis Van Oaks roared with voracious laughter, a reaction which caught Patsy Simpson decidedly off guard since she didn't consider herself a necessarily humorous woman.

By the time Fettis drove out with the new hot water heater, a special order item Jack Moss had not kept in stock, Ranger's greeting of teeth-showing and growling had given way to tail-wagging and the occasional lick. "Morning, Miss Patsy," Fettis said as he walked into her kitchen where she was unconsciously enjoying the spray hose feature of her new faucet by rinsing the sink needlessly in a counterclockwise motion.

"Good morning, Fettis. You know my husband, don't you?" Fettis was surprised to see Doug Simpson sitting at the breakfast table, a half-filled coffee cup in front of him. He immediately stood up.

"Well, sure I do. How you getting along, Doug?" Doug Simpson walked over to Fettis and grabbed his hand firmly in a shake.

"I'm doing real good, Mr. Fettis. Better, really, since you've been around here."

"Is that so?"

"It sure is. I got beans need spraying this morning, but I says to Patsy when I got up, I says, 'I'm not going to the field this morning till I've had a chance to shake Mr. Fettis's hand personally and thank him for all the help he's been giving us around here the last month or so.' Patsy told me you'd likely be bringing that hot water heater out."

"Yeah. Sure did. Got it on the truck."

"Well I know Patsy's asked you before, Mr. Fettis, if we could pay you, and I know you haven't taken a cent from her, but I want to ask you again. Please ... let us pay you for your trouble."

"It's really no trouble, Doug. I just saw some things needed doing around here, I got the time on my hands, and I'm glad to help out. Jack Moss is the one you'll be needing to settle with when the time comes," he laughed, and then was joined by Doug Simpson and Patsy.

"He's been real good about setting us up on some credit," Patsy said.

"Well, I just got to tell you straight out, Mr. Fettis. If it hadn't been for you being so neighborly, we'd like as not had to put off a lot of the fixing you've been doing around here. Least till the crops come in this fall. And we'd about forgotten what Mr. Cronkite was supposed to look like on the TV."

"No bother, Doug. Me and Elba Rae got us kind of a small place, over on the highway you know, and 'cept for the mowing, it just doesn't need that much doing. And I'm a retired man, you know. Does me good to get out and keep myself busy."

"Well, we sure do appreciate you. And if there's anything I can do for you— ever—you say the word."

"I will," Fettis allowed.

"Well I 'spect I better get on," Doug Simpson said. "Beans aren't gonna spray themselves. But thank you again, Mr. Fettis."

"You're welcome."

And then Doug Simpson was off to the fields and Fettis Van Oaks was alone in the kitchen with Miss Patsy. They shared orange juice and some coffee cake before he went back to the truck to roll the water heater down the makeshift ramp he'd crafted out of two-by-fours.

*   *   *   *

It was around the middle of August when Elba Rae Van Oaks, not long liberated from a houseguest who'd finally returned home to Hattiesburg, decided to treat herself to an afternoon of shopping and lunch with her cousin Hazel Burns. Elba Rae had picked Hazel up in the Galaxie and they'd headed to the Square to amuse themselves with possible selections of fall work clothes on display at F & F Fashions. Kathleen Fike had been glad to see them, and Elba Rae was genuinely reciprocal since it'd been ages since she was free to come and go without consideration to her cousin Begina Marie Chittum.

They decided, against Elba Rae's better judgment, to lunch at the recently opened All Seasons Restaurant located just off the south side of the Square in the old converted house that had, up until four months earlier when they'd relocated to their new modern facility out on the highway, been the long-time site of the Buford Memorial Funeral Home. Elba Rae didn't want to seem silly by expressing her discomfort with the thought of dining in such a familiar and somber setting and was relieved when her cousin Hazel said it first.

"You know, it's just a little strange sitting down in here eating a meal. Don't you think?"

"You mean because of the funeral home?" Elba Rae feigned surprise.

"Well, yeah. I mean, how many times have we been in here over the years?"

Elba Rae was busy cutting at a pork chop but finally couldn't contain her bemusement. "Well, I didn't want to say anything."

"What?" Hazel asked.

"I was fine with it till we went over to that salad bar."

"Yeah?"

"Well ... you know."

Hazel Burns put her head down slightly, and partially covered her face with her hand to conceal a smile.

"I just couldn't help but think," Elba Rae continued, "when I was getting my plate down at the far end, that's just where the bodies used to be laid out. Do you think they made that salad bar about the same length on purpose?"

"I was thinking the very same thing."

"And all I could see," Elba Rae went on, "is how the last time I was standing over there looking down like that it was at poor Miss Nita Perrymore. Right there where the lettuce is. Every time I scooped up a pile I could still see her in that pale pink dress and that ghoulish old lipstick Martha Betty let them put on her."

"She looked like a streetwalker," Hazel Burns whispered.

"Oh, Hazel," Elba Rae exclaimed as she looked around and tried not to laugh out loud.

"Well, it was your own momma that said so, Elba Rae. I distinctly remember Aunt Ethel saying Martha Betty ought to be ashamed for not taking a Kleenex to those lips."

"Goodness, she did though, didn't she?"

"She did," Hazel Burns was glad to confirm.

"But I'll still say it, though."

"What's that?" Hazel asked.

"Her hair," Elba Rae started out, "never looked any better than when they had her laid out here. It was always so thin, you know. Especially when she got on up in her years."

"Did Sue come up here and fix it?"

"No, Hazel—don't you remember? Martha Betty tried to get Sue, but she was so down in her back she couldn't get out of bed. I know she hated to disappoint Martha Betty, as long as Miss Nita went to her and all. But she just couldn't do it. So Martha Betty let them do it here. And honestly, I don't know what they did to her but she never looked better. Except for those lips."

"She was right peaceful looking, as I recall."

"It's a shame she wasn't coming up here all along to get her hair done."

"Do you think they take appointments, Elba Rae? I mean, just for hair?"

"I doubt they do if you're alive."

The ladies laughed out loud anyway, albeit with the restraint as though they still were inside a funeral home, and carried on with their lunch on a hot afternoon in Buford. Elba Rae was scooping up the last bite of her peach cobbler which had, according to Elba Rae's review, clearly been made with canned peaches and was a little too doughy for her liking, and was announcing without room for debate that lunch would indeed be her treat when they were greeted by the arriving Florine Moss and Willadean Hendrix. The foursome exchanged pleasantries.

"I don't guess it'll be long before school starts back, will it, Elba Rae?" Florine Moss asked.

"No, not long."

"The summer's just flown by," Willadean Hendrix joined in.

"And I hear you've been busy for most of it?" Florine said.

Elba Rae knew Florine Moss was politely wanting to confirm the departure of Elba Rae's summer houseguest from Hattiesburg. "I did have some company this summer, ah-huh. My cousin Begina, on my daddy's side, you know."

"I'd heard she'd been visiting," said Florine.

"But she's back in Hattiesburg now."

"Ah-huh. And goodness, Fettis has been the busy one too this summer."

Having gathered sufficiently the money she'd need to pay the check at the hostess area at the front door, Elba Rae snapped shut her pocketbook. "How's that?"

"Fettis," Florine Moss confirmed. "Jack says he practically moved in at the Simpson place."

"The … Simpson … yeah … ah-huh … He's been busy." She looked across the table at Hazel. "You 'bout ready?"

"Yeah, I'm ready," Hazel said.

"Jack says he's never seen Fettis work so hard in all his life. First one thing and then another. Course, that's the way it is with any old house. You start fixing one thing, you're gonna find five more that need something too. But Doug Simpson sure owes Fettis a big debt, what with all he's been doing out there this summer."

"Yeah …" Elba Rae stared at Florine Moss. "Let's us go, Hazel. I'm thinking I might want to go back to Kathleen Fike's and get that dress I was looking at."

"Okay," Hazel said, and they bid their adieus and were on their way.

"Do you want to just walk over?" Hazel inquired when they were out on the sidewalk in front of the All Seasons Restaurant that would always be the funeral home no matter what type of cuisine might be offered up within.

"What?"

"To Kathleen's."

"Oh. Never mind. I don't think I want to go back today."

"Are you sure? That brown dress was—"

"I'm ready to go home. I've got a lot to do at the house."

"Well, all right, but I thought you'd be wanting to make a day of it since you've been cooped up so long with Begina."

The cousins rode in practical silence to the Burns house where Hazel disembarked and Elba Rae continued on home. It wasn't like Fettis hadn't mentioned he was lending a hand here and there out at the Simpson place, Elba Rae thought, what with old man Simpson down and his son Doug back in Litton County trying to keep best he could the farm going without losing the whole she-bang. She didn't recall, however, his necessarily precisely mentioning the quantity of favors he'd lent. But then again, he'd made himself so scarce ever since word came of Cousin Begina's impending arrival they'd not really had an exact discussion of the subject.

That evening, Elba Rae Van Oaks wanted to have a discussion with her husband Fettis. She wanted to talk about the Simpson place and the overall nature of the work, so Fettis modestly summarized his accomplishments to date including the recently installed hot water heater.

"Trouble is," Fettis said, "the pipes underneath that house are near about rusted out."

"You've been under the house?"

"Well, yeah. I thought I'd better check it out."

"Why?" Elba Rae wanted to know, since she could not recall any occasion on which she had spied her husband Fettis in a kneeling position in preparation for surveying the underneath of their own home.

"Wouldn't do no good to change out one bad pipe under the kitchen sink if it was just connected to a heap of other bad ones under the house. Plus, not one of those pipes has got enough insulation around it to get through the winter. It's a wonder they haven't all froze up and busted before now."

"So what are you saying, Fettis? You got more things to do out there?"

"Well, I gave my word I'd come back and check out those pipes."

Elba Rae was silent—speechless as it were. It was not that she doubted her husband's latent talents in home repair; it was his zest and lack of a finite quitting point that confused her. Especially since the coast on the home front was clear of any visiting cousins.

Fettis Van Oaks left at his usual time the next morning to go about the plumbing inspection as promised while Elba Rae tried to savor the last few weeks of her summer vacation; she found herself, however, too restless to do so. Not even Lisa Hughes on the TV could keep her attention, even though Lisa was in the throes of one of her messiest affairs since Elba Rae had been watching.

At the Simpson place that morning, Patsy Simpson had been taken by surprise when Fettis Van Oaks arrived at her door not with his customary tool box or package from the Moss Hardware & Supply business, but presenting a small arrangement of yellow and white daisies.

"Daisies! They're so pretty, Fettis, and they're my favorite flowers. Did you know that?"

"Well, yes, ma'am, I did hear you mention it once when we were out in the yard and you were talking about what you wanted to put in your flower beds when you got the time. These won't fill up your yard, but maybe you can enjoy 'em a little in the house."

"Oh, I will! Thank you so much. I'll just go put them in some water." She started to walk away from the front door and toward her kitchen. "Have you had your breakfast?"

"No, I didn't stop at the café this morning."

"Well, come on in the kitchen and let me make you something. And we'll enjoy my flowers before you start messing under the house."

Fettis leaned against the cabinet next to the pantry door with his arms crossed for most of the time Patsy Simpson was frying up a couple of sausage patties and some eggs, and although he had to shift about accordingly when she needed access to the toaster, he mainly just watched her.

"Smells mighty good, Miss Patsy," he told her as she set the plate before him on the kitchen table.

"Nothing fancy, but it'll fill you up, I hope." She poured herself a cup of coffee before joining him at the table.

"I hate to eat in front of you."

"Oh, that's all right. I had my breakfast early. Before Doug left."

Fettis concentrated on the meal before him and savored the hot sausage and crusty toast.

"Fettis?"

He looked up, but continued to chew.

"What makes you want to get up in the mornings and come way out here? To work on this old house?"

He chewed a few more times and swallowed before attempting to respond, to be mannerly that is and avoid talking outright with a full mouth.

"Because."

"Because what?"

"Because you need lots of things fixed around here."

"So?"

He looked down at his plate and picked up a corner of toasted bread, raking it through warm egg yolk before ingesting it.

"Don't you have any hobbies to keep you busy during the day? I mean, isn't there something you'd rather be doing? Like going fishing, or hunting, or puttering around in a workshop making a birdhouse?"

"Well, that doesn't much sound like me."

"Then what about your family? I know you're married to Elba Rae, but what about your other family? Why didn't you ever have children? It seems like a waste to me, you know. There's so many things you could have taught a son. Daughter too, for that matter, but you're so smart the way you know how to do everything around here. Not all men are like that, let me tell you. My husband Doug may be good at some things, and for God's sakes let's hope farming is one of them, but he doesn't know how to do half the things you can. He'd never admit it—and he'd die if he ever knew I was saying it."

"Your husband's a good man, Miss Patsy. He's trying to do for you. And his daddy."

"I know. But …"

"But what?"

"Didn't you ever want kids?"

He stared across the table at her for a moment, almost unsure of the right answer. A query of favorite jelly flavors for his remaining piece of toast would have been more anticipated.

"Just wasn't meant to be, I reckon. Elba Rae and me … well, we talked about it. Back then. But it never happened. Just wasn't meant to be."

"That's a shame."

"We made out okay. Elba Rae's had her school teaching to keep her occupied all these years."

"Then tell me about your family, Fettis. Are they in Buford?"

"Well," he started before swallowing the last bite of egg, "there's not many of us left to tell you the truth. My momma and daddy are both gone. Daddy went first, and Momma ... well, she didn't get along too good after he went. Got the cancer not long after."

"Had they been married a very long time?"

"Forty-seven years."

"My goodness, that's a long time."

"Yeah."

"Did you grow up here?"

"Pretty much. Not always right in Buford proper, but near about. Always in Litton County."

"Did you ever want to leave?"

"And go where?"

"I don't know. Somewhere. Someplace—just away from here."

"Well, I guess I thought about it once or twice. When I was still a kid myself. But then you grow up, and you get a job. Next thing you know you're married and settled down. Too late to be thinking about up and leaving then."

"I don't think it should ever be too late, Fettis. Not as long as you've still got life in you."

Their eyes met across the table, and for a long time, neither of them said anything to the other.

✳   ✳   ✳   ✳

Hazel Burns had been hesitant to phone her cousin Elba Rae with the news. In fact, she'd downright pondered and pondered over the most appropriate course of action, knowing action of some degree was called for, but not sure of what nature because of the potential scandal. Maybe the words would come to her delicately once the subject was broached, she'd hoped, but it had to be done one way or the other and she was the one to do it. She and Elba Rae had been raised more like sisters than first cousins, and Hazel knew without question Elba Rae felt closer to her than she did her real sister, Lila Mae, and now there were too many people talking about it for Hazel to turn a blind eye. Hazel's mother had gotten wind of it and once that happened, Hazel knew, it was only a matter of time before it would be told as fact—that much was undeniable, since Hazel's mother Ruby Burns's knowledge of the situation meant the boundary of family had been penetrated.

She would disclose the information to Elba Rae as gradually and gingerly as possible, and would be there to lend support in the unavoidable aftermath.

"Elba Rae?" Hazel said as soon as Elba Rae answered the phone. "Fettis has taken up with Patsy Simpson."

$$*\qquad *\qquad *\qquad *$$

When Fettis Van Oaks came home and after he'd put his truck keys on the shelf over the sink, he realized the kitchen was atypically empty for the time of day, the time when he'd be expecting to see his wife standing over or near about the stove. He stepped into the den which was quiet and unpopulated as well, and switched on a table lamp to give the room its only light other than the rays from the late afternoon sun. "Elba Rae?" He called out. "You here?" The Galaxie was in the carport, but maybe she'd gone somewhere with one of her church lady friends or her cousin Hazel Burns. "Elba Rae?"

Down the hall and at the door to the bedroom, Fettis saw finally Elba Rae sitting on the edge of the bed. "Elba Rae? Didn't you hear me calling?"

"Yeah. I heard you."

"What are you doing?"

"Nothing."

"Nothing?" She looked up at him, expressionless. "Are you sick?" He asked.

"Why?"

"Because you're just sitting here on the bed. What's got into you?"

"You mean," she started, "because I'm not standing at the stove fixing supper, like I usually would be this time of day when you wander in?"

"Well, yeah. Cause you're just sitting here. Staring at the wall. What's the matter?"

"Nothing."

"Oh come on, woman. Tell me what's going on."

"That's rich. Coming from you."

"Are you sick in the head or something? Cause you're not making a lick of sense. You want me to call a doctor?"

"I don't need a doctor, Fettis."

"Well then, what? We gonna play some kind of twenty questions game till I find out what's wrong with you?"

Elba Rae stood up and methodically went around the bed to turn on the lamps on each side.

"You have disgraced me," she finally said.

"Is that so?" Fettis asked, with decided sarcasm.

"All summer. Right under my nose. And now everybody in the county's talking about it."

"Talking about what?"

"Oh, don't play dumb, Fettis. At least give me that."

"Well, just what is it that I've done to disgrace you now, Elba Rae? What's new?" He was past agitated and his temperament was advancing toward anger.

"My own aunt had to hear about it, Fettis. Do you know how that makes me feel?"

"Well if that's the best you can do for a clue," Fettis said, "it ain't much. Cause that dad-blamed aunt of yours hears just about everything about everybody! And what she misses, your cousin Hazel makes up for!"

"It's not like it's only Aunt Ruby doing the talking."

"Talking about what, Elba Rae? Are you gonna tell me, or do you want to sit on the bed all night and stew?"

"It just so happens Kathleen Fike saw you coming out of the florist shop the other day. With some flowers." For the first time in the short duration of the conversation, Fettis had no retort. His anger subsided, and he did somewhat fear what was coming next.

"So?"

"So? So Kathleen was thinking maybe we were having a special occasion, or worse, worried I might be sick or something. So she just happened to mention it to Mabel Moss who said something to Florine who, as it turns out, already had reason to suspect. So Florine called Aunt Ruby to have a general conversation and casually asked if I'd come down with something or whether maybe it was our anniversary or something."

"Bunch of old magpies."

"Course, you can't blame Kathleen Fike for naturally assuming if she saw you coming out of the florist toting a big bouquet of flowers in your hand like a school boy, that you'd be buying them for me."

"Is that what's got you so bent out of shape? A little bunch of daisies I stopped and picked up the other day?" She stood firm and did not answer his question.

"You're getting yourself lathered up about something when there's nothing to be riled about. And all because of some gossipy women who gotta report everything they see, like there was something to make of it."

A defense was useless as far as Elba Rae was concerned. "You know, I was wondering at first what would possess you to go to working and fixing and repairing like there was no tomorrow, especially since you hardly hit a lick at a snake around here unless I'm standing over you every minute. And then it struck me. It all made sense. How come you'd be up and out every morning."

"Did you ever think maybe there was a reason why I'd want to be up and out of here in the first place? Huh? Did you ever think of that?"

"What is that supposed to mean? That you just want to get away from me?"

"No, gosh dang it, but maybe I didn't want to be cooped up in this house all day from morning to night with that simple cousin of yours that don't know anything to do but stuff her face!"

"Don't go blaming this on Begina! She didn't put you in the truck and drive you out there to Patsy Simpson's lure!"

"Didn't anybody lure me anywhere, Elba Rae, I've told you that a hundred times! She came in the store and needed some help and I gave it to her. And once I got out there and took a look, it was plain they needed more than a new air conditioner. I'd have done the same for anybody else that needed a hand."

"Well, now, I doubt that."

"Of course you do! Cause I'm just no good, isn't that right? Cause ole Fettis never does anything for anybody, is that what you know?"

"Don't put words in my mouth."

"I don't have to. I know what you think about me, and what your momma and your aunt and the rest of you mighty Maywoods have always thought about me. That I'm just no good Fettis. Doesn't work Fettis. Sits home all day while Elba Rae works her fingers to the bone Fettis. Well I don't care what y'all think. You hear me? I'm not some no-count bum who's never done nothing for nobody. And I'd have a job if I could. But you know I can't work on account of what happened. The doctor said."

"And isn't that just too convenient for you, Mr. Fix-it! Cause it leaves you free to loiter around in Jack Moss's store and wait for somebody to need a helping hand. And the prettier she is, the more helpful you can be!"

"You're wrong, Elba Rae."

"Really? Well, I bet Patsy Simpson doesn't much think I'm wrong. Not when she's lounging around in her remodeled house enjoying her hot water and staring at her love posies she got from you! And I bet she's not even sorry!"

"That lady's got nothing to apologize to you for, Elba Rae."

"Oh, don't defend her to me. She's just as much to blame for this as you are. I'm a good mind to drive right out and tell her exactly what I think of her, too!"

"She is a good woman, Elba Rae. Who happens to be married to someone who doesn't have the time to pay her any mind."

"Is that so? And that's where you step in, is it?" Elba Rae paused. "Tell me something. I don't imagine you go over there to her house acting the way you would here at home with me. Am I right?"

"What are you talking about, Elba Rae? Acting the way I would at home? What kind of way is that?"

"You know what I mean."

"No, dang it, I don't! You're not making a lick of sense!"

"You want to know what I mean? I mean I just bet you don't go over there and stand up in the middle of Miss Patsy Simpson's fine parlor and let your wind go! The way you do with me! The way you've *always* done with me! That's what I mean!"

"Hell, woman, you are crazy!"

"It's true, isn't it?"

"None of this is true!"

"Go on. Admit it. In all this time you've been out there at the Simpsons's, I bet you've never once let yourself go in front of her. I bet you wouldn't dream of standing there and breaking wind like a hog in a pen!"

"Elba Rae, letting out a little gas every once in a while is a natural body function. I'd think you know that being the school teacher. It's the way God made us and most all the animals. Even you."

"He didn't make me to up and let go any time of the day or night wherever I might be standing at the time, without any consideration to who's in the room."

"Then maybe that's your problem, Elba Rae! The problem with you and the whole rest of your family! Maybe y'all need to let a little wind out and stop trying so hard to hold it in all the time!"

"Oh, Fettis, now you're just being crude!"

"I mean it, Elba Rae! I bet it'd make the whole lot of you feel a heap better! Lord knows, you've all been holding it in long enough! Ever since I've known you! That's a long time for anybody to hold their wind! Even for a prim and proper holier-than-thou Maywood!"

"Stop it! Stop this crude talk right now!"

"Go ahead, Elba Rae! I don't care! I'm not gonna judge you, like you do me! Go ahead and let loose with a little poot!"

"You're vulgar!"

"Go on—poot! There's forty years's worth waiting to get out!"

"Vulgar!"

"Poot!"

"Vulgar, vulgar, vulgar!"

"Poot! Poot! Poot!"

"I have put up with a lot from you over the years, Fettis Van Oaks, but this is just about the lowest of the low! I can't believe you'd dare to talk to me like this!" With that, she turned away and started to leave.

"Don't go away now, Elba Rae! Things are just getting good! You want to talk about low? I'll show you low! I'll show you just how low I can get, and then … then I'll …"

"You'll what?" She whirled back around to confront him.

"I'll …" he took a small step somewhat toward her, but also off to the side just a little.

"Well, go ahead," she demanded. "You've got my attention! I'm waiting to see just how much of a low-down dog you can be! As if I didn't already know! As if I didn't already know what you've been up to with Patsy Simpson all this time!"

"I …" and with that, Fettis Van Oaks dropped to his knees. He looked up into his wife's face for a few seconds before collapsing onto the bedroom floor face-first.

*   *   *   *

The waiting area of the emergency room at the Litton County Memorial Hospital always seemed like a busy place no matter the time of day. Elba Rae Van Oaks had filled out papers and given information and gone over forms before being patted on the forearm three times by a heavyset nurse who instructed her to take a seat and try not to worry—the doctor would be out to see her just as soon as he knew something. Meanwhile, Elba Rae thought, Fettis could be alive or dead or calling out for her with what might be his last breath on the other side of the big swinging doors and she'd be sitting out in a noisy room full of people trying to find a magazine that had been published some time in last two years and would never know the difference. She wanted to help herself through the big swinging doors and hunt Fettis on her own but was, comforted or not, leery somewhat of the heavyset nurse who exuded just enough of an authoritative air to discourage revolt.

With the notion of a good read out of the question, Elba Rae had selected the first of only three possible seating options next to a benign enough looking woman who wore white stretch shorts and a bright red blouse. She sat down and gently leaned her head backward against the softly painted cinder block wall.

"I'm here with my little boy," the white stretch shorts lady said. "His daddy's in there with him. On account of they thought it might be too self-conscious for him if I went in."

Elba Rae Van Oaks was not so much in the mood for being social, but did at most all times try to be polite to strangers. "Is that so? I'm here with my husband."

"He's into everything these days, that one is."

"How's that?"

"My little one. Hugh."

Elba Rae looked about the room for a sign of a doctor or a nurse or any official wearing a white uniform who might bear news of Fettis's condition. She saw none.

"I should know by now, since he's my second one and all, that they're just gonna mimic what they see. You should always pay close mind to what you're doing when a child is watching you, that's for sure."

Elba Rae was nervous. "Was it some kind of accident?"

"Not exactly," Hugh's white stretch pants-wearing mother said. "It's my own fault for leaving that stuff where he could get to it in the first place."

"Did he get into some poison?"

"No," she sighed. "Vapor rub."

"Come again?"

"Hugh's big brother—my oldest, Maynard—he had a touch of bronchitis last month and no doubt Hugh saw me putting the vapor rub on Maynard's chest at night. I guess he just thought it was something to play with. Well anyway, I was trying to get my supper ready this afternoon and I missed him—Hugh—after a while, and if you've ever had young ones in the house, you know they're the most dangerous when you can't hear them." Hugh's mother paused. "Do you have children?"

"No. We don't. It's just my husband and me and he's—"

"Well, when they get quiet, that's when you need to check on them. I learned that with Maynard. Anyhow, I got to looking for him and he wasn't in his room, and where do you think he was?"

Elba Rae supposed participating in the mystery of little Hugh Nobody's disappearance would help pass the time until she got word on Fettis, so she went along with Hugh's mother in order to learn the medical mishap which had obviously befallen him.

"Where was he?"

"He was in the bathroom," Hugh's mother suddenly realized she was speaking too loudly and lowered her voice to a more discreet pitch. "He was in the bathroom. With that jar of vapor rub and stripped down to nothing but one sock. Just a-rubbing it all over himself."

Elba Rae frowned in sympathy.

"I know. You'd think that god-awful smell would have made him want to stop, but he was going to town. And when I say all over himself, I do mean all. Now I know he didn't see me putting that rub on any part of Maynard except his chest area so I don't know where he got the idea to strip his clothes off and rub it in places where it's not intended to be used."

It had worked, Elba Rae thought to herself. This woman had definitely gotten her mind off Fettis even if but for a couple of minutes.

"I don't think there's really anything harmful in the stuff," Hugh's mother carried forth, "but once it got absorbed in good, it heated up and it started to burn him so. Course he'd used the whole jar by the time I found him at it."

"I expect if you rubbed in a whole jar it would get a little warm," Elba Rae offered.

"You know we've got a doctor over in Mount Olive, but I was afraid to wait on him to be in his office tomorrow morning. Hugh's daddy said we should've just let it take its course, but I couldn't stand thinking there might be the possibility he could have harmed himself. You know, permanently." Elba Rae Van Oaks was apparently giving Hugh's mother an expression suggesting she did not readily accept an overdose of vapor rub would have fatal repercussions.

"I mean, what if one day he couldn't have children? I'd never get over it if I knew I'd stayed home tonight while his reproductive organs burned off."

Elba Rae Van Oaks had just about had it.

"And, bless his heart, but ..." and she paused to survey the room, as though it would have been embarrassing to be overheard by a stranger of a greater variety than the one to whom she was already babbling, "but I think his little T-bottle must be worrying him something awful. Can you imagine?" She queried while shaking her head from side to side. "Well," chuckling, "of course we can't, but you know for a little boy it's got to be misery. Having something irritating his privates like that."

"Ah-huh," was all Elba Rae could manage. "I need to find out something about my husband," she said as she stood up and walked away from Hugh's mother.

"Nice talking to you," Hugh's mother said and Elba Rae gave her a wave but a mediocre one in nature since she didn't even turn back around to look in the woman's direction as she did it. After pacing back and forth a few minutes in front of the nurse's station, which right then was not being manned by the heavy-set nurse but by one too busy with phone calls and incoming patients to notice Elba Rae, the double doors swung opened and the first nurse was back.

"Mrs. Van Oaks?"

"Yes! Here I am!"

"Come on back with me, hon."

Elba Rae did as she was told and followed the nurse and then asked, as soon as the flapping doors were closed behind them, "Is he dead?"

"Oh, no, darlin', he is doing just fine," she said as they walked. "I'll let the doctor talk to you. He's in there with your husband right now. But he's going to be just fine. We might have to keep him a few days, to run some tests, but the doctor thinks it was a mild attack. As heart attacks go, that is. Could have been much worse."

With that news, Elba Rae slowed her pace and then came to a stop altogether. She leaned against the wall and let the constricted muscles throughout her entire body relax, and then followed the big nurse into a small room where a doctor was standing over the still-alive figure of Fettis Van Oaks.

*   *   *   *

A week later, Fettis Van Oaks returned home where he and his wife Elba Rae pretty much never again discussed the specifics of what had preceded the heart attack, although without need of clarification it was generally understood Patsy Simpson's name would not be mentioned there within nor would Fettis be available to undertake any sort of home repair or appliance installation unless it was within the boundaries of the Van Oaks's property or that of a blood relative on either side but preferably a Maywood's.

That fall at the faculty meeting held the week before school started outright, Elba Rae Van Oaks sat at the table with Irma Young, Louise Kinney, and Claude Pickle, and accomplished with great success her goal of not even making eye contact with Patsy Simpson, who, Elba Rae needn't have feared, had no intention of letting her.

When Fettis Van Oaks succumbed two years later to the strain of heart attack known as massive, Patsy Simpson, with hesitation, did accompany her husband Doug to the visitation at the Buford Memorial Funeral Home to pay their last respects. The other teachers would be there, she knew, and certainly Mr. Bailey would, and Patsy Simpson knew how much Mr. Bailey liked the word cohesiveness so she put on a nice black dress and her small strand of fake pearls and walked into the room where Fettis Van Oaks was embalmed and on display in a silver metal casket.

Elba Rae received them right after a sincere hug and brief exchange with Willadean Hendrix, whereupon Elba Rae thanked Willadean for the delicious pecan pie she'd brought by the house. There was an absence of emotion from any of them as Doug Simpson expressed his condolences and allowed as to how he'd always be grateful for the help Mr. Fettis had lent around their place.

"Thank you, Doug," said Elba Rae. Then, for what was possibly the first time in years, she purposely looked Patsy Simpson right in the face, and Patsy Simpson looked back. "I'm sorry," Patsy said.

Elba Rae stared into her eyes after Patsy offered the words. And then she turned back to look only at Doug. "Thank you for coming."

With that, the Simpsons stepped aside and Elba Rae was free to greet the next visitors who'd arrived to mourn with her.

THE TWO MAYWOOD
GIRLS

"Are you not close to your sister?" Dr. Yardley had been looking down and perusing Elba Rae's file when he spoke that afternoon, and she didn't even think he was ready to start. It was an unexpected question.

"Lila?"

He closed the file and looked up at her. "She is your only sister, isn't she?"

"Yeah ... she's my only one."

"But she lives out of town—up in Birmingham—and you don't spend much time together, do you?"

"Well, no. We don't. She's married, and has a family, and her own life there."

"Does she visit?"

"Visit Buford? Well, yeah, she visits. Our momma is here and if Lila Mae wants to see her she knows she'll have to come to Buford because Momma's just not gonna get too far away from home. I used to drive her up there ever once in awhile, but Momma doesn't like to travel anymore. If she gets out of her own house and her routine, she's a mess."

"Were you and Lila close growing up?"

There was a delay before she answered, because Elba Rae didn't consider it an uncomplicated subject. Not that anyone had, before that day, ever asked.

"I'm eight years older than Lila Mae, so we weren't really coming up at the same time, if you know what I mean." To Elba Rae Van Oaks, Dr. Yardley's placid face suggested he knew the relationship between the two sisters had been shaped by more than chronology.

*   *   *   *

Lila Mae Maywood did not appreciate being seen in public wearing the same or even similar outfits as her older sister, Elba Rae. It didn't matter that Elba Rae was nearly twelve and Lila Mae only four; she still knew the difference. But worse than the matching dresses and jumpers and little sun suits that were new, mostly gifts on Christmas and sometimes birthdays, were the ones Lila Mae knew for sure did not come from a store at all and were from the big smelly trunk her mother kept up in the attic. The big smelly trunk is where her mother went to get all the old clothes Elba Rae used to wear before she got too grown.

The most severe fit Lila Mae Maywood would ever throw about previously worn clothing was on Easter Sunday right before she turned five. Things had been decidedly going her way, that's for sure, up until about nine that morning. Her Easter basket was filled to its brim with colored eggs and jelly beans and a chocolate rabbit she made sure was not smaller than the one in her sister's basket, which did contain the same number of dyed eggs but had the one with the bad crack. She had been wearing the new little white gloves meant only for church off and on since she got up except for when her mother had insisted she remove them while handling her congruently formed bunny. And then her world collapsed. Right there across the foot of the twin bed in the room she shared with Elba Rae.

It was a light pink dress with little embroidered roses and a sash that tied in the back. It was neatly pressed, yes, and appeared to be clean, perhaps. But it smelled. It smelled like the trunk in the attic where her mother went to select from what was obviously a tremendous vault of clothing, the supply of which would never be extinct. Lila Maywood was stunned. The white patent leather shoes were new—she had gone to the Square with her mother herself to try them on—and the white ankle socks were still attached to their cardboard, and the petticoat had a price tag on its strap not yet snipped off. But in the middle of all her new was Elba Rae's old dress.

"Momma, no!" she screamed as she snatched the dress off the bed and ran down the stairs toward the kitchen, leaving a mild trail of mothball-scented fragrance in her wake. "Momma! Momma, no!"

"What in the world, Lila Mae?"

"It smells, Momma!"

"What smells? And what are you doing running around with your dress? You're gonna ruin it. Get back upstairs and start getting ready. I'll be up to brush your hair in a minute."

"No, Momma!"

Ethel Maywood did not suffer insubordination graciously, nor was she accustomed to making a request twice. "What do you mean, no?" She ceased her potato peeling and turned to face her youngest daughter.

"I'm not wearing this old dress, Momma! It smells bad! And it's Elba Rae's!"

"It does *not* smell bad and it is *not* Elba Rae's and don't tell me what you're *not* going to do!"

"It's Elba Rae's old dress, Momma, and you can't make me wear it on Easter! Elba Rae got a new Easter dress! It's not fair!"

"Lila Mae, hush up. That is a perfectly nice dress. It's been washed and ironed and it's pretty. And you've got your new shoes and your new little gloves, so you're gonna be the prettiest girl in Sunday School today."

"No!" was Lila Mae's resounding retort. About then, the bottom two stairs creaked like they did whenever anybody stepped on them and Elba Rae Maywood soon entered the kitchen dressed for church. Lila took one look.

"Momma, can you cut the tag off? It's scratching my neck," Elba Rae said, adding a squirm for effect.

"Come over here in the light," her mother said.

Lila could not endure the injustice another second. She thrust her pink dress to the floor and burst into sobs which quickly gave way to wails, the kind children somehow perfect around a certain age. "It's ... not ... fa–a–a–ir," moaned Lila.

Ethel Maywood was now incensed. "You pick that dress up right this second or so help me, Lila Mae!" A second passed, and then two or three with wails but no picking up. "I mean it! If you don't pick that dress up and go put it on right now, every bit of your Easter candy's going to the trash pile and I don't mean maybe!"

"You ... can't ... throw ... my ... ca–a–an–dy ... a–wa–a–a–ay ..." she cried.

"Where is my yardstick?!" Ethel Maywood asked, not expecting either child to answer since they were both accustomed to her rhetoric.

"It's in the broom closet, Momma, want me to get it?" Elba Rae was sometimes the helpful one.

"You stay out of this!"

"I didn't do anything!"

"No, you just had to come down here and parade around in your new clothes and tease your sister cause you know she doesn't like wearing your hand-me-downs."

"But Momma, I—"

"But nothing, Elba Rae. Go on upstairs and find your daddy and tell him I said to take that tag off with his shaving razor. And tell him I said not to cut your neck."

"Why are you yelling at me, Momma? All I did was come in here—"

"Go on, Elba Rae, before I knock the both of you into next week!"

Elba Rae was not one to cry in the face of adversity; rather, there was something about it that made her more bitter than it did melancholy. She frowned, understandably, but turned around and made the steps creak again on her way back up them.

"Lila Mae, pick that dress up this instant and get to your room. I don't have time for this today. We're gonna be late as it is. And on Easter!"

Still sniffling but resigned to her mother's mandate, Lila Mae Maywood snatched the pink dress from the kitchen floor and made a partial retreat, ascending about midway up the stairs before collapsing in a heap of defeat. She lay face down on the dress and cried.

*   *   *   *

At only five minutes after the official ten o'clock start of Sunday School, all Maywoods were present and accounted for at the First Avenue United Methodist Church in Buford, their morning tribulations seemingly repressed if not completely forgotten, except for the mild residual puffiness in Lila's eyes which had ceased tear production only as the family had left their home.

Most members were accustomed to lingering outside the church following preaching for general visiting and on Easter, as was the case on Mother's Day and near about Christmas, the lawn was at capacity what with the church's regular members and the addition of members who didn't regularly attend plus the ones who didn't regularly attend who weren't even members but who were, guided by the holiday's spiritual beckoning, making their rare guest appearances. At twelve years old and almost a teenager, Elba Rae Maywood was feeling much more grown up than she ever had before, and instead of gravitating toward the other children in the congregation to run around darting in and out of the old oaks while the adults talked, Elba Rae was more compelled to stand tall with her mother and father as they conversed with Mr. and Mrs. Perrymore. She was conscious of her appearance and, even with church over, didn't want to get dirty.

"Don't you look so pretty today and all grown up, Elba Rae," Mrs. Anita Perrymore remarked, which made Elba Rae blush.

"What do you say, Elba Rae?" Ethel Maywood didn't miss a beat.

"Thank you."

"And where's little Miss Lila Mae? I know she's got to be just cute as a button."

"Oh, she's off hooting and hollering and getting a mess I'm sure," Ethel said.

"You about ready, Ethel?" Raymond Maywood attended church most every Sunday and was never considered one of the holiday husbands, as some were, but he did not savor the fellowship on the lawn as much as his wife Ethel and was usually more anxious to get home and exchange his scratchy Sunday suit for a more comfortable wardrobe.

"I guess we do need to be going if I'm going to have everything ready for dinner."

"Are you expecting a big crowd today?" Mrs. Perrymore asked.

"Goodness yes, and I'm not near ready. Ruby and Hazel are coming, and we've got Ray's sister, Laveetra, and her family." She turned her attention away. "Where is Lila Mae? Elba Rae, go find your sister and tell her it's time to go."

"Yes, ma'am," Elba Rae responded pleasantly before heading toward what looked like a raucous game of tag from which she knew Lila would resist being extracted. It made her walk even a bit faster and with purpose.

Lila was still protesting when the girls joined their parents. "Lila Mae, just look at you!" her mother exclaimed. "Have you been on the ground? I will never be able to wash that out of your dress!"

"We were playing, Momma." Both Perrymores laughed.

"Well you sure are mighty sweet-looking this morning, Lila Mae," Mrs. Perrymore gushed and then looked at her husband. "Isn't she the cutest thing you ever saw? Those gloves ... you are getting to be a little lady, that's for sure."

Ray Maywood appreciated the irony. "She can be when she wants to."

"Oh, I miss having a sweet little girl like you to dress up."

"Why don't you get one?" Lila suggested, which sent all four adults into a fit of laughter.

"Well, you know what?" Mrs. Perrymore said after composing herself. "I had a little girl. But she's grown up now." She let out one last chuckle. "She is just precious, Ethel."

"She's a handful sometimes, but I guess we'll keep her," and everyone smiled. Except for Elba Rae Maywood, who didn't think it so very amusing that her sister was apparently being praised for rolling on the ground in her Easter dress, which Elba Rae knew full well wasn't really even new, not to mention the plethora of compliments being heaped upon her for wearing an ensemble she'd been threatened into with a yardstick. Elba Rae had not run off to frolic after church let out. She had stayed with the grown-ups and been polite.

"It's *my* dress," Elba Rae announced.

"Uh–uhhhh!" Lila protested. "It's *my* dress!"

"Is not! It was mine and Momma just got it from the trunk. Mine is new!"

"It's not your dress! Momma, make her stop!"

"Elba Rae, hush that," her mother demanded. "Let's go right now!" She grabbed Elba Rae by the upper arm and marched her away from the delightful Perrymores. "I am ashamed of you," Mr. Perrymore heard Ethel say as they left. "Why do you have to pick on her like that, huh? Answer me!"

"She got my dress dirty and I—"

"You don't care anything about that old dress, Elba Rae! Honestly! You act like you're more her age than she is sometimes! Always wanting to start something! Always stirring something up when you could just leave it be!"

Their voices fading, Raymond Maywood picked Lila up in his arms and carried her along behind, leaving both Perrymores to palaver elsewhere and amongst others.

*   *   *   *

"Elba Rae, help me set the table. Aunt Laveetra and Uncle Sammy will be here any minute and the table's not even set." Ethel Maywood was darting about the kitchen at full capacity, with a potato masher in one hand and a carving knife in the other.

"How come Lila Mae doesn't have to help?"

"Elba Rae, please—don't argue with me. I don't have time."

"But—"

"She's not even five years old and I don't want her handling my good dishes! Now get in there and take the plates out of the china closet and put them around the table. Mind to be careful with them. They were your grandmother's and they can never be replaced. And when you've done that, you can come in here and get the everyday ones for your table."

"The little table?"

"Yes."

"Momma!"

"What?"

"I don't want to sit at the little table with the kids! I want to sit at the big table! With you and Daddy!"

"There's not enough room at the grown up table, Elba Rae. We've got too many people coming."

"That's not fair!"

"Elba Rae, for the love of … please just help your momma today and put the plates around. And I promise you next year when you're thirteen you can sit at the big table. If I have to eat squatting on the floor to make room. All right? Will that make you happy?"

"I don't want to sit with Begina."

Ethel Maywood slowed her flurry and looked directly at her daughter. "Now Elba Rae, I have told you before."

"I don't care."

"You be nice to your cousin. If I catch you even thinking about making fun, I will blister you so you won't be *able* to sit down till next Easter! Do you understand me?"

"She's peculiar."

"I don't care what she is. She's your cousin and it's Easter and you be nice to her." Elba Rae turned around in disgust and walked into the dining room. "So help me, Elba Rae," Ethel projected, as the door swung back into the kitchen.

Alone in the rectangular shaped dining room, Elba Rae opened the closet door and delicately removed a stack of the china plates which were never used except on Easter and Christmas and sometimes Thanksgiving, depending on who was there. She stared at the big table before her eyes were drawn to the other small one at the end of the room, which had been set up in the bay window overlooking the side yard. She knew it was really her mother's tea cart with the leaves pulled up and not even a tablecloth over it made it look like anything else. It was there she'd be relegated to relish Easter dinner with her repulsive little sister, her cousin Hazel, and her other cousin Begina who usually got food on herself and talked with her mouth full. Begina's mother, Aunt Laveetra, was married to Uncle Sammy who Elba Rae found always to have an aroma, and although the other grown-ups usually just made out like it was the cigars Uncle Sammy smoked that were the culprit and not so much Uncle Sammy in and of himself, Elba Rae was not at all convinced that theory held truth.

Aunt Laveetra as a rule smelled fresher, but she never got on to Begina for anything, even if the other kids were being gotten on to by one of the grown-ups which was usually Elba Rae's mother Ethel or Hazel's mother, Aunt Ruby, and not even when Begina was smack in the middle of the trouble. Aunt Laveetra would just laugh and say, "She's got forty devils in her and none cast out sometimes," and go on about her business. Elba Rae had heard her own mother say to her daddy she believed Begina was simple but Elba Rae didn't really know what they meant exactly. That Easter Sunday, while she gingerly arranged the good china plates around the big dining table, she was just hoping Aunt Laveetra wouldn't play her cat joke. Elba Rae hated that without qualification.

"Elba Rae?" Ethel Maywood beckoned from the other side of the door. "Come get the everyday dishes for your table. Elba Rae?" Elba Rae obediently obliged and returned to the kitchen just as her mother was shaking the last glob of mashed potatoes off of the masher and into their pot on the stove.

"Oh, Momma, can I lick the masher?" Elba Rae hoped.

"I'm licking the masher!" It was the wee worrisome whine of Elba Rae's brat of a sister who'd managed to show up from somewhere.

"I said it first."

"Uh–uh!"

"Did too."

"Oh, Elba Rae, honey I'm sorry, but Lila Mae did ask a minute ago and I promised her."

"Momma!"

"Don't pout, Elba Rae, you can have the next one."

"But she always gets to lick it!"

"Now that's not true, but she asked me first this time while you were setting the table," Ethel Maywood pronounced, after which she without further discussion handed the masher to Lila Mae who delayed her first lick long enough to smile at her big sister. Then she did actually attempt to insert the entire potato masher into her mouth at once.

"It's not fair! I'm so hungry!"

"Good, cause we're about to have a big dinner. Just as soon as Aunt Laveetra and them get here. They're just running a little late."

"I can't wait that long! I'm hungry now."

"I don't think you're gonna starve in the next fifteen minutes. Now carry these plates in the dining room and put them around your table."

"But Momma, I am hungry! I haven't had anything all day!"

"Oh, Elba Rae, you ought to be ashamed. Why, you don't know what hungry is, and you never have. You know, there are children over there in China that really do have to go all day without so much as a morsel. And I bet they don't complain about it half as much as you."

"They would if they were this hungry."

"You had a good breakfast this morning and I know you've been in your Easter candy so don't make out like I don't feed you around here. What's the matter with you? Have you got a tapeworm?"

"I didn't have any breakfast!"

"Elba Rae Maywood, it is against the Lord's word to tell a fib and it's even worse doing it on the Sabbath."

"But I didn't. You didn't make me any eggs, remember?"

"No, but I fried nearly a pound of bacon this morning and made biscuits before we went to Sunday School. I can't help it if you won't come down to breakfast when I call. Maybe this will teach you."

"Lila Mae got all the bacon. I wanted the last piece and she ate it just to be mean." Whether Lila Mae Maywood had a defense prepared or not was immaterial at that moment, as her mouth was way too full of potato masher to talk out. "All I got was an old biscuit and some grapes out of the icebox."

"Elba Rae, what did I just say about telling fibs?"

"It's not fibbing, Momma! All I've had to eat all day is three grapes and a cold biscuit."

"I don't believe that for a minute but I can't do anything about it. Now are you gonna take these dishes in the dining room and help me or do I need to get the yardstick?"

"It's in the broom closet," Lila Mae Maywood announced with potato seething through her teeth. Elba Rae knew when her mother was not going to budge on a subject, be it a discussion about a school outfit or an undone chore. She knew, as well, when to take her leave to avoid a brush with the yardstick, although Elba Rae's daddy Raymond Maywood would be the very first to advise that if the yardstick made it out of the broom closet just half as many times as it was alluded to he'd have two perfect girls under his roof. So Elba Rae took the everyday dishes off the counter and she redirected herself back to the dining room but could not, even though it surely would have been the better of ideas, go quietly.

"I don't care what you say. It's true. All I've had to eat today is three grapes and a cold biscuit," and she stepped a little quicker before getting the last part out because she wanted to be mostly in the dining room before she got through talking back to her momma.

Muffled by the door swinging behind her, Elba Rae could still hear her mother in the kitchen. "Cold biscuit and some grapes. Lord have mercy. What am I gonna do with that girl?"

∗   ∗   ∗   ∗

Elba Rae could hear the shrill voice of her cousin Begina Chittum even before the car door was open. When her mother Ethel had spied the bedraggled vehicle making its way toward the house, she'd scurried through the halls to announce it so everyone could be in place outside to greet the contingent of relatives even before the motor was turned off. Aunt Ruby did not as a rule warrant such a welcome ceremony, as she was closer family than Aunt Laveetra—both physically and otherwise—and Aunt Laveetra and her family were considered company.

Begina was sort of bouncing up and down on the back seat and grinning really big, and as a measure of the cynicism being twelve had brought with it, Elba Rae didn't really know the reason to be so especially jubilant over an afternoon in Buford. Even through the car window she could tell Begina's mouth was dirty and her hair was stringy and the bouncing wasn't making either look any better. "We're here, we're here, we're here, we're here, we're here," Begina was semi-singing, in perfect synchronization to her bouncing.

"Momma," Elba Rae said. "Don't even start," her mother Ethel said back. Uncle Sammy opened the car door and a waft of cigar smoke followed him loyally.

After they'd all said their hellos and how was the ride over and gotten in the house good but mainly in the kitchen, Laveetra Chittum declared as to how she wished there was something she could do to help with the dinner and Ethel Maywood assured it was all pretty much done and Elba Rae'd heard her mother say to Aunt Ruby one time before if Aunt Laveetra really did want to help she wouldn't always make sure they were late every time they came over and Aunt Ruby seemed to insinuate the infraction was all the more compounded since Aunt Laveetra didn't even offer to bring a dish, not even the relish tray.

The four children sat at Ethel Maywood's converted tea cart with the tablecloth over it and set with the everyday dishes and had a rather somber dinner, as it were, while the grown-ups at the big table laughed and tee-heed and said to one another how delicious everything looked, which is to say until Begina Marie Chittum unconsciously or otherwise determined to liven things up.

In what was probably not her debut performance, Begina began to blow into her glass of iced tea rather than sip from it, which produced just a subtle enough stream of bubbles to both amuse Lila Mae Maywood and Hazel Burns and tickle Begina Chittum's nose. Lila Mae and Hazel's reactions naturally encouraged Begina to repeat so she blew in her glass some more and tickled her nose and the more she blew the more Lila Mae and Hazel laughed and the more Lila Mae and Hazel laughed the harder Begina blew which made enough tea go up her nose that she began to produce a rather unique snort. Elba Rae, meanwhile, was unamused by all of it. Until the snort. And then she could maintain her stoicism no longer and she giggled out loud and uninhibited and soon the small table was one solid disruption of happiness, as far as the girls were concerned, yet an unacceptable disturbance if you happened to be one of the grown-ups at the big table with the good china.

"What are you girls doing?" Hazel's mother, Ruby Burns, wanted to know. "Nothing, Momma," Hazel said, as the group contained their fun a bit. "Eat your dinner," Ruby said back.

"You too, Elba Rae," Ethel Maywood joined in.

The girls had resumed their eating for all of a minute before Begina was once again blowing into her tea, now made all the funnier due to the threat of scrutiny from the grown ups. Hazel Burns put her hand over her mouth to lessen the chortling sound but Lila Mae Maywood snickered without inhibition. Elba Rae then observed Begina's mother Aunt Laveetra watching and feared another reprimand was forthcoming. But instead of a scolding, Aunt Laveetra just smiled at Begina even as Begina was generating the biggest tea bubble yet, which translated as an official endorsement to Elba Rae, who spontaneously picked up her own glass of tea and blew into it wildly. Rather than laughter, however, Elba Rae's action drew a quick and collective gasp from her audience, as the excessive force of her blow displaced several ounces of tea out of her glass and onto the table.

"Elba Rae, what are you doing over there?" Ethel Maywood said as she pushed back from the table slightly for a better view.

"Elba Rae got tea all over the table, Momma!" Lila announced.

"What?" Ethel got up and walked over to the bay window.

"Why don't you shut up, Lila Mae?" Elba Rae said, but it was too late.

"Oh, for goodness sakes, Elba Rae," Ethel Maywood fretted, "all over my good tablecloth. What were you doing over here?!"

"Nothing," Elba Rae replied.

"Nothing my foot. You're over here playing instead of eating. Look at your plate—you've got tea all in your food. Bring that in the kitchen and scrape it and get a clean one." Elba Rae was embarrassed at the condescending tone in her mother's voice in front of her younger sister and cousins. "I don't know why you think I should let you sit with the grown ups. At this rate you'll be eating at the little table till you're married."

"Momma!"

"Come on, now, and bring your plate in the kitchen." Ethel Maywood went first and Elba Rae followed behind in sullied shame.

"You're in trou–u–u–ble," Lila Mae said under her breath not loud enough for her mother to hear but plenty good for Elba Rae.

"Shut up!" Elba Rae screamed back.

"What did you just say?"

"I wasn't talking to you, Momma, I was talking to Lila Mae. She—"

"Lila Mae hasn't done anything to you."

"Yes she did, she—"

"Bring that plate in here and don't open your mouth again except to eat." They continued the march into the kitchen. "You know, for somebody who was so hungry she was about to faint earlier, it looks like you could just sit at the table and eat your dinner instead of making a mess." In the dining room, Begina Chittum laughed aloud.

"Whatever you're doing over there," Ruby Burns said to her daughter Hazel, "stop it."

Ethel Maywood returned momentarily with a clean plate in her hand and Elba Rae in tow. Ethel went around the table to serve it with food and said excuse me to Sammy Chittum as she leaned over him to reach the green beans, after which she handed the replenished plate to Elba Rae. "Now take this over there and sit down and you'd better not spill another drop of anything."

"Yes, ma'am," Elba Rae said.

"Honestly," Ethel commented as she resumed her place at the table.

"They're just being kids, Ethel," Laveetra Chittum lamented.

Ethel was not going to agree. "That's no excuse for a twelve-year-old, Laveetra. She started out this morning tormenting Lila Mae about her Easter dress before we ever left home and she was still aggravating her about it after church. And if you could have heard her carrying on before y'all got here. Telling me some tale about not having anything to eat all day but a cold biscuit and some grapes. I don't know why she wants to be so ornery some days."

At the little tea cart with the soiled table cloth, Elba Rae absorbed her mother's summation of the day's events thus far and ground her teeth together slightly. "I hate you," she said to Lila Mae.

*   *   *   *

In the afternoon sunshine, Hazel Burns, Begina Chittum, and Lila Mae May-wood searched earnestly for eggs hidden by Begina's mother, who'd been cogni-zant of making the hiding places not too challenging, especially for Begina whose basket would turn up empty if she hadn't. Laveetra's husband Sammy stood under the shade of an elm tree puffing on a cigar, regaling Ray Maywood with the story of a catfish caught two summers prior by Sammy's cousin Willie Lynn Chittum.

"I told W'lynn that dang catfish was too big to waste on eating. Fish that size ought to be mounted."

"Did he mount it?" Ray asked.

"Ate it," Sammy Chittum said, exhaling at the same time.

Inside the house, Elba Rae was nearly through clearing the table but Ethel Maywood and her sister Ruby Burns still had an hour's work ahead with the dishes.

"How 'bout helping your aunt Ruby dry, Elba Rae?"

"You said I could go outside as soon as I cleared, Momma."

"I know I did but you don't care anything about hunting eggs. That's for little kids."

"Why do I have to always help? Why doesn't Aunt Laveetra do anything?" Ruby Burns dried the gravy boat and put it on the top shelf of the cupboard while sneaking a glance at her sister, knowing what Ethel likely wanted to say but curious how it'd come out.

"Aunt Laveetra is company and we don't ask company to wash dishes."

"Why not? You wash dishes when we go to their house."

"That's because I offer."

"Then why—"

"Get a clean dish towel out of the drawer and don't ask so many questions." Elba Rae did as she was told without further discussion and joined her aunt Ruby who was at the sink rinsing. Ruby handed her a wet plate and gave her a wink.

After the egg hunt was over and the kitchen repaired to its pre-dinner condi-tion, the families gathered in the parlor to visit some more and, at least for the benefit of Ethel Maywood and Ruby Burns, to rest. The younger children were in and out though Elba Rae sat on the floor at the end of her parents's long couch because she wanted to be a part of their adult conversation. Sometimes it was about things Elba Rae understood and other times not; the same held true with the various people whose names came up. It was always more fun when Elba Rae knew who they were. Elba Rae's mother and her aunt Ruby were doing most of the talking, with periodic contributions from her father and Uncle Sammy. Aunt Laveetra sat in the corner in a straight back chair next to Elba Rae, looking content but otherwise uninvolved.

"Whatever became of all those Maharrys?" Ruby Burns asked. "I heard somebody asking Martha Betty in Sunday School this morning about Ned's brother, but I didn't know he'd been sick."

"Oh, he's been sick for a long time, Ruby," Ethel confirmed.

"What in the world?"

"I expect it's his liver by now. You know he was always bad to drink."

"I thought that was the oldest one."

"He may have too, but the one that's so sick hasn't ever been able to keep work."

"Well, Ned's not like that."

"I don't imagine Martha Betty would put up with him if he were," Ethel stated confidently.

"Weren't there four of them?"

"I believe there were. Now that oldest one you're talking about is the one that married one of those Pickets."

"That'd be enough to drive you to drink," Ray Maywood injected.

"They say she was weaned on a pickle and I don't think Martha Betty cares a thing about her."

"Is that right?"

"Not at all."

"Now the one closest to Ned is the one that was in that bad car wreck coming back from Athens. They say he's just not right. And Martha Betty's never told this, but I don't think his wife has lived with him since they got him back from the hospital."

"Who takes care of him?"

"I don't know, exactly. That oldest one has two children who are on up there, so maybe they help look after him."

"That's right pitiful."

"I know."

Elba Rae was completely immersed in the very grown-up discussion taking place between her mother and her aunt and although not a participant herself, it was easy to forget others were also in the room, which made the meow all the more intrusive.

"She wasn't from Litton County, was she Ethel?"

"No, don't you know he met her in Virginia when he was stationed over there. Somebody said they thought she'd gone back there to her people, but Martha Betty's never mentioned it. I think she tries to look in on him some too."

"Martha Betty's a good person."

"Yes, she is."

And then it happened again. A meow.

"I saw a picture of one of those Picket girls in the paper a week or two ago," announced Ethel.

"I did too," Ruby said, "but it wasn't the one married to Ned's brother."

"No, this was the one that had the cleft palate. She was posing with somebody they'd had a bridal shower for at their church. Bless her heart."

"Wonder why she'd want her picture taken and put in the newspaper?"

"I don't know. And she was just grinning. Wasn't even trying to close her mouth."

"I don't imagine she can."

"No, but she could excuse herself from the picture."

"You know the one that married Ned's brother was no prize herself and there wasn't anything even wrong with her lips."

"Make a freight train take a dirt road," remarked Ray Maywood, which elicited a chortle from Sammy Chittum.

"That's not a bit nice," Ethel Maywood said, while laughing herself.

Meow. It was louder that time than the first two, enough so it broke Elba Rae's concentration and made her look up at the source: her aunt Laveetra.

"I hear a cat," Laveetra said to Elba Rae. Elba Rae turned away and hoped for the continuation of the discussion of unattractive ladies and pitiful injured men whose wives went away. Ruby Burns picked up.

"Those girls didn't have any mother growing up, you know. She died giving birth to the last one. And I think old man Picket liked to work them to death keeping that place up."

"I guess we shouldn't judge somebody unless we've walked in their shoes."

"No, but they all were a peculiar bunch."

"Meow," Laveetra Chittum said. Elba Rae looked at her. "I hear a cat, Elba Rae. Do you?" Elba Rae stared at her aunt and wondered why she had to be the recipient of the unwanted attention. "No," Elba Rae said, and looked away.

"I didn't see Miss Nita in church today," Ruby stated.

"She was there," Ethel said.

"She must have been keeping the nursery. You know she's always been good to take her turn on the special occasions and holidays when nobody else wants to."

"She does. But we saw both of them after preaching because she was making over the girls' Easter dresses. They're both sweet as they can be, but you know sometimes she is just silly as a goat."

"I know what you mean."

"Meow."

"Stop," Elba Rae said but without directly addressing Laveetra.

"Stop what, Elba Rae?" Laveetra asked innocently.

"Stop that sound."

"What sound?"

"That cat sound."

"That's not me, Elba Rae. I believe there's a cat in here. Do you have a cat?"

"We don't have a cat."

"You reckon somebody's let one in?"

"No!" Elba shifted her body around on the floor so as to have her back completely to her aunt, an act of defiance which did little to discourage Laveetra's playful teasing and, in fact, most likely served to prolong it.

"Meow," she said immediately.

Elba Rae jerked herself back around to face Laveetra. "Why do you always have to do that?"

"Do what, sweetie?"

"Make that sound!"

"What sound?"

"That meowing!"

"I told you, honey, that's not me. I believe there's a cat in here."

"Is not! It's just you going 'meow.' Meow, meow, meow, meow, meow, meow, I know it's you! I'm not a stupid little kid!"

"Elba Rae, what's going on over there? Are you raising your voice to Aunt Laveetra?" Ray Maywood was perturbed.

"Daddy, make her stop!"

"Stop what?"

"She won't leave me alone! She's making those meow sounds and saying there's a cat in the room!"

Ethel Maywood's relaxed demeanor quickly switched to recovery mode. "She's just playing with you, Elba Rae."

"She acts like I'm a baby, Momma! Like I don't know it's her making the cat noise."

"That's no reason to be disrespectful."

"Well, make her stop."

"Oh, I'm sorry, sweetie," Laveetra finally offered. "I was just playing with you. I wouldn't have done it if I'd known it was gonna get you so riled."

"Elba Rae," Ethel said, "tell Aunt Laveetra you're sorry for talking back to her."

"I didn't do anything, Momma!"

"Mind me, Elba Rae." Elba Rae, prematurely thinking the situation could deteriorate no further, suddenly realized her sister and cousins had come back in the parlor and stood transfixed by the tense standoff.

"Is Elba Rae in trouble again?" Begina Chittum asked.

"No, baby," Laveetra assured, yet not enough so to satisfy Begina.

"Then why is Aunt Ethel fussing at her?"

"Apologize, Elba Rae," Ethel Maywood insisted.

"Momma," Elba Rae whined. "Make them go away first."

"Why should they? They haven't done anything wrong."

"Elba Rae's in trouble," Begina laughed, which came out snort-like as though an undischarged amount of tea might still have been clogged in her sinuses. The snort made Lila Mae laugh and soon Hazel Burns couldn't help herself either, even though it was Begina's snort that was funny and not so much the discipline about to be levied upon her cousin Elba Rae.

"It's not funny," Elba Rae yelled at them. For all intents and purposes, however, it was to the other girls. Because they were all younger after all, even Hazel if just slightly, and they'd not been present for whatever had transpired as a prerequisite to the confrontation between Elba Rae and her mother and, not to mention, Begina was still snorting.

"Stop laughing!" Elba Rae insisted. And then she crossed the line. Not that she hadn't already been the focus of enough controversy, but her next act of rebellion permanently elevated her misbehavior to a level from which there could be no recourse.

Elba Rae began to mock Begina's snorting. She embellished, of course, and exaggerated with volume, naturally, but the basic vibrations in her throat were striking duplicates of the sort frequently made by Begina Marie Chittum.

Whatever Elba Rae's intention, Begina reacted pleasantly at first and laughed benignly, which made Elba Rae all the madder. She could feel rage coming on and it was intensifying. She repeated her imitation for a second round that was louder than the first and enhanced with the accompaniment of swine-inspired facial expressions delivered exclusively for Begina, who even in her simple mind, began to sense all was not well. She stopped laughing at Elba Rae, yet the attack continued.

"Quit that this minute, Elba Rae!" Ethel Maywood screeched.

But it was too late. Elba Rae was beyond the point of retreat. Begina Marie Chittum had often been made fun of, by the children at her family's own church and some of the ones at her school. It struck a very specific and isolated chord in her, however, when the source of aggression was from within—from her family, and from an older cousin she actually looked up to and wanted to be like. Elba Rae snorted at her some more and Begina started to cry.

"Now you *have* done it!" Ethel proclaimed.

"Come here, baby," Laveetra Chittum said to Begina as she extended her arms. "Come here to momma. It's all right." Begina ran to her mother's embrace and buried her face. "It's all right. Elba Rae's not mad at you, baby." Even her sobs had an underlying snort to them.

"What did I tell you about mocking and shocking?" Elba Rae did not respond to her mother. "Huh? Answer me! Didn't I tell you this morning before they ever got here I didn't want to catch you making fun of her?!"

"Yeah, but—"

"But you just don't listen, do you? You just talk back and give sass, and you mock and shock and aggravate and torment till you've made everybody miserable!"

"You told daddy Begina was simple and—"

"I never said any such thing and you ought to be ashamed! She is your cousin and they came all the way over here to spend Easter with us today. And all you've done is hurt her feelings! Laveetra, I'm sorry. She is just growing up to be nothing but trouble. Do you hear me, Elba Rae? You are nothing but trouble! Ray, take her upstairs this minute!" Raymond Maywood dutifully complied and pulled Elba Rae by the forearm toward the stairs in the hall.

Sammy Chittum, meanwhile, was gathering his last two cigars and his matches and surveying the room for any other personal effects. "We need to get on the road anyway, Laveetra."

"So soon?" Laveetra said, feigning surprise.

"We got a long drive back."

"Well, okay," she said, "but was there something you were going to talk to Ray about?"

"Some other time."

"Well, as long as we're already here, don't you think now would be good?"

"Some other time, Laveetra."

"Oh, I'm sorry, Laveetra," Ethel offered, "was there something you needed to talk to Ray about?" Ethel Maywood was not yet predisposed to suspect the request would be monetary in nature.

"As a matter of fact, there was something Sammy wanted to discuss with him. I hate to bother him with all this worry going on, but—"

"Another time, Laveetra." Sammy's voice was firm and absolute. "Let's go. Ethel, thank you for the delicious dinner. Ruby, always good to see you."

Ruby Burns stood to deliver her parting comments. Laveetra Chittum, though obviously reluctant, joined in with her own, and before they were all reloaded in the car, Begina had calmed down and was mostly back to her usually happy self. They repeated their thanks and their pleasantries again even as Sammy turned the ignition and the engine backfired twice.

*   *   *   *

For the sin of mocking her afflicted cousin, combined with the other implied infractions accrued throughout that Easter day, Elba Rae Maywood was expelled from the first floor of the house until the following morning, banned from leaving the perimeter of the bedroom she shared with her sister. She would not be called for supper because she would not be permitted to have any. That would hopefully teach her a lesson, her mother Ethel had droned after Uncle Sammy and Aunt Laveetra and Cousin Begina had gotten off and the lecturing had begun. She would stay in her room and think about what it really meant to be hungry and hopefully recall that discomfort the next time she was tempted to play with her food instead of eating it.

She would be subjected to isolation, so that on the next occasion for which company gathered around the dinner table and in the parlor for what should have been a pleasant afternoon, she could harken back to the still and the loneliness of her unpopulated cell and appreciate the inclusion unique to a family's bond. Even if that meant tolerating an immature sister or a simple-minded cousin.

In the end, however, it was the hunger which ultimately made the biggest impression on Elba Rae Maywood. She regretted the meanness she'd shown Begina, for certain, and given the opportunity to reflect, she truly didn't care if her little sister wore the dresses which had once been hers and reeked of the inside of grandmother Maywood's old steamer trunk anyhow. But mainly what Elba Rae Maywood thought about before floating off to sleep that Easter night when she was twelve was what she wouldn't have given for just three grapes and one cold biscuit.

HELMA VAN OAKS AND
THE LONG GOOD-BYE

After a nearly two-month absence from her classroom at the Homer T. Litton Grammar School, the week came when Dr. Yardley declared Elba Rae Van Oaks cured. Of course he didn't put it that way exactly, since no one had ever alleged her to be ill, that is, not in the clinical sense of the word at least.

He shared the outcome with her on a Wednesday in what was to be somewhat of a summation session executed in mostly a paternal manner. As he explained it, he had prepared a report and after conferring with the Superintendent during which Elba Rae Van Oaks's general state of mind was discussed but without compromise to the various disclosures previously made there within, Dr. Yardley professed Elba Rae Van Oaks was not a threat to the students or to the faculty at large of the Homer T. Litton Grammar School, and that as long as the principal did not especially plan activities for which they might be put together, Patsy Simpson should be reasonably safe as well. Howard Bailey agreed to accept Elba Rae back at school and on the same day he did coincidentally issue an immediate moratorium on potlucks.

During his concluding remarks, which as a rarity exceeded the customary hour he allotted for their visits, Elba Rae Van Oaks couldn't help but conclude herself that Dr. Marvin Yardley seemed innately fascinated with death, and if Elba Rae had been a psychologist herself, or had even a fourth of the credentials Dr. Yardley did, she might have felt qualified enough to voice as much to him out loud. She didn't, of course, because it really wasn't her place to analyze him. It hadn't been his place to analyze her either, she knew strongly, but Dr. Yardley hadn't been suspended from school and he hadn't needed Elba Rae Van Oaks's endorsement to get back to work as she had his, so that helped keep things in the appropriate perspective for her.

Yet no matter how much their conversation tended to wander, he would no doubt redirect them back to the morning in the teacher's lounge and Patsy Simpson and the Chicken Florentine casserole and the commonality he purported it shared with death. Elba Rae Van Oaks thought it a strange analogy. After all, it was just a casserole. She supposed, however, he had made much of its repeated mention when she'd recalled the untimely death of Earl Moss, the loss of Dewey Richardson, and the clement passing of Miss Nita Perrymore who'd perished after her last tragic fall at Restful Haven.

So during what would be their last mandated visit together, Elba Rae made a point to think for herself of a time when she had not carried a Chicken Florentine casserole to a bereaved family in their time of need, which was not an easy exercise, but one she mentally completed whether she chose to share it with Dr. Yardley or not. It hadn't been pleasant to remember, since so many memories directly involving Elba Rae Van Oaks's mother-in-law, Miss Helma, were tainted with an unpalatable flavor.

The disturbing recollection Elba Rae had that day was from late in what proved to be Helma Van Oaks's own last winter. Everybody knew she was dying from cancer, including Helma Van Oaks herself, but no one talked about it. Not even Miss Helma. It was a game the Van Oakses played wherein if they didn't talk about it, it wasn't real, and if they didn't talk about it in front of Miss Helma, she wouldn't know they knew, and if Miss Helma didn't know she wouldn't say the word in front of anyone else and then it would never happen. It did, of course, not that winter exactly but later on in the year just as the temperatures were saying it was summer even if the calendar didn't yet concur. But not before one last hurrah Elba Rae might have otherwise avoided, had she not known like everyone else in Buford and most of Litton County that Helma Van Oaks wasn't long for the world. Elba Rae had convinced herself it was the right thing to do, that later—which, based upon Helma Van Oaks's general appearance that February would more likely be sooner—when Helma was gone, she'd feel better about herself for going with them, whereas, under normal and less dire circumstance, she would have been excused with little fanfare since school wasn't out and everyone knew Elba Rae Van Oaks had to teach and couldn't be expected to just head off to Florida in the middle of the week like there was no job or consequence for leaving.

"Well, when will you be back?" Ethel Maywood needed to know.

"We're leaving in the morning," Elba Rae said back into her phone from the kitchen. "The service is on Thursday, then we'll be driving back on Friday so we'll be ready for the graveside Saturday morning."

"I don't understand why they don't just bring him on back here for the funeral in the first place, Elba Rae. It seems like an awful lot of trouble for you all to pack up in the car and drive all that way just to sit through a funeral they could have had in Buford in the first place. I could understand if they were going to bury him there, but why have everyone drag all the way down there just to sit through a funeral and then have to pull all the way back up here to bury?"

"Well, it sort of makes sense if you think about it, Momma. He's lived down there for so long, it was more his home than Litton County was."

"Then why aren't they burying him there?"

"I don't know. But I got the idea it was what he wanted. To be brought back here, I mean."

"I'm surprised that woman would have it."

"Now Momma, you know I didn't have anything to do with the arrangements. But I'll tell you something."

"What?"

Elba Rae Van Oaks looked about her kitchen, not wanting her husband Fettis to overhear discussion of the unsavory detail she was about to disclose. "Well, I don't think anybody really knew what his wishes were before he died last night, because Fettis as much as said he'd never heard talk of it before and I'm sure if Miss Helma had known, she'd have let it out before now."

"What?"

Elba Rae cupped both hands about the mouthpiece of her telephone. "They cremated the body."

"Oh, my word!"

"Miss Helma is awful upset."

"She didn't know?"

"Apparently not. Only that wife knew. And she'd never let on, not this whole time he's been sick. And now Miss Helma is beside herself. Cause she'll never get to see him again, you know. And I kind of feel sorry for her. He was her only brother and they hardly saw each other after he left Buford."

"Well, I can't much blame her for being upset," Ethel sympathized. "Bless her heart. And here she is with one foot in the grave and the other on a banana peel herself."

"I know it. It's right pitiful. That's why I felt like I needed to go. At least I can help Fettis with her and see they get down there and back in one piece."

"And they're just sending his ashes up here to bury?"

"That's right."

"Is that what they usually do with them?"

"Well, I don't know, Momma. I've never known anybody to be cremated."

"Don't they usually sprinkle them somewhere, or pour them out of a boat?"

"I guess you could. I don't really know."

"I read in a magazine at the beauty shop one time where one of those movie actors in California had died and in his papers he'd left instructions to be cremated and that they were to hire a plane and throw the ashes right out the door while they were flying over some mountains, and just let them blow where they might."

"Well, thank goodness all we have to do is go to the cemetery Saturday morning and bow our heads for a few minutes and be done with it. I sure don't want to be taking off in a plane with Miss Helma or trying to hang over the side of a boat somewhere with her. Can you imagine?"

"No, I can't. And I don't even want to think about it. You know there's just something not right about decimating the human body after you've passed, Elba Rae. I don't care if you are dead and it's just your fleshly home that the soul has left. It's disturbing to me."

"I know, Momma, being cremated isn't something pleasant to think about."

"Do you think it was that wife's idea? You think she talked him into it?"

"I don't know. Maybe it was something he decided all on his own."

"Well, do you think it was something he decided a long time ago, before he got down sick so bad he couldn't hold his head up nor think for himself anymore?"

"I don't know, Momma, and it doesn't much matter at this point. The arrangements have been made and they are what they are. And wherever they go to have it done … the cremating … they've already done it."

"Well, I hope it doesn't go giving you and Fettis any wild ideas."

"About being cremated? Oh, Momma, please."

"I mean it, Elba Rae. Lord willing, I'll have gone on long before either one of you and won't have to face it. But I'm like poor Helma, now. I just don't think I could ever stand the idea."

"Well, it's not something you've got to worry about because even if you outlive the both of us, we've got our plots out at Glory Hills side by side and I have no intention of being cremated and I'm certainly not spending my eternity laying there next to a pile of Fettis's ashes either."

"Good."

"So don't worry. We'll be back sometime Friday."

"How'd you get a substitute on such short notice?"

"Inez Young is coming."

"Inez Young. You know she can't do a thing with those children."

"I can't help it. It's the best we could do with no more time to plan than this."

"Well, I hope Fettis and Helma appreciate you for going, Elba Rae. Taking off from school, and losing pay."

"I do too, Momma, but even if they don't, I'll feel better knowing I went."

By Sunday, the benefit of hindsight would enlighten Elba Rae Van Oaks to know differently.

*   *   *   *

Stooks Willard had starred in what was one of the earliest scandals Elba Rae Van Oaks could remember to have taken place right there in Litton County—which is not to say there hadn't been scandals before Stooks Willard; it was just he was one of the first Elba Rae had been old enough to know about more or less as it unfolded as opposed to just hearing about later in some diluted and distorted versions as told by her mother Ethel Maywood or her aunt Ruby Burns. The fact that Stooks Willard was somewhat of a relative of Elba Rae's made her well beyond interested from purely a prurient standpoint and more of a witness almost. Stooks Willard was the only brother of Fettis Van Oaks's mother, Miss Helma, who worshiped the earth Stooks tread upon and never faltered in her defense of him, not during or even after the scandal. He was older than Miss Helma, and Elba Rae always got the impression he had looked out for her during a childhood fraught with unloving parents and too little money to provide necessities, much less comfort.

He'd left Litton County the morning after graduating high school and joined the Army, and Willard family legend had it the only tear he shed when he got on the train was when he hugged his little sister Helma good-bye; thereafter, until his return to Buford, the only inquiries he made about their folks were done so through the letters he addressed directly to her.

It was understandable, then, when Helma Van Oaks took his side during the scandal that was Stooks Willard's divorce from his first wife, Dorothy, even though, from all appearances obvious to Elba Rae, the two women had not previously been cross with one another that anyone knew. Dorothy Willard was a short little woman who wasn't known to assert herself or raise her voice or ever, in anyone's account, disagree publicly with anything to do about Stooks. She was unassuming and minded her business and kept a home for Stooks, who'd worked his way up at the Litton Power and Light Company after his discharge from the Army.

In a turn of events which proved first embarrassing and then downright devastating for poor, short, meek, and unassuming Dorothy, Stooks Willard had made the acquaintance of a young secretary at Litton Power and Light named Lola du Vasier, whose real name was Lola Duvazier but who, on her own and after having been exposed to conversational French in the eleventh grade, had taken to spelling it differently than any previous Duvaziers because it decidedly sounded more worldly, which Lola had desperately always yearned to be. Lola had most boldly sought out the companionship of Stooks Willard without regard for the existing Mrs. Willard, and by the time Dorothy had had enough and sought legal counsel who rightfully named Lola du Vasier as a co-respondent in the divorce suit, all of Buford and most of Litton County were aware to some degree of the illicit goings-on.

A year later, when Stooks Willard had been eased out of his job at the Power and Light and rendered basically homeless thanks to the shrewd barrister diminutive Dorothy had managed to engage as her representation, it was not so terribly surprising when he took off for Florida to join Lola du Vasier, who had since retreated there herself because she'd always wanted to live near the ocean and because she knew with unfailing clarity she was no longer welcome in Buford, but also because her sister Etta Jean did reside in her own mobile home there which had two bedrooms. Perhaps no one was more despondent over Stooks's departure than his sister, Helma; not even Dorothy who, as it turned out, owned her house free and clear as well as all rights to the pension benefit theretofore accrued by Stooks Willard at the Litton Power and Light Company. Helma Van Oaks vehemently blamed Miss Lola du Vasier for beckoning her brother out of state and vowed to never accept their union, turning down the invitation to their nuptials, acknowledging it only to immediate family, and not even sending a gift though Lola du Vasier was known to be registered, it being her first wedding and all.

On the rarified occasions which brought Stooks Willard back to Buford in the years following his affair and remarriage, the new Mrs. Willard did most certainly never accompany him, nor was she spoken of unless Stooks outright did the speaking himself. But even when he did, the conversation would be brief, as though mentioning Lola would somehow implicate the other party after the fact in the scandal. Over time, the invitations he extended to his sister Helma to visit them in Florida, done so in the strictest sense of politeness only since neither he nor Lola du Vasier ever expected her to accept, stopped altogether and Helma Van Oaks would never see the unit he and Lola at first rented and then eventually purchased two rows over from Lola's sister Etta Jean at the Shady Palms Mobile Home Community just outside the Panama City limits. That was, she would never see it until after Stooks was dead.

Elba Rae Van Oaks didn't doubt for a second there would be tensions when they arrived in Florida, unavoidable as they'd been brewing and festering and gone completely unpurged for all the years since Stooks and Dorothy had broken up and Stooks had run off to Panama City to take up permanently with that woman, who graduated to that wife, who—officially and forever, whether Miss Helma or Fettis or Dorothy or anybody else minded it or not—was now the widow. Elba Rae dreaded the trip like she'd not dreaded anything for a long time. Because besides the tensions, there was Miss Helma's condition to be mindful of, which was, by the morning they departed Buford, all one big aggravation of illness and grief and bitterness on top of the usual layer of what was her normal everyday disposition that was somewhat prone to unpleasantness.

Fettis Van Oaks went first that morning to fetch his mother at her house. Elba Rae had advised that would be best, since she likely would need special assistance, which did also serve the purpose of allowing Elba Rae just a few minutes of solitude longer in her own home with a cup of coffee to gather her thoughts. By the time Fettis arrived back with his cargo of Miss Helma, she knew her constitution was as strong as it was going to get. She carried her own suitcase to the driveway to meet them and save time, clutching under her arm a parcel of sorts.

"What've you got there, Elba Rae?" Helma Van Oaks inquired, before Fettis could even maneuver the car back onto Highway 29 and point it south. They were traveling in Helma's dark brown Plymouth Fury at Helma's insistence, because she was unconvinced any other vehicle could possibly offer comparable comfort.

"It's some chess squares Hazel made for us to take on the road. She brought them over last night."

"Well, wasn't that thoughtful of her?"

"And she said to tell you she and Aunt Ruby are thinking about you."

"She's a sweet girl, Elba Rae."

"Yes, she is."

"Chess?"

"I believe she said they're chess, yes, but to tell you the truth I haven't looked at them." She paused. "Did you want one?"

"Oh, lands no, not yet. But thank you."

"Well just let me know. I'll have them back here."

Her curiosity satisfied, Helma turned her attention to her son across the front seat from her. "Which way are you gonna take us, son?"

"South," was his reply.

"Well, I didn't figure we were gonna head north to get to Florida from here."

"We've got to hit 231 and then we'll head on through Troy and then down to Panama City. Now just try to relax. Are you comfortable? Did you bring a pillow?" Fettis looked in the mirror and made eye contact with his wife. "Elba Rae, did you pack a pillow?"

"I didn't really bring any kind of a pillow, Fettis, but if you—"

"I don't need a pillow, son." She turned around to face Elba Rae. "I don't need a pillow, Elba Rae."

"Well … okay then," said Elba Rae, who leaned back on the seat and took in a big deep breath, hoping Miss Helma wouldn't feel the need to navigate, knowing, as Elba Rae did, how Fettis resisted any suggestion of directions when he was behind the wheel. "I've been driving an awful damn long time, Elba Rae," he'd say to her whenever they rode together and she questioned his route, "and obviously I ain't lost myself yet cause here we are!" Fettis Van Oaks and his mother had a tendency to quibble when confined to close quarters for too long at a time and their sudden journey to Florida made conditions ripe.

As the morning sun warmed the car and the miles began to disappear behind them, Helma Van Oaks dozed on and off, sometimes fitfully but repeatedly. Elba Rae was glad and surmised it was, most likely, the residual effects of medication Miss Helma had already inventoried a couple of times in her purse since they'd left Buford. She'd told Fettis it was something the doctor had prescribed for her arthritis and when he inquired as to what the other two bottles were for she'd told him one was for her blood pressure, which she reminded all was just sky-high, and the other was for her cholesterol, a number equally as perilous. Elba Rae Van Oaks was no pharmacist but bet if she had half a chance to read the labels, she'd be able to put two and two together and know Miss Helma was taking medicines to ease her condition—the cancerous one. But it wasn't her place to say, of course, and if Miss Helma wanted to pack a trunk full of pills and swallow them six at a time, Elba Rae didn't care as long as it kept her mother-in-law quiet and diverted her attention from Fettis's driving so they could just get to Panama City and attend Uncle Stooks's service without a major calamity.

Helma roused briefly on the approach to Troy long enough to read aloud a billboard sign welcoming tour buses to the cafeteria located at the forthcoming intersection, noting with glee that a complimentary meal awaited the bus driver, whereupon Fettis Van Oaks clarified to her completely that the head count of the Plymouth under no stretch of the criteria constituted a tour nor would it be reasonable to expect he'd dine for free, and tour dining rules notwithstanding, he had already decreed some thirty minutes earlier that the Van Oaks family would be partaking of their meal at the Shoney's Big Boy which was definitely the intersection after the cafeteria. Helma Van Oaks muttered something to the effect of apparently having missed the announcement because she must have dropped off to sleep for a minute, and Elba Rae thought it was more like two hours but stayed out of it.

∗   ∗   ∗   ∗

Fettis Van Oaks had begun to scout Highway 98 for suitable lodging even before they arrived in Panama City proper. He had, in fact, already pointed out several prospects which were met with an objection by either Elba Rae or his mother Helma, with one in particular adamantly vetoed by both despite its promise of color TV and air conditioning in every room. Elba Rae knew he was probably weary from driving and just wanted to stop and be done with it, but she could not with reckless abandon forgo at least a minimal standard of cleanliness and safety whether they were on a funeral trip or not. Nonetheless, when he pulled into the Sandy Dreams Motor Court before even soliciting an opinion from either of the women, she didn't object. Miss Helma was looking peaked and Fettis was getting cranky and her own legs were in need of a stretch.

It had already been established by Miss Helma back at the Shoney's that they would check into their motel first for a period of repose in lieu of going directly to call at the residence of the late Stooks. Elba Rae suspected Miss Helma wanted to put off seeing Lola for as long as possible due to the likely awkwardness of their meeting.

They settled in adjoining rooms on the first floor of the two-story structure which looked older close up than it had from the road. Elba Rae's observation that the rooms smelled musty went more or less unacknowledged as Miss Helma declared she was going to lie down for a while. Meanwhile, in an unprecedented move, Fettis Van Oaks went back down to the office to inquire of the desk clerk if he knew exactly how to get to the Shady Palms Mobile Home Community, which the clerk did because he'd off and on gone with a fine woman from over there.

When it could not plausibly be deferred any longer, Helma Van Oaks walked into Fettis and Elba Rae's room through the connecting door and reasoned it was time they went on over to the house. There was, briefly, some discussion over whether they should—or were expected to—telephone Lola first to confirm their pending visit, with sensible points brought out supporting both sides, but Miss Helma had ultimately decided they would not after making note of the Sandy Dreams Motor Court's surcharges for locally placed phone calls which were strategically glued right onto the receiver.

"But you know," Helma Van Oaks fretted once they were in the car and motoring down Highway 98 again, "maybe we should have just gone on and called her to get the directions right. I'm not sure if I remember how she said to get there."

"I know how to get there," Fettis assured. And off they went.

After a twenty-minute drive during which they had decidedly been traveling away from water, Fettis turned the Fury into the entrance of the park, which was marked by two festively painted wagon wheels each adorned by strikingly lifelike replicas of flamingos, probably once pink but now somewhat lighter after years in the Florida sun. The desk clerk's instructions had been as precise as could be and Fettis intended to thank him before they checked out.

"Well, how do you know which one is theirs, Fettis? They all look alike in the dark," Helma observed.

"Because she told you the other night they lived on lot thirty-three."

"How do you know which lot is—"

"Because," he cut her off, "the number is painted on that big white rock in the yard. Everybody's got one. See?"

She peered out the car window and squinted. "Well, it's a good thing they do. I'd never find my way home if I lived in here. Especially at night." Elba Rae looked out her own window from the back seat but didn't particularly study the painted rocks so much as she gazed up at the stars and fantasized she was somewhere else.

"This is it." Fettis stopped the car in front of lot thirty-three, on which was anchored an orderly-looking home with the porch light turned on.

"This is it?" Helma asked.

"This is it," Fettis repeated.

"Oh, Lord …" Helma sank into the back of her seat.

"What's wrong? Are you feeling sick?"

She didn't answer at first. "Momma? Are you getting sick? Do you need to go back to the motel?"

"I'm sick, son, but it's in my heart." In the moonlight, Elba Rae could tell Miss Helma was bordering on tears. "When I think about what your uncle Stooks gave up …"

"That's water under the bridge now, Momma. We need to let it rest in peace. Like Uncle Stooks."

"A good job with a retirement … a brick house … a wife, such as she was. And for what?" She looked about their surroundings. "This? A little trailer down here in the middle of nowhere? Away from home and all his people?"

"Did you ever think he was where he wanted to be?" Fettis asked, without sounding overly argumentative. "I mean, didn't anybody hold a gun to his head and force him to run off down here with her."

From the backseat, Elba Rae piped up. "Fettis—"

"No, Elba Rae, now, really. Maybe it's time some things were said that should have been said a long time ago. The poor man is dead and he's not coming back, and no amount of dredging up his mistakes is gonna make a bit of difference at this point. We need to just let it go so we can mourn him proper."

"He was my only brother, Fettis! And I've missed him every day of my life since the minute he said he was leaving Buford," Miss Helma proclaimed.

"Then why didn't you ever come visit him? Huh? It's not like he didn't beg you enough times. Hell, I'd'a driven you down here if you'd ever wanted to come."

"Why are you talking to me like this in my worst hour? When I am just prostrate with grief and suffering?"

"Miss Helma, we—"

"You don't have to get in this, Elba Rae! Let Fettis say his peace if it makes him feel better to be hurtful to his momma!"

"I was just going to say," Elba Rae insisted, "I think we should get out of the car and go in now. Look."

Deep in the throes of their sensitive conversation, they had not noticed the open door of the trailer or that Lola du Vasier had stepped outside and was staring at them.

*   *   *   *

The trio emerged from the Fury and took slow, deliberate steps toward the front door, in single file, with Helma Van Oaks in the lead. Prostration of grief and suffering aside, Elba Rae did have a morbid curiosity of how the two women would get on, given the circumstances, but was relieved when Miss Helma simply extended her arms and gave her brother's wife an embrace. It was no loving embrace, mind you, and both women were noticeably stiff during the gesture, but it was an embrace nonetheless. "Come on in out of this night air, y'all," Lola du Vasier said, and only when they were all inside did she exchange greetings with Elba Rae and Fettis.

The trailer was small and narrower than Elba Rae imagined it would be, but appeared neatly kept and homey. It wasn't necessarily comparable to the home Stooks had lived in with Dorothy, which indeed was of brick construction as Miss Helma had specified before they exited the car, but it still had a certain ambience about it that made Elba Rae perhaps feel less sorry for Stooks Willard than she'd previously felt. About the walls and on the end tables were various framed photographs of the Willards together, as well as group shots with what were obviously a variety of friends from over the years. The kitchen was compact but clean.

Lola wasn't as tall as Elba Rae remembered, though she surely was bigger than Stooks's first wife little Dorothy. She'd obviously made an effort to try keeping up her appearance and her hair looked freshly dyed. Elba Rae didn't think the burnt orange tint was necessarily flattering for a woman seventy years old and could only imagine what was going through Miss Helma's mind. When she spoke, it was with a voice flavored by unfiltered cigarettes.

"Y'all must be hungry and I want you to fix a plate here in a minute," Lola du Vasier offered. "I've got more food in there than I can say grace over, what with Etta Jean and the neighbors and the people from the church. I don't know what I'm gonna do with all of it."

"Why don't you freeze some of it?" Miss Helma suggested.

"I guess I'll have to do that, Helma, because I'm running out of places to put it. I had to take a couple of things down to Etta Jean's trailer already as it is. Fettis, don't you want to go in there and fix a plate? I've got some casseroles in the oven and they ought to be heated through by now. Helma, let me get you a plate."

"I can get me a plate."

"Well, you look worn out. Was it a bad drive?"

"No, it wasn't that bad and my car rides real good. It's a Plymouth."

"Momma, you take it easy there and visit with Aunt Lola and I'll get you something." Fettis Van Oaks lifted himself from the sofa and took the several steps necessary to render him fully in the kitchen, and Elba Rae took his lead and went after him. The countertop was teeming with foil-covered dishes and plastic containers and before they'd had the chance to pry the paper plates apart, Lola du Vasier was opening the oven door and extracting the hot selections. She set them on the stove top and peeled away their aluminum covers.

"Here's some serving spoons for these, and the tea is yonder there in the pitcher," she said, motioning toward an orange plastic pitcher on the two-seat dinette table under the window. "The glasses are in that cabinet next to you, Fettis, and help yourself to the ice."

"Thank you," Elba Rae said. "It all looks delicious."

"Well, y'all dig in, now."

"Thank you, Aunt Lola." Elba Rae found it odd to hear the word. In all the years Uncle Stooks had lived in Florida, she had never heard Fettis refer to Stooks's wife as Aunt Lola and it was surreal to hear him address her as such then. Lola seemed to like it, though, Elba Rae surmised, because she broke the slightest of smiles before stepping back to the living room and joining Miss Helma where Elba Rae expected they'd get down to the business of discussing the particulars of the arrangements for Stooks.

"What's this?" Fettis whispered discreetly, as he stuck a big spoon in a browned casserole, the incision releasing a big puff of steam.

"Looks like a …" Elba Rae wasn't really sure. "Stir it up a little so I can see."

He obliged, and Elba Rae thought for a second she spied a chunk of fruit, although the exact species of which was not discernable. "It's some kind of casserole."

"Well, no kidding," Fettis replied, and then he elevated a spoon full of it slightly so they could better study the content. "Is that a pineapple?!"

"Shhhh!" Elba Rae said, as audibly as she could without rousing Lola or Miss Helma's attention. "It looks like pineapple, and that other big piece must be some chicken."

"What kind of mess is this?"

"Put it back and cover it up if you don't want any."

"Are you gonna have some?"

"No," Elba Rae said. "Cover it back up." They then turned their attention to another selection that—while easily recognizable as eggplant—baffled them both due to its pure simplicity. It was, in fact, just eggplant. Sliced, drizzled with an unidentifiable liquid, and baked into a crisp. "Give me a little spoon of that."

"It looks like plain old eggplant."

"I don't care," Elba Rae sighed, "I've got to have something."

"What kind of food *is* this?" Fettis sort of asked to himself. Elba Rae, meanwhile, was wondering the same as she looked about the tiny kitchen and took a more detailed inventory of the offerings. Nothing right off the bat impressed her as readily familiar at all. It was not that Elba Rae Van Oaks was unsophisticated or unopen to new culinary experiences, and just a few months earlier she'd even cut out the recipe from the *Ladies' Home Journal* for something called a Teriyaki which she distinctly recalled involved a can of pineapple rings. But she'd not yet planned the occasion to actually try it and whenever that might turn out to be, she knew, a death was no time to experiment with unproven or exotic creations. She considered that perhaps the unusual array of food was just a cultural phenomenon. They were, after all, far away from Buford; they were all the way into another state.

Then it struck Elba Rae she'd never really heard Fettis or Miss Helma clearly distinguish what denomination of church it was Lola du Vasier and Uncle Stooks had been attending all the years since leaving Buford. Elba Rae knew, of course, that Stooks had been a Methodist, but then that was before he'd been tempted by Lola du Vasier and before he'd gotten himself divorced from meek Dorothy and before he lost everything he owned and left Litton County for a life in the sun with Lola. By contrast, Lola du Vasier's religious affiliation was somewhat of a mystery as no one in any family Elba Rae knew of had ever associated with a Duvazier until, that was, Stooks associated all the way out of town with her—and there was just no telling what-all she might have lured him into since.

Elba Rae glanced around the kitchen one more time just to confirm her suspicions, and was eager to share the theory with Fettis but knew it would have to keep until they were safely enclosed back in their room at the Sandy Dreams Motor Court. And maybe by then she'd have actually nailed down the exact kind of church it was whose members would cook such fare for a death. Based upon what she'd observed so far, Elba Rae could most definitely and without question rule out Methodist, with Baptist and Presbyterian both doubtful. Even in Florida.

She and Fettis managed to procure enough samples to give the appearance of a full plate and avoid arousing suspicion. Miss Helma, thankfully, was apparently so generally overwhelmed by her grief and the fatigue brought on by her own illness and probably the overall awe of the fact she was, lo so many years later, actually sitting in Lola du Vasier's very parlor, that she nibbled at the food on her plate without so much as a query of what it was or who'd brought it. She and Lola had been talking about the order of events as it pertained to Stooks's service, as well, and that had kept her mind off what she was chewing.

The memorial service would be the following afternoon at two at the church, the full name of which Elba Rae had missed, probably while she was perusing a ham so stuffed with cloves it looked more like a beef roast. After that, there would be a reception in the family life hall (also at the church) and then it'd be over. There was not to be any additional formal gathering at the Willard home, making it evident Lola du Vasier might be as anxious to cut the unfortunate family reunion short as the rest of them were. She also made it perfectly understood to all, albeit tempered with a sympathetic tone, that she had no plans to travel to Buford for the interment of Stooks's ashes at the graveside service scheduled for Saturday. Elba Rae could tell Miss Helma disapproved.

"It's not that I wouldn't want to be there, Helma," Lola explained. "But there's no way I can make that trip up there and back by myself."

"Do you not drive anymore?" Helma Van Oaks was not pleased, even though she'd not relished the idea of sharing the front row of chairs at the grave with Stooks's second wife.

"I do around here, Helma. Just to get to the store and the doctors and wherever I have to go. Etta Jean and them usually carry me to church. But I wouldn't dream of starting out on the highway trying to get all the way to Buford and back on my own."

"Can't your sister bring you?"

"Oh, lands no, Helma. To be honest, I trust my own driving more than I would hers. But don't tell her that."

"Well, isn't there a bus that—"

"Momma, I think Aunt Lola's trying to tell you she's just not up to making the trip." Elba Rae was impressed at her husband's mediation. "We understand, Aunt Lola. After all, Uncle Stooks is gone and the place where we bury the body is just a symbol and … well … in his case, under the circumstances and all, he really is pretty much gone already."

"I knew having the grave there in Buford would be important to you, Helma," Lola consoled. "Stooks and I talked about it for a long time one day and we both always felt like Buford should be his final resting place. It was his home. But this …" she paused and pensively looked around the trailer's living room. "This was *our* home and I'll always have a part of him here, too."

Helma Van Oaks thought about it for a minute. "If you think that's the thing to do, I'll let anybody that asks know you're just not able to travel."

"It's best," Lola confirmed.

"Let's try some of that dessert, Fettis," Elba Rae interrupted, in a not-so-subtle attempt to defuse further tension. "What do you want?"

"Oh, please do, Elba Rae. Just help yourself." Lola du Vasier was back to playing hostess. "Helma, how about a piece of pie?"

"No, thank you," Helma Van Oaks said sternly.

"Well I believe I will," Elba Rae said as she stood up and repeated the four steps back into the kitchen, optimistic the dessert selections would be less confusing than the main course had been. Even in other sects, she hoped, surely a pie was just a pie.

Elba Rae observed an angel food cake and what appeared to be a strawberry pie, although it clearly had failed to set properly because the one hole where a slice had previously been removed and served had filled back in with red goo. There were some sugar cookies on a plate but, generic though they might have been, they looked dry. Toward the back of the table in between the sugar cookies and the orange tea pitcher was a plastic container with a tightly sealed but semi-transparent lid attempting to reveal what could have been a batch of brownies or a banana nut bread. Unimpressed by neither the angel food cake nor the seeping strawberry pie, Elba Rae decided to take her chances and go with the undetermined confection in the covered container. She was decidedly startled by Lola du Vasier's sharp voice directly behind her just as she was about to snap open the lid.

"Oh, no, hon, you don't want to open that one."

"What?" Elba Rae was suddenly flushed and embarrassed, as though she'd been caught taking something that didn't belong to her. "I was just seeing what it was."

Lola du Vasier put her hand on Elba Rae's shoulder. "That's Stooks."

*   *   *   *

"She looks tough," Helma Van Oaks declared before Fettis had the key fully inserted into the Plymouth's ignition switch and Elba Rae still had one leg hanging out the car door.

"I imagine she's tired," Fettis offered.

"She looks worse than tired. I believe she must not wear the first sign of anything on her head when she's out in the yard."

Elba Rae had managed to get herself fully contained within the Fury before Fettis began pulling away from lot thirty-three. "I did notice she must like to take the sun," Elba Rae said.

"But I can't figure," Miss Helma continued, "what she could be doing. There's not enough yard out here to spit over. It wouldn't hurt things for her to plant a flower or a bush, but that wouldn't keep her busy long. Reckon she's got room in the back for a garden?"

"Oh, I don't know, Momma, and I don't much care. Maybe she likes to go to the beach."

"The beach?!"

"Well, yeah, Momma, we are in Florida after all! There's an ocean out there in case you hadn't noticed!" Sometimes the fervor with which Fettis Van Oaks accelerated when he drove was directly proportionate to his mood, and Elba Rae could tell he'd had enough togetherness by the way he whizzed by the bedraggled flamingoes on their route back onto the main road.

"Well, if she can manage to drive herself out to the beach and blunder around all day, it looks like she could make an effort to go to her own husband's burying."

"The beach is just a little closer to her house than Buford is, Momma. And it's not like you wanted her to be there anyhow."

"Who said I didn't want her there?"

"You didn't have to say it out loud. I know you got no use for her."

"That's not the point. Stooks was her husband and you'd think she could get herself to the cemetery to see him buried. She just doesn't want to. He's dead and gone and she's through with him now. I guess she'll be too busy going to the beach to be bothered with her husband's funeral Saturday."

"The funeral is tomorrow, Momma. We won't be out at the cemetery ten minutes Saturday and it's a long way for her to drive just to—"

"You know, Miss Helma, she might not even go the beach at all. And not this time of year anyway. It's still right cool down here." Elba Rae Van Oaks said it with a most pleasant of tone while wondering if there was any branch of the Nobel Prize for which she might be eligible.

"Well, I don't know where she's been, but she needs to stay out of the sun. Her skin's gonna be ruined."

Elba Rae was grateful for the cloud between her and the moon that had come up as they sped down the highway because it hid the distress she wore on her own face. By the time Fettis returned the Fury back to the Sandy Dreams Motor Court, it appeared more populated than it had been when they'd left for Aunt Lola's and Elba Rae thought it odd people would wait until so long into the evening before securing their lodging. It was practically nine thirty and she observed the office to be nearly full of people as they drove by it on the way to park in front of their rooms. She sighed, and hoped the onslaught of new guests would not guarantee a noisy night, but then she knew it would be a while before she could get to sleep on any account, what with the news she had to share with Fettis, which she would do just as soon as they got Miss Helma settled and were sure she was out of earshot.

Elba Rae and Fettis said their goodnights to Miss Helma, three times as it were, since every time they'd bid her what they believed to be a final good evening, she seemed to remember just one more item she wanted to mention and would open the adjoining door and stick her head back through it, the final time with it fully engulfed in some type of sleeping device meant to salvage a hairdo but which Elba Rae found, due to the severity of the elastic, much more reminiscent of the complimentary shower cap found in each bathroom of the Sandy Dreams Motor Court.

"Yes, Momma, we've got a clock in here," Fettis had told her. And, "Yes, Momma, I've got the directions to get to the church," he'd reassured. And, "For God's sake, yes I locked my door—now go to bed," was his last piece of advice.

"Lock that door," Elba Rae snapped as she paced around the foot of their bed.

"The damn door's already locked, Elba Rae. Momma! Don't you start too!"

"I'm not talking about the outside door. I'm talking about the one to your momma's room. I don't want her popping in here unexpected."

"Well, I imagine she'll knock in the morning to make sure we're decent before she just barges in." Fettis was unbuttoning his shirt and paying no heed to his wife. Consequently, she promptly stomped over to the door and secured the latch herself.

"When did you get so modest, Elba Rae? It's not like we're gonna be tearing the sheets up in here tonight."

"Oh don't be vulgar. I've got to tell you something, and I don't want her to hear. And unless she's knocked out unconscious, I can't be sure she won't pitty-pat in here six more times to tell us to brush our teeth or make sure we've excused ourselves one more time before getting in bed."

"What's got you so fired up?"

"I just don't want your momma to hear. That's all. I found out some things tonight. About Uncle Stooks. And the … arrangements … and I think it would upset your momma to know."

"Is that what you and Aunt Lola had your heads together about for so long in the kitchen? When you were whispering so?"

"Yes! Did your momma hear us?"

"No, but she knew you were whispering about something. She didn't ask me what it was, but she could tell something was up. She gave me that look."

"Well, let's not tell her."

"What is it we're not gonna tell? Uncle Stooks is dead. She knows that. The service is tomorrow, we all know that. He was cremated and the ashes are on their way to Buford to be buried on Saturday, she already knows the whole story. What's to tell?"

"He's not on his way to Buford. At least not yet."

"He's not?"

"No." Elba Rae was clearly nervous about the situation and alternately peered toward the door to Miss Helma's room to be sure it was still closed, and toward the ceiling of their own room from whence a definite racket was originating. It sounded as though the travelers in the room directly above theirs were rearranging the furniture. In her state, it didn't occur to her that the occupants in the room above might not even be travelers at all, at least not the kind with license plates issued from another town.

"Well," Fettis pondered, as he systematically wadded his shirt into a ball and tossed it to the floor beside his luggage, "long as the funeral home down here gets the ashes to Buford before Saturday morning I don't guess it matters much. I mean, it's not like we're having any kind of visiting or anything up there."

"The funeral home down here's not sending them to Buford, Fettis."

He had been on the verge of extracting his belt, but stopped. "What do you mean they're not sending them to Buford? We're burying him there. We're having a graveside Saturday morning. Momma's got her heart set on it. And Aunt Lola said so herself—tonight. All that talk about how important it was to bury Uncle Stooks in Buford."

"What I mean is," Elba Rae was treading in uncharted waters, "we have to do it ourselves." Fettis Van Oaks sat down on the side of the bed and looked at his wife. He didn't have much of an expression, but Elba Rae knew he was puzzled.

"What do you mean we've got to do it ourselves?"

"Just what I said. Apparently, the funeral home doesn't take care of the ... of the ... shipping ... unless you ask them to special. That's what Aunt Lola was telling me in the kitchen. She said when the cremating was done, they just gave the ashes to her. In a box."

"Aunt Lola's already got Uncle Stooks's ashes?"

"Yes," Elba Rae said, and knew for a fact.

"In the house?"

"Yes."

"Well how do they get to Buford? For the burying?"

"We have to take them. Friday, when we leave."

"You're shittin' me!"

"Hush that talk, Fettis!"

"You mean we've got to put Uncle Stooks in the car with us? And drive him all the way back to Buford?"

"Unless you want to stop by the post office and mail him, we do."

"Oh, Lord." He stood back up and joined in the pacing. "You're right, Elba Rae. I'm glad Momma didn't hear any of this. It'd have just gotten her more stirred up than she already is and she's not real happy about this whole cremating thing to start with."

"That's why I didn't want her walking in on us."

"Well, unless she's got a hatchet over there, I think we're safe."

"It's not funny, Fettis."

"I'll say it's not. How are we gonna pack a box with Uncle Stooks in it and not let Momma see? Because I definitely don't want her to see. That would be too upsetting for her. I'd rather her just think the funeral home took care of the ... the shipping."

"I agree. We'll just have to figure out a way to be sort of sly about it, and get them in the car without her knowing. And then, after we get home, you can take him on over to the funeral home. That way, they can bring him out to the cemetery in the hearse like they're supposed to and your momma will never know any difference."

"When are we supposed to pick him up?"

"Well, that's some of what Lola and I were discussing in the kitchen, when I went to get some dessert. She doesn't want to make it any harder on your momma than it has to be, either, so she suggested you slip back over there tomorrow night—after Miss Helma's gone to bed—and get them."

"It's kind of giving me the willies, Elba Rae."

"Not as bad as I got them in that kitchen, I promise you."

"What are you talking about?"

She sat down on the edge of the bed and stared at the dark green TV screen which, free or not, wasn't even turned on. "Aunt Lola's only giving us half of him."

"What?!" Fettis screeched.

"For heaven's sake, don't wake up your momma!"

"What are you talking about, Elba Rae?"

"Do you remember what she said tonight? When she was going on about how Buford was Uncle Stooks's home, and how they'd talked about it, and how he'd wanted to be buried there?"

"Yeah, I heard all that but what—"

"And do you remember her saying something like this was his home too, and how she'd always have a part of him here?"

"Maybe, something like that, but—"

"Well, she's already got her part of him. In a box. Back in her bedroom."

"You're shittin' me!"

"Fettis Van Oaks, I told you I don't want to hear that word!"

"I don't care, Elba Rae! If there was ever a time in our lives to say 'shittin',' I'd say this was it, don't you think?"

"Being common and vulgar's not gonna help anything." About then, their conversation was disturbed by a solid thump from the room above. "What kind of place *is* this?"

Fettis walked over to the lone chair in the room, to the far side of the bed, and sat down in it to help him absorb the situation. "She divided him?!" He said it, but unconvincingly.

"She did. Poured half of him in a Tupperware bowl to give to us, and she kept the rest. And the worst part?"

"It gets worse?"

"She had him right out there on the kitchen table, next to that sorry strawberry pie."

"No ..." Fettis was in an official state of disbelief.

"If she hadn't come up behind me when she did, I'd have opened the lid and stuck my hand right in there and grabbed a handful." She shook her head gently from side to side. "Banana nut bread indeed."

Elba Rae walked with deliberately soft steps to Miss Helma's door and put an ear to it.

"She can't hear us through the walls," Fettis said.

"I don't want to take any chances."

"She's the cool one, Elba Rae."

"Who? Your aunt Lola?"

"She's not my aunt."

"Whatever."

"Having us over ... sending us in there to fix a plate ... and all the while my uncle Stooks is laid out on the kitchen table next to the cobbler."

"It was a strawberry pie, I think, but I can't even be sure it was that because—"

"Oh hell, it don't matter what kind of pie it was, Elba Rae. The point is my momma could have seen that—it—him, and she's like to've never gotten over it, especially with her not even well herself."

"I know it."

"That's why we've got to be extra careful with him on the way home." He stood up and had a mild look of relief on his face. "We'll put him in the back seat with you. And Momma will never know."

Elba Rae said, "Well … okay," because, after all, what else could she?

$$* \qquad * \qquad * \qquad *$$

Elba Rae Van Oaks slept poorly that night at the Sandy Dreams Motor Court and she could tell her husband Fettis did too, his tossing about uncommon for a man who usually slumbered so soundly she routinely checked for a pulse several times a week. The bed was strange and it was uncomfortable and the thing inside the case that passed for a pillow by Sandy Dreams's standards was featherless and flat and worn out. And it seemed every time she managed to doze enough to get a dream going it would have her in the midst of some bizarre setting with mostly strangers except for Lola du Vasier and Uncle Stooks who kept telling Elba Rae he didn't want to get in the car with her, whereupon Elba Rae would look everywhere for Fettis to lend assistance but he was nowhere to be found. It was such a relief when the apparent passion coming from the room above woke her from the worrisome dream she didn't even fret over the circumstances, those mainly being she and her husband Fettis were in bed only one floor underneath active fornication that, were she to allow her mind to go there, probably wasn't even between man and wife. Elba Rae missed Buford and was homesick for it.

Just after dawn, she fell asleep after ascertaining Fettis was, in fact, breathing, after he'd ceased his tossing and become eerily still on the other side of the bed. Their collective peace was terminated by the familiar sound of tapping on the adjoining door.

"Are y'all up?"

Elba Rae heard Miss Helma, but didn't readily answer.

"Fettis?" Helma persisted, from the other side of the door.

Elba Rae glanced at Fettis, whose eyes were still closed. "Fettis, your momma's calling."

"Huh …" he mumbled, but didn't open them.

"Your momma's calling."

"I don't hear her. Go back to sleep."

And then it got louder. "Fettis. Elba Rae," followed by three more taps, stronger than the first ones. "Are y'all up in there?"

"You hear her now?" Elba Rae said, pulling the cover to her chin and rolling over in the bed and adding as she did, "This is the worst pillow I've ever seen in my life. The goose must have just flown over it and shook."

"Fettis! Are y'all up or not?"

"No, damn it, Momma, we're not up!"

"Well what are y'all doing in there? It's nearly seven. Don't you think we should be getting some breakfast?"

"Lord, give me strength," Fettis said softly, more awake by then and not wanting to lay into his mother so early in the day. "Give us a minute!" He hollered out and then looked over at his wife. "Rise and shine."

Elba Rae did not want to rise and knew it would be particularly difficult that day to shine, considering the agenda before them. There was a funeral to attend with a dying woman who despised the deceased's wife and there would be the whole business of covering for Fettis that evening should, by any stroke of misfortune, Miss Helma discover the Fury gone when Fettis went on his covert errand to collect their half of Uncle Stooks. In the midst of it all, she wondered what Inez Young would be teaching her pupils and how behind she'd be when she got back the next week.

By seven thirty, the trio was seated at Eddie's World of Pancakes a short drive from the Sandy Dreams. The sign on the highway which had beckoned them promised more varieties of pancakes than one could eat in a week, while also making motorists fully aware Eddie did not take checks. Elba Rae was weary from lack of sleep and knew Fettis must have been too; neither of them was very hungry, nor were they in the mood for the perky waitress named Bonnie who was vigorously attacking a piece of chewing gum while she talked. Miss Helma, on the other hand, appeared to be benefitting from a restful evening and was more than willing to engage the cheerful Bonnie in conversation while she proceeded to order a short stack of strawberry pancakes with the side of link sausage. The thought of a strawberry made Elba Rae quiver and relieved her of whatever appetite she might have been able to conjure. She ordered coffee and some toast, just so she wouldn't have to answer any questions from Miss Helma.

No sooner had they returned from their breakfast outing, the one upon which Miss Helma had been so eager to embark, when Helma retreated to her own room deciding she was feeling a little tired and thought she'd better lie down for a spell, which Elba Rae took as somewhat of a code for meaning she needed to get to her pill stash and commence swallowing. Elba Rae and Fettis alternately made use of the free TV and dozed, achieving both without much effort simultaneously, knowing Miss Helma would give them the tap signal when it was time to meet the next item on her schedule.

The service for Stooks Willard began promptly at two at the Church of Holiness Praise, a name meaningless to Elba Rae in an aggravating sort of way because it offered no more clues as to its denomination than had its members' odd way of expressing condolence. The sanctuary was small and the pews weren't very long, so Elba Rae and Fettis took their seats in the second row and let Miss Helma sit in the front with Lola du Vasier, Lola's sister Etta Jean, and a man introduced to them as Etta Jean's friend, T. W., which immediately suggested to Elba Rae a connotation she didn't want to think about in church—not even one without a sanctioned affiliation.

When the service concluded, at the part where the minister would have been directing the congregation to the cemetery were they back in Buford at a normal funeral, he instead thanked them for coming on behalf of Lola du Vasier and the Willard family and invited them to the Family Life Center where there was some brief mingling but no refreshments. Lola du Vasier and Miss Helma bid one another a cordial and likely forever final good-bye, and then it was over. For as much as Miss Helma knew, anyway.

Fettis and Elba Rae had both taken to putting their ears to the wall that night at the Sandy Dreams to determine the degree to which Helma Van Oaks was still stirring. Elba Rae had no doubt Miss Helma was packing some type of rest medicine to ease her sleeping, and Elba Rae knew Fettis knew, but she was too concentrated on the mission to procure Uncle Stooks to distract Fettis by opening a discussion of his mother's failing health. Maybe when they got back to Buford, she thought, but at that moment, they just wanted to know Miss Helma was down for the night. When they were reasonably sure, Fettis quietly slipped out of their room and into the Fury and disappeared down the highway.

Elba Rae tried to get interested in the TV program she found but, among their lodging's other shortcomings, the reception just wasn't that good on the set. Each time she heard the motor of a nearby car engine she hoped it was Fettis, and was relieved when finally she heard his key in the lock. He walked in and took his jacket off without saying a word.

"Did you get him?" Elba Rae asked.

"Yeah. I got him."

"Did she say anything to you?"

"Lola? No, not much. Just said 'Bye' and something like, 'Take care of your momma, she don't look too good,' something like that."

"Well, where is he?"

"I left him in the car. Where do you think he is? I wasn't gonna bring him in here and set him up on the dresser with us all night."

"Did you cover him up?"

"No. He's in the floor. In the backseat."

"Well, you better cover him up." He pondered her suggestion briefly.

"Yeah … I guess you're right. We got to get through this without Momma getting all hysterical on us," he said and went into the bathroom, returning quickly with a Sandy Dreams Motor Court hand towel.

"What are you gonna do with that?" Elba Rae seemed disturbed.

"I'm gonna take it out to the car and put it over the container."

"You can't use that!"

"Why not?"

"Because it's stealing!"

"Oh for God's sake, Elba Rae, I got bigger worries on my mind than taking one lousy old rag from this dump. They'll never miss it. And besides, people do it all the time. They darn near expect it, and I bet we're paying for new ones in the rates they're charging us anyway."

"That still doesn't make it right."

"Well, when we get home, you can mail it on back to them with a sweet note about how it got in your suitcase by mistake. How's about that?" And out he went. She heard the car door open and momentarily close back, and when Fettis came back in the room for that second time, they more or less didn't talk about it—or anything else—anymore that night. They were both exhausted and even slept a little better because of it.

Elba Rae awoke first the next morning and got herself ready before Miss Helma even had opportunity to start her knocking and when she did, Elba Rae's first thought was how forward she was looking to being in her own house and in her own bed by day's end, away from the Sandy Dreams Motor Court and away from Florida and away from her mother-in-law Helma Van Oaks, and so relieved was she to have the worst part of the trip over with that she ordered the tall stack of hot cakes and the country ham on the side and ate most all of it when they stopped by on the way out of town for day two at Eddie's World of Pancakes. Miss Helma even seemed to be in better spirits, the weight and the anticipation of encountering Lola du Vasier behind her. Bonnie told them to have a safe trip and hurry back but Elba Rae Van Oaks was certainly in no hurry to comply with the latter.

*   *   *   *

"Yes, Momma, we made it in just fine. About thirty minutes or so ago," Elba Rae Van Oaks said into the telephone.

"Well how did Helma hold out?"

"She did okay, I guess, under the circumstances. She slept a lot in the car on the way home today but that suited me just fine. Fettis too, I expect."

"They didn't get into it bad, did they?"

"Well … Miss Helma had a little fit the other night when we first got to Lola and Stooks's trailer. Going on about the past and Stooks running off with Lola and how he was her only brother and all such as that. Fettis just doesn't have much patience with her when she starts that."

"I imagine it would take a lot to live with her, Elba Rae. I'm sure she had a dog's life with Fettis's daddy, but she's never been any picnic either."

"I'm just glad it's over. Fettis has gone to take her home—oh, I think that's him pulling up now. I've got to get my supper started, Momma."

"Well, tell Fettis we'll see y'all tomorrow at the cemetery."

"All right, Momma," and the conversation ended. Elba Rae wanted to tell her mother Ethel Maywood the truth, but knew for the interests of all concerned it would behoove her to keep the details of their return trip a secret. But maybe later, Elba Rae thought. After Miss Helma was gone. Bless her heart.

When Fettis had stopped at the house to drop Elba Rae off and to remove their luggage, Helma Van Oaks had not left her perch in the Fury, which had made it fairly uncomplicated for Fettis to extract the towel-wrapped parcel from the floor of the back seat and slide it indiscriminately right into the back seat of Elba Rae's Galaxie without detection. They had already decided Fettis would go first thing the next morning to the Buford Memorial Funeral Home and deliver the partial remains of Stooks Willard for his local interment.

Elba Rae Van Oaks fried a chicken that night which she and Fettis consumed with a pleasure missing from their meals of the several days prior. It would be a long time before either of them would hunger for hot cakes, and Elba Rae was still disturbed by the misuse of an eggplant she'd witnessed in Florida. They were glad to be home and when Elba Rae's head hit her pillow that evening, she appreciated its fluffiness as perhaps she'd not fully done before.

*   *   *   *

The February sky was overcast on Saturday morning in Buford and Elba Rae Van Oaks decided it was appropriate weather for a burial, because it was a somber occasion after all, even if it was just a graveside service and even if they were only burying half of Uncle Stooks—and that is to say if anyone could even be certain Lola du Vasier had especially divided him into equal portions. Elba Rae didn't want particularly to think ill of Lola du Vasier, but in the bigger scheme of things, she was dubious Lola had taken the care to be precise in her allotment for them unless perhaps she'd used a measuring cup and Elba Rae did consider the real possibility they might have taken possession of no more than a third of Stooks Willard, if that. Fettis had taken out right after breakfast and Elba Rae was anxiously relieved when he returned.

"Who did you talk to? Was Charles Robert there?" Charles Robert Tully was the director at the Buford Memorial Funeral Home and had grown up in the business under the careful tutelage of his father, also Charles Robert Tully who went by Charles whereas Charles Robert Tully the younger went by Charles Robert so no one was ever confused about which Tully was which. Charles Robert had been pretty much running the place on his own since his father Charles had retired, although Charles Senior did occasionally drop by the visitations, even when the deceased wasn't necessarily a relative or close friend. Charles Robert knew it was mainly to check up on him to ensure that the standards set forth by Charles Senior's father, Charles Victor, were still being upheld. After such a long history, most inhabitants of Litton County knew the only way Charles Tully Senior would truly retire would be the day he became a customer of the business itself.

"Charles Robert wasn't there. One of those Dickerson boys was. Dick or Denny or one of them."

"Well, let's see. There were three of those Dickerson boys."

"This was the tall one."

"They were all big boys. I believe Dennis is the one Momma told me was working up there with Charles Robert."

"Then that's who I saw."

"Oh, I hate to hear that. I always feel better when I know Charles Robert is overseeing the arrangements himself."

"Well, there's not much to it. He told me they dug the hole yesterday, they got the tent up, and they'll put the chairs out this morning. Main thing is they're going to bring Uncle Stooks out there in the hearse so Momma doesn't know he rode all the way home with us in the backseat. What we got of him that is."

"Fettis …"

"What?"

"I just thought of that."

"Of what?"

"What Lola put him in. That container. Did you have to buy something? An urn, or some kind of box?"

"Hell, no! I wasn't buying no damn urn! I mean, enough is enough! This whole thing's somehow been all on me since the minute Uncle Stooks died. I took Momma down there, I sat up in that woman's living room and ate her nasty food, and I skulked out in the night to go get a box of ashes. Think about it, Elba Rae! Haven't I done enough? Do I have to pay for something to bury him in too?"

"Well, you can't just leave him in a plastic bowl! It's not right! And it's tacky besides!"

"They're not leaving him in a damn plastic bowl, Elba Rae! Calm down!"

"Don't holler at me, Fettis Van Oaks, I am just as sick of this as you are!"

"I'm not hollering!"

"You are too hollering!"

"Well if I am, it's because I am worn out with this! And besides, they're not gonna bring him out there in the stupid bowl! Give me credit for having just a teaspoon of sense, will you?"

"Then what are they going to do with him?"

"He's wrapped up in the towel."

"He's *what*?!"

"The towel, remember? The one you didn't think we should bring?"

"Yes, for heaven's sake, I was there too, remember?"

"Well, when I got over there, I wrapped him up real good in the towel before I took him in. And when I let that Dickerson boy know I had no intention of springing for any of their overpriced boxes, he said that wouldn't be any problem at all. He went back to the flower room or some place and he came back with a nice big piece of ribbon. Black. And he tied up a right pretty knot around the towel so it looks real proper and it'll keep it covered."

"I don't believe you, Fettis Van Oaks."

"Well, if you knew how much those grave diggers wanted for a plain old wooden box, you'd change your tune, let me tell you. And hell—it's not like

Uncle Stooks was even going to take up a whole one. It would have been highway robbery, is what it would have been."

"I don't care. It still sounds tacky."

"It'll be fine. He was real careful about how he made up the ribbon, so the part of the towel with the motel name on it doesn't even show."

"Well thank goodness one of you was trying to be tasteful."

"Oh ... give me strength, Lord ..." Fettis Van Oaks mumbled to himself, as he walked away from his wife and back toward their bedroom.

As was usually the case, Helma Van Oaks had insisted on being motored to the cemetery in the Fury so Elba Rae and Fettis left the Galaxie at Miss Helma's and made their way to the small graveyard in the old part of Buford. It was mostly filled up by the time Stooks Willard died and if you didn't already have your plot there or know some family members who did, it was likely you'd be relegated to the newer but bigger Glory Hills Cemetery which was outside of Buford proper.

By the time they arrived, the Buford Memorial Funeral Home hearse was already in position on the narrow road that meandered through the grave sites. There were a few cars pulled over to the side as best they could which barely allowed Fettis room to ease by and park the Fury in its rightful place behind the hearse. Elba Rae thought she'd spied the tall Dickerson Dennis at the wheel of the hearse and was glad when Charles Robert Tully emerged from the other side and approached the Fury. Fettis rolled the window down.

"How y'all doing?"

"Hey Charles Robert," Fettis replied.

"How you doing, Ms. Van Oaks?" He said to Miss Helma.

"I'm doing okay, Charles Robert."

"I'm real sorry for your loss," he said.

"Thank you."

"I knew Mr. Stooks. Way back when. Fine man ... fine man."

"Yes, he was," Helma Van Oaks agreed.

"Whenever y'all are ready, my associate will carry Mr. Stooks's remains over to the grave and then you will follow and take your seats in the front row." Fettis looked across the seat at his mother and noticed her fading pallor and how thin she suddenly seemed, and if only for the first time that week, he felt sympathy for her.

"Are you ready, Momma?"

"Yes, son."

Charles Robert Tully looked toward the back of the hearse and gave a nod to Dennis Dickerson who was standing by with his hand on the door handle. Elba Rae imagined it was a look they gave one another many times over in the course of a month while the rest of Litton County went about their lives unaffected. Tall Dennis opened the door and extracted the terrycloth-covered container and in the light of day, the ribbon didn't look all that bad, Elba Rae observed, although she had no intention of retracting her earlier disdain for Fettis's frugal decision or complete absence of decorum.

"Is that it?" Helma Van Oaks asked, looking at Fettis and then back at Dennis Dickerson and the white towel with the black ribbon tied around it.

"Uh ... yeah, Momma."

"Well what kind of thing did she send him up here in?"

"Huh?"

"What kind of box is he in?"

"I don't know, Momma. Must be something they use for ashes. I just don't know."

"I've never seen anything like that in my life. What's that white thing it's wrapped in? And is that a bow tied around it?"

"Uh ... looks like it might be, yes."

Elba Rae sat motionlessly in the back seat and could feel herself possibly becoming faint.

"I should have known not to trust that woman!" For all the deterioration one could have observed in the physical condition of Helma Van Oaks by that February, it was obvious her dislike of Lola du Vasier was going to be one of the last senses to fade.

"What do you mean, Momma?"

"I shouldn't have just taken her word for it that the arrangements were being made. I should have gotten in there myself the first day in Panama City and found out what she'd done. I know I could have ordered up something that looked better than this!"

"It'll be all right, Momma. Now try not to get worked up. We need to be spending this time saying our final good-byes to Uncle Stooks."

"He looks like a birthday present, all wrapped up with a bow. Oh–h–h–h," she let out a semi-wail and leaned her head against the car window.

"Momma, we've got to get out. Try to get yourself together."

"Those Duvaziers were always low class, Fettis. Every one of them. Still are. Lola down there in that old trailer in the middle of nowhere ... that fat sister of hers laying up with a man she's not even married to ... it looks like she could have let my brother have one day of dignity at the end of his life. He had to die to get back home as it is. Why did she let them tie him up in a sheet?"

"Well I don't really think it's a sheet, Miss Helma," Elba Rae injected, "it looks more like some kind of soft cloth. It's probably something they use when the loved one's been cremated. She probably didn't mean any harm when she picked it."

Even though Fettis was surprised by his wife's attempt at disarming the situation, he knew there would be no convincing his mother that Lola Duvazier who became Lola du Vasier had made a suitable selection of burial containers for the late Stooks, all the more worrisome of course since for once, Lola du Vasier wasn't the culprit. But inasmuch as neither Fettis nor Elba Rae surmised Helma Van Oaks would be speaking to Lola du Vasier ever again, they felt generally secure in letting the assumption go unchallenged. They were both in too deep to start talking by then anyhow.

"Oh, Stooks, forgive me for leaving you down there," Helma Van Oaks declared, as she practically kicked the car door open and rolled herself out.

∗   ∗   ∗   ∗

With little more commotion and even less spoken about the unsatisfactory arrangements attributed to Lola du Vasier, Fettis and Elba Rae managed to get Miss Helma away from the cemetery and back to her house after the brief service. A few assorted distant relatives and friends had dropped in, and Elba Rae's mother Ethel Maywood did also pay a visit to the house, accompanied by Elba Rae's aunt Ruby Burns and her cousin Hazel.

"Are you all right, Elba Rae?" Hazel asked while standing in Miss Helma's living room eating a chicken leg off a plastic plate.

"Oh, yeah, I'm okay."

"Well, you sure looked like you were worried about something out there at the cemetery."

"Me? Just tired, I guess. It was a long few days down there and back, Hazel, and someday …"

"Someday what?"

"Well, someday I'll tell you about it. After things are settled down a little bit, you know. And when we're not here, if you know what I mean."

"I see," Hazel Burns nodded, and knew that meant there was a forthcoming tale which would more than likely be worth the wait. "Miss Helma seems like she's holding up."

"Yeah, she's the pistol all right. She can still get up and go when she sets her mind to it."

"How is her health, Elba Rae?" Elba Rae did not answer right away because she knew the subject of Helma Van Oaks's condition mandated delicacy, making her exact choice of words all the more important, although she ultimately decided a few suggestive hints might be all right as long as the volume at which they were spoken was sufficiently muffled.

"She's not well, Hazel."

"I didn't think she was. Aunt Ethel came over and had supper with Momma the other night while y'all were gone and she told Momma she just didn't think Miss Helma was too well."

"She's not," Elba Rae repeated, but softly.

"And of all the times for this," surveying the room and the sparse gathering, "when she's already poorly herself."

Elba Rae leaned in closer to her cousin Hazel Burns. "Believe me, Hazel. We could have all done without this past week."

"That was an unusual-looking container they picked out for the burial," said Hazel.

"Did you think so?"

"Momma said in the car on the way over here from the cemetery she imagined it was something Stooks's wife had got up."

"Yeah," Elba Rae said. "It was."

* * * *

On Sunday mornings, Fettis Van Oaks did not customarily attend worship services at the First Avenue United Methodist Church with his wife, Elba Rae, on account of the back injury he'd sustained which did on occasion also travel into his neck if he sat just the wrong way, which a pew most usually threatened to be. Rather, he absorbed the quiet as he was accustomed to doing and knew upon her return he'd be the audience for Elba Rae's recital of the most recent news and announcements for which, he'd never let on to her, he had decidedly less of a hunger for than she.

Elba Rae Van Oaks, as it was, seemed in an unusually cheerful mood that morning even though the skies were still overcast and the wind was in the north. They were just both glad to be home, Fettis knew, with the trip and the funeral over. She'd hollered down the hall something akin to "I'm gone," and he'd distinctly heard the carport door close presumably behind her. It was nine forty-five and she wouldn't be back until nigh on twelve thirty. Fettis had just made his final selection of periodical for what was to be a peaceful stay in the lavatory when he heard Elba Rae scream out.

*   *   *   *

They stood in the kitchen at opposite ends of the harvest table, each staring at the object in the center. Neither's eyes dared to leave it, as though unattended it would cease to be inanimate and take on an unnatural power. It was so quiet Elba Rae could hear the hum of the electric clock which hung on the wall above the chair Fettis usually sat it but at which he then stood.

"Fettis, how could you?" Fettis continued his watch and seemed to ignore her all together. "Fettis!"

"What, damn it? I hear you!"

"How could you do this?!"

As Fettis Van Oaks had shuffled through the *National Geographic* and then the *Field and Stream* before finally settling as he mostly did on the *Look*, Elba Rae had indeed projected down the hallway that she was leaving when, in fact, she'd decided to delay her departure briefly after considering she should find alternative storage for whatever remained of the chess squares Hazel Burns had thoughtfully baked so as to wash up and return the dish to her after preaching was over. In the flurry of activities since they'd gotten home, she'd not even thought to get them out of the Galaxie where Fettis had so quickly dashed them a couple of days before.

Elba Rae knew, of course, as soon as she opened the back door of her car and looked down at the floor. She knew she was not looking at Hazel Burns's chess square parcel at all because she recognized instantly the distinctive Tupperware bowl belonging to Lola du Vasier. And as she and Fettis looked at it together on the kitchen table, the horror of the mistake had begun to settle over her like a pall.

"How could you not look at what you were picking up?"

Fettis shook his head slowly from side to side. "I didn't want to look at it! I just wanted to get it out of your car and into my truck and over to Charles Robert Tully before anybody saw!"

"Well, who was going to see you in our carport, Fettis? Who was out there that you couldn't take one second to look at what you were picking up?"

"It had the towel over it! I didn't unwrap him first, I just picked it up towel and all! How was I supposed to know he was on the bottom under the damn cookies?!"

"Because you're the one that picked him up the other night, remember? And you're the one that took the towel out there so your momma wouldn't spy it in the car! So she wouldn't get herself in another hissy fit when she found out we had to ride Uncle Stooks up here in the back of the car like a box of … of … of chess squares! Do you remember any of that?!" Fettis sat down in the chair under the humming clock and put his face in his hands. "We'll just have to call Charles Robert," Elba Rae continued "and tell him what's happened. Maybe he can switch them without anybody else ever needing to know."

"No," he said.

"No? Fettis, we've got to fix this!"

"Go to church."

"What?"

"Go. Now. Tell your cousin you forgot her damn bowl or tell her you left it in the motel or don't tell her nothing at all—I don't care. Just go."

Elba Rae picked up her pocketbook from the counter by the stove and pulled the scarf she'd had on back out, tying it quickly under her chin. She was far too distraught by then to concentrate on a Sunday School lesson, much less a long-winded sermon, but was eager to flee the kitchen and its completely unacceptable situation nonetheless.

Hazel Burns did not particularly ask about her container that day at church but so as to finalize whatever loose ends she could, Elba Rae did take Fettis's suggestion and relayed to Hazel with regret how they'd checked out of the Sandy Dreams Motor Court sans the chess squares which they'd all so enjoyed. Hazel Burns joked that maybe a maid somewhere in Florida was savoring her efforts and then wondered why Elba Rae didn't even see fit to smile, never considering her delicious chess squares had been wrapped in a hand towel and tied up in a bow with care and delivered with reverence to the cemetery by Charles Robert Tully and the Dickerson boy where they were now interred and awaiting a permanent marker.

Elba Rae drove the Galaxie extra slow when she pulled back into the carport that Sunday after church and entered the house with similar trepidation. Fettis Van Oaks sat before the TV in the den, his lounge chair partially reclined with the foot rest outstretched. Some type of sporting event was being broadcast but Elba Rae didn't really think he was studying it too closely.

"It's done," he said to her, without taking his eyes off the TV or adjusting the position of his chair.

"Did you call Charles Robert?"

"No. I took care of it myself."

Elba Rae sat down on the couch and put her pocketbook in her lap. The scarf was still tied to her head when Fettis got through extolling his solution.

"Oh, Fettis, no ..." she said.

*   *   *   *

Helma Van Oaks grew weaker and weaker in the days after Stooks's death and by late April she could no longer stay by herself. The family took turns attending her at home as best they could and for as long as was medically merciful with the help of Dr. Bud's frequent visits, and she lasted another full three weeks after finally being taken to Litton County Memorial Hospital, not acknowledging to even a nurse that her time on earth was concluding.

Miss Helma went to her grave without ever learning of the unspoken travesty which had transpired on the day everybody thought her brother Stooks was laid to rest. And true to the pact they made with each other, Fettis and then eventually Elba Rae were able to go to their own without anyone else ever knowing either, although most people who happened down Highway 29 in the springs that followed would always marvel at the hardiness and the vivid color of the crocus Elba Rae Van Oaks could raise in her flower bed out by the mailbox, even if the buttercups were usually late to bloom.

ON THE WAY TO GLORY

Elba Rae Van Oaks did not like snakes. She wasn't particularly prejudiced against any certain species because she hated all of them equally and without favoritism. No one had ever known why she was so adamantly opposed to their presence on earth, whether it was mortal fear or a distrust born of the serpent in the scripture as found in Genesis, but whenever anyone heard Elba Rae Van Oaks tell a story that began with a snake sighting, the listener could generally bet his week's pay there would be a reptile missing his head before it was over. She'd never been bitten or threatened by one to any degree beyond its mere act of trespassing in her path, yet she'd never encountered one she wanted to let live all the same.

By Labor Day weekend in 1988 the heat had taken its toll on the grass and the trees, even the mature ones surrounding Elba Rae Van Oaks's house out on Highway 29. It didn't feel much like fall even though the Halloween costumes were already stacked on the shelf at the entrance of the new dollar store on the Square, where Elba Rae had ventured on a Saturday to pick up a few staples like some washing powders and a pair of pantyhose, as well as a couple of less critical things like a box of Little Debbie Swiss Rolls and a copy of her new favorite weekly newspaper which she'd folded up quickly and stuffed directly into her purse as soon as the checker had rung it up, even though anyone halfway looking would still have been able to see the big "Brave Last Days" headline proclaiming the impending demise of a famous Hollywood star whose ill-mannered habits had finally come to claim their baggage. The air conditioning was cold in the LTD and right before Elba Rae turned off the road and into her driveway, she'd smiled to herself when she thought about her dear late mother, Ethel, and how chilly she used to get whenever she rode with Elba Rae. By then she mostly did smile when she thought of the dear late Ethel Maywood. Time had seen to it.

The grin lingered unconsciously as she eased the golden Ford toward its place in the carport. Until, that was, she spied the thing curled and coiled on the steps just below the kitchen door. Instinctively, she pounded the brake propelling the sack with the Little Debbies into the floor board. She stared at it for a minute first, to be certain she was indeed seeing what she thought she was seeing, and once confirmed, reckoned the concrete steps under the shade of her carport must be especially cooling to the underbelly of a snake on a hot afternoon. But she would kill it, nonetheless.

She reversed the car and backed several feet out of the carport, turned off the motor, and eased open the door, verifying after each motion the creature who'd dared invade the sanctity of her property hadn't attempted retreat. She moved with such a combination of stealth and grace the gravel didn't dare crunch under her weight. She didn't take her eyes off the steps until she'd gotten around the side of the carport and headed out back behind the house where she kept what remained of Fettis's tools. Out of the snake's view, her grace broke into a rather awkward gait as she ran toward the door of the old shed, in as much as Elba Rae Oaks could still run in her sixty-fifth year.

At first she had trouble finding the hoe which historically was her weapon of choice when it came to snake decapitation but wasn't panicked just yet since she knew the shovel would get the job done if time were of the essence. Fettis had never had the old shed wired for electricity even though he talked about it for years and Elba Rae cursed him a little that afternoon because she surely needed a good burning light bulb in there sometimes. All the years he'd puttered around and wasted hours in Jack Moss's hardware store and not to mention the generous amount of time he'd donated to practically remodel the Simpson place before Elba Rae put her foot down but no, never had he found a day to wire up their old piece of shed. She had her fingers touching the handle of the shovel when she spied the hoe hanging on a nail from its blade. She snatched it off and loped back toward the carport, cognizant enough of her approach to slow down before startling her prey.

She tiptoed to the door step where the unsuspecting creature waited, as if in a welcoming capacity. It did not move; it did not raise its head. It lay there, coiled and practically posed, so that Elba Rae Van Oaks could lurch toward it in one polished swoop and chop its head off with a hoe blade potentially too dull to have done so with just one swing, had it not been assisted by the hard surface of the concrete step beneath which made for an excellent if impromptu cutting board.

Elba Rae finally felt a slight breeze move through the carport as she stood there and watched the snake's life writhe from its body while debating whether it'd be worth the trouble to hook up the hose to wash the evidence off her steps or whether she could manage it with a dishpan of warm pine sol water and a sponge. With either method, the first order of business was of course to remove the remains which she planned to do by hooking the headless body on the blade of the hoe and marching out back to the edge of the big gully where she'd give it flight with one swift sling. And ordinarily, she would have done so without further delay. But that Saturday afternoon as she leaned over the dead snake she noticed for the first time its unusual appearance which she'd not especially studied in her adrenalin fueled rush to park the car and kill it. Its color wasn't particularly striking; it was the dark brown shared by so many of its departed comrades whose place of eternal rest was the same big gully soon slated to receive a new member. It was the markings on its back that struck Elba Rae Van Oaks as out of the ordinary.

They were distinctive and rather impressive once she had the chance to look at them up close, a perfect and repeating pattern of amber diamonds one would expect on a lovely manufactured fabric and Elba Rae vaguely recalled seeing a set of sheets in the Penney's catalogue which were similar. Although she'd never consider sleeping on something that looked like a snake she did think just for a minute it would make a handsome throw pillow for the settee but then her marvel turned to curiosity if not outright concern for discovering exactly what nature of snake had come to rest mere inches from her kitchen and before she flung it toward the gully to rot in the sun, she decided she wanted to know. So she hooked it on the hoe and pulled it off the steps and uncoiled its body in a straight line on the carport floor, and when she glanced back over at the mess generated by the execution, she made the decision right then to get a sponge and some hot pine sol water because the hose alone just wasn't going to cut it.

Several years after Fettis Van Oaks had died and been buried in his plot at Glory Hills, Hazel Burns was visiting one Sunday after church and was surprised to see the *National Geographic* magazine neatly stacked on the coffee table in Elba Rae's den along with other reading materials and publications found in the homes of most Buford women. It was not that Hazel Burns considered the *National Geographic* inappropriate or terribly rare, it was that the subscription label was addressed to Fettis Van Oaks who was dead and therefore no longer in need of his magazines, this particular one of which Hazel Burns happened to know had never been necessarily enjoyed by her cousin Elba Rae. Elba Rae had, in fact, complained of its increasing subscription cost one day when she'd opened the notice and advised Fettis Van Oaks of as much with a recommendation he cancel his order since the only purpose receipt of the *National Geographic* seemed to serve was to create a pile of unread magazines, a feat which could be accomplished by the several others he renewed on an annual basis and never looked at either. Fettis Van Oaks mostly did not deliberate her suggestion and instead informed Elba Rae he was a grown man and was, as a matter of record, perfectly capable of deciding which magazines he'd choose to subscribe to and which magazines needed to be cancelled and pointed out to her in an impatient tone of voice that she had no way of knowing what he read and what he did not read when he was in the bathroom having his private time in the mornings, and for good measure he even had the nerve to challenge the literary value of the *Redbook* as long as they were factoring the fiscal aspects of it all. Elba Rae Van Oaks told him she just hoped they had *National Geographic* in hell and vowed never to speak of it again.

So Hazel Burns found it odd to see the latest issue on the coffee table that Sunday afternoon but Elba Rae just explained to her as to how the subscription was already paid up and she'd just never gotten around to cancelling it and every once in a while she did come across an article or some pictures which were a good supplement to the social studies book she taught with at the Homer T. Litton Grammar School. What Elba Rae Van Oaks did not tell her cousin Hazel was that ever since he had died, she'd found an unexpected comfort on the days she opened her mailbox and discovered something addressed to Fettis. Hazel Burns had never married and Elba Rae just didn't think she'd understand why Elba Rae found it reassuring for Fettis to continue receiving mail after he was gone and she never intended to tell Hazel that not only had she purposely failed to cancel the subscription, she had renewed it herself since his death. Over time, the frivolous pieces of mail like the advertisements and the solicitations for charitable donations Fettis used to get had become all the less frequent, but it was always a pleasantly reflective moment, if not altogether happy, on the day when the *National Geographic* came to the house addressed to Mr. F. Van Oaks on Highway 29 even if he did happen to be out at Glory Hills and not at all at home.

With a dead snake on her mind, Elba Rae perhaps for the first time since Fettis had died surmised the *National Geographic* might finally have a practical use for her since, as long as she clawed through them long enough, she was likely to eventually come across some pictures of snakes and some information about them which might help to identify the make and model as it was of the one lying in state out in the carport. So she poured a glass of tea and dabbed a little bit of sweat from her brow with a paper towel before settling at the kitchen table with a collection of the dated periodicals.

By the second glass of tea her ice was all but melted, she'd been through seven issues, and had yet to come across so much as a reference to the word snake. And the more she looked the more unlikely it seemed to her Fettis Van Oaks had ever really derived a scholastic benefit in the least from his continued subscription to such content and she didn't care how good a speech he'd made about his time in the bathroom, she knew full well he wasn't sitting in there reading any laborious articles about the Aborigines or the plight of some woodpeckers in drought plagued areas of Texas. The more reasonable explanation was that he'd kept it coming simply because she'd asked him to stop it and mailbox memories or not, she was a good mind to send in the cancellation notice herself and purge whatever remained of the sentiment attached. That was when she flipped over to the page with a picture which changed everything.

It was not a snake that got Elba Rae Van Oaks's attention. Not at all. It was a full page photograph of some men and women standing in a semicircle with the men holding spears and the women holding pottery, wicker baskets containing some unidentified fruit, and bundles of what looked like wheat but could have just as easily been unassembled broom straws. Their faces had some kind of paint on them, both the men's and the women's, with more on the men than the women which Elba Rae Van Oaks found completely out of order since, regardless of the occasion, the women should have been more made up than the men. Some of the men's heads were topped with a headdress of feathers and twigs with the center man's being the larger of the group indicating clearly to Elba Rae Van Oaks—without even reading the caption—he was the leader. The women's heads were covered too, not with the ornate looking creations the men got to wear, but with colorful sheaths of material twirled around and around completely covering their hair like a big soft serve cone from the Dairy Castle drive in right off the square in Buford. However, in the greater scheme of things, it was not so much what the men and women were covered in as it was what they weren't that ended Elba Rae's snake search that day. The men wore loin cloths and nothing more and Elba Rae Van Oaks suspected the length of them was absolutely insufficient to cover anything if they weren't really careful when they sat down, unless they had some underwear on that just didn't show up good in the picture but she had no intention of hunting the magnifying glass to find out. Yet, being the educator she was, she could appreciate the wardrobe of the endemic men onto whom she was glancing as they posed in their far away village. It was the women who wore nothing above their wastes either which at first disgusted Elba Rae until, to her horror, she slowly began to entertain an association between the disrobed women and Fettis Van Oaks's loyalty toward his subscription and she wondered how many more like photographs had been published over the years and years he'd been receiving the magazine not to mention the ones she'd paid for since he'd been dead. Before another second passed, she crossed over to the telephone on the wall and tore off a page from the notepad attached to the caddy which hung with it and wrote cancel National Geographic on the paper.

She said 'ye gods' to herself but out loud as she sat back down at the table, the page still open to the spear holding men and the Dairy Castle-headed women. She had strayed far off course by then and didn't much care anymore about what kind of snake she'd hacked to death in the carport and was even a little mad she'd wasted so much time and hadn't even begun to mix up her pine sol water. But she still couldn't take her eyes off the picture of the men and women standing in the semicircle, thousands of miles away. She imagined she might even have wanted to read the story if they just had their clothes on, to find out who they were and where they lived and what it was they were celebrating, not that Elba Rae Van Oaks knew for sure it was a celebration, but she did know a thing or two about geography and about social studies and she knew enough to know the men and the women didn't just make up their faces and come together in a semicircle with the women bearing what were obviously some gestures of a gift unless it was for a reason. So she looked at the photograph a little closer the next time, made more palatable by pretending to herself the women were really wearing black blouses with little short skirts and she found when she squinted just enough, it wasn't so hard to do.

In the foreground of the picture, in fact around which the semicircle formed, there was an assortment of bright orange gourd looking vegetation arranged in a manner such that they resembled something of a primitive shaped pyramid and upon further review, ironically aided perhaps by the squinting, Elba Rae took note for the first time the women indeed were holding their pottery and their fruit baskets and their broom straws in an outstretched fashion as if offering them to the gourd pyramid like a present. As she shook her head from side to side, she looked down one more time and saw the caption on the page opposite the photograph: "Native women offer sacrifices to bountiful crop." There it was, she thought. Her suspicions confirmed. A bunch of barren women standing around with presents for a pile of pumpkins. Educational responsibilities aside, Elba Rae Van Oaks took pause for a moment to be glad she lived in Litton County and accepted there were some places on earth she really did just never care to visit, and by the time she'd gotten the water hot enough and made her way back to the carport with a bucket and sponge, a swarm of big green flies was already gathered around the still unidentified corpse.

✳   ✳   ✳   ✳

"I wonder if we'll ever get another drop of rain," Hazel Burns said to Elba Rae Van Oaks when they sat down in the Clara Battles Babcock Sunday School Room the next morning at church.

"I don't know, but my grass is just dead," Elba Rae Van Oaks replied. "There's no need to even cut it again until we get some."

"I know what you mean. This heat makes you want to stay in the house all the time. I didn't even want to go to the grocery store yesterday, but I finally made myself."

"Me either," Elba Rae said. "I went to the dollar store and by the time I got through, my clothes were nearly wet. And—oh, I didn't even tell you—when I got in home yesterday, there was an old snake in my carport."

"O-o-o-h-h, Elba Rae! Did you kill it?"

"Yes, ma'am. I took the hoe to it."

"I'm surprised the car didn't scare it off."

"Me too, but it didn't act much afraid. It was all the way up on my back door step like it was just waiting for me to get home and let it in the house!"

"O-o-o-h-h, what kind was it?"

"You know, I couldn't tell. It was a brown color but it had some markings on it I've never seen on a snake."

"Reckon it was a moccasin?"

"No, it wasn't a water moccasin."

"Wasn't a copperhead, was it?"

"Not like one I've ever seen."

"What'd you do with it?"

"I gave it a sling in the gully. But you know before I did, I tried to study it for a minute and figure out—"

Before Elba Rae Van Oaks could finish her story, the salacious details of which she had no intention of including, Mrs. Ulgine Babcock entered the room and took her place at the lectern to begin the lesson and Elba Rae thought it just as well since she didn't really want to revisit the whole *National Geographic* subscription issue with Hazel Burns anyway.

The lesson that morning was about Ruth and Elba Rae alternately listened to Mrs. Ulgine Babcock and alternately thought about her curriculum for the week to follow at the Homer T. Litton Grammar School, then listened to Mrs. Ulgine Babcock and the lesson about Ruth but also thought about her tool shed that needed cleaning out as soon as it cooled off enough to tackle, then heard somebody say something about Ruth, which drew Elba Rae back to the lesson before concluding it would behoove Mrs. Ulgine Babcock not to forgo a girdle, especially on those Sundays she found herself standing at a lectern in front of a group.

After prayer, Ulgine Babcock delayed dismissal with her reminder of the upcoming Halloween youth party for toddlers to grade eight to be held in the fellowship hall the Saturday before Halloween, an annual event enjoyed by the children and their parents and by members alike who chose to attend even if not always so much by the volunteers who came to help put on the event with the youth Sunday School teachers. Elba Rae had done her share over the years, but knew that wouldn't necessarily exempt her from making some punch or baking cupcakes for the children. So it didn't come as any surprise Ulgine Babcock was extolling the virtue of helping out in front of a decidedly past child-bearing age Sunday School class. Hazel Burns could appreciate the injustice as well and even said as much to her cousin as they walked out of the Sunday School room and down the hall toward the sanctuary for preaching. "Why do I need to be up here on a Saturday throwing a Halloween party for the young people?" She said, her lips pursed together so tightly she resembled a ventriloquist.

"I know it," Elba Rae Van Oaks agreed, careful to make sure she wasn't overheard. "Looks like if enough of the parents won't step up and take care of it, they just don't need to have a party."

"That's right," Hazel Burns said, walking but still pursed.

"Here I am sixty-five years old, without a child or a grandchild in this church nor any sign of a relation to a child and I'm having to get up something for them to have a party. That's just not right," Elba Rae reasoned.

The two ladies continued on and took their customary pew, relishing the few minutes between the end of Sunday School and the beginning of the service to visit with members in adjacent pews, some of whom had been occupying them longer than Elba Rae Van Oaks or Hazel Burns either one. The sanctuary was small but befitting its setting, with beams crossing the steeply vaulted ceiling. Elba Rae wondered some Sundays if the beams had ever been dusted but didn't imagine she'd ever be up there to know. Martha Betty Maharry sat one pew behind Elba Rae and Hazel Burns and though thin and fragile by Labor Day Sunday in 1988 and looking every one of her eighty years, she rarely if ever missed preaching, although she'd given up Sunday School some time back because it wore her out too much to sit through both. Martha Betty liked to lean forward just a bit into Elba Rae's pew before it got to be eleven o'clock in case any news had been shared during the ten o'clock hour.

"Morning, Elba Rae. How are you?"

"I'm fine, Martha Betty. How are you doing?"

"I'm up and going, and that's more than some folks I guess."

"That's the truth. How's Ned feeling?"

"Oh," Martha Betty Maharry took pause, "he's just not getting around well at all. He wanted to come to preaching this morning but he's so down with the gout."

"I hate to hear that, Martha Betty," Hazel Burns joined in. "He has such a time with it, doesn't he?"

"He does. He'll try to get out and do a little work in the garden and before I know it, he's back in the house. He told me the other day if it wasn't better next spring he wasn't even going to plant another one."

Hazel Burns immediately turned around to face the front toward the pulpit, not so much because she wanted to see the pulpit but because she didn't want Martha Betty Maharry to see her or the little smirk she wasn't able to overpower. Hazel Burns did not find humor in Ned Maharry's suffering nor in his wife's recounting of it yet the repeating of Ned's vow that the end of his gardening days was drawing nigh got her tickled since he'd been threatening to put down his seed sack every spring since 1979, which was the year the tiller had gotten away from him and caused near devastation before he was finally able to catch onto the kill switch. By then, however, he'd been pulled completely out of the garden proper and tilled a trail through two of Martha Betty's hydrangea bushes and right past her most fruitful gardenia until he came to rest under the clothes line where he'd all but caught the hem of one her best delicates she'd only moments earlier hung on the line to dry in the April air and to hear Martha Betty tell it, she'd barely escaped being tilled herself. So Hazel Burns just had to excuse herself from hearing one more time that Mr. Ned Maharry was planning to retire from gardening.

"Well they're trying to get up people to help with the Halloween party," Elba Rae conveyed to Martha Betty Maharry.

"Oh, goodness, Elba Rae, I wish I could, but you know I don't drive after dark anymore," lamented Martha Betty apologetically.

"To tell you the truth, Martha Betty, I just don't think it's right to depend on some of us for it anyway. It's time more of the younger ones get involved and take some of the responsibilities."

"That's right," Hazel Burns chorused.

"You've always been good to help, Elba Rae," Martha Betty offered. "Nobody can say you haven't done your part over the years." Whatever retort Elba Rae Van Oaks may have been ready to render was interrupted by the conclusion of the organ prelude and the Call to Worship which was just as well, Elba Rae thought, because they were in church after all and she didn't want to sound unwilling to help. She turned around to face the altar and Hazel Burns who was still smirking and left well enough alone. Though not necessarily for long.

*   *   *   *

The scripture reading was from First Thessalonians. Beyond that, truth be told, had someone held a gun to Elba Rae Van Oaks's head ten minutes after church was over that afternoon and demanded she recount the finer points of the sermon, her life would surely have been in peril. She had nothing against either of the Thessalonians or Reverend Timmons, as it was, and as preachers went, knew him to be godly and capable. She supposed she was amongst some of the older members of the congregation who would always long for Reverend Bishop and for his warmth and reassurance, and for an era in the church as well as their own lives which was passing if not already completely gone. So she tended to day-dream a bit during the preaching hour some Sundays, her drifting having usually gotten warmed up good during Sunday School, depending of course upon who was teaching the lesson.

Elba Rae especially struggled that Sunday to follow Reverend Timmons and didn't really realize it—or why—until the epiphany which came to her in the form of a dream that evening. She would later call it a divine intervention because that was the only way to make sense of it, since she'd not particularly been think-ing about the people from the *National Geographic* or their offerings to the pile of gourds before bed that night, at least not consciously anyway, because she'd been entirely too involved in thinking about the mystery Miss Angela Lansbury had found herself unexpectedly involved in on her TV show, although, had Elba Rae Van Oaks been more rational about it, it wasn't so very unexpected since she stumbled into one most every Sunday night.

In the dream, Elba Rae was in a faraway place completely unfamiliar and strange and the faces of the people she encountered were vague even if their bod-ies were absolutely in focus. They wore the same outfits as the men and women from the magazine, such as they were, because the women once again were unclothed above the waist. Elba Rae struggled in the dream to look down at her own body, desperate to ascertain the status of her blouse or absence thereof, yet crippled by the incapacities which commonly encumber the dreamer she was unable to bend her neck to see. Everyone was holding an armful of vividly orange gourds and seemed to be taking them somewhere.

Then, amidst the crowd of African tribes people, there emerged a face Elba Rae knew. It was a woman who, like the others, was bare-breasted but did at least have on a clean white girdle and Elba Rae recognized her instantly to be Mrs. Ulgine Babcock.

"Ulgine!" Elba Rae Van Oaks attempted to shout but in dream sounds, it came out more of a whisper.

"Elba Rae. I'm glad you're here," Ulgine Babcock said pleasantly.

"I don't know where I am, Ulgine, do you?"

Ulgine Babcock was cradling something in her own arms, too, but it wasn't the indigenous looking fruit the other people were holding; it was a fully carved jack-o-lantern complete with a lit candle whose flame Elba Rae could make out inside between its snaggled teeth.

"What are you doing with a pumpkin, Ulgine?"

"It's for the youth party, Elba Rae. We're here to worship. And I'm so glad you've come to help. Did you bring your offering?"

Even though she still could not look down, Elba Rae could tell her hands were empty and devoid of her pocketbook or so much as a coin purse. "I don't have any offering, Ulgine." Elba Rae was fretful.

"But it's Halloween, Elba Rae. You must bring your pumpkin to help us make the offering. You said you would help us, Elba Rae. Remember? In Sunday School? You said you would help."

"I will help, Ulgine, but I thought you'd want me to bring some food or make the punch, or help the little ones with their games. I didn't bring any money."

"The children are depending on us, Elba Rae. And Reverend Timmons, too. We have to help him make the altar. You'll have to bring your pumpkin if you want to help the children."

"I don't understand, Ulgine. We've never done this at the Halloween party before."

"We've always done it this way, Elba Rae. We have the Halloween party every year and we have to bring the pumpkins. You said you would help."

"I will help! I told you I would help! But I don't know what you want!" Ulgine Babcock walked past Elba Rae and never looked back. "I will help, Ulgine! I've always helped! But I don't know what you want! I don't have a pumpkin!"

Elba Rae clearly heard herself say the word pumpkin out loud as she woke up from the confusing and distressing dream. Her digital clock on the night table read 2:18, and it would be nearly four o'clock before she got back to sleep.

She was restless until dawn and once, during a broken doze, even determined a pumpkin was sitting on her dresser right next to the monogrammed powder box that had belonged to her late mother Ethel Maywood, but reasoned after a moment of lucidity it was instead the sleep cap she'd never put on the night before, so it was a relief to awaken at last to the holiday because Elba Rae Van Oaks was in no shape to teach fifth grade at the Homer T. Litton Grammar School that day.

She paced in the morning while drinking her coffee more so than reading the newspaper which is what she normally would have done in a leisurely manner on a non-school day. She was tired, from lack of sleep, but disturbed, too, and not just from fatigue. The weekend repeated itself to her over and over, from the time she went shopping at the dollar store until she got home and beheaded the unbeknownst breed of snake, to the point where she sat at the harvest table searching through the pages of Fettis's *National Geographic* before being greeted by uninhibited Africans praising their harvest. And then the blood rushed to her head at once because it all had perfect reasoning; the dream, Ulgine Babcock, and the upcoming Halloween party at the First Avenue United Methodist Church. She took her coffee cup to the kitchen sink and put it there without even rinsing, and went right away to the bathroom to run water in the tub. She knew it was a holiday for most, but she'd try anyway and if Reverend Timmons wasn't in the church office, then she'd go straight to the parsonage and talk to him there.

*   *   *   *

The parsonage of the First Avenue United Methodist Church was not on First Avenue, although it once had been before the fire which destroyed the original church building back in 1940. That structure had been erected of oak and pines from Georgia a few years after the church itself was organized in the 1870s, and in the early part of the century, a small residence for the minister had been added on the property not exactly connected to the church though close enough that when the big blaze of '40 took down the center of their worship, the house was also left little more than a smoldering uninhabitable shell. It was the kind of two-fold tragedy that occurred when there was the first, notable tragedy—the church catching fire—compounded by the realization that while the sanctuary loss may have been in the Lord's hands, the slack response time of the Litton County Volunteer Fire Brigade had most likely been in the hands of Clara Battles Babcock since she enjoyed talking on her new party line so well the parsonage was already fully engaged by the time someone could get through on the phone to Mr. Winton Babcock, into whose custody the only fire engine was bestowed.

After much deliberation and studying and praying and financial consultation amongst the elders, it was decided a bigger church would be constructed to replace the old one which would include an education building to house the Sunday School rooms even though it required displacing the site of the former parsonage all together to fit it all on the lot. But just as the Lord giveth and the Lord taketh away, Miss Gladys Pendergrast made it known to all she had modified her documented last will and testament so as to bequeath her modest dwelling a couple of streets over on Third Avenue to the Trustees of the First Avenue United Methodist Church upon her passing for the express use of a new parsonage. Practically everyone said 'bless her heart' at least once when the Lord saw fit to taketh Miss Gladys Pendergrast away a mere week after the first services were held in the new church and much was made of the mysterious working ways of the Lord Himself, although Miss Gladys Pendergrast's only living blood relative, a cousin from Huntsville who'd all but assumed the inheritance of a house was imminent, was less philosophical about the whole thing.

Elba Rae Van Oaks had not always been a consummate pillar of the First Avenue United Methodist Church, but after her husband's disability left his life revolving more around the Lodge and the coffee club at Jack Moss's hardware store and bowling in Tallapoosa County on Tuesday nights than it did around his wife, she sought her own solace in the bosom of her church family and if anything, the dedication only strengthened after Fettis went to glory and she didn't even have part of his life anymore. She couldn't recall a time when her calling had been any more clear than it was that Labor Day morning when she went hunting for Reverend Timmons to share the revelation and when she saw no sign of his brown pickup truck in the parking area next to the church, she directed the LTD straight to the parsonage donated by the late Gladys Pendergrast. He seemed genuinely surprised to see her, or much less anyone, at the front door when he came to answer the bell ringing.

"Why ... Elba Rae ... what a surprise."

"Good Morning, Reverend. I hope I didn't get you at a bad time. And I'm sorry I didn't call first."

"Well not at all. Come in, come in," he said as he held the door open for her. She did not hesitate to enter. He stepped out of the entry and into a tastefully decorated parlor which to Elba Rae always looked like a public room she suspected the Timmons never set foot in unless they were entertaining the company of a church member. "How about a cup of coffee? Lorraine's gone out to the Piggly Wiggly already this morning, but I believe the water's still hot on the stove."

"Oh, no, thank you, but I've already had mine."

"Well, all right. Would you like to sit down?"

"Yes. Thank you." Elba Rae suddenly felt awkward but knew it probably would just take her a few minutes to get comfortable with what she was about to divulge. She sat down on the sofa and Reverend Timmons was opposite her in a formal looking wingback.

"I sense there's something on your mind this morning, Elba Rae."

"Oh, there is."

"Are you troubled about anything?"

"No, I'm not troubled exactly but … well … yes, maybe I am. It's about the Halloween party at the church next month."

"Oh, yes. It's getting to be that time again, isn't it?"

"It is, but it really shouldn't be."

"Excuse me?"

"What I mean is, Reverend Timmons, we shouldn't be having the Halloween party. We've got to stop it. That's why I'm here."

"I beg your pardon?"

"I believe it would be sinful to continue having it at the church."

"Well, Elba Rae, correct me if I'm wrong, but we've been hosting a party for the children since before I ever came to Buford. Reverend Bishop told me so himself one time, and—"

"That is true. We've been doing it a long time and I guess I'd have to say we just didn't know any better. But now we do. Or at least I do, and I believe the Lord sent me a sign so I could do something about it. And I plan to. It's my duty."

"Elba Rae …"

"Yes?"

"Are you sure you don't need some coffee?"

"No, thank you."

"Well I think I do. Will you excuse me for just a moment?"

"Of course. You go right ahead." Upon her endorsement, Reverend Timmons tentatively stood up and walked around the corner and into the parsonage kitchen. Elba Rae kept her seat but she could hear the lid being opened on the jar of instant coffee and even wondered what brand the Timmons favored, whether it was the extra dark Folgers Elba Rae usually preferred unless something else was especially on sale, or whether they might be partial to the freeze-dried kind Elba Rae just hadn't been brave enough to ever try, due to its lightened pallor. She heard the tea kettle being put down on the eye of the stove and anticipated Reverend Timmons's eminent return.

"Obviously," he said as he re-entered the room serving somewhat to announce, "something has happened to make you question the appropriateness of our having a Halloween party for the children."

"Yes, it has. Just last night."

"Why don't you tell me about that?"

"Well … all right. It started, really, when I got home from the dollar store Saturday. I'd just run up there to get some washing powders and some panty hose and, well, a few other things, but I when I got home there was a snake in my carport." And so it went. All the details, in saturated clarity with the major omission, of course, being Elba Rae Van Oaks's stark resolution that the *National Geographic* would never again count a penny of her money in their till, and concluding with her divine message.

Reverend Timmons leaned back in the wing chair and put his empty coffee cup on the side table near a lamp. "And so you see this as a message of sorts."

"I do, yes," she confirmed. "From the Lord. I believe He put that snake on my doorstep Saturday so there was no way I could miss it. It was His way of leading me right to that page in Fettis's old magazine so I could see those heathen natives in there worshiping their pumpkins."

Reverend Timmons smiled at her, albeit benignly and without judgment. "Elba Rae, in all fairness to the children in our congregation, your magazine didn't exactly identify the fruits in the picture as being pumpkins, did it? The kind as we know them? As the children know them?"

"Well no," she went on, "but I don't expect they have exactly the same kind as we do here. You know it's awful hot over there and I don't imagine they get near enough rain. But I could bring the magazine to you and you could see for yourself. It's as plain as day. And that's why we can't allow the church to be used for a party that's going to glorify something so ungodly. It's like worshiping a molten image, and it's just downright pagan."

She wasn't near about through. "If the parents want to let them dress up in costumes and carve pumpkins, that's their business. But it doesn't mean we have to let them use the church to do it."

"Have you considered that not everyone will agree with you, Elba Rae?"

"Well, I don't guess everyone would understand right off. But you know what they say, Reverend. A picture really is worth a thousand words and I bet anybody that sees my magazine can't help but feel the same."

The way the reverend looked at her, Elba Rae couldn't positively tell how he was leaning. "Some may see the connection," he said, "but I doubt you'll convince everybody about this, Elba Rae. The children look forward to the Halloween party for a long time. The parents do too. And, if I'm being honest, I've always enjoyed the fellowship myself."

"Even if it's wrong?"

"Are you absolutely certain about your conviction, Elba Rae?"

"I know what I saw, Reverend. Those people were huddled together to worship some pumpkins. And if we allow it to go on here in Buford, then we're just no better than they are. Why, if the Baptists ever got hold of my magazine, they'd be getting up a mission trip or at least donating to one to send people over there to save them. The least we can do here is not promote the same sin."

He leaned against the back of the chair and briefly glanced at his empty coffee cup on the side table before deciding he was stimulated enough by his guest and didn't need a refill. "I can't make a pronouncement about this right now, you understand. But I will take it under advisement and I may discuss it with a couple of the elders. To gauge their opinions about the appropriateness of allowing it to continue at the church."

"Tell them to call me if they want to see the magazine."

"Yes … I will do that. And I'll be in touch with you about it."

"Well, thank you," she said as she stood up, noticing as she did Mrs. Lorraine Timmons pulling into the driveway. "I better let you go now so you can help Lorraine get in the groceries. I hope you have a good holiday today," to which Reverend Timmons thought it had already been compromised.

Elba Rae respected Reverend Timmons's advice and knew he'd take the distressing matter under advisement and was confident he'd talk to the elders like he said he would, but as she navigated back home that morning in the Ford, she was not content to leave resolution entirely in his hands, fearing to a degree the urgency of the situation might lose something in his translation. And that's when she decided, not so much in a gesture to circumvent, but more in an effort to complement Reverend Timmons's actions she needed to have a few conversations about Halloween and pumpkins and the irreverent use of the fellowship hall on her own. Her primary ally, she knew without fail, would be the queen bee of the First Avenue United Methodist herself. Mrs. Ulgine Babcock.

*   *   *   *

Hazel Burns sat at the harvest table in Elba Rae's kitchen later that morning, Fettis's *National Geographic* before her. "Merciful heavens, Elba Rae. I can't believe a respectable magazine like the *National Geographic* would put pictures like this in it. For just anybody to pick up and see."

"But it's clear, isn't it? To you?"

"Absolutely! Those women are all but naked and the little skirts those men have on aren't big enough to flag a handcar either!"

"I'm not talking about their clothes, Hazel, I'm talking about the pumpkins! The way they're standing around trying to offer them gifts."

"Oh ... well, yeah, I can see what you mean now." Hazel Burns read the caption. "Yeah, it even says so right here. Says they're offering sacrifices to the crop. You know, I guess we go about our lives over here and never realize what goes on in other parts of the world. It's shocking sometimes."

"Now doesn't that make you think twice about us having a party at the church where the children are carving up some pumpkins? Can you honestly say you'd feel right with the Lord if you were icing up a pan of cupcakes for *that*?"

"Well," Hazel Burns hesitated ever so briefly, "no. I don't think I do feel right about it anymore. But what can we do? You know they'll just go on with it anyway."

"Not necessarily."

"Do you really think Reverend Timmons will put a stop to it?"

"Maybe not on his own he wouldn't. But if enough of us complain about it, the elders are bound to listen."

"Well at least I won't feel so bad if I tell Ulgine I'm not dragging up there with food this year," Hazel declared while nodding her head in an affirmative motion.

"Ulgine is exactly who'll end up putting a stop to this."

Hazel Burns looked unsure. "You think?"

"Who else has got her hand in everything that goes on up there?" Hazel Burns did not reply but Elba Rae could gage she was pondering. "Think about it, Hazel. She's the Sunday School Superintendent and she's president of the Women of the Church and you'd have to knock her in the head with an urn to get her off the flower committee. And I don't imagine anybody's ever told her she had to take on directing the Halloween party, but you know she's the one every year getting up the food and the helpers."

"You're right about all of that," Hazel agreed.

"Of course I am. The Reverend told me this morning he'd make some phone calls to the elders to discuss it, but I'm going to discuss it too. And when I get through with Ulgine, she's sure to understand."

"What are you going to do?"

Elba Rae pointed to a small brown paper sack on the counter top next to the sink. "I'm going to take her those late this evening."

"What is it?"

"Some tomatoes Martha Betty left over here the other day."

"You're giving Ulgine your good tomatoes?"

"I need something to take and good gosh, Hazel, I know Martha Betty means well but if I ate nothing but tomatoes every meal I couldn't use up all the ones she gives me. Ned really ought to thinking about cutting back next year whether he's crippled up with the gout or not."

"Well good luck."

"You know what?"

"What?" Hazel Burns said as she got up from the table.

"It couldn't hurt if you went with me. It'd show her this isn't just my idea."

Hazel Burns, as history had proven, was not as confrontational as her cousin Elba Rae Van Oaks and did not immediately liken to the idea of joining the pumpkin banning crusade, at least not publicly. "I don't know, Elba Rae."

"Why not?"

Hazel Burns did not have a good answer. The truth was, no matter how long it had been since the misfortune Elba Rae had suffered as a repercussion of the unpleasantness with Patsy Simpson, people in Litton County would never forget it. It didn't matter that Elba Rae had paid her penance by attending sessions with Dr. Yardley and had eventually been cleared to go back to her job, or even that she had continued to teach in the years since without a hint of further incident. Symbolic closure had not even come when Doug Simpson finally lost his daddy's farm to the bank and went to selling equipment at the John Deere dealership on the highway, after which Patsy Simpson divorced him and made her return to Paducah where it was assumed she was still teaching though nobody much ever wanted to query Doug. Elba Rae's reputation was never completely restored and whether she knew it or not, Hazel Burns knew. Hazel hadn't suffered the consequences like Elba Rae had, but she'd experienced just enough of a burden from their work and familial associations to be leery of jumping onto what would no doubt prove to be an unpopular band wagon being pulled by the woman known even in contiguous counties as having once assaulted another teacher with a casserole dish. In the end, nonetheless, Hazel Burns could not hurt her beloved cousin's feelings. "Okay," she said. "I'll go."

"Good," smiled Elba Rae.

*   *   *   *

Mrs. Ulgine Babcock had not simply decreed herself to be the reigning monarch of the First Avenue United Methodist Church at random; rather, everyone just surmised she felt it her rightful position to assume even though she wasn't a Babcock by birth and was only one by marriage, but since there were no female born Babcock heir-apparents, no one could sensibly dispute her claim. Ulgine Babcock had inherited the appointment from her late mother-in-law, Mrs. Clara Battles Babcock, and anyone who'd ever attended regularly at the First Avenue United Methodist knew the Babcocks.

Mr. Winton and Miss Clara had been prominent citizens in Buford, as well as faithful members of the church who, as many knew, were in their day its strongest financial contributors—giving far beyond their obligatory tithes. Mr. Winton's family had been in the timber business with interests in Alabama, Georgia, and parts of Mississippi. They had acquired significant wealth before the Depression came and the demand for lumber dried up like most other peoples's incomes and savings. It was well known throughout the congregation just how critical his monetary assistance had been after the fire in 1940 took down the church and the parsonage next to it, and even those not grown or even alive at the time had heard the stories about how the Babcocks practically rebuilt the church out of their own pockets. Of course, the respect and reverence bestowed upon all Babcocks since then was never officially tarnished by the assumption that some of the excess donating was a means by which to offer recompense for the destruction itself, since the rumors of the significance Miss Clara's telephone hogging had on the fire's spreading never totally died out. And while that connection might have been openly discussed at times, no one much ever wanted to speak too loudly of the actual likely source of funds for the construction since those in the know at the time had heard the gossip about just how poorly a state the Babcock timber business was really in.

Because neither Mr. Winton nor Miss Clara ever let on—Miss Clara, it was assumed because she didn't know or because she chose to turn a blind eye—most people continued to believe the Babcocks were unaffected by the hard times everyone else endured. Miss Clara never went without the latest luxury for their home and Mr. Winton, it seemed, always had a big modern car to drive around

Buford. The Babcock children were never without new clothing when the seasons changed. But some of the men around town had well-founded suspicions otherwise and, as it turned out, a few had good reasons to know first hand Mr. Winton Babcock was engaging in an unseemly enterprise in order to maintain the family lifestyle.

It was erected so far back up in the Georgia woods even Mr. Winton Babcock himself sometimes had trouble finding it if he wasn't paying any attention to the markings along the path. Unlike so many of the farmers and area landowners who lost their spreads to the banks in the early '30s, the Babcocks owned their vast acres mortgage-free and while there might not have been anybody to buy their lumber, they at least still held onto their property. Mr. Winton was a proud man and reasoned if he couldn't use his assets for the purpose intended he had a right to use them for whatever means necessary to feed his family and to provide for them and if producing a product from the ingredients God already put on the earth was the way, he had the will. He'd kept up the fleet of unsuspecting looking trucks bearing the BABCOCK TIMBER COMPANY logo on their doors, which made distribution possible across a wide swath. And the fact that he could sell his whiskey at a profit margin much greater than he could his lumber was an added benefit.

When the new church building was nearly complete and the congregation began discussions of what form the dedication service would take, there was unanimous agreement that the Babcock family should be particularly honored for their support. The stained glass artisan was contacted and told of the desire to add the "In Honor of Mr. Winton Babcock" inscription at the base of the large round window which would be the focal point in the rear wall of the sanctuary. And ever since, countless Methodist women had received spiritual enlightenment within the surrounds of the Sunday School room so dedicated in honor of Miss Clara, whose full name was engraved in the brass plate on its door.

The Babcocks had two sons and no daughters. The oldest had disappeared somewhere over the Pacific during the War, his plane and his body never recovered. After the War was over and the Babcock Timber Company was back operating at capacity, more profitable than it ever had before, the youngest boy had married one of the Morton girls, Ulgine, and while he eventually took his rightful helm in the family business, his bride was indoctrinated into the goings on in the church as an understudy to Miss Clara to make clear the line of ascension.

They all lived under the expansive roof of the Babcock home and generally got along while Ulgine raised her own family in the church. Mr. Winton for all intents and purposes took complete leave of his senses in the '60s and required round the clock attention at the house, as he was bad to want to drive the car into town even though he'd forgotten pretty much how to drive and since even when the skill came back to him, as much a blessing to those already on the highway as to Mr. Winton himself, he rarely ever remembered how to get back home. Miss Clara eventually resorted to disconnecting the spark plug rather than merely hiding the car keys, since a car that wouldn't crank seemed to agitate him less than the strain of hunting the keys she had once buried in the back yard inside an old lard can. By the time he died in '65 he recognized no one in the family except for Miss Clara, which she knew in her heart even though he was prone to addressing her as Kitty most of the time. Miss Clara survived him until two months before her own eighty-eighth birthday when her body just gave out one morning after breakfast and she announced she was returning to her room to lie down. When Ulgine went to look in on her a little while before dinner time, she was reclined on her bed just as pretty and sweet as she'd ever looked but was indeed quite dead. Ulgine Babcock had become, at long last, the mistress of the manor.

Ulgine Babcock never officially served as Treasurer of the church but managed nonetheless to procure just enough information from the person who did to know which members pledged what and which members did not. She was not overly concerned with the amounts in and of themselves, since she was privy to the church budget overall and knew with certainty its members were funding it, and with excess at that, but mainly felt the need to know who the largest contributors were in the era following her famous in-laws. For whatever the strongest member felt compelled to offer, Ulgine would usually see to it the Babcock check was for just a slightly higher figure. She had learned well, it seemed, from the late Clara Battles Babcock.

"Did you call her and tell her we were coming?" Hazel wondered, as she sat on the passenger's side of Elba Rae's LTD.

"I debated, but went ahead and called because I wanted to make sure she was home. She said Winn, Junior was over at one their plants around Montgomery and probably won't be in till after dark."

"Elba Rae?"

"What?"

"What if Ulgine doesn't see the same things we see when she looks at the picture?"

"Unless she's blind as a bat or gone off her rocker like Mr. Winton was, she'll see it. But if you're worried about it, just let me do most of the talking."

Hazel Burns was not opposed to her cousin Elba Rae doing the talking as long as the recipients of which weren't too unreceptive. By that Monday afternoon, two full days as it were since Elba Rae'd come home to the snake in the carport, she was on a mission and there would be no stopping her until she heard what she wanted to hear. Hazel feared for the fallout should Mrs. Ulgine Babcock not agree to Elba Rae's out and out demand of the Halloween party being called off. On the other hand, Hazel considered, if Ulgine Babcock should take offense of equal or greater proportion than Elba Rae Van Oaks had to the whole pumpkin scandal, the deal would be pretty much sealed. With Elba Rae's conviction and her Maywood temper that Aunt Ethel swore to her last days came from Raymond's side combined with Ulgine Babcock's clout, the doors of the fellowship hall of the First Avenue United Methodist would never again be darkened with another pagan pumpkin, carved or others, although Hazel Burns suddenly had a distressing thought when considering the forthcoming traditional menus for the Thanksgiving Harvest Supper held the Wednesday before the holiday, and was unclear exactly how the food committee would convey—especially to the older members—that pumpkin pies were off limits. It would be disastrous, she feared, to inadvertently create an overstock of mincemeat as an unintentional byproduct of Elba Rae's campaign, but soon calmed herself with the assurance the two holidays weren't usually associated and assumed pumpkins would be welcomed by November, as long as they were baked in a pie.

The Babcock house was old and rambling with obvious additions made over the years, both while Mr. Winton and Miss Clara were still living and some since they weren't. Yet, many of the furnishings were original and for the most part occupied the same spots they'd had since being carried into the dwelling. A maid named Artice greeted Elba Rae Van Oaks and Hazel Burns after they rang the bell and announced Miss Ulgine had gotten tied up on the telephone out in the kitchen but just to make themselves at home in the living room and she'd soon bring in some iced tea. The ladies said thank you to Artice and strolled into the expansive room to the left as if carefree. They stood at first, in case Ulgine Babcock was nearby, but decided to go ahead to the settee when it became clear she wasn't and Elba Rae Van Oaks said quietly to Hazel, "they haven't changed this wallpaper since Miss Clara set up house," right as they sat.

Artice came back momentarily with a tray holding three glasses of tea and with Ulgine Babcock directly on her heels which couldn't help but suggest to Elba Rae the whole entrance had been staged, especially when Ulgine declared, "Oh, Elba Rae, I'm so sorry for making you wait! Hazel, how are you?" They exchanged their greetings and they took their tea and Artice went back to the kitchen.

And so it had begun, as Hazel Burns would lament many times over for the rest of her life, the final undoing of Elba Rae Van Oaks.

*   *   *   *

The endorsement from Mrs. Ulgine Babcock had not come as quickly or effortlessly as Elba Rae Van Oaks anticipated it would, given especially the profound evidence of the color photograph from Fettis's old magazine which was, by then, becoming mildly tattered. Ulgine committed to give Elba Rae's suggestion some thought the afternoon she and Hazel Burns visited but fell short of promising support. After a few days of apparent introspection, however, during which time she was also contacted for exploratory purposes by Reverend Timmons, Ulgine Babcock did finally also agree the full out celebration of Halloween might not be an appropriate church activity and she vowed to endeavor with Elba Rae Van Oaks to persuade the elders to stop it.

"I've prayed about it, Elba Rae," she said to Elba Rae Van Oaks on the telephone toward the end of the week, "and I agree with you" whereupon the two ladies commenced a thorough summarization one more time to justify their cause.

"Do you think we can get Reverend Timmons to go along, Ulgine?" Elba Rae inquired.

"I'll tend to him," Ulgine Babcock replied and Elba Rae smiled on the other end of the line knowing, as she did, the fight was officially over.

*   *   *   *

The First Avenue United Methodist Fall Festival was certainly not what Elba Rae Van Oaks had in mind the morning she'd gone seeking Reverend Timmons. It was, however, ultimately the end result of her efforts. While the elders had reluctantly indulged Ulgine Babcock's request to officially cancel a party with the name Halloween in it, they had not been so ready to abandon the youth of the church completely by offering nothing as a compromise. They consulted Reverend Timmons and, as an understood courtesy, reported to Ulgine Babcock and everyone agreed it would be okay to have a party for the children albeit with no costumes, witches, or pumpkins. Elba Rae Van Oaks felt a slight sting when she first heard the news and even considered she'd been betrayed by Ulgine Babcock but after pondering the overall situation, couldn't help but concur there wasn't anything blatantly irreligious about hosting some games and activities for the children in the fellowship hall and so ultimately satisfied was she with herself for spearheading the whole thing she volunteered without question to bake four dozen cupcakes and bring two bags of chips.

By the latter part of October, the weather in Buford was finally tolerable with the days offering a comforting warmth and the nights switching to an autumn chill. Elba Rae Van Oaks had an especially worrisome class of fifth grade pupils that year and for the first time she was serious when she'd hint to Hazel Burns in the lounge at school she was considering retirement. Hazel Burns had heard it before but knew there was something different in her cousin's voice. She actually meant it, Hazel thought.

"That Cummings boy is the worst child I've ever had in my room!" Elba Rae declared one afternoon as the two ladies sat in their regular corner table of the teacher's lounge, the tile floor of which having been refinished some years back after the old carpet was taken up.

"I was on the phone with Mary Alice at the Board when you brought him over this morning, and Mr. Bailey kept the door closed the whole time," Hazel said. "What did he do now?"

Elba Rae Van Oaks had a carton of cottage cheese on the table from whence she took a scoop and shook into a cling peach half that was sliding around in its syrup on her plate. "He is just vile, Hazel. If a child of mine behaved like that, I'd blister him so good when he got home he wouldn't be able to sit in the desk 'till this time next year. But that's the problem now," she exclaimed before forcefully hitting the peach half again with a follow up wallop of cottage cheese. "The children aren't gonna be any better than the parents they've got at home! And you know what I got to thinking?"

"What?" Hazel Burns was busy spreading her own tuna salad over a saltine which she removed from their sleeve one at the time.

"Well you know those Cummings have always been white trash. And I believe somewhere on his momma's side they're related to the Duvaziers."

"You know," Hazel said before biting into her cracker, "I think you're right. His momma was from down around Prattville and seems like her mother was a Duvazier before she married."

"I recollect something like that too."

"Well what did he do today?"

"You know he never pays a lick of attention during the lessons."

"Yeah, that's what you've said," nodded Hazel.

"He's usually looking off and out the window and fidgeting with his hair and his clothes, and that's when he's not whispering and just out and out talking aloud to that ole Pennington boy that sits right next to him. I've a good mind to separate them tomorrow. But anyway," she paused briefly to take a bite of peach, "this morning during English he had his book open and propped up on the desk and he wouldn't take his eyes off of it. I knew something was up because he's usually not paying me a lick of attention."

Neither Hazel Burns nor Elba Rae Van Oaks even noticed Claude Pickle had come into the lounge until they heard the soft drink can falling down into the pick-up tray. "Ladies," he said, to acknowledge their glance, whereupon he popped open the tab of his cola. "Claude," they said back in unison.

"Looks like we're about to get cooled off here in the next few days," he continued.

"How's that?" Asked Elba Rae.

Claude Pickle remained standing beside the drink machine and apparently had no intention of taking a table, even though there was no one else in the lounge. "Weather man on channel four said last night we're getting a cold front through here by the weekend."

"Did he?" Elba Rae said. "I tried to stay up for the news last night but I got so sleepy I don't think I ever heard the first word."

"Yep," he reiterated. "Supposed to start raining tomorrow and then turn off cold by Saturday."

Elba Rae Van Oaks and Hazel Burns weren't either one particularly interested in a weather report during their lunch which, undoubtedly, Claude Pickle sensed. He drank one short sip of his cola and took his leave from the lounge.

"There's another one that ought to be thinking about getting out," Elba Rae decreed while gesturing toward the door. "I walked by his room the other day and there was so much commotion coming from inside, I didn't even think he was in there."

"Was he?"

"Why sure. But those kids just run all over him. They do everything but tie him to the flagpole and he can't do a thing with them. And I've just about had it myself."

"Well what about the Cummings boy?"

"Well like I said, I knew something was up because he was studying that English book way too hard. So I decided to call on him. Just to see what he was really reading. And do you know what?"

"What?"

"I had to call his name out three times before he even heard me. So I walked down that row to just see for myself and there he was, sitting right up in my class with one of those awful smut magazines opened up inside his English book."

"He had the *National Geographic?*"

"Lands no, Hazel, it was one of those with the naked woman just spread out all over everywhere! Just vile, that's what it is! Just vile! I snatched that thing out of his English book so fast he didn't even have a chance to open his mouth first!"

"Well I wondered what that was folded up in your hand when you brought him over to Mr. Bailey this morning."

"Well, now you know."

"Where would he get such a thing?"

"Where do you think?" Elba Rae asked rhetorically. "Don't think I didn't ask after I got him out in the hall away from the other children. And do you know what he said?"

"What?"

"It's his daddy's. Said he keeps them in the bottom of his big tool box out in their garage."

"My word," Hazel Burns shook her head back and forth slowly.

"So it's no wonder the children are all devils when they haven't got any more example than that at home. I'll tell you, Hazel … I'm giving it serious consideration. I think it's time I whistled my dogs in home."

"Goodness, Elba Rae. It's hard for me to think about being here if you were gone."

"If I was over there in the office with Howard Bailey, I wouldn't be so quick to go. But it's just not the same in the classroom, Hazel. Not anymore."

Hazel Burns didn't much say anything else that day during lunch. She was somewhat pensive while she twisted up the empty end of the sleeve of crackers tightly and put them into a brown sack for the next meal.

"Do you 'spect he knows what he's talking about with the weather?"

Hazel Burns shrugged her shoulders. "I didn't see the news last night either. I turned the TV off early and went to bed with a book."

"Well if it's going to go to raining tomorrow," Elba Rae said, "I guess I'll try to get to the Piggly Wiggly this afternoon on the way home. I've got to get my cake mix and my chips to take to the church Saturday."

Elba Rae then went about cleaning up her own lunch apparatus by first snapping the lid back on her cottage cheese. "Elba Rae?" Hazel said softly.

"What?"

"I'm proud of you."

Elba Rae stopped snapping and looked across the table at her cousin. "Huh?"

"I'm proud of you."

"For what?" she said sincerely, while wiping cottage cheese remnants out of her spoon with a napkin.

"Just everything."

"What are you talking about, Hazel?"

"The party at the church. The way you stood up for yourself and got that all changed. The way you've always stood up for yourself."

"Well I don't know about that."

"I do. And I know it wasn't always easy. Back when people didn't want to think anything but bad about you."

Elba Rae stared at Hazel but didn't really want to open the door to further conversation. "Why in the world would you want to dredge up all that old mess?"

"Because like I said. I'm proud of you."

Elba Rae Van Oaks was utterly and completely void of a response. She was, it seemed then and perhaps for all of her life, ill prepared for a compliment.

*   *   *   *

Elba Rae first ran into Kathleen Fike at the Piggly Wiggly who, apparently, also watched the late news on channel four because she as much as announced she was shopping on Thursday afternoon rather than her usual Saturday morning because she'd heard it was going to be rainy and cold by Saturday. Elba Rae had not been down the baking goods aisle when she encountered Kathleen Fike but indeed had by the time she rounded the corner to Mabel Moss, who Elba Rae knew for a fact did mostly shop on Thursday afternoons because it was right after Mabel's regular appointment at the beauty shop and who couldn't help from commenting to Elba Rae that she must be planning on a lot of cake baking since there were a noticeable quantity and assortment of mix and frosting boxes in Elba Rae's basket.

"We're having our fall festival at the church this Saturday," Elba Rae explained. "I'm making cupcakes for the children."

"Is that right?" Mabel said. "Seems like I'd heard y'all weren't gonna have the Halloween party this year but you were doing something different."

"That's right," Elba Rae's voice got just ever so subtly deeper.

"Well good luck with your baking. I've got to get in home. Florine and Jack want to carry me over to the steak house for supper tonight."

"Tell them I said hello."

"I will," Mabel Moss said. And off they rolled but in different directions.

As Claude Pickle predicted or, actually, as the portly weatherman on channel four had, Elba Rae Van Oaks awoke to rain Friday morning and though not yet cold she could tell there was a chill in the air when she went out to the carport and got into the LTD for school.

She had dreamed about Fettis Thursday night and though much of it hadn't made sense, of note the part where the two of them were driving through the middle of Panama City but on a tractor, something about seeing him in her dream had made more clear the decision to retire from the employ of the Litton County Department of Public Instruction. It was not anything she could especially rationalize since the only part of the dream she remembered in detail was how she'd kept asking Fettis where they were going and all he would say is 'dang it, Elba Rae, I ain't never lost us before,' but it was all so obvious to her nonetheless. Before she got to the parking lot of the Homer T. Litton Grammar School that morning, she'd made up her mind. She'd wait until they came back from Christmas holidays but she planned to tell Mr. Bailey first thing after.

The low temperature Friday night was a brisk thirty-seven degrees and the high on Saturday under continued overcast skies didn't rise much above forty-five according to the indoor – outdoor thermometer hanging on the wall right beside the window over Elba Rae's kitchen sink. While the second pan of cupcakes was in the oven, Elba Rae thought to go hunt for the thermal underwear she'd ordered from the catalog but not had occasion yet to wear. She wondered if maybe her mother the late Ethel Maywood had experienced a similar change in her own chemistry by which she chilled more easily the older she'd gotten.

She lay down on her couch in the den after finally getting the last batch of cupcakes frosted and likely went sound to sleep but didn't remember any particular dreams later. At a quarter after five, feeling snug in the new set of thermals yet in some crevice of her mind wishing she'd just let them have their old Halloween party so she could have been spared participation, she gathered all her baked goods and her two bags of chips and got them loaded into the Ford. The last thing she did before leaving the house was check one more time the handy thermometer she'd bought at Jack Moss's store and said out loud to herself, "thirty-nine. I'll be in a rigor."

Naturally Ulgine Babcock had taken ownership of the fall festival once the decision was rendered and had decorated the fellowship hall with crepe paper and balloons and even several bales of hay in the corners. Elba Rae Van Oaks thought that was taking things a little bit too far and worried there might be spiders in them.

There was an assortment of games set up for the younger children and a few things meant to appeal to the older ones as well, such as a dart board and something that looked like a makeshift staging area. No telling what Ulgine had in mind for that, Elba Rae scowled slightly, as she put out a bowl of chips. In the center of the hall was a round table with a new aluminum washtub sitting on it. The Dawson girl was busy placing apples in it which would quickly float to the surface of the water with which the tub was mostly filled.

By six o'clock the fellowship hall was full of children and more parents than had typically come to the Halloween parties and Elba Rae Van Oaks couldn't help but be pleased with herself one more time for achieving the eradication of a sinful ritual while obviously not hindering the ability of her church family to come together for fun and food. It must have been all her stirring around and walking back and forth from the kitchen, which was also crowded, but Elba Rae thought it terribly warm in the fellowship hall and began to regret her decision to wear thermals, sheer though they were. She picked up a paper napkin from one of the buffet tables and wiped her forehead that was uncharacteristically moist with perspiration.

Ulgine Babcock had clearly put the Dawson girl in charge of the apple-bobbing table because as soon as Ulgine whisked by and spoke something in her ear, the Dawson girl nodded yes and stepped up on a hay bale right beside the table and began to clear her throat for an announcement. It took nearly a minute, but after saying excuse me, excuse me everybody enough times the room got quiet and gave her their attention.

"We're just about ready for the apple-bobbing competition," the Dawson girl said. "But we're going to do it a little different." Everyone looked around and smiled and talked softly with each other and laughed a little.

"We're gonna give all of you kids a chance to play later, but first, we're going to get just the parents and the adults to have a little game of their own." There was more talking and a bit more laughter. When the fellowship hall had been called to order and most everyone stopped what they were doing, Elba Rae Van Oaks had found herself standing next to Mrs. Ulgine Babcock. "It's a good party, isn't it, Elba Rae?"

"Yes. It is," Elba Rae said and smiled. She clutched a soaked napkin in her hand.

"Now who wants to go first?" The Dawson girl teased. "Who'll be the first one to get a little cooled off in the washtub? Hummm?" She surveyed the room back and forth and while greeted with nothing but obvious friendly faces and happy parents, no one readily came forward.

"You know what?" Ulgine Babcock said loudly enough to be heard by all. "We have a lot of people to thank for helping put on the party this year and for even having it at all, and one of the hardest workers we have in our church is standing right beside me." Elba Rae looked to Ulgine's right to see who she was talking about, not considering Ulgine was looking to the left.

"I think Miss Elba Rae deserves to get to go first." Conversation erupted for a few seconds but was suddenly taken over by applause, led by none other than Mrs. Ulgine Babcock. Elba Rae Van Oaks was somewhat stunned. Her family—her church family—was applauding her. Even the children joined in. It was if they, too, were proud of her, if not for a lifetime of devotion, at least for taking the initiative to speak her mind. Elba Rae felt a lump in her throat and was sorry Hazel Burns had made an excuse of the weather to stay home and not come on anyway to help with the food.

Elba Rae Van Oaks did not necessarily want to bob for apples on that Saturday evening in the fellowship hall of the First Avenue United Methodist Church nor on any other evening for that matter because she suspected there was no way to be effectively competitive without getting her hair wet, which was absolutely not a consequence to be taken lightly. And besides that worry, as if it wasn't reason enough, she'd been feeling what she thought was a mild wave of nausea coming on for several minutes. She could still hear the applause and decided it was just a combination of nerves and the emotion she was feeling from the unforeseen adulation.

She didn't care, she decided. It was unfortunate she'd probably ruin her hair for church the next morning but she just didn't care. This was her moment and she deserved it. She stepped forward and the applause started all over again.

*   *   *   *

The Dawson girl would recount she'd asked Elba Rae Van Oaks if she wanted the shower cap the game committee had not been so thoughtless as to not have on hand. Elba Rae Van Oaks had replied with something but the Dawson girl couldn't really understand or recall what she'd said other than something about catching her breath. She'd distinctly shaken her head no back and forth, the Dawson girl was clear on when she'd held up the shower cap, but in hindsight she wasn't even sure Elba Rae had seen it or what it was she was shaking her head about.

The children had been giddy to see a grown woman standing before the washtub apparently willing to stick her face in it, especially an old woman—to them—like Elba Rae Van Oaks. They had sort of squealed with little bursts of excitement when she'd gripped her hands onto the sides of the tub. And when she put her face in and came up the first time with the water pouring off of it and from her hair, they screamed with laughter even though her teeth hadn't managed to get around the core of an apple. The Dawson girl would make a statement later it didn't seem like Elba Rae Van Oaks even paused to take a breath good before plunging back headfirst into the washtub, creating quite the splash when she had.

She'd stayed under longer the second time around, bobbing up and down still but failing to emerge with either a red apple which was worth three points or even a green one worth two and Ulgine Babcock was later adamant she'd heard Elba Rae gasp before submerging that last time so fully the water covered her ears. Because she'd maintained such a consistently firm grasp on the washtub throughout the horrid few minutes, it had not been of immediate concern to even those closest the table when Elba Rae's bobbing had become less pronounced and her head was nearly all but completely under the water, partially obscured, even, by a cluster of apples floating on the surface behind her neck. The children hadn't noticed, of course. They were still too amused. It was the Dawson girl, finally, whose expression changed from delight to anxiety.

"Miss Ulgine?" She'd said with a slight quiver. "Is she still moving?"

Ulgine Babcock stepped closer. "What?" She said to the Dawson girl who was looking at the submerged figure of Elba Rae Van Oaks. "I don't think she's moving, Miss Ulgine!" Ulgine Babcock leaned over the washtub.

"Elba Rae?" She said somewhat softly at first. "Elba Rae? Can you hear me?" Elba Rae Van Oaks could not. "Elba Rae!" She said louder but not screaming yet. She turned around to look at the Dawson girl and then, in fact, had begun to scream. "Oh my Lord, I don't think she can hear me!" The Dawson girl had rushed forth, she'd repeat for days, and with the help of one of the teenaged boys who was, technically, beyond the intended age group for the fall festival, she and Ulgine Babcock delicately pulled Elba Rae Van Oaks's head from the washtub. Her eyes and her mouth were open but her gaze was unfocused. The grown ups were startled but instinctively stepped back to allow room on the floor sufficient to spread Elba Rae Van Oaks. The children hadn't really known what to do.

*   *   *   *

The power of chaos is its ability to strike in even the most sacred of places and during the most unanticipated hour. The congregation of the First Avenue

United Methodist Church had not prepared for chaos on the evening of their very first Fall Festival of Fellowship and nearly five minutes went by with Elba Rae Van Oaks's dripping body on the floor before anyone had thought to call Dr. Bud who, in turn, dispatched the ambulance even though Dr. Bud got to the church first. He had asked few questions before going to work on Elba Rae Van Oaks because it was obvious the situation was serious. Several minutes into the CPR a pint of water had come gushing from her mouth, the expulsion of which had brought encouragement to the adults left in the room who had not helped the others herd the children up to the sanctuary. But when the ambulance had finally roared up the street and the Dawson girl had met the two men at the door to direct them to the fellowship hall, Dr. Bud had been overheard to tell the first attendant in the room Elba Rae Van Oaks had no pulse and he could not detect a heartbeat.

Dr. Bud rode in the ambulance with Elba Rae Van Oaks and didn't stop trying to save her all the way to Litton County Memorial Hospital even though it had been unmistakable to him, a renowned physician, she had been dead on the floor of the fellowship hall before he'd ever gotten there in his new Cadillac.

*   *   *   *

Howard Bailey, with the permission of the Superintendent, out and out closed the school on Monday afternoon to allow the faculty and any students who were so inclined to attend the service for Elba Rae Van Oaks. Lila Mae Fessmire sat in the front pew as the rightful next of kin with her husband Bucky and most of their immediate family including some grandchildren. Hazel Burns sat in the second row.

Reverend Timmons's remarks were brief and mostly filled with scripture readings and several long-winded prayers. In between were two piano solos but no vocalist and Hazel Burns regretted she hadn't discussed Elba Rae's preferences with Lila because she knew for a fact Elba Rae Van Oaks hated *In the Garden*, especially at a funeral, and *A Mighty Fortress* wasn't much better because both women had a long-standing agreement it was entirely overused. But Lila hadn't asked and Hazel Burns thought maybe it wasn't appropriate to insinuate herself into the actual decisions pertaining to the particulars of the arrangements.

By the time they got to the shorter rows of chairs set up at the grave site, Hazel Burns had to take a spot in the third row after deferring to all the Fessmires. She tried to think of the last time she'd been out to Glory Hills much less past Fettis's grave and decided it must have been when she and Elba Rae had come out on Mother's Day to visit the late Ruby Burns and Aunt Ethel.

Lila wasted no time getting Elba Rae's house cleaned out and sold but in a final acknowledgment of the bond the two cousins had forged all of their lives, did offer to Hazel Burns the possession of a few personal items. They were nothing of extraordinary value; whatever those might have been Hazel knew the Fessmire children and grandchildren would be beneficiaries. But Lila did give her some costume jewelry for which Hazel was grateful since there was no piece in the collection her memories couldn't place on Elba Rae if she closed her eyes and thought long enough. And until the switch finally gave out, Hazel's living room was illuminated by a large ceramic lamp with a clock inset in the base which Elba Rae had, indeed, repossessed from Mabel Moss years earlier.

There were also a few odd kitchen items Lila had apparently decided would be of no use to her or any future Fessmire households she'd no doubt be helping to establish. Among them was one heirloom Hazel Burns politely accepted but which she never actually put to use. It was a Pyrex dish with a clear glass lid and whenever Hazel came across it in back of the cabinet, it would alternately make her smile even if a tear was likely to follow. She imagined up in heaven the angels were dining on Chicken Florentine casserole, some of the freshest they'd ever had.

A P P E N D I X

▼

Cousin Begina's Favorite Waffle Batter

1 & 3/4 cup flour	3 eggs
2 teaspoons baking powder	7 tablespoons vegetable oil
1/2 teaspoon salt	1 ½ cups buttermilk, room temperature
1 tablespoon sugar	

Preheat the waffle iron. Sift the dry ingredients into a medium sized bowl. Separate the eggs, putting the egg whites in smaller bowl. Beat the egg whites until they are stiff. (If you are using an electric mixer, you can beat the egg whites first, then beat the batter without having to wash the beaters. The reverse is not true. If you beat the batter first you'll have to wash the beaters before beating the egg whites.) Add the egg yolks, oil and milk all at one time to the dry ingredients. Beat until there are no lumps in the batter. Fold the egg whites into the other batter using a spatula or other flat utensil. Put a full ½ cup of batter in your waffle iron to make a 9-inch round waffle.
Serves 4.

(Unless one of your guests is Cousin Begina, in which case, double).

Chocolate Chess Pie
Courtesy of Routy's Hot Pit Bar-Be-Que

1/2 cup butter	2 tablespoons all-purpose flour
2 oz chocolate, unsweetened	1 & 1/2 teaspoons vanilla extract
1 cup sugar	1/8 teaspoon salt
3 eggs, lightly beaten	1 pie shell, baked
1/4 cup crème de cacao liqueur	vanilla ice cream or whipped cream for topping

Preheat oven to 350 In a saucepan over low heat, melt butter and chocolate. Remove from heat. Blend in sugar, eggs, liqueur, flour, vanilla and salt. Beat until smooth. Pour into the pie shell.

Bake for 30 to 35 minutes or until set. Cool on a wire rack for at least 30 minutes.

Eggplant Parmesan
Courtesy of unknown member, Church of Holiness Praise

Panama City, Florida

1 large eggplant, cut in 1/4-inch slices	dash of garlic powder
1 tablespoon olive oil	1 teaspoon dried leaf oregano, crumbled
3 tablespoons grated Parmesan cheese	1 can (8 ounces) tomato sauce
1/2 teaspoon salt	4 ounces shredded part-skim mozzarella cheese
1/4 teaspoon pepper	1/4 cup Italian seasoned bread crumbs

Spread a little tomato sauce mixture over the bottom of a 9-inch square shallow baking dish. Arrange eggplant sliced in layers with mozzarella cheese. Pour remaining sauce mixture over the eggplant and cheese; top with bread crumbs. Bake eggplant Parmesan at 350° for 50 minutes, or until bubbly.

Note: May not be appropriate as a condolence dish

Virginia Millford's Gin Gimlet

1 1/2 ounces [45 mL] dry gin

1/2 ounce [15 mL] lemon [or lime] juice

Ice cubes

1/2 slice of lime

Pour dry gin and lemon [or lime] juice, over ice cubes, into a shaker. Shake; pour into a cocktail glass. Decorate with lime.

(Virginia recommends enjoying her favorite refreshment in the comfort of home.)

Edith Bishop's Famous Pea Salad
A favorite of the Buford Home and Garden Society

4 cups cooked and drained black-eyed peas

1 green pepper, seeded and diced

1 red pepper, seeded and diced

1 small onion, diced

2 jalapeno peppers, seeded, with the ribs removed, finely diced

2 tablespoons olive oil

4 tablespoons red wine vinegar

2 cloves garlic, minced

1 tablespoon cilantro, chopped

Salt and pepper to taste

Combine all the ingredients in a bowl and taste it for seasonings. Add more vinegar if the salad does not seem moist enough. Let the salad rest in your refrigerator overnight if possible.

May be served in a paper cup to those too infirm to hem up on a fork.

Chicken Florentine Casserole

2 packages (10 ounces each) frozen chopped spinach

1/4 cup butter

1 clove garlic, crushed and minced

dash dried basil

dash ground thyme

1/4 cup all-purpose flour

1 cup grated Parmesan cheese

1/3 cup half-and-half or whipping cream

5 cups cooked chicken, sliced

3/4 cup half-and-half or whipping cream

3/4 cup chicken broth

salt and pepper

6 thin slices ham

Cook spinach according to package instructions, drain well. In a skillet, melt 1 tablespoon butter; add minced garlic, basil, and thyme. Cook over medium low heat, stirring constantly, for about 5 minutes.

Add 1 tablespoon flour and blend well. Add 1/3 cup half-and-half and the spinach; simmer for 5 minutes, stirring constantly. Put spinach into the bottom of a lightly buttered 2-quart casserole or baking dish. Cover with cooked chicken slices. Over medium low heat, melt remaining butter and blend in remaining flour, stirring until smooth. Gradually stir in 3/4 cup half-and-half and 3/4 cup chicken broth; continue cooking and stirring until thickened. Season to taste with salt and pepper. Cut sliced ham in strips. Add to sauce and pour over chicken. Cover all with grated Parmesan cheese. Bake at 400' for 20 minutes, or until cheese is lightly browned. Serves 6.

Caution: Using this dish as a weapon may have most unfortunate repercussions.

978-0-595-48620-5
0-595-48620-7

Printed in the United States
118458LV00001B/10-12/P

International Armed Conflict
Since 1945

SERIES ON
STATE VIOLENCE, STATE TERRORISM, AND HUMAN RIGHTS

Series Editors
George A. Lopez, University of Notre Dame
Michael Stohl, Purdue University

International Armed Conflict Since 1945:
A Bibliographic Handbook of Wars and Military Interventions,
Herbert K. Tillema

World Justice? U.S. Courts and International
Human Rights, edited by Mark Gibney

State Organized Terror:
The Case of Violent Internal Repression,
edited by P. Timothy Bushnell, Vladimir Shlapentokh,
Christopher K. Vanderpool, and Jeyaratnam Sundram

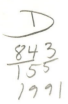